Praise for *The Pawn*

"Riveting . . . a gripping plot and brisk pacing will win James some fans eager for his next offering." —*Publishers Weekly*

"[An] exceptional psychological thriller. Steven James writes at a breakneck pace, effortlessly pulling the reader along on this incredible thrill ride. With this first installment of The Bowers Files, Steven James has left his mark as a writer to watch for." —*Armchair Reviews*

"A very interesting story. This is the first of a planned series, the second of which is *The Rook*. If that is as tightly drawn and paced as *The Pawn* already is, John Sandford might have to start looking over his shoulder." —*Crimespree Magazine*

"*The Pawn* is an intense, *CSI*-like thriller. This is not a story for the weak of stomach or faint of heart; the killers' histories and crime scene descriptions spare no detail. With his first novel, James steps into Christian fiction with a bang." —*Christian Retailing*

Praise for *The Rook*

"Best story of the year—perfectly executed."—*The Suspense Zone*

"Fans of *CSI* and *Law & Order* will enjoy the police work and forensics, but this jacked-up read feels more like an explosive episode of *24*; it's a wild ride with a shocking conclusion." —*Publishers Weekly* starred review

"Steven James writes short, snappy chapters, and his action-packed book is filled with many twists and turns." —*ChristianBook Preview*

"*The Rook* is suspense thriller writing at its highest level with complex storylines, unpredictable plot twists, and characters who engage the reader in many different ways." —*TitleTrakk.com*

Praise for *The Knight*

"Top-notch suspense." —*RT Book Reviews*

"There's a nice balance to *The Knight*, from the intrigue of the cleverly devised plot to the thrill of the investigation, and from the tense courtroom drama to the loving relationship Bowers has with his stepdaughter. It's a smart, thoughtful, and satisfying novel." —*Mysterious Reviews*

"Page after page, the suspense never ends. This book is highly recommended." —*Midwest Book Review*

"*The Knight* is a fabulous, fast-paced thriller full of surprise and suspense—and I highly recommend it." —*5 Minutes for Books*

"If you haven't read any of the books in this series, what are you waiting for? I've never had a more enjoyable time reading a suspense novel, and I am dying until book 4 comes out. VERY HIGHLY recommended." —*Books, Movies, and Chinese Food: Book Review*

"I'm continually in awe of Steven James and his mastery of story. If you are looking for top-notch thriller writing laced with suspense, action, mystery, and emotion, then look no further. Steven James is your guy." —*Fiction Addict*

Praise for *The Bishop*

"James writes smart, taut, high-octane thrillers. But be warned—his books are not for the timid. The endings blow me away every time." —Mitch Galin, producer, Stephen King's *The Stand* and Frank Herbert's *Dune*

"Move over, Alex Cross, there's a new FBI special agent in DC, Patrick Bowers. Steven James joins the ranks of James Patterson in his spine-tingling thriller *The Bishop*. Patterson fans are going to love Steven James." —Kathleen Antrim, bestselling author, *Capital Offense*

"Steven James's *The Bishop* should come with a warning: don't start reading unless you're prepared to finish this book in a single sitting. Riveting!" —Karen Dionne, International Thriller Writers website chair; managing editor, *The Big Thrill*

"*The Bishop*—full of plot twists, nightmarish villains, and family conflicts—kept me turning pages on a red-eye all the way from New York City to Amsterdam. Steven James tells stories that grab you by the collar and don't let go." —Norb Vonnegut, author, *Top Producer*; editor, *Acrimoney.com*

"Steven James locks you in a thrill ride, with no brakes. He sets the new standard in suspense writing." —*Suspense Magazine*

"Incredible." —Ann Tatlock, award-winning author

"Forget what you know. Steven James turns everything upside down in *The Bishop*. This is thriller writing at its absolute best." —*TheChristian Manifesto.com*

"Breakneck speed doesn't even begin to describe the pace of *The Bishop*. Absolutely brilliant." —Jeff Buick, bestselling author, *Bloodline*

"As thrilling and unexpected as any five-star action movie. James delivers a new take on crime and the criminal mind that's both eye-opening and heart-pounding. A high-energy read that delivers a jolt to the senses again and again." —John Tinker, Emmy-award-winning writer

THE QUEEN

THE QUEEN

THE BOWERS FILES #5

A PATRICK BOWERS THRILLER

STEVEN JAMES

Revell

a division of Baker Publishing Group
Grand Rapids, Michigan

Published by Revell
a division of Baker Publishing Group
P.O. Box 6287, Grand Rapids, MI 49516-6287
www.revellbooks.com

Printed in the United States of America

Library of Congress Cataloging-in-Publication Data
James, Steven, 1969–
    The queen : a Patrick Bowers thriller / Steven James.
        p.   cm. — (The Bowers files ; bk. 5)
    ISBN 978-0-8007-1920-3 (cloth) — ISBN 978-0-8007-3303-2 (pbk.)
    1. Bowers, Patrick (Fictitious character)—Fiction. 2. Criminologists—
Fiction. I. Title.
PS3610.A4545Q44 2011
813'.6—dc22   2011014738

The quote on p. 233 is taken from P. Kreeft, *Back to Virtue* (San Francisco: Ignatius Press, 1986), 37.

11   12   13   14   15   16   17   7   6   5   4   3   2   1

On October 1, 2003, at 03:25 a.m., hackers broke into the Naval Ocean Systems Center in San Diego, California.

An unknown amount of data was stolen.

Since that day, there have been over six dozen confirmed instances of malware and logic bombs found in the Department of Defense's Joint Worldwide Intelligence Communication System (JWICS), the United States military's most secure, dedicated intranet for sending critical and top secret information to combat troops and first-strike weapons systems worldwide.

The United States government continues to deny that these events ever occurred.

PART I

- ICE -

PROLOGUE

Present day
San Antonio, Texas
10:13 p.m.

Kirk Tyler turned the computer monitor to face his captive.

The video image showed a young woman leaving the Authorized Personnel Only entrance to Lone Star Mall. The mall had closed more than hour ago. No one else around.

Nighttime.

The girl was the man's daughter.

Dashiell Collet wrenched against his bonds, but the duct tape held him securely to the steel chair and he wasn't going anywhere. The empty warehouse loomed around him.

"This doesn't have to end badly for her," Kirk said, enjoying the view of the seventeen-year-old cheerleader sashaying to her car. Erin was obviously unaware that she was being followed, that she was being recorded, that her life was balancing on such a razor-thin edge. "Just answer my question."

Dashiell was silent.

"Well?" Kirk asked.

"If you touch her." Dashiell's teeth were clenched. "I swear to God—"

"Let's leave God out of this." Kirk stared at the screen. The video feed came from a camera hidden in the top button of the oxford of his associate, now twenty paces behind the girl. "I just want you to tell me the name of the person you've been in touch with at the Pentagon. That's it. Just your contact's name, and this will be all over."

"I told you before, I don't know what you're talking about!"

"You worked at the facility for fourteen years."

"What facility?"

"Dashiell, please. Enough. I want to know the name of the person in charge of the project."

Dashiell shook his head adamantly. "You've made a mistake. I'm the wrong man."

Considering Dashiell's situation, Kirk was surprised by the amount of resolve in the man's voice. Apparently his training was serving him well.

So, a little convincing.

Kirk's partner was wearing a hands-free Bluetooth earpiece, and Kirk spoke to him, said two words: "Take her."

On the monitor he could see the distance between the camera and Erin shrinking as his associate moved swiftly, silently, toward her.

"No!" Dashiell cried.

Erin was fishing her car keys out of her purse.

"This will stop," Kirk said, "when you want it to stop."

Dashiell strained heroically to get free, but the way he was bound, his struggles only constricted the duct tape more tightly around his ankles and wrists.

"I don't know anyone at the Pentagon!" he yelled. "I'm telling you I'm an insurance adjuster! That's all!"

Erin reached the car.

Opened the driver's door.

The camera was a yard away from her back.

And then.

She must have noticed the person in her side-view mirror or heard the rustle of movement behind her because she turned abruptly and opened her mouth to scream, but Kirk's partner was on her before she could.

"I don't know anyone!" Dashiell hollered.

On the video feed, Kirk could see a hand clamped over the girl's mouth as she was shoved brusquely into the car. The images became quick, jerky.

"I swear!"

"I don't believe you, Dashiell."

"Leave her out of this! Let her go!"

It was hard to tell what was happening in the vehicle. A struggle, yes, but for the moment everything was a blur of arms and colors and cries. Then, the screen showed the flash of a hand backhanding the girl and then, as she called out weakly for help, Kirk watched as her left arm was pressed down and punched with a hypodermic needle.

"Stop this!" Dashiell shouted. "Call him off!"

"Tell me."

Erin's eyes rolled back. She drifted down in her seat.

"Okay, I will! Just tell him to stop!"

Kirk spoke into the phone. "Hang on."

An arm positioned the girl's now limp body in the front passenger seat, strapping the seat belt across her waist and chest. The driver's door clicked shut, then the video image remained stationary, the camera staring patiently out the windshield at the stretch of vacant parking lot surrounding the car.

"All right," Kirk said to Dashiell. "Talk to me."

"If I tell you, you have to promise you won't hurt her." Dashiell was unconsciously wetting his lips with his tongue, nervous. Desperate.

"I promise."

"Swear to me that this man will let her go. That he won't touch her. You have to—"

"Listen to me, Dashiell, I swear that if you tell us the name, I'll let both you and Erin go. You have my word. I'll have my man leave her in the car, and she'll wake up in a couple hours with a headache, but other than that she'll be fine." He sat at the table and faced Dashiell, carefully steepled his fingers, and leaned forward. "However, if you don't tell me what I came here to find out, he's going to bring her back here, and I'll make you watch as the two of us occupy ourselves with her for the rest of the night."

Dashiell was breathing heavily, defiantly, but Kirk could see defeat in his eyes. "Rear Admiral Colberg."

"Colberg."

"Yes. Alan Colberg. He lives in Alexandria, Virginia. Works for the Department of Defense. You can look it up. Now, tell him to leave her in the car."

"Just a minute." Kirk tapped his laptop's keyboard, verified the name against the list of potentials his employer had sent him. Yes, the rear admiral had been an employee of the Pentagon's Project Sanguine, but based on Colberg's work schedule and job responsibilities, the computer told Kirk there was only a 61 percent likelihood of a match. Not enough to go on.

"I need more." He held up the phone. "Prove it or—"

"All right, listen. Colberg helped design the extremely low frequency technology back in the eighties. He was on the original team. The first one to man the station."

"That's not proof."

"Check his background. He wrote a paper back in 1979 on 3 to 76 Hertz radio waves and the use of the ionosphere in transmission technology."

It took Kirk a few minutes before he found anything online, but at last he was able to pull up a PDF of the symposium paper written by then Lieutenant (Junior Grade) Alan Colberg.

It wasn't 100 percent conclusive, but in this business, very little was. He would confirm everything when he met with the admiral.

Good.

The person who'd hired him for this job would be pleased.

Kirk spoke into the phone, to the man with Erin. "All right, bring her back and we'll get started."

"What?" The blood drained from Dashiell's face. "You said you'd let her go!"

"Yes." Kirk pocketed the phone. "I did."

"I'm telling you"—Dashiell's voice was taut with fear, with the revelation of what was happening—"it's Colberg. You have to believe—"

"I do believe you."

"But you swore you'd—"

"Mr. Collet," Kirk interrupted. "Part of my job involves telling people whatever is necessary to convince them to give me what I want. It's nothing personal." Kirk unholstered his Italian-made .45 ACP Tanfoglio Force Compact and pressed the end of the blue steel barrel against Dashiell's left thigh. "This is for wasting my time with your stalling."

"No, you have to—"

Kirk squeezed the trigger, and Dashiell Collet screamed.

Then screamed even louder when Kirk fired another round into his other leg.

Judging by the position of the barrel, Kirk was pretty sure the second bullet had shattered Dashiell's femur. The bleeding from both wounds was steady, not gushing, and Kirk didn't think the femoral arteries had been torn. Untreated, he would eventually bleed out, but he should survive at least a couple hours. Long enough to watch.

Kirk set the gun on the table to his left. It took him only a moment to gag him. "You could have stopped all of this if you'd just told me right away what I wanted."

Dashiell's eyes were bleary with pain from the gunshots. His head sagged, and Kirk feared that the blood loss was affecting him more quickly than he'd anticipated. He slapped his cheek. "Look at me!"

The man seemed to refocus.

"You need to know that Erin's death and everything that precedes it will have been your fault for inconveniencing me for the last three hours."

Although obviously disoriented, Dashiell pulled against his bonds once again but then winced terribly as his leg tensed. He tried to cry out in pain, but the gag swallowed the sounds.

Kirk unlocked the side door so the building would be accessible to his partner. As he was returning to the table, he felt his phone vibrate in his pocket. Only one person had the call-in code for this number.

Valkyrie.

Precisely the person he needed to talk to.

Kirk tapped the phone's screen, but before he could speak, the electronically masked voice on the other end said, "I was watching the video feed. I saw your man take the girl."

"He does good work," Kirk said. "We got what we wanted. Dashiell's contact is Rear Admiral Colberg. At the Pentagon." Kirk arranged the items he would be needing for his time with Erin. The tape. The ropes. The cuffs.

"You should have left the girl out of this."

If there was one thing Kirk Tyler did not like, it was having to explain himself. "I wouldn't have done it unless I believed it was the most prudent course of action." He decided not to mention his plans regarding the girl.

"The most prudent course of action."

"Yes."

"That's what you thought."

A pause that made Kirk somewhat uneasy.

"You should have left the girl out of this," Valkyrie repeated. But this time the words had a tighter edge to them. "This was sloppy."

"It was efficient."

"Efficiency means limiting collateral damage, decreasing exposure—"

"You weren't here." He had never cut Valkyrie off midsentence before, but he wasn't in the mood for a lecture. "Don't question my decision."

A longer pause this time. "In lieu of what I've seen tonight, I've decided to have someone else finish the job."

Kirk felt his grip on the phone tighten. "That wouldn't be wise."

"I told you when we started that there would be consequences if anything was mishandled. This situation with the girl—I consider it mishandled."

A warning flared through Kirk's mind.

He's watching you.

Kirk drew his Tanfoglio again, scanned the shadows of the warehouse. "You do not want to do this." He clicked through the possible

places Valkyrie or one of his men might be hiding. Saw nothing.
"You pull me from this and I'm coming for you."

"Good-bye, Kirk."

And before Kirk Tyler could respond, the cell phone he was
holding beside his ear exploded, ripping off his forearm and most
of his head, sending a frenzy of blood and brain and splintered
skull across the table. As his body dropped clumsily to the ground,
tiny globs of gray matter dribbled onto the concrete, and Dashiell
watched in horror—thinking only of what would happen to Erin
and to him when the dead man's associate arrived.

Alexei Chekov was halfway through the Grand Inquisitor scene
in *The Brothers Karamazov* when he heard from Valkyrie asking
him to come in and clean up a mess.

"You remember Kirk Tyler?" the voice said.

"I'm familiar with him, though we've never actually met." Alexei's
English was impeccable, as was his Russian, Arabic, and Italian.
When Valkyrie had first contacted him, he'd noticed a sentence
structure that suggested someone who'd either studied in or grown
up in the States. Because of this Alexei had chosen American English
for their conversations.

"I'm afraid you won't have the opportunity."

"He disappointed you."

"Yes."

Alexei placed a bookmark and set down the novel.

Valkyrie.

In early Norse mythology, a Valkyrie was a goddess who flew
over the battlefields deciding who would live and who would die—a
job strikingly close to his own. The myths evolved over time and
turned Valkyries into beautiful, angelic creatures who rewarded
fallen heroes in paradise.

Death and rewards. Who lives and who dies—the ultimate
decision.

Valkyrie filled Alexei in concerning Dashiell Collet and his daughter and all that had happened at the warehouse. "It's not far from where you are," Valkyrie explained. "I want you to dress Dashiell's gunshot wounds, take care of Tyler's body, then call an ambulance for Mr. Collet. I want him alive in case we need to speak with him again."

Valkyrie's comment about the warehouse being nearby told Alexei that his own location wasn't as secret as he'd thought it was, and he realized that he might have underestimated Valkyrie, a person he had never met, didn't even know the identity of.

"What about the girl?"

"She'll wake up in an hour or two. I'm afraid the man who tried to abduct her won't be so lucky."

Alexei knew a little about the calculated synchronization of Valkyrie's work, and he imagined that the would-be abductor's Bluetooth earpiece had been wired to detonate just as Kirk's phone had been.

He tried not to picture what the girl would see beside her when she awoke.

Over the years Alexei had developed a professional objectivity toward these things, but still, images like the one Erin would awaken to were deeply disturbing, and he found himself sympathizing with her, for the nightmares that would undoubtadly chase her for the rest of her life. Maybe he could get there before she awoke, move her someplace safe.

"Do you need me to clean that up as well?"

"I'll have someone else take care of it. Just get to the warehouse. Tonight I'll have a plane take you to Alexandria, Virginia. I want you to have a chat with Rear Admiral Alan Colberg. Tell him we need the access codes to the station. He'll know what you're talking about."

"All right."

"By the way, providentially, Tyler had a Tanfoglio with him. I know you lost one last year in Italy. Keep it. It's yours. For the inconvenience of being called upon so late in the evening."

Once again, impressive. How Valkyrie could have known about the incident in Italy was a mystery to Alexei. He had the sense that

Valkyrie had mentioned it just to show him that his past was no secret. "I don't use guns," he replied. "Not anymore."

"Not since your wife's death."

How?

"Yes."

A pause. "Of course. Contact me when you've finished with Colberg."

"I will."

The conversation ended.

Though Alexei did not carry a handgun, he did carry something else.

He slipped the cylindrical object into the breast pocket of his suit coat and left for the warehouse.

Valkyrie should not have known about the Tanfoglio or about Tatiana's death. It showed Alexei that Valkyrie had pried into his past, and when people poke around like that, they inevitably leave evidence of their presence.

On the way out the door, Alexei put a call through to one of his contacts in the GRU, Russia's military intelligence directorate, to see if he could find out who might be using the code name Valkyrie.

Based on the work Alexei needed to do at the warehouse, the flight time to Virginia, and the time change, he anticipated that the rear admiral would be just sitting down for breakfast when he arrived.

Hopefully, Colberg would be cooperative and Alexei wouldn't have to put the object he now carried in his pocket to use.

1

18 hours later
Thursday, January 8
Lorelette Mobile Home Park
Merrill, Wisconsin
4:21 p.m.

I scanned the trailer park through the binoculars I'd borrowed from FBI SWAT Team Leader Torres.

Most of the task force had agreed that we should go in light, but FBI Director Wellington didn't want to take any chances. So, even though we hadn't been able to confirm that Travis Reiser was actually in the trailer, she'd ordered a full SWAT team present on site.

Now I was a quarter mile away with Team Leader Antón Torres, a rock-jawed jock I'd worked with on a dozen previous cases, by my side.

Eight inches of crusty snow covered the ground, but mounds at least four feet deep lay pushed up on the shoulders of the roads and at the ends of the parking areas.

A low pressure system was sweeping down from Canada, leaving a foot of snow in its wake. It would arrive tomorrow afternoon, and I was glad we were here today and not in the thick of the storm.

Most of the trailers in the park had paint that was faded or peeling, ripped screen doors, or rusted sheet-metal roofs telegraphing the economic demographic of the people living here. Nearly a third of the sixty trailers had abandoned toys, discarded sleds, or half-melted snowmen sandwiched in the tight quarters between the homes. A lot of children lived in this park. Not good.

The sun edged toward the bottom of the sky, lengthening the

late-day shadows around us. Nearby, Torres's snipers waited for his go-ahead to take up position before twilight swallowed the park.

"Well?" he asked.

Once again I directed my gaze at the yellow single-wide trailer where we believed Reiser was staying. "Still no movement."

"His car is there."

"Yes." An eyewitness had seen Reiser enter the trailer last night. I didn't need to tell Antón that. We'd gone over all this earlier.

I handed him the binoculars, and while he studied the trailer I surveyed the area, noting entrance and exit routes and evaluating their relationship to the roads that wandered through this part of the county.

"All right." Torres set down the binoculars. "What are you thinking?"

"I see four possible exit routes." I gestured toward the west end of the park. "There, near the quarry, but if we put Saunders and Haley on the ridge, they'll have that one covered; the main entrance, one sniper can take that. There's a break in the metal fence to the south, but it looks like Reiser would need to cross the field behind his trailer to get there, so, unlikely." I pointed to the east. "I'd say that based on the layout of the park, if he rabbits he'll most likely head south, past that home—"

"With the snow angels."

"Yes."

Torres's jaw was set. "Kids are easier to handle than adults."

"And Reiser is experienced. He'll know it's a lot harder for snipers to take a shot if they see a child in the scope along with the target."

"They'll hesitate."

I nodded.

He studied the park. "I'm telling you, Pat, you have an instinct for this. You should've been SWAT instead of all this theoretical geospatial bull—" He cut himself off mid-curse, no doubt realizing that he was inadvertently turning his compliment into an insult. He corrected himself: "I'm just saying."

"I appreciate it."

Actually, the FBI's SWAT program wouldn't have been a bad choice, but I was born to work for the Bureau's National Center for the Analysis of Violent Crime, or NCAVC, and the last ten years had been a perfect fit for me.

"I'll go in first," I said.

He shook his head. "The director was clear. She wanted us to send in SWAT before you or Jake access the trailer."

"That's not the way to play this." This was not the only thing I disagreed with the director on. "People react in kind. When they feel threatened, they respond accordingly. You go in heavy, he's going to respond to meet the threat. I can talk him out." My experience as a field agent and as a homicide detective before that gave me street cred with Torres, and he didn't argue with me, just took a moment to peer through the binocs again. "Those are trailer homes," I added. "A shoot-out would mean—"

"Yeah. Rounds flying through the walls," he said grimly.

While he considered what I'd said, Agent Jake Vanderveld, the NCAVC profiler who was working this case with me, sauntered toward us. Broad shoulders. Blond hair. Meticulously trimmed mustache. I was thirty-seven, he was a few years younger. He nodded a greeting and slapped Torres on the shoulder.

"Where're we at?" Jake asked.

"Still deciding." Torres lowered the binoculars.

"Play it safe, Antón," I said. "Have people in place, but then—"

He made his decision, shook his head. "No. I'm not comfortable with it. I want my men in there first. You can follow close, right after the team, but I want to secure the premises first."

"Hang on," Jake spoke up, a little too authoritatively. "This is all a game to Reiser. He'll want to taunt Pat." Jake had helped lead us here and knew Reiser's file better than almost anyone. "If we send in a man in civilian clothes, Reiser'll think he has the upper hand. Play to his weakness, his arrogance, and you'll get close."

It was unusual for me and Jake to agree about anything, but apparently this time we were on the same wavelength.

Torres worked his jaw back and forth for a moment, then let out a small sigh. "All right. Listen. I go in with you, Pat. But I enter the trailer first."

"Plainclothes?" I said.

He nodded.

"Agreed." I stood. "And Travis Reiser might be the only key to finding Basque, so tell your team minimum force. We need to take him alive."

"That's not the priority here."

Basque had eluded us for six months now, and if we were right about Reiser, he might flip on Basque, turn him in. "Keep him alive, Antón."

"If this little prick takes any aggressive action, we're dropping him."

Though I wanted more reassurance that the SWAT team would hold off from taking Reiser down, they'd been trained, as I had, to fire at a target until it's no longer a threat. That wasn't the outcome I was looking for, but I knew Torres was right. You don't take chances, especially with someone like Reiser.

"All right," I said. "Let's go."

We all quieted our cells, one of the SWAT guys distributed radios to us, small, nearly invisible patches you wear just behind your ear, and while Torres changed into civilian clothes, I went to get some body armor.

2

Torres by my side.

Reiser's pale yellow trailer sixty meters ahead of us.

The air—crisp, bitingly cold.

We knew if we pulled our guns at this point it would increase our perceived threat level, so we kept them holstered as we walked, as we scanned the area. "So, you asked her yet?" Torres said, keeping his voice low.

"Asked her?"

"Lien-hua."

I glanced his way. "Who told you about that?"

"Little birdie."

"Ralph."

"Okay, a big birdie."

I went back to scrutinizing the park. "If you must know. I'm waiting for the right time."

"The right time."

"Yes."

"I'm telling you, don't be nervous, bro. You'll do fine."

"I'm not nervous."

"Mm-hmm." He crunched along the road beside me, sturdy, confident but not brash. I realized I was glad he was with me. "Just don't put it off too long. You only live once, you know."

"I'll keep that in mind."

Forty meters to Reiser's trailer.

Though I didn't want to, I eased aside thoughts of Lien-hua and carefully observed the park.

Despite the weather, several small faces were staring at me through the torn screen door of the trailer home that lay directly across the road. Abruptly, a woman pulled the children back into the shadows and swung the screen door, then the trailer door shut.

I didn't like this.

Any of it.

The trailer park brought back a swarm of dark memories from a crime scene fourteen years ago when I was a Milwaukee police detective and was forced to view the kinds of things no one should ever have to see: the body of Jasmine Luecke in her trailer home—or more precisely, what was left of her body, laid out gruesomely in the hallway.

The aftermath of one of Richard Devin Basque's crimes.

There were sixteen victims that we knew of. All young women. He kept them alive for as long as twelve hours while he surgically removed their lungs piece by piece and ate them, making the dying women watch as he did.

When I finally cornered him in an abandoned slaughterhouse in Milwaukee, he was holding his scalpel over his final victim, Sylvia Padilla. She was still alive when I arrived. Which, even after all these years, made the memory even more troubling.

Thirty meters.

I hadn't been able to save her—I doubted anyone could have—but I did manage to apprehend Basque, and he was eventually convicted, sent to prison, and spent thirteen years behind bars, most of it in solitary confinement.

But then, just over a year ago, the Seventh District Court announced Basque was going to receive a retrial after "a careful review of the culpatory DNA evidence and eyewitness testimony pertinent to the case."

And unbelievably, at the conclusion of his retrial last May, he was found not guilty and released from prison with official apologies from the judge, the warden, and even the governor.

Less than a month later, Basque started killing again.

This time with an accomplice.

Fifteen meters to the trailer.

Upon review of the digitized case files, Jake discovered that

DNA found at the scene of the June homicide matched previously unidentified DNA at four of Basque's earlier crimes, and that's what led us to Travis Reiser.

I was forced to concede that Basque might have had an accomplice all along.

Since June I'd linked three other murders to Basque and Reiser, and if they really had been working together from the start, I couldn't help but wonder how many other crimes Reiser might have committed by himself in the years since Basque's arrest and initial conviction.

"Listen," I said into my mic. "This man can lead us to Basque. Be prudent. Don't get trigger happy."

In the silence following my words, Torres reiterated, "You heard him. Wait for my signal."

The team confirmed over the radios that they understood, and Torres and I arrived at Travis Reiser's jaundice-colored trailer. "Puke yellow," Torres muttered. "How appropriate."

We took the steps up to the front door slowly, but my heart was racing.

My friend Ralph Hawkins—an ex-Army Ranger who now headed up the NCAVC, and apparently the guy who'd mentioned my engagement plans to Torres—once told me that fear was one of the key ingredients to courage. "If your life's in danger and you're not afraid," he said, "you're just a freakin' moron, and you're a liability."

Right now I was not a liability.

I knocked. "Travis, are you home?"

No answer.

"Mr. Reiser," I said. "Please open the door."

Still no reply. No movement inside the trailer.

A nod from Torres and we drew our weapons. He carried a Glock 23, I unholstered the .357 SIG P229 I've carried with me ever since starting in law enforcement fifteen years ago. Reliable. Accurate. An old friend. It felt at home in my hand.

I tried the doorknob. Locked.

We had a warrant to search the premises, but if you break down a door, you run the risk of contaminating evidence or inciting adversarial action, so it's always better to find an alternative. However, in this case, that wasn't going to happen. I signaled for Torres to move aside, then positioned myself in front of the doorway.

I kicked the door hard, holding nothing back, planting my heel directly next to the lock. It blistered apart, the door flew open, and Torres whipped through the entrance. I followed closely on his heels.

The living room was dark, lit only by the muted daylight that managed to seep through the heavy curtains drawn across every window. The trailer smelled of mold, of cigarette smoke, of stale beer.

No sign of Reiser.

Torres hooked left toward the bathroom, I moved right, down the short hallway to the bedroom.

The door was closed.

"Travis?" Gun ready, heart racing, I pressed it open.

The room was strewn with dirty clothes and discarded Michelob cans. A mattress lay flopped on the floor, covered with a crumpled mess of sheets and blankets. An old TV sat on a wooden crate in the far corner. To the left, a small dresser was pressed against the wall near the closet, which I now approached.

I raised my SIG just below eye level. High ready position.

Opened the closet door.

Clothes, shoes, boxes. That was all.

I let out a small breath then looked around the room one more time. Nothing.

He wasn't here.

Just moments ago, I'd been amped with anticipation, but now I felt the all-too-familiar plummet of disappointment that comes from running into an investigative dead end. Highs and lows. The roller-coaster ride of hot adrenaline and cold letdown. Story of my life.

When I returned to the kitchen I found Torres waiting for me.

"Place is empty, Pat."

"Right."

Dirty dishes filled the sink. Beside them I noticed a wooden block bristling with knives. Basque and Reiser typically chose scalpels and knives rather than guns, and I tried not to consider the grisly thought that these blades had been used for something other than cutting vegetables or fruit here in the kitchen. The Bureau's Evidence Response Team would find out. "Have your team check the rest of the park," I told Torres.

Based on what I knew about Basque and Reiser, it would've been unlikely for Travis to bring a body back to his home, but still, I found myself carefully sniffing the musty air. I caught no hint of the odor of human decomposition.

It wasn't my job to process evidence, the ERT would do that, but I didn't want to contaminate anything before they arrived. I holstered my SIG, turned on my phone, and pulled on a pair of latex gloves. Then I went to the ashtray beside the couch and inspected the burnt ends of the butts. All cold.

Torres spoke into his mic. "Sweep the rest of the park. Cordon it off. You know how much is riding on getting this right. No mistakes."

Then he called in for local PD to send marked cars to the roads leading from the park.

I studied the room. Cheap cabinets, a Formica kitchen table, countertops strewn with unopened mail—two bills, a paycheck from the factory, two credit card offers. The most recent postage was stamped on Tuesday.

Yet he entered the trailer last night.

According to the eyewitness.

Something to follow up on.

Just as I started looking through the bathroom cabinet, my phone rang. This cell was a temporary replacement for a prototype of a new smart phone the National Geospatial-Intelligence Agency had been letting me use. Last week I hadn't been quite gentle enough when I slammed it onto my kitchen table after a rather big setback on a case. So now, for the time being, I was left without my 3-D hologram projector for mapping crime scene locations. I don't have a very good history with phones. Hopefully I've learned my lesson.

Probably not.

When I checked the screen I saw that FBI Director Margaret Wellington was on the other end of the line.

Oh, this day was just getting better and better.

3

I let the phone ring.

Six years ago when Margaret and I were both on staff at the Academy I'd noticed some discrepancies in a case and, not knowing who was responsible, I'd brought it up to the Office of Professional Responsibility. After an inquiry, she was discreetly transferred to a North Carolina satellite office—not a career move in the right direction for her—and she'd blamed me for it. But then, a little over a year ago, after landing back in the good graces of the administration, she rose quickly through the ranks, looking for a reason to fire me every step of the way.

It rang again.

Last summer, Margaret's predecessor, Gregory Rodale, found himself caught in the middle of an insider trading scandal. Shrewdly, Margaret, then the Executive Assistant Director, had positioned herself to be on the short list for the director position even before he was asked to resign.

The approval process in the Senate went astonishingly smoothly, and now a woman I'd never gotten along with and never really trusted was at the helm of the most powerful law enforcement and domestic counterterrorism agency in the world.

Mid-ring, I finally answered. "Pat here."

She bypassed a greeting, got right down to business. "What do we know about Reiser?"

"He's not here, but his car is parked outside. We're working from the premise that he's not far. Torres and the team are searching trailer by trailer."

"All right." She didn't sound dismissive, just perfunctory. "In the meantime, there's another matter to attend to. There's been an accident not far from you. I need you to have a look around."

"What accident?"

"An ice fisherman found snowmobile tracks leading to a stretch of open water. Law enforcement didn't find any footprints to or from the break in the ice. Whoever was driving the snowmobile went down."

"Where?"

"Tomahawk Lake. Just outside of Woodborough."

A chill swept over me. That was only fifteen miles from my brother Sean's home in Elk Ridge.

He's a snowmobiler.

The moment went deeper. "Who? Do we have a name?"

"It's not Sean, Pat. Don't worry."

Her words caught me by surprise. I couldn't remember ever mentioning Sean's name to Margaret, or even indicating to her that I had a brother, so unless she'd been reviewing my personnel files I was at a loss as to how she made the connection so quickly.

A random snowmobile accident would be an issue for local law enforcement to look into, not something for the FBI to investigate. Also, here was the Bureau's director rather than my direct supervisor on the line. There had to be more or she never would have called me. "What else?"

"A rather astute young deputy took pictures of the tracks and emailed them to the FBI Lab. We identified the type of snowmobile—a Ski-Doo 800 XL—and that led us back to the owner. Forty minutes ago the sheriff's department found the man's wife and daughter at the house. Both dead. The woman shot in the back. The girl in the chest."

My brother didn't have a daughter, so the dead woman wouldn't have been his wife Amber, but still I sank onto one of the chairs in Reiser's trailer. "What are their names?"

"I assure you, Patrick, this has nothing to do with Sean."

"Margaret, what are their names?"

A small pause. "The missing man is named Donnie Pickron. His wife is Ardis. Their four-year-old girl's name is Lizzie."

I felt a deep stab of pain. Knowing their names made the crime all the more real, and hearing Lizzie's age was almost unbearable.

I tried to process Margaret's words. It seemed highly unusual for a sheriff's deputy to call on the FBI in the first place, and even more unusual to ask for their help with something like this right off the bat. "Margaret, I'm not sure I see what this has to do with the Bureau."

Only after I'd finished my sentence did I realize I'd been calling her by her first name this whole conversation. Over the last eighteen months as she'd moved up the career ladder it'd taken me a long time to get used to referring to her by her title rather than her first name, and I still wasn't used to calling her Director Wellington. Probably never would be.

"Donnie was ex-military, and the Navy is pressuring us to have someone investigate it. They want to know if this was a murder/suicide, or if his death was accidental."

"So his death was confirmed?"

A pause. "No. Not yet."

"So he might still be alive?"

"We don't know much of anything at this point." She dodged my question. "That's why I want you to look into this."

I imagined that the pressure from the Navy had a lot to do with her decision to make this a Bureau matter, but still, I couldn't figure out why she'd mentioned the snowmobile accident first, considering it was much less serious than a double homicide. Things just weren't adding up here. "I want you to go up there," she went on, "have a look around. I'm sending Jake with you. He's good at what he does."

It went unstated, but I guessed she'd added that last comment because she was aware of my history with Jake Vanderveld, how reticent I was to work with him. I left the topic untouched.

"I can't leave the Reiser case right now, Margaret," I said. "We're closing in. He's in the area."

"Torres and his team will find him. I need you in Woodborough."

"I work serial offenses, Margaret, not—"

"You're the most experienced agent anywhere in the area," she told me bluntly. "You notice what needs to be noticed." Coming from her, the words were a sudden, unexpected compliment.

I rubbed my head. "A sheriff's deputy who's investigating what appears to be an accidental drowning contacts the FBI Lab—and within forty minutes of identifying a missing man's deceased wife and daughter, the Navy brass is pressuring the Bureau to look into the case? What's really going on here, Margaret? There's something you're not telling me."

"You know everything I know," she said tersely. "Woodborough is eighty-five miles north of you. Go up there, have a look around, and clear this up. There's a storm moving into your area. Interstate 94 is already shut down east of Fargo, and you're going to get hit hard." She paused for a moment as if to process what she'd just said. "I'll send up one of the ERT agents from the Reiser investigation later tonight to process the scene of the Pickron homicides, but I want you to head up the investigation."

"Margaret, this is all—"

"Patrick, I'm very busy. I'm not pulling you from the Reiser case. Just go to Woodborough. Figure this out. I'll talk with you in the morning. I've told the sheriff's department to hold the scene and wait for your arrival."

I looked around the trailer, exasperated. "What about Reiser?"

"If SWAT finds him I'll have Torres watch him until you and Jake can drive back down. Beyond that, it'll take the ERT a couple of days to go through the contents of his trailer. Until then, look into the double homicide."

"Or triple."

"Triple?"

"If Donnie was murdered too. We don't know yet. Not until we find his body."

"Of course. I'll call Jake. Inform him of what's going on." Without saying good-bye she hung up.

Frustrated, I jammed my cell into my pocket. Torres had pulled the shades open to get more light into the trailer, and now, outside the window, I saw Jake answer his phone.

A glance at my watch.

4:46 p.m. I could hardly believe it was just over twenty minutes since we'd moved on the trailer.

From my infrequent visits to my brother's house, I knew that from here most of the drive to Woodborough would be on county roads rather than interstate, so depending on how icy the roads were, we might not get up there until 8:00. And only then would I be able to start looking over the scene.

This was going to be a long night.

But then there was the matter of Sean.

I'd only be fifteen miles from his house.

Yesterday when I met up with Jake in Madison and drove over here, I'd convinced myself that Merrill was far enough away to justify not getting together with Sean. But now that I'd be just minutes away, I couldn't come up with a way to politely avoid at least inviting him out for coffee. And I imagined that Amber, his wife, would also want to see me.

And seeing her would be even harder than meeting up with my brother.

4

I took one more look around the trailer, then stepped outside.

The sun had dipped below a silo nestled on the horizon, and the Wisconsin countryside was draped in one long winter shadow. In the day's fading light I could see the SWAT guys moving methodically through the trailer park, stopping at one door after another.

Until I had a chance to assess the situation in Woodborough, I wouldn't know how much time I'd actually have available to see Sean, so I decided to put off calling him for the time being. However, since I'd been planning to meet my stepdaughter, Tessa Ellis, here in Merrill tomorrow afternoon so I could show her around some of the areas I'd lived in as a child, I figured I'd give her a shout right away to tell her about my change of plans.

This week she was visiting the University of Minnesota for a special weeklong three-credit winter session for academically gifted seniors considering attending in the fall. After seeing her SAT scores, the U of M was so bent on recruiting her that they'd sent an admissions officer to meet with her at our home in Denver in October, before her dramatic grade point slide this last semester.

With her academic record, I doubted she needed a class on research methodology, but since her parents had attended U of M, I wasn't surprised she'd agreed to sign up for the class, at least to check out the campus.

Of course, maybe now that both her mother and father were gone, it could have simply been a way for her to honor their memory.

Four members of the Bureau's Evidence Response Team entered the trailer, and I walked toward the driveway to get some privacy for the call. Last weekend I'd decided my investigation took precedence over chauffeuring Tessa around the Midwest, so I'd arranged for a rental car for her, and though someone her age wasn't officially supposed to drive one, the Bureau has an arrangement with rental car companies at every major airport. With my credentials I was able to swing it.

She didn't answer, so I left her a voicemail explaining what was going on. "If this storm hits early, I may need you to stay in the Cities for another day or two. Talk to you soon."

Then I returned the body armor to the SWAT guys, and by the time I arrived at the car, Jake was waiting for me.

"Well," he said, "I guess this is another case we'll be working together."

"Yes."

Being over six feet tall I had to stoop to get into the rental car. I slid into the driver's seat, Jake climbed in the other side. "Director Wellington says you have a brother in the area."

"Does she?" I started the engine.

"I didn't know you had a brother."

"Yes." I turned the car around and headed for the highway. "I have a brother."

"What's his name?"

"Sean—but if you don't mind I'd rather stick to the case right now than talk about—"

"Right. Of course." He overdramatized the words. "Didn't mean to pry."

A moment passed. "It's all right. Did Margaret mention which ERT agent she was sending up to process the scene?"

"Natasha Farraday. She had a few things to wrap up here; should get to Woodborough around 8:30."

What Natasha lacked in experience, she made up for in persistence. A good choice.

Jake positioned his iPad 2 on his lap. "Director Wellington had the deputy who sent in the photos of the snowmobile tracks to the Lab, guy named Bryan Ellory, send us the crime scene photos of the house."

"So, preliminary police reports?"

He tapped the screen. "Looks it, yeah."

"Read me what we have."

Jake opened the files, I found the highway and headed north as the glow along the western horizon drained slowly into night.

Alexei collected his baggage from carousel 6 in the Minneapolis–St. Paul International Airport and headed to the Avis reservation desk. He was traveling under the name of Neil Kreger and had a midsized sedan waiting for him.

Neil Kreger.

He mentally reviewed this identity's family history, work experience, previous residential addresses, habits, interests. The sum of a life never lived.

It was just over a four-hour drive to Elk Ridge, Wisconsin. He'd hoped to arrive earlier, but as it turned out, the day's work schedule had not allowed for that.

It'd been a busy morning, first chatting with Rear Admiral Colberg and then setting everything up for his regrettable fatal car accident near Cedarville State Forest in Brandywine, Maryland, not far from his home.

Before boarding his plane to the Twin Cities, Alexei heard that, unfortunately, Dashiell Collet had not survived the night. Erin had, however—awakening just as Valkyrie predicted she would—only to learn of her father's death. Situations like that were one of the painful downsides of Alexei's line of work, and though he tried not to dwell on them, he could not help but feel sympathetic toward the girl's plight.

Ideally, arriving tonight would give Alexei enough time to look into the background of the three Eco-Tech members before his 1:00 meeting with them tomorrow afternoon at the Schoenberg Inn, famous as one of the northwoods locations gangsters used back in the early 1900s when they traveled up from Chicago to northern Wisconsin to elude the law.

With the hidden prohibition-era poker rooms and underground

escape routes into the neighboring national forest, the Schoenberg had served John Dillinger and his men well. As far as Alexei knew, Valkyrie had arranged to use it for the meeting, no doubt paying the manager more than enough to obtain full access to the parts of the hotel no longer open to the public.

Alexei's GRU contact still had no leads on Valkyrie. Nikolai was well connected and even had ways of getting into the US government's federal agency databases, but so far had come up empty.

That surprised Alexei.

And intrigued him.

He arrived at the Avis desk. "Neil Kreger," he said with a smile. He handed his license to the frizzy-haired, baggy-eyed woman behind the counter. "I'll be the only driver."

5

As we passed the Chequamegon-Nicolet National Forest on the way to Woodborough, Jake gave me his thoughts about the information contained in the police reports.

"Looks like we have a single EAMD," he said, referring to the four locations every murder includes—the site of the initial *encounter* between the killer and the victim, the *attack* (which might include abduction), the *murder* itself, and the *dump site*.

When all four occur in a single location, it makes it harder to develop a geoprofile since you have only one site to work with. On the other hand, when a body is found in a home like this, evidence is preserved, making the site an ideal crime scene from a forensic standpoint.

Jake spoke for a few more minutes about the reasons why husbands shoot their families. Textbook, fill-in-the-blanks profiling that might or might not be pertinent to this case. I did my best to give him my attention, keeping my points of contention to myself.

"From my experience," he said, "with a crime like this he won't have spent too much time with the bodies."

Jake had been in the Bureau eight years, a second career after working as a forensic psychologist in the Midwest: Rockford, Madison, a short stay in Cincinnati. With a master's in abnormal psychology from Cornell, experience consulting with law enforcement, counseling rape victims, and an impressive curriculum vitae, the Bureau was glad to have him. Now he was based out of Quantico, Virginia, at the National Center for the Analysis of Violent Crime. But he was a man who tended to jump to conclusions too soon based on gut instincts and "experience" rather than relying solely on the evidence, and I avoided working with him whenever I could—but he'd requested the Reiser case, Ralph had approved it, and here we were in Wisconsin together.

In the conversational lull following Jake's words, I called Deputy Ellory, the officer who'd contacted the FBI Lab to see if they could identify the snowmobile tracks. The whole situation struck me as incongruous. Multiple homicides in a rural area and a possible suicide, and a deputy rather than the sheriff was taking the lead on this? It didn't make sense.

Ellory picked up. A quick greeting, then I asked, "What made you think to call the Bureau?"

"I figured they'd have the fastest ways to look up the model of the sled. You know, like when they have tire track databases or something." He sounded young enough to still be in high school. "How they do all that stuff on *CSI*."

Honestly, it was a good idea. Most agents I've worked with wouldn't even have thought of it. "Okay. Tell me about the house."

"Well, actually, I wasn't there too long. Your director told us to leave. Lizzie, we found upstairs. Mrs. Pickron—Ardis—she was on the steps. She was shot in the back. Probably with a .30-06."

There was no mention in the police reports about the murder weapon being found. "Did you find cartridge casings?"

"No. That's just what it looked like."

"What it looked like?"

"The bullet hole, the entry wound. I hunt. You get to know gunshot wounds pretty good."

He would have to know GSWs incredibly well to distinguish between calibers on an entry wound—I wasn't even sure it was possible. Exit wounds yes, but—

Jake waved a couple fingers to get my attention. "Ask him about Donnie."

I said to Ellory, "Have you found Donnie Pickron or recovered his body?"

"No."

If the stretch of water was wide enough, we might have a chance at getting divers in to find him. "Any divers up there who can search the area?"

"Far as I know there's just one guy around here who dives—Denny Jacobson. But he's down in Florida this month. Visiting relatives, I think. Parents moved there last year, you know. But Donnie's body is obviously down in that lake *somewhere*."

We didn't have nearly enough facts yet to know what was obvious and what was not, but I decided that pointing that out might not get us off on the right foot. "I was told there were no boot or shoe impressions, just the Ski-Doo tracks."

"That's right."

"Has it snowed recently? Is there any chance footprints might have been covered or obscured?"

"No."

"Are you a snowmobiler?"

"Everyone around here is."

Growing up in Wisconsin I'd ridden my share of snowmobiles, but I hadn't been on a sled in over fifteen years. Putting the question of the sled's weight and the thickness of the ice aside for the moment, I said, "I understand this will depend on the speed, but how far do you think a Ski-Doo 800 XL would go without someone squeezing the throttle?"

"Let's see . . . the trail along the lakeshore is pretty steep. I'd say he couldn't have been going more than thirty miles per hour. Forty tops. That would mean . . ." He paused, obviously evaluating how that would relate to my question. "I guess it would cruise twenty, thirty yards maybe. But it went under a hundred yards from shore."

Tonight when we arrived it would be too dark to get a good look at the lake, at least not with respect to its orientation to the surrounding terrain. We could check it out in the morning.

"We'll be at the house in about twenty-five minutes. Does it work for you to meet us at the Pickrons'?"

"You betcha."

End call.

The full moon, the first of the year, had risen, and from where it hung low in the sky it looked impossibly round and bright, like an unblinking orange eye staring at us from the heavens. Its light reflected boldly off the snow, lending a surreal feeling to the evening, a spectral glow whispering across the fields.

Jake broke the brief silence. "So, they haven't found him yet?"

"Not yet. No."

He typed a few notes into his iPad. I hopped off Highway 77 and began winding down the county roads that led to the Pickron residence just outside of Woodborough.

6

We'd missed supper, but Jake and I swung through a gas station and grabbed some snacks to tide us over. Now, I crumpled up my Snickers bar wrapper, set it between the seats, and turned onto the long winding driveway that led to the Pickron house.

A frozen marsh bordered the house on the north and west sides, and in the headlights I could see vast clumps of dead marsh grass cutting through the crust of snow. From the maps Jake had pulled up, I knew a forest lay south of the house.

The closest residence I'd seen on the way here was about half a mile down the road.

The house lay at the top of a rise that would have given the family a beautiful wide-open view to the north. We parked beside one of the cruisers out front, I grabbed my laptop bag, and as we walked up the snow-packed path toward the porch, I took a moment to note the snowmobile tracks on the side of the house closest to the woods. In the brisk moonlight I noticed that two pairs of boot prints led to them from the side door.

Deputy Ellory, a baby-faced twentysomething guy with sandy-colored hair and slightly vacant eyes, was waiting for us by the front door.

Two state troopers flanked him, and I asked them to wait outside. They nodded without saying a word, but the hard look on their faces told me how deeply the murders had affected them. How committed they would be to catching the killer.

Good.

Ellory, Jake, and I entered the home. No sign of forced entry. The temperature in the house was cool. Fiftyish. I set down my computer bag.

To avoid tracking dirt or snow into the house and contaminating the scene, the three of us took off our shoes, or in my case, boots, in the mudroom just inside the entrance. Ellory asked me, "So, you gonna process the scene then?"

"An agent will be here shortly to do that," I answered. Eight pairs of shoes and boots were positioned neatly against the wall—some men's, some women's, two for a little girl.

Lizzie will never use those pink boots again, never again run out into the snow to play.

I looked away, asked Ellory, "Any other officers here? Any other troopers?"

"We tried to keep the scene clear, like they said."

"What about the sheriff?"

"He's down with the flu," Ellory told me.

Down with the flu? With a case this big?

He must have been deathly ill or remarkably negligent.

"So," Ellory went on, "if you're not processing the scene, you're here to . . . ?"

I slid my boots toward the wall and donned a pair of latex gloves. "I'm here to take a look at the temporal and spatial aspects of the crime. See where that leads us."

He looked at me quizzically.

"I'm a profiler," Jake offered. "We track violent serial offenders: arsonists, rapists, mostly murderers."

"So you two hunt serial killers?"

"Yes," Jake said.

"So you're like a team or something? Like on TV? Like on *Criminal Minds*?"

Jake straightened out his shirt. "We work together whenever we're called upon to do so." He sounded like he was at a press conference.

"And you think this crime is . . . that there's a serial killer?"

"You never can tell on these things."

"Actually," I cut in, "at this point we have no reason to believe that the killer or killers are linked to any other crimes."

Ellory looked at me, then at Jake. "Okay," he said. "Good." He indicated the doorway to the main part of the house. "It's right through here."

7

The three of us entered the living room.

White carpet. Nicely appointed. The room was color-coordinated in light green, apart from the recliner, which didn't quite match the walls and couch. The vast, drapeless plateglass window facing the marsh had three spread-out bullet holes with an expansive network of cracks fingering away from each of them. The police reports Ellory had sent us had mentioned these bullet holes but had not included a photo.

Jake glanced around briefly, then headed toward the kitchen, where I noticed a purse on the table.

I studied the scene. No sign of a struggle. Neither room had been ransacked. No disarray of drawers, papers, or furniture that might indicate the killer was searching for something.

Following Jake momentarily, I went through the purse, confirmed it was Ardis's. Memorized its contents.

A laundry room lay just off the kitchen and contained the side door that, based on the tracks outside, the killer or killers apparently used to exit the premises. I surveyed the room, layering it into the mental map I was forming of the interior of the house, then returned to the living room.

On the east side, a flight of stairs led to the second level. Through the railing I could see Ardis's body lying grimly on the steps. According to the police reports, her daughter Lizzie had been killed on the second floor landing, in the bathroom doorway.

I felt a wash of nausea. Considering the number of bodies I've seen over the years, you'd think I would have gotten used to this by now, but each time I work a homicide, it hurts just as much as it did the last.

Ellory saw me gazing toward the stairs. "They told us you wanted us to leave the bodies alone, so I had one of the guys turn off the thermostat. Figured that'd help keep the bodies cool. Preserve 'em."

I faced him. "When did you do that?"

"I don't know. Couple hours ago."

"What was the temperature set at when you turned down the thermostat?"

Silence. Then, "I don't know. I don't think we checked. Why?"

Jake answered from the kitchen. "Knowing the room temperature and the current temperature of the bodies would have helped us narrow down the time of death."

Ellory looked confused. "But we already know that: 1:48 this afternoon."

I stared at him. This information hadn't been in the police reports. "How do we know that?"

"One of the neighbors heard five gunshots and thought it might be Donnie out target shooting." He gestured toward the window with the three bullet holes. "Turns out he was killing his family instead."

"Is there any indication that he wasn't target shooting?"

"That he *wasn't*?"

I approached the window. "Yes." I studied the three bullet holes in the window and the cracks spiderwebbing away from them. The holes were in an off-centered, downward-sloping triangular pattern. The maze of cracks covered at least a third of the window.

Hmm.

I turned and looked at the sight lines to the landing. A five-meter-long open hallway stretched the length of the living room, revealing the three doors on the upper level. From the police reports I knew two of them were bedrooms; the bathroom door lay at the end of the hallway just to the right of the stairs, although from here I couldn't see Lizzie's body.

"Well, Mrs. Frasier heard five shots." Ellory was watching me. "There's three bullet holes right there in the glass. And each of the two victims was killed with a single shot. That's five shots."

"Yes, it is." I went back to examining the window, thinking about the shot progression.

Timing and location.

Mrs. Pickron is on the steps, her daughter was killed in the doorway to the right of the stairs.

The bedrooms are on the left.

The bullets had traveled through the window as well as the storm window, another sheet of glass several inches away that was meant to seal the room from the cold Wisconsin winters.

This window covered most of the wall and with the marsh outside—

Someone might have been able to look in and see the killer.

Or killers.

Ellory seemed to read my thoughts. "We figured the perp might have been shooting at someone out there—or maybe someone fired back. We looked for footprints in the snow before you came. Nothing."

"Always strive to separate evidence from coincidence." The words of my mentor Dr. Calvin Werjonic echoed in my head. *"Truth often hides in the crevices of the evident. Be always open to the unlikely."*

In high-velocity impact fractures, glass on the exit side of plate glass will have a larger opening than the entry side, and I could tell that the bullets had been fired from inside the house. In addition, when fired through plate glass, a bullet will create a cone-shaped fracture called a Hertzian cone that surrounds the hole on the downrange side of the glass. The Hertzian cones for these three holes confirmed that the entry point for all three bullets came from inside the house.

From inside the house.

A bullet passing through glass will cause radial cracks extending away from the entry point, but they'll terminate when they meet other cracks already present. So when you have multiple gunshot holes, by studying the pattern of cracks you can deduce the order in which the bullets passed through the window. In this case, the webbed cracks in the glass caused by the hole on the far left met the cracks from the bottom hole, but did not pass them. The cracks caused by the remaining bullet hole stopped at the cracks caused by the other two.

This pattern told me that the bottom bullet had passed through the glass first, the one above it to the left had been fired second, and the remaining bullet third.

"There was a pause before the final shot," I said quietly. "Did Mrs. Frasier mention that?"

Ellory was staring at me. "How did you know?"

"The angles. What did she say exactly?"

"She heard five shots—two in succession, then a pause and then two more. A little bit later she heard the fifth shot. But how did you know?"

"The angles," I repeated. "She remembered it that distinctly?"

He shrugged. "I guess she's got a good memory."

Once again I gave my attention to the web of cracks in the glass.

"What are you thinking, Pat?" Jake asked from somewhere behind me.

"Just trying to compare what we know with what we're assuming," I said.

"You said angles." Ellory sounded confused. "What are you talking about?"

We didn't have any wooden dowels or laser pointers, but I could use something else to show him. "Do you have a pen?"

He handed me one from his pocket.

Taking a pen of my own and one from Jake, and using a chair so I could get to the holes, I slid the pens into each of the three bullet holes' entrance and exit holes so that the men could see the angles from which the bullets had been fired.

"When you eye up the angles against the layout of the room, you can see that the last bullet must've been fired from somewhere on the landing at the top of the stairs. The other two were fired from the ground floor."

I headed for the steps.

"What is it?" Jake asked me.

"I need to see the bodies," I replied softly.

8

Jake said nothing but joined me at the base of the stairs.

Ardis lay sprawled awkwardly a few steps above us, facedown, her head turned sideways toward the railing, her left arm extended above her head in a way that looked like she was reaching forward, almost like someone trying to win a race, lunging toward the finish line. Reaching for eternity.

She'd been descending the stairs when she was killed.

Seeing her corpse brought the harsh reality of death home again.

Right here, lying before me was a woman who, earlier today, had been breathing, thinking, existing—alive—and now she was gone. That quickly.

It struck me that one day I'll die in the midst of something just as she did—a dream, a hope, a doubt, a relationship. And that'll be it. Such a simple truth, such an undeniable truth, yet one we desperately avoid addressing in our lives. As one of the mathematicians I've studied, the seventeenth-century philosopher Blaise Pascal, bluntly put it, "The last act is bloody, however fine the rest of the play. They throw earth over your head and it is finished forever."

The last act is bloody.

However fine the rest of the play.

I knelt beside Ardis's body.

Late forties. Slightly overweight. Blonde hair, now splayed sadly across the steps. She had gentle-looking features, wore jeans, wool socks, no shoes. Earlier, I'd found no phone in her purse. I felt her pockets. Nothing.

The pattern of blood spatter on the carpet confirmed that her body hadn't been moved. Based on the angle of the blood droplets on the wall and railing, the shooter would have been positioned directly behind her near the top of the stairs when he—or she—fired.

She was fleeing when she was killed.

Her flannel shirt was a mess of blood from the fatal gunshot wound to her back, centered almost directly between her shoulder blades.

From the police reports I knew that Donnie was forty-eight, and, with the age of the couple, I wondered briefly if Lizzie might have been adopted. Something to check on later.

I inspected Ardis's hands. She had short unpolished fingernails that might contain the DNA of her attacker if she'd been able to scratch him. We'll see.

No visible defensive wounds on her hands or forearms.

Behind me I heard Jake asking Ellory if they'd moved anything. The deputy said no.

"This is how you found her."

"That's right."

I looked into her unblinking eyes.

Ardis.

Her name was Ardis Pickron.

Anger tightened like a knot in my chest and I was glad. Forget objectivity. I like it when things get personal. I want to feel grief and want it to be like a hot knife inside of me. It keeps me focused on why I do what I do.

I'd been dreading this next part of the investigation ever since Margaret had told me about the crimes.

Viewing the body of the four-year-old girl.

Carefully, I stepped over Ardis. It wasn't easy because of the narrow staircase and the position in which her body had fallen. Crossing over her like this felt uncomfortably intrusive, and I had the sense that I should apologize, even though there was no one to apologize to.

Still, in my thoughts, I did.

At the top of the stairs I noted the two bedrooms to my left. The door down the hall would be the master bedroom. I would check on that in a minute. The room closest to me was obviously Lizzie's and looked just as you'd expect a four-year-old girl's room to look—a pile of stuffed animals on the bed, posters of horses covering the walls, a Dora the Explorer play set in the corner, a stack of Dr. Seuss books on a shelf near the window. A small pile of little girl's shirts lay folded neatly on the bedcovers, a dresser drawer still sat open.

Lizzie's body lay in the doorway to the bathroom on my right.

She had blonde hair like her mother's and wore pink tights and a flowery red dress that didn't seem quite appropriate, considering the season. Lizzie lay face up, and the front of her dress was stained with blood.

I closed my eyes.

It's always hardest when it's children.

Over the years I've known more than one street-hardened cop who was assigned to a child homicide case and was never the same again. Some quit. Some ask for transfers to desk jobs. One FBI agent I knew took his own life. It affects you deeply and forever and you're never the same again.

I took a breath, opened my eyes again, then forced myself to examine the position of Lizzie's body. Based on the location of the doorway in relation to the stairs and the adjoining walls, the killer would have been on the far side of the landing when he shot her. He hadn't posed or repositioned her.

The cold, calculated nature of the crime appalled me.

Did your father do this to you, Lizzie? Did he kill you?

Seeing the young girl's body like this hurt so badly that I had to fight hard to keep from losing it.

A girl. A four-year-old girl.

Could a father really do that to his daughter?

You know he could. You know how often this happens all over the country.

I tried to shake that troubling thought, found it nearly impossible. Finally, I turned away from the girl and went to the far door, the master bedroom.

Staying in the hall, I peered inside.

The bed was neatly made, covered with a checkered quilt. Light purple walls brought a calm mood to the room. The closet door stood slightly ajar. On the bed stand: a Thomas H. Cook novel, and a cell phone charging beside a small lamp.

Closing my eyes again I tried to picture how things might have played out, but I was interrupted by Jake, who'd joined me on the landing. "So that's the girl." He spoke softly, with a reverence I wouldn't have expected.

I opened my eyes. "Yes."

He was looking at Lizzie. "I hate it when it's kids."

For the second time today we agreed about something.

"So do I."

A small moment passed between us, and I sensed that neither of us could think of the right thing to say.

"All right," I said at last. "Let's reconstruct this, try to figure out what happened here at 1:48 this afternoon."

9

Jake's gaze moved toward the staircase. "Well, it's pretty obvious Lizzie was leaving the bathroom and Ardis was on her way down the stairs. Probably fleeing."

I nodded. "The killer was back here near the master bedroom when he shot Lizzie. I think Ardis was in Lizzie's bedroom when he did. Probably putting the laundry away."

"Why do you say that?"

"The shirt drawer is still open, there are folded shirts on the bed. Someone was interrupted putting them away. And if Ardis had been in the master bedroom and tried to flee, she would've had to get past the shooter and most likely would've been killed on the landing."

"Hmm," Jake reflected. "So the killer ascends the stairs, positions himself where you are, and the bathroom door opens. Lizzie appears. He shoots her."

"That alerts Ardis"—I was thinking aloud—"who leaves Lizzie's bedroom, sees her daughter lying in the bathroom doorway."

It was possible that Ardis had been descending the stairs and the killer shot her first before Lizzie left the bathroom, but it seemed more likely that a child would be frightened by the sound of a gunshot and stay in the bathroom, hoping that her mother would come to check on her. For now, I proceeded as if the order of events was along the lines of what we were thinking. "What's the first thing you do," I said, "if you hear a gunshot and then find the body of your daughter?"

"Run," Jake said. "Call 911."

I evaluated his answer. "Before that you'd check to see if your child was alive, then you'd look around to see where the shooter is. To see if you're in danger too. And if you are—"

"You'd run."

"Or hide." I was studying the angles of the staircase and the location of Lizzie's body. Would you respond differently if you knew the shooter? If it was your husband? I imagined you would but thought the specific response would depend on the state of the relationship. At the moment, postulating any further bordered on trying to decipher motives, which is something I try to steer clear of doing. "Remember, it's possible Lizzie wasn't dead when Ardis found her."

Jake looked at me questioningly.

"It seems probable that Ardis didn't see the shooter or else she would've hidden in the bathroom or been killed on the landing rather than making it nearly all the way down the stairs."

"Okay," he said. "So the killer steps into the master bedroom, then hears Ardis descending the stairs. He rushes out and shoots her before she reaches the bottom." He contemplated that for a moment. "So what about the bullet holes in the window?"

"The neighbor heard two initial shots. Those were the kill shots."

He looked at me skeptically. "And how do you know the shooter didn't fire the shots through the window first, then kill Ardis and Lizzie?"

"The angle of the first two bullets through the glass shows that they were fired from the first floor," I explained, "but if the killer fired those before ascending the steps, it would have alerted Ardis and Lizzie, who would have hidden in a room since the only exit route is down the steps. Additionally—"

"He would've shot Ardis from the ground floor," Jake said, tracking with me, "rather than from the landing."

I nodded. "Yes."

"Huh." He gestured toward the plate glass. "You knew all this earlier, didn't you? Just by looking at the trajectory of the bullet holes and knowing the position of the bodies? That's why you were so concerned about the angles in the glass when we first got here." He sounded impressed, but I noted a thread of contempt in his voice. "You knew it already back then."

Well, I didn't quite know it.

"I had my suspicions."

When he replied I sensed that he'd taken offense, as if reconstructing the crime scene had become some kind of competition between us: "So then, after killing them, he fires the shots through the window." Jake was pretending to take aim at the window, here from the landing.

"First he descends the stairs," I corrected him. "The single shot fired from the landing was the final one to pass through the glass. He would've had to go to the ground floor and fire the two shots through the window first."

"Why would he do that?"

I shook my head. "I have no idea. But I'm really wondering about that last shot the neighbor heard—the final bullet to pass through the window. The trajectory tells us it was fired from the landing. That means that after coming down the stairs, the killer would've had to return to the landing—stepping over Ardis's body as he did—before firing again through the window."

Mentally, I played out a few other scenarios, but at the moment I didn't come up with any other event progression that took into account the timing and trajectory of the shots as well as the location of the bodies and their position.

"When the shots were fired, where Donnie shot 'em from," Ellory called from the base of the stairs, "what does any of that matter, anyway?"

"Everything matters." I didn't like that he was referring to Donnie as the killer.

I pressed the master bedroom door open the rest of the way and stepped inside.

10

I studied the carpet for any evidence that someone might have entered the room.

"What is it?" Jake asked.

"We have no footprints leading from the front porch to the side of the house where the snowmobile was parked, so, assuming the killer rode it from the scene, he exited the scene through the laundry room. The family left their shoes, not just their boots, near the front door. Neither Ardis nor Lizzie was wearing shoes, so it appears the family habitually—"

"Takes off their shoes in the house."

"Yes."

Jake went on, paralleling my thoughts: "And if Donnie was the shooter, he would've had his shoes off in the house."

"It's likely."

"However, if someone else was the shooter, he wouldn't have taken off his shoes. After all, why would he?"

"That's right."

"So, mud on the carpet?"

Or water stains or shoe impressions . . .

It was more likely we'd find mud or impressions by one of the entrances to the home or on the pristine white living room rug. "Maybe."

I inspected the carpet but couldn't tell if the shoe impressions I saw were the same size as Donnie's boots in the mud room. Natasha should be here any minute to process the crime scene. I'd have her check it out.

I descended the stairs, stepping past Ardis's body as reverently as

I could. "We'll want to check the neighbor's clock," I told Ellory. "See if it has the correct time. If we really are talking about 1:48 p.m."

"I'll have an officer do it." He stared past me toward the landing. "You think he forgot something maybe?"

"Who?"

"The shooter. That he might have been on his way out, realized he forgot something upstairs, went back to the landing to get it, and then fired the last shot through the living room window when he got there."

"I really couldn't say."

Jake, who was still on the landing, answered, "That would make sense."

While Jake came down the stairs to join us, I questioned Ellory about some of the issues that the rather disappointing and incomplete police report had left unanswered.

"Were the lights in the house on or off when you arrived?"

"They were on. All of them, except the study."

"Were the exterior doors locked or unlocked?"

"The doors were unlocked, but that's not so unusual." He said the next few words with uncertainty, as if he'd stopped believing them: "There's not much crime around here."

"Appliances. Which were on?"

"You mean like the oven?"

"Yes, and the computer, television, the washer, dryer, a cooking timer—anything." All of these things tell us what was happening, where people were, what they were doing, or when they were doing it.

He thought. "Not the washer or dryer. Or the TV. We checked the computer for a suicide note; didn't find one though."

"The computer is in the study?"

"Yes."

I retrieved my laptop from the mud room. "Do you by any chance know the last webpage that was opened?"

He was looking increasingly disappointed in himself the more we spoke. "I didn't look."

"It's okay. Thanks."

In the small office nook attached to the living room I clicked to the internet history while Ellory asked Jake, "You're a profiler. What's your take on this?"

The web history was password protected. The Bureau has ways past that, however. I surfed to the Federal Digital Database and entered my ID number.

"Rage," Jake said. "Donnie's—or whoever committed these crimes—their behavior exhibits uncontrollable rage. We find this type of thing with people who snap. Something pushes them over the edge—job loss, marital problems, the death of a child."

I downloaded the program I needed, and a few seconds later, using a 32-byte MD5 hash, I'd cracked the password and I was in.

Jake continued, "Almost always in cases like this, we find what we call a trigger event or a precipitating stressor. Do we know if there was any sudden trauma in his life recently?"

"No," Ellory answered. "If there was I don't know what it would be."

The web history had been deleted, but the hard drive hadn't been wiped. It wasn't difficult to click into the terminal window, enter a few lines of code that Angela Knight, my friend in the Bureau's Cybercrime Division, had taught me, and pull up the files.

Someone had been surfing through the naval archives of Ohio Class fleet ballistic missile submarine, or SSBN, deployment records from the 1980s. I could hardly believe the information was made available to the public, but then again, the data was three decades old. A few mouse clicks told me that the Cold War archives weren't considered matters of national security any longer, and a Freedom of Information Act request had apparently been filed by a group known as Eco-Tech four months ago.

Interesting.

Following up on that, I discovered that Eco-Tech had done some consulting for half a dozen Fortune 500 companies and two foreign governments—Brazil and Afghanistan.

Meanwhile, Jake kept his questions coming to Ellory. "Did Donnie have any mental or emotional problems that you're aware of?"

"Not that I know of."

I checked the time the sub archives were last opened.

Just minutes after the murders.

After the murders.

Odd.

Donnie was in the Navy. Maybe he was searching the sites.

But why then?

I heard a car crunch to a stop out front, possibly Agent Farraday. After I finished downloading the web history and email records to my laptop, I headed for the front door.

"Job dissatisfaction?" Jake asked Ellory behind me.

"Nope. He works at the sawmill over on Highway K. Far as I know he had no problems at work. Nothing like that."

Boots on again, I stepped onto the porch. The frigid air bit at me, and I tugged on my wool hat. Natasha Farraday exited the car.

Natasha smiled. Early thirties. Dark hair. Demure. Spot-on professionally. Even though we'd never dated, I'd sensed for a while that she had a thing for me. However, because of my relationship with Lien-hua, who also worked for the Bureau as one of its top profilers, I'd made sure to keep things with Natasha completely on the friends-only level.

After she greeted me, a stern-looking fiftyish man with shaggy, wolfish eyebrows followed her out of the car, stuck out his hand, and introduced himself as the county coroner. "Jeddar Linnaman, good to meet you."

I wasn't sure I'd heard that right. "Jeddar?"

"Full name's Jedderick, like Frederick but with an extra *d*. Everyone just calls me Jeddar."

"Nice to meet you."

"Agent Farraday told me all about you, Dr. Bowers. It's an honor to work with you."

The PhD wasn't something I liked drawing attention to. "Thank you. Just call me Pat."

After filling in the two of them on what we knew, I asked Natasha to pay special attention to the carpet fibers in the house and prints on the laundry room doorknob. "We'll also want to compare the boots by the door to the size and visible wear patterns of the sole impressions outside the laundry room."

"Got it."

"The computer was accessed after the murders, websites having to do with submarine deployments. I'm going to want to pull all the sectors to get a byte-level data analysis."

"That'll take time," she said, mirroring my thoughts.

"Yes."

Depending on the size of the files and the computer's processing speed, it could take up to twenty-four hours to upload the entire drive to the Cybercrime Division's FTP server.

"Go ahead and do a cursory review of recently accessed files," I said. "I'll get the emails and web history to Cybercrime, but I'd like your eyes on the registry as well; see what else you can find."

She agreed, then, carrying her forensics investigation kit, she entered the house with Jeddar Linnaman.

Already there was a lot to think about, and I needed to sort some things through. Taking a walk helps me collect my thoughts, so I stayed outside, zipped up my jacket, donned my leather gloves, and stepped into the night.

11

The two state troopers who'd been stationed on the porch had left when Natasha and Linnaman arrived, and with no one else around, the night closed in on me, embraced me, stinging and cold and quiet and still.

I headed down the driveway, mentally evaluating the clues.

Every crime occurs at the nexus of five factors:

(1) offender desire
(2) target availability
(3) location
(4) time
(5) lack of authority figure or supervision

Take away any of the five and you have no crime. Entire schools of criminological theory have sprung up over the last 130 years focusing on how to eliminate one or another of the factors from the crime equation.

Some investigators, mostly profilers and forensic psychologists, focus on the first issue—the offender's motivation: Why does he do it? What's going through his head at the time of the crime? Personally, I've found it's more helpful to just accept the fact that this person was motivated, for whatever reason—and probably for more than one—to commit the offense.

Other theorists study victimology or location: Who was victimized? How can you keep these people from being in high-risk areas at high-risk times? Some researchers study how people perceive public and private spaces and the likelihood of crime in those locations. Others track the temporal fluctuations of crime. And, of course, some criminologists try to increase (or give the appearance of increased) law enforcement presence, such as leaving empty police cars on busy roads or installing fake video surveillance cameras in conspicuous places.

Five factors.

Stop one, stop the crime.

Yet even though it's vital to deter crimes whenever possible, I've always been more in the business of solving them after they do occur.

Like today at 1:48 p.m.—if the recollection of Mrs. Frasier was correct.

Three initial questions rolled through my mind: Why then? Why there? Why Ardis and Lizzie?

As I walked toward the mailbox, I clicked through what we knew so far about the progression of events:

1:48 p.m. Shots fired—Still need to confirm the time.

2:41 p.m. Snowmobile tracks veering off the trail are discovered entering a stretch of open water on Tomahawk Lake. Deputy Ellory photographs the tracks, then calls the FBI, emails the photos to the Lab.

3:30 p.m. The Lab identifies the tracks, and local law enforcement narrows down the pool of possible victims to four people in the area who own that model snowmobile.

4:02 p.m. Officers follow up on the owners and find Ardis and Lizzie Pickron murdered; Donnie missing.

4:30 p.m. Admiral Winchester, the Chief of Naval Operations, is already pressuring FBI Director Wellington to have agents look into the case.

A thought: *So why the FBI and not NCIS?* But the answer was immediately obvious: the Naval Criminal Investigative Service only investigates crimes involving active duty military personnel, and Donnie was retired military rather than active duty.

That left the Bureau rather than NCIS, but still—why the high-level interest in a sawmill worker's disappearance?

That was the big question. The hinge upon which all the other facts swung.

The Navy's interest in the crime and the recently accessed websites on Ohio Class submarines didn't support the theory that the snowmobile's trip off the ice and Donnie's disappearance were the result of a simple suicide or a haphazard accident during a flight from a crime scene.

It didn't appear to be a robbery gone bad either.

When you move through a case, it's best to ask the sensible, obvious questions first, just like a reporter might do: Who? What? Where? When? Why? How?

So, where had Donnie been earlier today? Did he show up at work? If this was a setup to make him look guilty, why would he be targeted? What had he done or what did he know that caused him to end up in someone's crosshairs? And what might decades-old submarine deployment records have to do with anything? And why would Donnie—or anyone else—have been so careless as to look them up on his computer *after* the murders?

And of course, what about the three shots through the window? Either they were fired out of necessity or they were not. But what necessity?

Questions, questions.

Too little data.

I started back for the house. The moon had slipped behind a stray cloud, leaving the stars to rule the night. Seeing them reminded me of the times in college when I worked as a wilderness guide in North Carolina. After enough nights out on the trail you begin to know which stars will appear first, emerging slowly through the late twilight. *There you are, Vega, and Castor and Arcturus, so good to see you. How've you been? How has the night on the other side of the world been treating you?*

Everything was so simple in those days, life bared down to the basics of survival. Eat. Sleep. Climb. Paddle. You're forced to put all the niceties and creature comforts of modern life behind you and get back to the essentials. Survival. Relationships. Encountering the real.

I looked at the house again.

Encountering the real.

Life.

Death.

Two bodies. A missing snowmobiler.

Pausing at the side of the house, I bent and took a picture of the two sets of boot prints with my phone. Committed the imprint patterns to memory.

Then, leaving the stars behind, I quietly ascended the porch steps.

After a body is moved, the crime scene is altered forever, so contrary to what you might see in the movies, forensics examiners and evidence response teams are not typically in a hurry to remove bodies from a scene. Unless there's something present that would contaminate or destroy evidence (wind, water, etc.) they'll leave the corpse, sometimes for several hours, as they photograph it, check the core temperature to establish time of death, look at bloodstain patterns, and study the degree of and locations of the pooling of blood inside the body before removing it for an autopsy.

I spent another hour or so studying the scene, evaluating what I did know and comparing that to what I did not, then when Natasha and Linnaman were preparing to remove the bodies I realized it was almost 9:30 p.m. and I still hadn't called my brother.

I went into the study, eased the door shut. Hesitated for a moment.

Then pulled out my phone.

12

I imagined that even if Sean didn't invite me to stay at his place, Amber would, so I decided it might be best to try his work number first.

No one answered at the bait shop, which surprised me, since, with his beer and liquor sales, I'd expected that he would be open until at least 10:00 or 11:00.

I confirmed the number and tried again. Nothing.

He didn't own a cell, so that left his home number. I didn't have him on speed dial, but I found the number and tapped it in, hoping Sean would answer instead of his wife.

Amber picked up after two rings. "Hello?" I heard the splashing clatter of pots in water, and I could picture her standing beside the sink doing the dishes. Her honey-colored hair tied back in a loose ponytail.

"Amber, it's Pat."

"Pat."

"How are you?"

"I'm good." Her tone was impossible to read. "This is a surprise."

"I'm sorry to call so late, but I found myself in the area and I wanted to see if you and Sean were going to be around tomorrow. So we can get together."

"You found yourself in the area?" No more dish sounds now. "Where are you?"

"Woodborough."

"Woodborough," she repeated slowly. Then, "Do you need a place to stay?"

"No, I'll get a motel room."

A pause. "You're welcome to stay here, you know."

Even though I figured it wouldn't matter to Jake or Natasha if I stayed with my family, I declined. "Thanks, but I'm actually here on business and should stay close to town. I need to go to Tomahawk Lake first thing in the morning."

"Oh." Now, sadness in her voice. "The Pickrons." Of course she would have heard about them. By now, word of the homicides would've been all over the news.

"I'm assisting the sheriff's department," I said.

"Pat, it's so terrible what happened. I can hardly believe it. Things like that just don't happen here." I thought she might add, "Just in the big cities," or something along those lines, but she left it at that.

Since Amber was the only pharmacist in Elk Ridge, the next closest town over, I wouldn't have been surprised if, in these small, close-knit communities, she'd known the Pickrons or at least been peripherally familiar with the family's name.

At last I said, "Is Sean there? I tried the bait shop."

"No one picked up?"

"No."

"Figures. He's out ice fishing. He doesn't always get someone to cover the store. You know how he can be."

I didn't know how to respond to that. "Yes."

"Really, Pat." I sensed a subtle shift in her tone. A softer quality. "You know you're welcome here."

"I know." Based on my history with Amber it wouldn't be a good idea for me to head over there, especially if Sean was late in getting home. Additionally, because of my relationship with Lien-hua I didn't want to give anyone the wrong impression. "I'll be tied up all morning, but I should be able to get away for lunch. Do you think that would work? For the two of you?"

"I'll talk to Sean." I heard the clink of glasses in the background. She'd gone back to doing the dishes. For the moment at least, she'd given up on convincing me to come to the house tonight. "It's business," she said, "so Tessa didn't come along?"

"I was hoping she could come over tomorrow, but with this storm, we'll see. She's in the Twin Cities this week."

"I hope she can make it." More dishes. "We've never met, you know. Your stepdaughter and I."

Now that I thought about it, I realized she was right. Amber hadn't made it to my wedding with Tessa's mother and had been in the hospital with food poisoning the weekend of Christie's funeral nearly two years ago. "I'll try to make that happen. I'll call you in the morning. We'll set up a time to get together." I was stumbling for a way to gently ease out of this conversation. "After you talk to Sean."

"It'll be good to see you. It's been too long."

I wondered if it'd been long enough.

"Good night, Amber."

"Good night."

We ended the call, and I slowly lowered the phone.

Hearing her say good night to me again brought back a rush of memories and emotions that I really didn't need surrounding me at the moment.

A few months back, when Lien-hua and I had started to get serious, she'd told me that she wanted us to look forward and not backward. In lieu of this, she'd proposed that we not talk about past loves, past mistakes, past regrets, and as it happens, Amber fell into all three categories. So, although I would've been glad to discuss things with Lien-hua, I'd never spoken to her about Amber. Never even brought her up.

But now, I thought again of what had happened five years ago between me and Amber when she and Sean were engaged. Even though Lien-hua was the one who'd suggested not dredging up the past, in light of our potential future together, I felt a vague wash of guilt just thinking about Amber, and our relationship seemed like something Lien-hua should know about.

This week Lien-hua was on-site in Cincinnati profiling a case of three missing women.

I was about to tap at the phone to speed-dial her but then had second thoughts. It would probably be best to think through how to delicately broach the subject of Amber first, before getting on the line with Lien-hua.

I held the phone for a moment, staring at it, thinking about why the shooter might have returned up the stairs a second time after the murders.

The phone. Hmm.

Yes, check on that first, then call Lien-hua.

Using my laptop I logged into the Federal Digital Database, found that Donnie and Ardis Pickron had only one cell phone between them, registered in her name. I entered my federal ID number again and pulled up Ardis Pickron's mobile phone records.

13

Elk Ridge, Wisconsin

From his vantage point in the log cabin nine hundred meters from the Schoenberg Inn, Alexei Chekov monitored the entrance using the US military issue night vision binoculars he'd purchased last month on the black market in Afghanistan.

He didn't like surprises, and he wanted to have at least a cursory idea of how many people he would be dealing with at the meeting at 1:00 tomorrow afternoon. He'd been told three, but he anticipated a lot more had to be involved, at least at some level.

Through his sources, he knew that the team would be arriving tonight.

To monitor them, he'd taken the liberty of accessing this cabin. It'd been empty when he arrived, and he was hoping the owners wouldn't return or he'd be forced to make sure they would not be a problem. That might get messy, and that was a situation he would prefer to avoid.

So far he'd seen nine people arrive at the Schoenberg Inn, a sprawling, stylish hotel that looked out of place here in the northwoods.

All of the people he'd seen had parked in locations that allowed the lights from the front of the Schoenberg to illuminate their faces from more than one direction as they entered—an indicator that told Alexei they were either innocent civilians or, if they were operatives, they were inexperienced.

Using an infrared camera, he'd photographed all nine and was currently running their photos through the Federal Digital Database's facial recognition to confirm their identities. So far he'd identified four people from Eco-Tech—three men and one woman.

Because of their carelessness while entering the hotel, Alexei was surprised someone as meticulous and careful as Valkyrie was working with them.

Already, $2,000,000 had been wired to their account: Valkyrie had informed him of this. Alexei was here to deliver $1,000,000 more as well as the access codes he'd gotten from Rear Admiral Colberg that morning. The final payment of $1,000,000 would be delivered upon completion, after the message had been sent to and received by the US government at 9:00 p.m. Saturday night. That was all he'd been told—a message sent to the government.

He would pick up that money from a drop point tomorrow prior to the deadline.

When his phone rang and he saw who it was, he quickly answered.

Nikolai Demidenko, his contact at the GRU.

"In reference to Valkyrie, all I have found, my brother," Nikolai said, "are some suspect ties to an Islamic charity based in Pakistan. But that is all."

"Pakistan?"

"Yes."

"Send me the details and keep looking. I will forward the usual amount to your account."

"Yes, yes, of course."

Islamic charities?

Informative.

Alexei had been on a few cases in Pakistan himself over the years. Perhaps he and Valkyrie had associations with some of the same people. Something to keep in mind. Wait and see what else Nikolai could dig up.

Alexei had grown used to getting very little sleep but decided he would watch the Inn for two more hours and then go to bed.

Until then he would observe the premises, doing the job he had been hired to do.

Simply.

Professionally.

To the best of his ability.

The phone records confirmed my theory.

At 1:54 p.m. an incoming call had reached Ardis Pickron's cell phone.

The conversation hadn't ended until 1:58 p.m.

Before the state troopers left, one of them had driven to Mrs. Frasier's house and found out that the oven clock she'd looked at when she heard the last shot was six minutes slow, so the murders would actually have occurred at 1:54 rather than 1:48.

Someone had called Ardis's cell almost immediately after the murders.

And yet, now, the phone was charging in the master bedroom.

So the killer went back upstairs to answer the phone?

Possible.

The call had come from an unknown, unregistered number from someone in Egypt, one that had never called, or been called from, this phone before.

Although the country of origin appeared on the phone company's records, no actual number did, which meant someone knew what he was doing when he covered his tracks.

I took a moment to go tell Natasha to dust for prints on Ardis's phone, then I returned to the study for some privacy.

If the killer didn't talk for four minutes on the phone, who did?

Was more than one offender present? After all, there were two sets of boot impressions in the snow outside the laundry room door.

Truth often hides in the crevices of the evident. Be always open to the unlikely.

Considering both the location of the phone in the master bedroom and the timing of this call, it seemed at least possible that it had rung shortly after the murders, and that the shooter had gone upstairs to answer it.

If so, he or she would've had to have been expecting the call. Why else answer the phone at the home of a person you just killed? Why else have a four-minute conversation?

Unless it was Donnie after all.

When you're working a case, you arrange the pieces like a jigsaw puzzle, and I had the feeling I was looking at a straight-edged piece that might help frame in part of the perimeter. But how it related to the other facts of the case was still a mystery.

It's getting late, Pat. Call Lien-hua, tell her about Amber.

I hadn't really taken the time to collect my thoughts like I'd hoped, and I still wasn't sure exactly how to tackle this, but I knew I'd better call her now, tonight, get it off my mind.

I speed-dialed her number.

14

When Lien-hua picked up, she promptly told me she was busy going over case files with one of the local detectives. At first I thought it seemed a little late in the day for a business meeting like that, but then remembered I was the one calling her from a crime scene.

With the ambient noise in the background it sounded like she might be at a restaurant.

"I'm sorry to cut this short," she said, "but I really have to go, Pat. Ashton's got some notes we need to go over."

"Ashton."

"Ashton Rivera. The detective I'm consulting with."

"Of course."

I was quiet, searching for what to say, for a way to gracefully bring up Amber. "I had to drive up here to Woodborough. Margaret handed me another case."

"I heard."

I gave Lien-hua the rundown, and when she spoke again her tone had softened. "I wanted to tell you that I'm sending a surprise up there for you. It should arrive tomorrow."

Lien-hua's surprises were always intimate and always memorable. "Hmm. I suppose it won't do any good to ask what it is?"

"If I told you what it was, it wouldn't be—"

"Sure, I know—a surprise—but I won't hold full disclosure against you this time. I promise."

"Nope. You're going to have to wait. But I have a feeling you're really going to like it."

Okay, now my curiosity was getting piqued.

"Really, Pat"—urgency in her voice again—"I need to go. Ashton and I need to finish some things up. I'm glad you called, though."

"Yeah." I wanted to mention Amber, tell Lien-hua the story of what had happened five years ago, explain that Amber wasn't a threat, but all that came out was, "I'll look forward to that surprise, then."

"Good. Call me tomorrow."

"I love you," I said.

"You too."

After we hung up I was still thinking of Amber, of the incidents from my past that I hadn't shared with Lien-hua. The phone felt heavy and awkward in my hand, and I nearly missed slipping it into my pocket.

"Pat?" Jake's voice. He was standing in the doorway. I wondered how long he'd been there.

"What?" Even to me, my tone sounded somewhat sharp, but I figured if he'd been listening in on my conversation he deserved it.

"We should probably find a motel before it gets too late."

I heard Linnaman's voice from the living room: "You staying in Woodborough, then?"

"If possible," Jake said.

We joined Linnaman by the couch.

"Only one there is the Moonbeam Motel. The Schoenberg's in Elk Ridge, but the Moonbeam's a lot closer."

"That's it, then." Jake looked at me expectantly.

"All right." I tossed him the keys. "I'll be right out."

I did one final walk-through, trying to do what Margaret said I was good at—noticing what needs to be noticed—but didn't feel very successful at all.

At last I returned to the night and left with Jake for the Moonbeam Motel.

━━━━━━━━━━ ◆ ━━━━━━━━━━

In her dorm room at U of M, Tessa listened to Patrick's voicemail from earlier in the day—holding the phone to her right ear because of the hearing loss she'd suffered in her left ear last summer, when it all happened.

When the message ended, she set her phone on the dresser. The mirror above the sink caught her reflection, and she whisked away a strand of black hair from her eyes so she could see to wipe off her mascara.

Over the past couple years she'd flirted with the Goth look, wearing black lipstick, fingernail polish, and mascara for most of her sophomore and junior years. However, this year she'd eased up on all that, moving into more of a neo-Bohemian thing. But the dark mascara had stayed. As her friend Cherise sometimes said, "Fashion trends may come and go, but black is always sick."

As she was washing up, she brushed her fingers across the line of thin, straight scars on her right forearm, emblems of her cutting stage in the wake of her mom's death. They marked her search for release, narrow red lines that each brought a thread of pain while also letting a different kind of pain out.

But these days, despite being totally into screamer bands like House of Blood, Trevor Asylum, and Death by Suzie—and being pretty much addicted to gothic horror stories—she wanted nothing to do with blood or dead bodies in real life.

Nothing at all.

She'd had enough of that.

Instead, lately, she let her pain weep out onto the pages of her notebooks, filling one every week or so as she passed through the quotidian rhythm of life.

But still, the notebook wasn't quite enough.

She took the bottle out of her overnight bag.

Stared at it for a long time.

Slipped two pills out.

She caught herself glancing at the phone as she swallowed them and decided to return Patrick's call in the morning rather than tonight. She shed her clothes, pulled on her pajama pants and one of the old T-shirts Patrick had given her, an XL Simon Fraser University tee from the days he'd done his postgrad work in Vancouver.

Leaving the dorm room's bathroom light on, she swung the door only partly shut, then climbed into bed and grabbed the teddy bear she'd brought with her. Occasionally over the past year Patrick had given her a hard time about sleeping with Francesca, but she had the feeling that beneath it all he was glad she hadn't grown up completely yet; that at least in a few small ways she was still a little girl.

And he was probably relieved she was sharing her bed with a stuffed animal and not some guy.

Even if the pills did help, Tessa didn't expect to sleep much tonight, since she barely slept at all these days, and when she did, her dreams were harsh and scraped raw with images of her being chased by a man with a cold face and barren eyes and a wide unnerving grin that still gave her chills whenever she thought of it.

She'd been a part of something last summer that she could not forget and would never forgive herself for, something she tried not to think about every night when she lay down to go to sleep.

And every day when she awoke.

But the memory of that gun beside her ear, of squeezing the trigger, of the sound of the man who was about to kill her dropping to the floor, of seeing—out of the corner of her eye—all that blood splattered across the wall . . .

It had all happened so fast, so—

It was way too much.

She slid the memory to the side. Buried it.

Refused to let it crawl to the surface.

A distraction.

That's what she needed.

She flicked on the light beside her bed, pulled out one of her notebooks, propped herself up, and picked up a pen, *as carefully as if she were pulling out a scalpel to do surgery,* the words whispered through her mind, seemed to hover in the air before her, *against the black insidious tendrils of shame tentacling through her heart.*

Okay, that was too much. Too melodramatic. Definitely in need of editing, but something else would come.

She placed the tip of the pen against the virgin page, but hesitated. When she opened herself up like this on paper, she could be certain it would bring everything to the surface again, paradoxically making her feel worse and better at the same time.

Just like the razor blades.

But leaving different kinds of scars.

However, when she didn't write, when she kept everything inside, the dreams only got worse. She began with a few disjointed thoughts, then wrote,

> my soul is famished,
>   yet feeds on phantoms.
> my stomach grumbles
> at me, starving for
> something real.
> i lift another forkful
> of vapors to my mouth.
> when my diet is made up of so much
> illusion and mirage,
> the more moments i devour,
>   the emptier i become.

She tinkered with the words a little, then wrote for half an hour, poems stained with the past, but the harder she tried to forget, the clearer she seemed to remember.

At last, clicking off the bedside lamp, she put the notebook aside, drew Francesca close, and stared at the light easing from the bathroom doorway. *"She knew it was important that she rest,"* she thought, visualizing the words again, almost as if they were scribbled on a page, *"but Tessa Bernice Ellis did not close her eyes, lest the sleep she needed, the dreams she dreaded, would find her once again."*

15

After picking up our room keys at the motel's front desk, Jake and I agreed to meet tomorrow morning in the lobby at 8:00, when it would finally be light enough to view Tomahawk Lake. Natasha, who would also be staying at the motel, told us that she was returning to the Pickron house in the morning but would meet up with us later in the day.

In my room, I stowed my suitcase in the closet and gave Torres, the SWAT Team Leader, a call. He told me they hadn't found Reiser. "Don't worry, Pat. We're on this. We found blood on two of his knives. We checked the DNA. Matched that of two missing persons—one in Milwaukee, one in DC. The DC victim was female, but the one from Milwaukee was male. Doesn't fit the pattern. And no prints on the knife. He must have wiped it clean."

DC? He brought the knife in the knife block back here from DC?

"I'll be back down there as soon as I can," I told him.

"I know," he replied. "What are you thinking about the case up there? Double domestic homicide? The husband the shooter?"

"It's too early to tell," I said honestly.

After hanging up, I realized that I was becoming more and more concerned about the approaching snowstorm. I tried Tessa's number again but only reached her voicemail.

Not a fan of texting, I left another vm for her to call me first thing in the morning: "It's supposed to start snowing in the early afternoon so I need you to leave the winter session early, by 8:30 or so. Either that or I'll reserve a room for you at a hotel there . . . Okay, so talk to you in the morning." Out of habit I found myself calling her by the nickname I'd given her a year ago, a small way of acknowledging her independent spirit and her insatiable interest in Edgar Allan Poe: "I love you, Raven."

I said nothing about hoping she would sleep well.

It was a topic best left untouched.

Ever since the day last summer when her father had been accidentally killed and I shot a man who was threatening Tessa's life—was in fact about to shoot her—she understandably hadn't been able to sleep well, rarely making it through the night.

I'd suggested a counselor, but that didn't go over so well. She'd scoffed at the relaxation exercises I looked up online and tried yoga once but hated it.

Being a vegan and not wanting to use any drugs that had ever been tested on animals, she'd tried all the natural and homeopathic cures she could find. Then practical, commonsense things: no caffeine or food within four hours of bedtime, calming music, different ambient lighting combinations in her bedroom, candles and incense, getting up and doing something else rather than lying there dwelling on the fact that she couldn't fall asleep. Nothing had really helped, at least not in the long-term.

Obviously, it's not healthy for a high school senior to be unable to get more than four or five hours of sleep a night, and her GPA had taken a dive. In just one semester her cumulative 4.0 slipped to 3.65—pretty traumatic for a girl who'd never gotten a B on a report card in her life.

Her resultant testiness had also eroded her budding relationship with a new guy friend. He stuck with her for a while, but as she became more and more moody he finally broke things off just before Thanksgiving, which only made matters worse.

It seemed like the more I tried to find something to help her sleep, or the more I asked her how she'd slept, the more upset she became, so last month I stopped bringing it up. As long as she wouldn't take medication or see a therapist, I wasn't sure what else I could do for her.

Now, I set down the phone, but I left the ringer on just in case she called back.

After cranking up my room's heater, I sent Cybercrime the emails and web history I'd downloaded from Donnie Pickron's computer, searched through our online files for other instances of three shots through a window at a crime scene to see if that was the signature of any known criminal, but came up blank. Then I took some time to familiarize myself with the online maps of the miles and miles of snowmobile trails that intersect Tomahawk Lake and weave through the surrounding forests.

I found out that nearly all of the national forest service staff are seasonal and the ranger's office closes down most of the roads once winter hits. It didn't take me long to realize that, based on the location of the sawmill in relation to the Pickron residence and the long, looping county roads that wound around the marsh, it would have saved Donnie time and money if he rode his snowmobile to work through the Chequamegon-Nicolet National Forest rather than driving his car.

I committed the trails to memory.

Finally, emotionally drained from the events of the day, especially from seeing the four-year-old girl Lizzie's body, I put my laptop away and headed to bed, unsure, with all of this on my mind, if I would be able to sleep any better than my stepdaughter.

16

Friday, January 9
6:05 a.m.

I awoke later than I'd expected, a black slit of night still hanging between the curtains.

The motel didn't have an exercise room, but I threw myself into an old-school workout of push-ups and crunches and ended with pull-ups on the door frame to the bathroom—a way to keep my grip in shape for the climbing trip in Patagonia I was planning this summer. Ever since my days as a wilderness guide, I've slipped out to go rock climbing whenever I got the chance, and this summer was going to be my first trip to Patagonia in more than a decade. I needed to crank up my finger strength or I'd never be able to pull down the 5.12 routes I was eyeing.

After a shower, I saw that it was 7:08 a.m., less than an hour before my trip to Tomahawk Lake with Jake.

I flipped on the TV to catch the weather, and a life insurance commercial popped on.

Life insurance: an oxymoron. After all, life is the one thing that cannot be insured, a fact that's all too obvious to someone in my business.

"Planning for the unthinkable, made simple and secure," the announcer said.

I barely held back a head shake. A culture that calls the inevitable "unthinkable" is simply a culture in denial. However, when he assured me that I would "never have to face the future alone," his words brought to mind something a little less disheartening: a conversation a few months ago with Tessa, the talk that had led to my decision to take things with Lien-hua to the next level.

My wife Christie died of breast cancer almost two years ago. At the time I didn't know who Tessa's biological father was, and neither did she, so, as her guardian, I began caring for her as if she were my own daughter. From the start, things had been rocky, but eventually we'd grown as close as a real father and his daughter might be, and I wouldn't trade the time with her—even the rough spots—for anything.

Tessa liked Lien-hua a lot and wanted me to get together with her, but Lien-hua had been drifting from me, and when Tessa asked me how things were going I'd been honest and told her, "She seems a little aloof lately."

"What are you doing about it?"

I shrugged. "I don't know. I'm wondering if she's not that interested in me after all."

"Patrick, women want to be pursued. They want to play hard to get, but the last thing they want is to succeed in getting away."

I stared at her. "That doesn't make any sense."

"That's 'cause you're not a girl."

"Why don't they just—"

"How old are you again?" An arched eyebrow. I was having a conversation with Mr. Spock. "Thirty-seven? And you still have no clue about women?"

"Do you know a guy of any age who does?"

She considered that. "Good point. But when a girl distances herself from a guy it's a test to see how serious the guy is."

"So, let me get this straight. Women pretend they don't want guys to pursue them so that they will, and they act like they're not interested in them when they are."

"Exactly."

"And the more ambivalent they act about making things work, the more they want to get got?"

"Pretty much, yeah."

"You're a teenage girl. How do you know all this?"

"I'm a teenage girl."

So, I'd pursued Lien-hua as Tessa suggested and found that her counterintuitive observations about women were correct. Consequently, things with Lien-hua had progressed, and this coming week I was planning to propose.

If I could only work up enough nerve to actually pop the question.

I surfed through the channels until I came to some cable news weather. The cohosts chatted for a minute about the balmy weather in San Diego while the scrolling news at the bottom of the screen announced that Secretary of State Nielson had arrived in Tehran for "groundbreaking bilateral talks about sanctions and Iran's controversial nuclear research program."

That's what the media was reporting, but I'd heard through my friends higher up in the government that his trip was really precipitated by Israel's recent statement, "Any nuclear aggression by Iran will be met with immediate and unequivocal force." Israel has never officially acknowledged that they have nuclear weapons, but to everyone in the know, it's a given. The story caught my attention only because Nielson is a friend of Margaret's and his name comes up now and again. According to her, she helped him get started in politics years ago. I had the sense that she liked having friends in high places who owed her.

The ticker scrolled: the stock market was down forty-four points, the Celtics beat the Lakers, and then finally, the meteorologist addressed the national weather scene. He started by encouraging everyone in the upper Midwest to fill up on gas and groceries before the storm arrived. And to stay off the roads if at all possible.

I only needed to watch a few moments to realize that it'd be best if Tessa left by nine or not come up at all.

After clicking off the television I decided to call her during the drive to Tomahawk Lake to sort things out.

Whenever possible I like to visit the scene of a crime at the same time of day as when the crimes occurred in order to gain a temporal understanding of that location. If that isn't practical, as in this case, I could at least orient myself spatially in reference to the snowmobile tracks, open water, and the sawmill Donnie worked at across the lake.

At the scene, I try to consider what the killer and the victim saw, smelled, or heard. What would I be responding to if I'd been there? If I'm the victim, am I resisting? How does the environment affect that—either facilitating or hampering my efforts to get away?

Timing and location.

And frankly, the crime scene at the Pickron house didn't make sense, especially if Donnie were the shooter. After all, surely he would've known that he'd be a suspect, whether or not he bothered to remove the spent casings. Why take the cartridge casings if you're simply going to commit suicide?

While it's true that people often don't think clearly during and immediately following their involvement in violent behavior, removing evidence is a form of staging, and you only do that if you're trying to cover something up, derail an investigation, or shift suspicion onto someone else, which—if Donnie had been planning to kill himself—didn't seem likely.

I pulled up the emails I'd downloaded from the Pickrons' computer, checked the times they were last opened, and found that almost all of Donnie's emails on Mondays and Fridays were last accessed before 6:00 a.m. In some of them he'd written that he was "on his way out the door" so it seemed reasonable to move forward with the working hypothesis that he checked his email and left for work soon afterward.

I made a note to find out when he was expected to arrive at the sawmill on those days, then reviewed my notes, specifically what we knew about the murder weapon.

Apparently, Donnie had a gun cabinet in his basement. An empty rack and .30-06 cartridges told me that Deputy Ellory's guess about the type of gun used was probably correct. Two handguns were still in the cabinet.

Why take the rifle with you on the snowmobile? If you wanted to either kill yourself or protect yourself, why not just take one of the handguns along?

I couldn't help but think that a hunter like Donnie would have chosen a shotgun or maybe a handgun for the crimes. Rifles are better for long distances. Why use a rifle in the close quarters of a house? Did the shooter fear that Ardis or Lizzie would flee and want to be able to pick them off before they got away?

And where was Donnie now? At the bottom of Tomahawk Lake? And if not, who drove that snowmobile off the ice?

That last one was the key question to address this morning.

At last, at 7:55, with all of this cycling through my mind, I laced on my boots, gathered my coat, gloves, and cap, and headed for the lobby.

The continental breakfast offered at the Moonbeam Motel consisted of sludgy, cold coffee and a box of day-old donuts. Instead, I opted for two large glasses of orange juice, telling myself that it was the equivalent to a plateful of fruit. As I was finishing the second glass, my phone rang.

Tessa's ringtone.

"Hey, Raven, how are you?"

"Good."

"How was the winter session yesterday?"

"Lame. I bailed so I could check out the places Mom wrote about in her diary when she went here. So that's been cool."

I wasn't excited about her skipping the class, but knowing Tessa, her reply didn't surprise me. "Has the food gotten any better?"

"They have, like, no vegetarian dishes. Just hamburgers or steak, or whatever, every day. It's troubling." I would've expected that the university would offer vegetarian alternatives, but I took Tessa's word for it.

As a big fan of cheeseburgers myself, I'd been trying for months to come up with good reasons to get her to expand her culinary interests to include animals. I had a zinger. "Tessa, if God didn't want us to eat cows he wouldn't have covered 'em with meat."

"He covered you with meat."

Okay, that was not a bad comeback.

"Um." I had to take a second to regroup. "So you got my messages then? About leaving early? Are you on your way up?"

"You said it's like a four-hour drive?"

"Maybe a little longer to get to Woodborough."

A pause. "There're still some places here I want to visit. I'm not sure when I'll be back in the Twin Cities. I'd like to see 'em before I leave."

I flipped open my laptop and checked the weather one more time. "I can understand that, but if you're going to come"—NOAA was now calling for up to eighteen inches—"you should probably leave right now."

A small, tight silence. "The Walker Art Center doesn't open until 9:30. Mom used to go there all the time."

"Then I guess it makes the most sense for you to stay there in the Cities. I can try to catch up with you later this weekend before you fly back home." Actually, because of the storm, I was a lot more thrilled about this scenario. The last thing I wanted was for Tessa to get stuck somewhere on a back road in Wisconsin in a blizzard.

"Listen," she said, "I'll just swing by the center, then get going. I shouldn't have any problem."

"Just stay in—"

"Patrick. We live in Denver. I can deal with a little snow. Besides, I've never met Amber and I haven't seen Sean in like forever."

As a girl who often seemed four years younger emotionally than her real age and yet four years older intellectually, Tessa had always been an enigma to me, and now I couldn't tell if she was excited about driving over or not. "All right," I said, "here's how we'll play this. For now, as long as you leave by 10:00 I'm good with you driving over. But if the storm moves in faster and I give you the word, you need to stay there in the city."

"Yeah. Okay."

"And on the way you'll stop at a hotel if the roads get too bad."

"Yes, Dad."

Dad—lately that word had been coming out more and more often and sounding more and more natural and welcome to me each time.

"So," she said, "we're staying at a hotel there, right? I mean, instead of at Sean and Amber's?"

She knew a little about my history with my brother and his wife, but we'd never talked specifics. And now she was displaying a little more intuition than I liked. "A motel. Yes. It'll give us all some privacy."

"Privacy."

"Yes."

"They invited us to stay with 'em, didn't they?"

I tapped my finger against my leg. "It's better if we don't." I tried not to be too stern but to also make it clear by my tone that we were done discussing the topic. "Text me when you leave and call me if anything comes up."

"I will."

I reserved a room for her, and as I was slipping the keycard into my pocket, Jake emerged from the doorway. After a quick "Good morning," he filled up a coffee cup, grabbed two donuts, and we headed for the car.

It had to be close to zero outside, and the windchill made the air feel like a wire brush scraping across my face.

"Gonna be a cold one," he said.

It already is.

"Yes," I replied.

Though the sun was still low, the day had started shockingly bright, with the early morning sunlight splintering sharply off the snow. It didn't look at all like a blizzard was on its way.

Looks can be deceiving.

I used the voice recognition on my phone's GPS program to ask for directions to Tomahawk Lake, and we took off.

17

Snowmobile trails paralleled us on either side of the road, just beyond the snowbanks that had been shoved onto the shoulders by the plows.

If you've never seen a snow-covered field or forest in the North, you might imagine that the snow all looks the same, but it doesn't. Because of the various angles of the flakes reflecting the sunlight, the woods look like they have thousands of tiny diamonds winking at you as you drive by.

Although we were a little north of Wisconsin's prime farm country, I still saw a few cement silos resting beside barns nestled on rock or concrete foundations to help the boards weather the snow.

But most prominently, I was impressed by the sight of the forests all around us, rolling dense and thick over the hills. Birch and poplar filled in the gaps between the picturesque pines, most of which were burdened with a thick layer of postcard-worthy snow. And, from growing up in this state, I knew that beyond those trees, hidden deep in those woods, were impenetrable marshes and countless isolated lakes—Wisconsin has over fifteen thousand lakes, more than nine thousand of which still remain unnamed.

But the one we were going to was not.

We arrived at Tomahawk Lake and parked at the north shore boat landing.

No state troopers or sheriff's deputies were there yet, and I was glad because it gave me the chance to look around uninterrupted.

Rather than police tape, yesterday's responding officers had set up wooden blockades and orange highway cones enclosing the snowmobile tracks that led to the broken ice. Considering the locale and the likelihood that this was the scene of an accident rather than a homicide, it was about all they could do.

A twelve-foot extension ladder was chained to a sign beside the boat landing. I guessed the officers or state troopers had laid on it in order to get closer to the break in the ice when they were placing the cones.

From my research last night, I knew that the lake's open water was caused by a series of powerful underground springs. The ribbon of water, at least a hundred meters long and a dozen meters wide, looked like a giant eel twisting along the ice, rolling over whenever the sharp wind troubled its surface.

Though we weren't far from Highway K, the snow-laden trees lining the shore softened the sound of cars and distant snowmobiles, leaving a deep silence that only a few birdsongs tapered into.

Jake avoided the ice for the moment and walked along the shoreline. I saw that he was on the phone.

I took some time to study the lake before heading onto the ice. Tomahawk Lake was vaguely oval-shaped, a mile or so across and nearly four miles long with a series of inlets on the western shore. To the south, the water beneath the ice dispersed into a flowage that eventually fed into the Chippewa River.

Mentally overlaying the trail system against the topography of the area, I decided that the most direct route from the Pickron house to Tomahawk Lake would have been the Birch Trail, which led along the hilly northern shore stretching away from me on either side.

On a snowmobile it would probably take fifteen minutes or so to get to the lake from his house.

Although the tracks to the open water had been noted by an ice fisherman, based on the absence of ice fishing shanties, I could see that there wasn't much interest in this side of the lake from sportsmen, probably because of the unpredictable currents that carried the warm spring-fed water from this area westward, causing invisible and deadly fault lines of thin ice to finger across the surface.

However, snowmobilers apparently weren't scared off the ice along the other shoreline because, in the morning sun, I could make out tracks stretching across it. I imagined that if you started at one end of the lake and let loose you could hit the sled's top speed before reaching the far shore. I wasn't certain how fast that would be, but with the advances in the last few years, some of the newer sleds had engines as powerful as compact cars and could probably reach speeds of 110–120 mph. I figured if you could top out at those speeds anywhere, you could do it here.

The only set of snowmobile tracks leading toward the open water were the Ski-Doo 800 XL tracks the FBI Lab had been able to identify.

Somewhat tentatively, I stepped onto the frozen lake.

As a kid growing up in Wisconsin, I'd had an almost pathological fear of falling through the ice. The idea of dropping into the terrifyingly cold water was disturbing enough, but the thought of coming up beneath the ice and not being able to find the place you'd fallen through was even worse—that frantic and desperate search while your air gives out horrified me back then and, honestly, still did.

After I'd taken a few steps onto the ice, the morning stillness broke open with the harsh grind of the blades at the sawmill across the lake as they powered through logs to get them ready to be shipped to the paper mills in Neenah and Menasha. At first the sound gave me a start as I thought it might have been the ice cracking underfoot, but then I realized it was just the sawmill Donnie worked at, the one I was planning to visit later in the day.

I'd been told there were no footprints near the break in the ice when Ellory first arrived at the scene yesterday, but now I counted eight different sets of boot imprints that led toward it. All of them stopped ten to fifteen meters from the water, now writhing in the escalating wind.

Some of the impressions were undoubtably left by the law enforcement officers and first responders, but I wouldn't have been surprised if some came from curious civilians stopping by last night to have a peek at the site after all the officers left.

I studied them closely, photographed them with my phone. We

would need to confirm it, but one set of boot prints appeared to match the ones found outside the laundry room door at the Pickron home.

The high-pitched whirr of a snowmobile on the other side of the lake caught my attention, but then it was overwhelmed by the sharp whine of a blade at the sawmill ripping through another log.

Jake joined me. "How could this have been an accident, Pat? Anyone going under here would've had to be aiming for that stretch of open water. I'm thinking suicide."

It certainly appeared that he was right, but I said, "I think it's a little premature to go there, Jake."

"I don't think this case is as complex as you seem to want to make it." The friction in his voice was no doubt sharpened by our past and how infrequently we agreed about the best approach to solving the cases we worked. Two investigations in particular stuck in my mind. In each, his cocksure insistence on the accuracy of his profile had detoured the investigation, wasting precious time. Three people were dead now who might have been saved had local law enforcement broadened their investigative strategies and not given two serial killers more time to abduct those final victims.

To top things off, at the press conferences Jake had emphasized how his profile had helped crack the case wide open. Personally, I couldn't care less about press coverage or credit for a case, but I did care about murders being averted.

And I did care about the arrogance of the people I worked with.

"Either Donnie came home," Jake said, "and found his family dead, then snapped and took his own life, or for whatever reason, he shot his wife and daughter and then killed himself. Think about it, Pat, a man kills his family then himself—not that unusual." Then he added, a tight thread running through every word, "As you're so adept at pointing out, we may never know his motives, but his actions speak for themselves."

"You're assuming too much, Jake."

He folded his arms. "Then give me another scenario that fits the evidence."

Alternate scenarios were not the problem—sorting through them to find the truth of what happened was.

"First of all, we have no body so we don't even know if Donnie or someone else was riding the snowmobile when it went under."

"You're thinking someone jammed the throttle or tied it off?"

"I'm not thinking that yet because I have no reason to. I'm just considering it as a possibility."

He shook his head. "Pat, the water is a hundred yards from shore."

He was right. And the tracks were straight, aimed directly and unfalteringly at the open water. It seemed hard to believe that the sled would go that straight and that far without a rider on it, even if someone had secured the throttle.

"Jake, how many suicides have you worked that involved someone purposely drowning himself?"

"It's rare," he admitted.

"What about through a hole in the ice?"

He was quiet.

"If Donnie intended to commit suicide," I said, "why not just turn the gun on himself or shoot himself with one of the handguns he kept in his gun cabinet? I'm guessing that most people would consider drowning in ice-cold water in a frozen lake a lot more frightening way to go than a quick, fatal gunshot wound. The open water is clearly visible, so it's unlikely the rider accidentally went in. Also, the killer made no attempt to cover the bodies, and—"

"I know," he said impatiently. "Killers with close relationships to the victims normally position them in more reverent ways. I thought of that yesterday at the scene."

I let his rough tone go unchallenged. "Also, why would Donnie remove the spent cartridges and the murder weapon? And what about the nuclear submarine records and the Navy's interest? Why would they even get involved if they thought it was either an accidental death or a suicide?"

Jake didn't reply.

Four patrol cars turned onto the road leading to the boat landing.

Jake turned his face from the wind to look at them. The black eel of water rippled uneasily behind him. "So what exactly are you saying?"

"I'm saying that at this point we don't know who, if anyone, went down with the snowmobile. We don't know if Donnie is alive or dead. We don't know who called Ardis's cell phone at 1:54 or why the Navy is interested in this case. We don't know how many people were present at the house when Ardis and Lizzie were killed, and we don't have any idea who they might have been."

"So you don't think it was Donnie?"

"If you set aside assumptions about domestic homicides and look at this case objectively, everything *except* Donnie's relationship with the victims and his disappearance points to someone else as the shooter."

Ellory and the two officers who'd stood sentry at the house last night crossed the ice toward us. Four more officers followed them.

Often when the Bureau gets involved in joint investigations, local jurisdictions feel as if we're stepping on their toes. It can become a point of contention that only serves to hinder the investigation, but so far I'd seen no indication that we were going to run into trouble with that here, and I was thankful.

Far behind the officers, a bank of low, gray clouds was crawling into the western horizon.

As Ellory approached, he followed my gaze. "Here comes the storm."

It made me think of Tessa again.

A slight tickle of concern.

"Listen, we need to get some divers down here as soon as possible."

"I told you yesterday, there's no one around here who dives."

"What about Ashland? That's less than an hour and a half away. With all the shipwrecks in Lake Superior there'll be plenty of cold-water divers up there."

A question rolled through my mind: *If the Navy is so interested in this, why haven't they sent a SEAL team over to the area for body recovery?*

I had no answers.

He was quiet.

I waited. "Right?"

"Yes."

"Well, let's get a couple of them down here before the storm hits, see if we can recover the snowmobile or the body of the driver."

My phone wobbled in my pocket and I checked the screen. A text from Amber—she and Sean would be able to meet at the Northwoods Supper Club just down the road from Tomahawk Lake. "11?" she'd typed.

While Ellory assigned one of the officers beside him to radio the sheriff's department in Ashland, I texted Amber that later—noon or 1:00—would be better.

Jake and the remaining officers went to shore to look over the Ski-Doo's tracks before they reached the ice. I walked beside the ones leading toward the open water, Ellory beside me.

I made sure neither of us disturbed the boot sole impressions paralleling the snowmobile tracks.

"Sheriff still down with the flu?" I asked him.

"Yup."

The uniformity of the snow clods kicked up by the snowmobile's treads told me that whoever drove the snowmobile had done so at a steady speed. No accelerating or decelerating. No swerving.

If this were an accident, he would've swerved to avoid it.

But if it were suicide, wouldn't he have accelerated toward the water?

When someone commits suicide by cutting her wrists she'll often slice her skin several times, trying to get up enough nerve to drive the blade deep enough to kill herself. Law enforcement and medical personnel refer to those wounds as hesitation marks.

Conversely, when the decision has been made, she'll draw the blade quickly, deeply, often in an uncontrolled manner.

Despite the low number of nerve endings in the flexor surface of the wrist, almost no one draws the blade steadily and slowly across the skin. If it appears she has, it's a good indication that it wasn't a suicide.

When people see pain or death coming, they either swerve to avoid it or despairingly accelerate into it. In a sense, almost no one drives uniformly toward the open water.

It was yet another indication that this wasn't a suicide.

Or a haphazard accid—

"You're famous," Ellory said, jarring me from my thoughts.

"What?"

"I looked you up. Consulted all over the world. Two books. Articles in more than a dozen professional journals."

He looked me up?

I wasn't sure how to respond. "Thank you," I said awkwardly.

"I'm impressed." But he sounded faintly sarcastic rather than dazzled. "I didn't know who you were."

I ignored his comment. "The only thing we need to do right now is make some headway on this case before that storm hits."

We'd made it only a few more steps when he said, "So, geospatial. What is that exactly?"

Though I wasn't really excited about giving a briefing at the moment, I guessed that this was as good a time as any to talk him through it. "Basically, I study the temporal and spatial patterns of serial offenses and then work backward to find the most likely location of the offender's home base."

He stared at me blankly. "Okay."

I paused and he stopped beside me. We were twenty meters from the water.

"We take everything we know about a crime—time of the offense, location of the bodies, likely offender characteristics and patterns of behavior, add in geographic factors such as urban zoning, population distribution, roadways, topographic features, and traffic patterns as well as weather conditions at the time of the crime, and then compare that data to the way human beings spatially understand their surroundings and form mental maps of their area of familiarity. Then, by applying what we call journey-to-crime models, I'm able to narrow down the region from which the offender most likely left when he initiated the crimes."

"So you need a bunch of crimes, then; I mean, to make this work."

Very astute. "That's true," I said. "The more locations I have to work with, the more accurate I can be."

We started for the water again.

"But here you only have the house and the lake. Two locations." I sensed more than a slight challenge in his words.

"Two locations, yes. That we know of," I agreed, but I was no longer concerned about his understanding of geospatial investigation because I saw a glimmer of something round wavering in the water. Then it disappeared. "Did you see that?"

"See what?"

It reappeared in the waves again. A black, shining circle about the size of a basketball. I jogged toward the break in the ice. Five meters from the water I realized that getting any closer could be a bad idea and—

Yes.

I stopped. It was a snowmobile helmet bobbing in the waves.

"Ellory, get that ladder out here. Now."

"But—"

"Go."

He finally saw the helmet, hesitated for a moment, then hurried toward shore.

I tried to reassure myself that laying the ladder on the ice would distribute my weight over a larger surface area, just as it does in mountaineering when you're crossing crevasses. The weight distribution would reduce the chances of the ice cracking.

But it still might.

I shook the thought.

It seemed odd that the helmet should resurface today.

Of course, it might have been planted there earlier this morning, but regardless of when the helmet entered the water, the waves might still overwhelm it and take it under.

I watched it for a moment, weighing the implications, then Ellory, the officers, and Jake arrived with the ladder.

"Lay it down," I said. "I'm going for the helmet."

18

"Pat," Jake said, "I think we should wait for a diver."

"We need to see whose helmet that is, and you know as well as I do that it could—"

"Go under. Yes, I get that."

"It wasn't there yesterday?" I asked Ellory.

"No."

"You're sure?"

"I think so."

"But," Jake interjected, "divers from Ashland can be down here in a couple hours."

"Too long." Patience is not my specialty. "We don't know if the killer is still at large, and if he is I don't want to wait any longer than absolutely necessary to get a clue that might lead us to him." I pointed toward the water. "I've done this before, mountaineering. It'll be all right. Lay it down and slide it out there."

"So you really don't think it's Donnie?" Ellory said.

"Whether it's Donnie or not, we need to vigorously pursue all leads as they arise. And I'm going to get a look at that helmet."

Finally, they extended the ladder to its furthest position and laid it on the ice. I knelt and then crept out on it while the team held the end that lay farthest from the water. The section in front of me poked out slightly over the waves.

It'll adequately disperse your weight. It will.

But still, I could feel my heart racing.

The wind stung my face.

Two meters to the end of the ladder.

All those childhood fears of going under the ice came rushing back, and I took a breath to try to calm myself. I paused. Regrouped. Crawled forward again, slower this time.

I watched the waves take the helmet toward, then away from the broken lip of ice.

"Pat, this is stupid," Jake said.

"It'll hold," I replied.

Just a meter farther.

I heard no hint of the ice cracking beneath me.

Edging forward, I stared at the short stretch of ladder hovering in front of me, the black water rippling just inches beneath it.

Thankfully, the wind had shifted slightly and was now coming toward me, so the helmet was being washed against the ice rather than drawn into the open water.

The rhythm of the waves made me think of a heartbeat pulsing blood through a body, mocking my attempts to reach the helmet's strap.

Backward. Forward.

Backward.

I came to the end of the ladder, lay down so I could extend my arm farther, and then reached for the helmet, but it was too far to my left.

Behind me, silence from the men. Unsettling in its depth.

The water splashed toward me, then receded, easing the helmet forward and backward with each throb of wind-driven water. But it didn't appear that the helmet was going to come close enough for me to grab it.

I inched closer.

"Easy," Ellory whispered behind me.

Nope. Still too far.

"You need to swing me out." I spoke softly, as if louder words would land too heavily on the ice and shatter it.

I heard Jake say, "No, Pat."

"Just do it," I told him.

After a moment, I felt the ladder rotate to the left, and I moved farther out over the waves.

The beating heart of the lake.

Forward. Backward.

Careful, Pat. Easy.

Still lying down, I hooked my feet around a rung and gripped the edge of the runner with my right hand, then outstretched my left, but still couldn't get to the helmet. A few rampant waves rushed forward and soaked through my sleeve, my glove, while others licked up at me and splashed against my chest. With the wet clothing came a shock of cold, and I knew I needed to hurry. Steadying myself, I eased out farther.

Faintly, I heard Ellory say, "Careful," but I was concentrating on keeping my balance. I told myself that my grip, earned from years of rock climbing, would be enough to hold me in place.

The wind carried the helmet toward me.

The water, black and terrifyingly cold.

I timed the waves, and as they swelled toward me I dipped my hand into the water and managed to snag the strap of the helmet, still buckled in a half circle.

"Got it."

And then.

The sound was subtle, not sharp like I would have thought it would be. Over the years I've heard some people describe the sound of cracking ice to be similar to that of a gunshot—distinct, explosive, ricocheting through the air. But this was different. It was more like a deep groan stretching to both sides of me across the frozen lake.

"Pull him back!" one of the officers yelled.

As the ice along the edge of the water splintered apart beneath me it must have caught the men holding the ladder off guard, because my end dipped into the waves. I clung to the sides of the ladder, tried to scramble backward, and managed to keep from sliding in, but the surging water drenched my face and jacket and made my grip on the ladder more slippery, more tenuous.

Hurry!

Thankfully they'd managed to catch hold of the ladder and now quickly pulled me backward.

But from my waist up, the front of my jacket was soaked.

As they drew me back, my heart hammering in my chest, I watched the cracks finger out beneath my weight.

And then, at last, I was past the fractured ice and safely away from the water.

I dropped the helmet onto the ice and rolled off the ladder. Juiced on adrenaline and caught in the grip of the cold, I found myself shivering fiercely. I didn't realize how tense I was until I heard Ellory saying to me, "Nice job."

I closed my eyes, took a deep breath, and then tried to quiet my frayed nerves.

You made it. You're good. It's all good.

Opening my eyes again, I pushed myself to my feet, then borrowed Ellory's jacket sleeve to dry my face and tried to shake some of the water from my clothes.

Softly, but not so softly that I couldn't pick up the words, one of the officers muttered to his partner, "I don't know how long he would've . . ." He must have noticed me glance his way because he let his voice trail off into silence. Looked away.

Jake stared at me. "You better get changed."

He was right. In these clothes, in this weather, hypothermia could set in within minutes. I'd gotten what I came here for—a spatial understanding of the scene, and a clue I hadn't expected. At the moment there wasn't anything more for me to do here at the lake. However, before I swung by the motel to get into some dry clothes, I wanted to have a look at that helmet.

At the moment, Ellory was inspecting it. "It's got Donnie's name on it," he said quietly.

"Let me see it."

He handed it to me. "He's down there." Ellory was staring at the water.

Curious.

Would a person about to crash, at any speed, take off his helmet?

Black, with a gray cushioned interior, the helmet had a slight crack in the faceplate. On the rear of the interior was Donnie's name, printed in black permanent marker.

"We'll compare the handwriting"—a wave of uncontrolled shivering chopped up my sentence—"to Ardis's and Donnie's to confirm that one of them wrote the name."

No one said anything, and I had the feeling the discovery of the helmet had closed the case for them.

"You don't think it's his?" Ellory remarked.

I pointed to the strap. "Whether it's his or not, how could a helmet strap that's designed to sustain a snowmobile crash pop off someone's head in the water—and then rebuckle itself together?"

That seemed to get their attention.

It certainly had mine.

Man, I was cold.

On the way to the car I called Amber to cancel lunch, refraining from mentioning my near-miss with the open water. "It's just that this case is taking a few turns I hadn't expected," I explained, doing my best to keep the shiver out of my voice.

"I see."

"Anyway, maybe we could connect later on sometime."

"Have you eaten yet?"

The lack of a substantial supper last night and my missed breakfast this morning wasn't helping anything, and discussing lunch only reminded me of how hungry I really was. "Not yet."

"Well, you need to." It wasn't a mothering tone, but that of a friend. "You don't know how long you'll be in the area, so let's get together while we can. Besides, you sound tense. Are you okay?"

"I'm not used to the cold."

We got into the car, Jake started the engine, I cranked up the heat.

Honestly, stepping away from the case for a few minutes would give me a good chance to decompress and mentally shift gears before my trip to the sawmill. And Amber was right, I did need to eat.

She pressed me once again and I finally agreed to meet her and Sean at the Northwoods Supper Club at noon, giving me enough time to drive to the motel, change, and get to the restaurant. I decided I could take one hour for lunch, then head to the sawmill.

Jake directed the car toward the road. After hanging up, I told him my plans and he said he was glad I could see my brother. "I'll grab something to eat on my own. That way you and your family can reconnect." Then he mentioned offhandedly, "I spoke with

Director Wellington a bit ago. It's just a local affiliate, but there's going to be a press conference at 12:30."

"Here?" I shed my coat so the car's heat would actually reach me. "In Woodborough?"

"The station is in Ashland. They sent a correspondent down yesterday to cover the Pickron homicides."

Even though Margaret had put me in charge of the case, I like dealing with the media about as much as I like the idea of falling through the ice. "All right, well, make it brief. No specula—"

"Pat." His voice was sour. "I've done press conferences before."

"Yes. I know."

I thought he might respond sharply to my comment, but instead he just said, "Besides, I need to follow up on a few things at the sheriff's office in Woodborough."

"What about the sawmill?"

"Maybe I could meet you there? You could catch a ride with your brother?"

Jake didn't know about the state of affairs between me and Sean, and it wasn't something I felt the need to address.

"Sure," I said. "Meet me at 2:00."

"I should be able to make it by then."

As we pulled onto the county road I called Tessa to tell her I really wasn't comfortable with her driving over. "In this case I think we're better off safe than sorry," I told her. "Stay at the college or a hotel if—"

"Are you shivering?"

"I'm not used to the cold," I said, repeating what I'd told Amber. "Use the credit card I left with you to reserve the room. If they hassle you, just have 'em call me."

It took her a long time to reply. "Okay."

"Talk to you soon."

"Bye."

After we hung up, I told Jake to keep an eye out for a store or gas station.

"For?"

"I'm gonna need to pick up a dry coat."

19

Alexei fast-forwarded through the footage that his cameras had taken of the entrance to the Schoenberg Inn last night after he'd gone to bed, but found that no one else from Eco-Tech had arrived.

He verified that the tracking threads in the seams of the duffel bag containing the $1,000,0000 were working properly. The transmissions were untraceable, undetectable—unless you knew specifically what to look for. This tracking system was not part of his arrangement with Valkyrie, though. This was for himself, and he'd kept it quiet.

Valkyrie had given him limited intel about the project, so Alexei still wasn't exactly sure what the significance of this target was.

But he planned to find out.

He took some time to research Eco-Tech. On their website they described themselves as "an international coalition of like-minded environmentalists with a progressive agenda to defend Mother Earth from anthropocentric shortsightedness." Bloggers on the other end of the political spectrum called them eco-terrorists.

Which was probably a more accurate description.

After all, with millions of dollars in cash and some hard-to-obtain access codes, they were obviously not here in the northwoods to simply stage a protest or have a sit-in.

Interestingly, there were eight pending lawsuits against them for alleged hacking activities into government and corporate computer systems. Some right-wingers were labeling them "hacktivists" (hacker activists), and it seemed like there was enough evidence to make the charge stick.

With roots in the radical Deep Ecology movement popularized by Edward Abbey's novel *The Monkey Wrench Gang* in the seventies, and then sharpened by the radical ecological writings of Derrick Jensen, Eco-Tech pulled no punches in making their agenda clear: global population control, income redistribution, drastic carbon emission reduction, and most importantly, nuclear disarmament. Their motto said it all: "A New Breed of Green—Dialogue When Possible, Action When Necessary."

A new breed of green.

Hacktivism.

As their website put it:

Human greed and selfishness have caused irreparable damage to the biosphere. The only chance for the long-term stability of the planet is a radical change of attitude and action, and despite the currently fashionable "Green Movement," that change is not going to come simply from people replacing their lightbulbs or carpooling to work.

To love your children you must leave them more than the legacy of your self-indulgence, the devastation of a world raped of its dignity to make your life more comfortable, more convenient, more consumer-friendly. We are committed to leaving the next generation a planet well cared for, a garden well tended. That is what we strive for. That is why we act.

Despite their muddied philosophical roots and alleged hacktivism, Eco-Tech's goal was certainly noble—fighting for more sustainable lifestyles and more conscientious, environmentally friendly corporate and political policies.

At first Alexei wondered if maybe they were here to combat logging of old growth forests in the area, but he found confirmation online that virgin forests in Wisconsin were now pretty much all part of national forest land and weren't logged at all.

Still, something had to be here in this area or else Valkyrie would not have hired him to get access codes from Rear Admiral Colberg, would not have assigned him to come here to the middle of nowhere to deliver two million dollars.

In preparation for his meeting, Alexei slipped the one weapon he carried, his specially modified spring-loaded bone injection gun, into his pocket.

For close-quarters combat the device was one of the most useful weapons he'd found.

Not much larger than a Mini Maglite flashlight, the bone gun was typically used by paramedics to quickly start IVs, especially in patients in cardiac arrest or with difficult-to-locate veins. Because of the amount of force generated at the tip, it easily perforates bone and is used to implant a needle into the marrow, usually below the kneecap. After removing the needle, a catheter is left behind and then used to administer the appropriate drug.

However, Alexei didn't typically use his bone gun to implant a catheter to administer medication. These days, when circumstances dictated it, he used it on adversaries to break bones, and in some cases, shatter them entirely.

His bone gun had been modified so that if used properly it could cripple, or even kill—although he had never gone that far with it. But he had used it twice on the C7 vertebral prominence, once while on an assignment in Amman, another time in New Delhi.

That vertebra was low enough to allow the subject to continue to breathe on his own, but that was about all he would ever be able to do on his own again. After six months both men on whom he had used the bone gun in this manner were still alive. Thinking of them in that condition had been unpleasant for Alexei, and he had anonymously paid for both men's medical bills.

Now, on his laptop, he pulled up satellite images of the region surrounding the Schoenberg Inn and got started connecting the uplink from the transmitter in the bag to the GPS tracking device.

Unfortunately, fifteen minutes ago when Patrick called her, Tessa was already on her way to Wisconsin.

She'd decided not to bring that up.

The Walker Art Center had been closed for some sort of renovation, and the more she thought about it, the more she realized she wanted to see Sean, whom she almost never spent time with, and at least get a chance to finally meet her stepaunt. It'd be nice, after all, to connect a little more with Patrick's family, the only one she had left.

Maybe she could even find out why Patrick and his brother didn't exactly get on famously with each other. She'd always been curious about that.

Besides, she knew that Patrick wanted to see her, and she figured she'd have time to cruise around the Cities a little on Sunday before flying back home to Denver in the evening.

A little while ago it had started to snow, but the roads looked good to her.

Only a dusting so far.

Even if the trip took a little longer than four hours, as long as the snow didn't slow her down too much, she would arrive in plenty of time for supper.

Tessa merged onto I-35 and headed north.

20

As Jake drove away, I walked up the snow-packed path toward the historic Northwoods Supper Club.

I wore my new camouflage coat, the only jacket the combination gas station/convenience store/gift shop had in my size. I didn't really want to think about what Tessa might have to say about how stylin' I was.

On the way here Amber had called to confirm the time, and when I asked about the location, she'd launched into a short history of the place: the site of the Northwoods Supper Club had been used as a lumberjack mess hall nearly one hundred years ago before it burned down in the 1970s. The current restaurant had emerged from the ashes and had benefited from the nostalgia of the site's past.

A large vinyl sign hung out front with a picture of a man dressed in a blaze orange jacket eyeing down the barrel of a gun. Bold lettering announced "Welcome Hunters." I wondered which hunting season was open in the middle of January. Bear maybe. Possibly small game—squirrels, rabbits.

I pressed the door open and stepped inside.

Huge pine logs formed the walls, and stout handmade oak tables and chairs filled the restaurant. A bar, peppered with a few customers in snowmobile suit overalls and flannel shirts, took up most of the west wall. Though I doubted it was still legal to smoke in the restaurant, the residual smell of years of cigarette smoke lingered in the air.

More than a dozen broad-antlered whitetail deer heads and one elk head had been mounted on the walls of the restaurant. Tessa, to put it mildly, was not an advocate of sport hunting, and I could only imagine her reaction walking into a place like this. I remembered the two trophy bucks mounted in Sean's living room and wondered how I was going to navigate that situation if she did end up making it over here, but then I saw Amber seated alone near a window at the far end of the restaurant, and my thoughts of how to deal with Tessa's potential reaction to mounted deer heads disappeared.

Amber had glanced down at her menu, and the sunlight from the window warmed her face, giving her a soft, warm glow, making her seem almost otherworldly. Angelic.

She hadn't changed much since I'd last seen her three years ago. Amber was thirty-three now but looked at least five years younger. I'd never thought of her as beautiful in the way that a movie starlet or a model is—with perfect features smoothed over with careful layers of makeup. Rather, she made up for her relatively anonymous looks with an infectious vitality, a contagious love for life, and a disarming flirtiness that she tended to weave, without realizing it, into her frequent and endearing smiles.

She set the menu aside and looked around. When she saw me, her eyes lit up. "Pat!" I gave her a small wave and made my way to her table. She'd already stood to greet me by the time I arrived.

And then she was in my arms. Surprisingly, she still wore the same perfume—gentle and delicate and femininely alluring. The scent seemed so familiar to me. I backed away just as she turned her cheek for me to give her a kiss of greeting. Though it might have been impolite, I refrained, said instead, "It's good to see you."

"You too."

I gestured for her to have a seat, but she hesitated slightly, and we ended up sitting down almost simultaneously, as if we'd planned it that way. This brought a light smile from her.

"Well." She placed both of her hands palm-down on the table as if she were accentuating that we were officially beginning our conversation. Her coral fingernail polish looked freshly touched up. "We have a lot of catching up to do. Where to begin?"

"I'm not sure." I looked around the restaurant, even though I'd already scanned it when I walked in. "Is Sean here?"

"He's coming. Should be here any minute."

"Okay."

"You look good, Pat."

"So do you." The compliment was out before I realized that it might not have been the wisest thing to say.

"Thank you," Amber replied. A small grin. "I like your jacket."

"Thanks. It's new."

"I see."

A server appeared, an anxious-looking woman in her late twenties. Her eyes darted around the room like tiny trapped sparrows. "Welcome to the Northwoods Supper Club." As she spoke, she tapped incessantly with her thumb and forefinger at her stack of menus. "Do you know what you want?" Her name tag read "Nan."

"I'll take a menu," I said.

She laid one on the table for me. I was going to ask for another for Sean, but Amber cut in. "Two coffees," she told Nan. "Specialty roast. And kindly bring some cream." She caught my eye. "And honey."

She remembered.

"Yes." Nan backed away. "Okay." Turned. Disappeared.

"Honey and cream," I said to her.

"That's still how you take it?"

"It is."

Normally, I wouldn't have chanced drinking coffee at a restaurant like this. Undoubtably roasted and ground months ago. Canned. Stored. Stale. More than likely brewed without using filtered water and with no real concern for the number of tablespoons of beans per six ounces of water. Trying not to think about all that, I changed the subject. "Your pharmacy. How's it going?"

"They opened a Walgreens in town, so that hasn't helped. But we're hanging in there. And you're still in Denver?"

I was ashamed she would even have to ask such a question. It underlined how poorly I'd stayed in touch with her and Sean. I decided to take the "you" in the plural sense. "We're still in Denver. Yes."

"And Tessa? How is she?"

"She's doing okay. Considering."

Amber had sent her condolences and spoken with Tessa on the phone several times after her father's death last summer. "I'm glad to hear that," she said softly. "I've been praying for her."

Okay, that was a side of Amber I'd never seen before.

"That means a lot. Thank you."

"Is she going to make it up here?"

"Actually, no. I was worried about the snow and told her to stay in the Cities for a couple extra days. Hopefully, though, we can arrange a visit sometime soon."

"That'll be nice."

Seeing Amber, being with her alone at a restaurant again, made me realize my feelings for her had never completely gone away, and that made things all the more uncomfortable.

This was one time I wished I could just turn off my emotions, but it's never worked that way with me. Sometimes my feelings come uninvited, when I don't want them to; sometimes they leave despite my best attempts at hanging on to them. It can be disconcerting.

She smiled again in her free and affectionate way, and I wished she hadn't. It brought too much back.

Sean, where are you?

"It's possible we'll be moving to DC," I commented. "There's an opening at the Academy, and they're asking if I'd be interested in teaching again."

"Would that keep you out of the field?"

"The Bureau wants its instructors to keep working cases every week."

"To stay sharp."

"Yes."

I looked away, first toward the door to see if Sean might have arrived, then to Nan, who was bringing our coffee.

"Now," Amber warned her, "he'll tell you if this coffee is any good."

"It should be." Nan looked concerned. "They just made it."

"I'm sure it's fine." I took the cup, added a touch of cream and honey, but before I could try it Nan asked me urgently, "Have you decided what you want?"

"Well, there's one more person in our party."

Amber waved her hand dismissively. "Sean told me to just go ahead and order. I'm not sure if he'll be eating anything or not." She tapped the menu and told me, "The Reuben's good."

I hadn't even had a chance to look over the menu. "Well, I'm a cheeseburger guy at heart," I replied. Then to Nan, "Give it the works, except—"

"Hold the mustard and pickles," Amber interrupted.

"Yes. Hold the mustard and pickles."

Nan wrote it down.

"I'll go for the Reuben," Amber told her.

"Fries or chips?" The question was directed at both of us.

"Fries," I said.

"Fries for me too," Amber told her.

Nan left for the kitchen, scribbling notes to herself as if her life, or at least her job, depended on correctly writing down word-for-word our rather unremarkable order.

Amber watched me expectantly. I braced myself and took a sip of my coffee.

Wow.

Nice.

"Well?"

Though I wasn't a big fan of flavored coffee, this wasn't bad. "I like it," I replied. "Air roasted, Mexican beans. They added undertones of caramel, a hint of butterscotch. Graceful acidity, respectable body."

She smiled. "It's called Highlander Grog. There's a roaster down in Watertown. Berres Brothers. They do mostly internet orders. This is the only local place that uses their coffee."

A thought.

"That's why you suggested we meet here."

She held up her hands in fake surrender. "You got me."

Sean entered the front door, stowed his snowmobile helmet and gloves in one of the wooden cubicles just inside the entryway. Thank goodness.

Amber tried some of her coffee. "I can hardly believe you knew the country of origin from just one sip."

Sean was weaving between the tables on his way toward us.

"Maybe I was making that up," I said.

"I doubt that."

Then Sean arrived.

21

My brother had grown a thick beard since the last time I saw him. Wild brown hair. Dark retrospective eyes. Decades of fishing and hunting trips had left the skin around his eyes tough and weathered. He'd always seemed like the kind of guy who would've been at home in frontier times forging his way west through the untamed wilderness.

We've seen each other twice in the last three years—once at my wedding and once at Christie's funeral. He likes to bowl, volunteers with the Jaycees, enjoys relaxing in his jon boat with a six-pack of ice-cold Old Style, and we never talk on the phone because we never seem to have anything to say.

"Good to see you, Pat." He shook my hand. Brisk. Firm.

"You too."

"Hey, Amber," he said with a quick look in her direction.

"Hello, sweetie."

Sean was two years older than I was and had been married once before. His wife left him, though, eight years ago, taking their son with her. She'd moved to Phoenix and only let Andy visit Sean for a few weeks every summer. Andy was nine now. Sean preferred not speaking about that part of his life, and I knew better than to bring it up.

He took a seat beside Amber, then drew in a heavy breath. "I gotta say: terrible thing, though. You having to come in under these circumstances."

There was no good way to reply to that. "It's heartbreaking what happened."

"I knew 'em, Pat. Donnie and his wife." He shifted his gaze to the window. "And Lizzie."

"I'm very sorry."

"We used to go out muskie fishing on Tomahawk Lake, Donnie and I."

I noticed that he was referring to Donnie in the past tense. "How long have you known him?" I tried to frame my question in the present tense.

"Eight, ten years, I guess. I just can't see him doing something like that. Not Donnie."

Whether or not Donnie had anything to do with the killings, Sean's words didn't surprise me. Over the years, every killer, every rapist, every arsonist I've caught has been friends with somebody, trusted by somebody, loved by somebody. Then, after the facts came out about the crimes, those people are shocked and dismayed. Family members, lovers, friends, none of them can believe what the offender did.

For a moment I thought about pointing this out to Sean, telling him that you can never really know someone, not really; that at times every one of us acts in ways that are inconceivable to others and, in retrospect, unthinkable to ourselves; that, in essence, no one lives up to his own convictions or aspirations. But from past experience I realized that bringing any of that up at the moment wasn't going to help.

"We really don't know who's responsible for the murders," I said as tactfully as I could. "Until we find Donnie, it's best to avoid assuming too much. He might be all right. There's still a lot to figure out."

Sean looked at me oddly. "Aren't most domestic homicides committed by husbands and lovers?"

"Yes."

"And he's missing."

"Yes, he is."

"The logical conclusion is it's him."

"We lack confirmatory evidence, and the logical conclusion when you lack evidence is to suspend judgment." The words had a cold and impatient professionalism to them, and I immediately regretted saying them. I tried to tone things down. "I'm just trying to say I think it's a little early to conclude anything."

He looked like he was going to respond, but held back.

When Nan arrived with our food, Sean went ahead and ordered a bratwurst. Soon she brought that too, and the conversation during the meal felt stiff and forced, the past—both my history with Sean and my history with his wife—weighing down every word.

It hadn't been an affair, at least not a physical one, but you can sleep with someone and never fall in love with her, and you can fall in love with someone without ever sleeping with her. From what I've seen, the second scenario is a lot harder to get over than the first.

And a lot harder to know how to deal with.

I've heard people throw around the term "emotional affair," so maybe that's what we'd had, but I'm not even sure what the phrase means. How many text messages or phone calls or smiles or secrets do you have to share before you're having an emotional affair?

And is it something you should even admit? Do you go up to your brother and say, "Hey, five years ago I fell in love with your wife. But don't worry, we never actually slept together"?

As far as I knew, Sean had no idea what had happened, and as time wore on, I could think of fewer and fewer reasons to bring it up. Contrary to the popular mantra of pop psychologists, I've always thought that when you apologize it shouldn't be for your own benefit but for that of the other person. I don't think you should ask someone to forgive you just so you can get something off your chest or quiet your guilty conscience. If an apology isn't in the other person's best interests, it's not serving to reconcile anything. It's just a subtle form of selfishness.

And in this case, I couldn't see how my true confessions would serve Sean. After all, he'd had one marriage fall apart, and I would never forgive myself if I were the cause of his second one disintegrating.

But in truth, Amber wasn't the only issue that stood between Sean and me.

My gaze shifted from her to the deer heads on the wall, and as

Amber tried to navigate Sean and me through the conversation, I became lost in my thoughts.

Because a deer was what caused the rift between me and my brother.

Or maybe there was no deer at all.

22

It happened twenty years ago on New Year's Eve when I was seventeen.

We were driving home from Amy Lassiter's party.

A stark and cold and moonlit night.

Sean was behind the wheel and I'd closed my eyes, exhausted from cross-country skiing most of the afternoon.

I knew Sean had been drinking a little at the New Year's Eve party, but we hadn't been hanging out together and I wasn't sure how much he'd had.

I never saw the deer.

He swerved, lost control of the car on the icy road, and we spun into the other lane, where an oncoming vehicle struck us, smashing into my side of the car and whipping us around toward the shoulder. We skidded toward the side of the road into a snowbank, which was probably the only thing that kept us from rolling over.

Sean and I both walked away from the crash, but the driver of the other car, a fifty-one-year-old woman named Nancy Everson, didn't make it.

I never saw the deer.

At the time, the responding officers hadn't questioned Sean's story about why he swerved and, as far as I knew, hadn't asked him if he'd been drinking at the party or done a Breathalyzer test. If they had, none of it raised any suspicions.

In the flickering swathes of emergency vehicle lights, I'd watched the paramedics roll the gurney with Mrs. Everson's motionless body onto the ambulance. Then, troubled and deeply saddened, I looked away to the side of the road.

The moon was bright, and I expected to see deer tracks, but the field of snow looked pristine, unblemished.

Excusing myself for a moment from the paramedic who'd just checked Sean and was now approaching me, I walked closer to the side of the road.

No tracks.

I crossed the road and took some time to study the snow stretching beyond the other shoulder but saw no sign that a deer had recently fled across the field on that side either.

A week later, after Mrs. Everson's funeral, I'd brought it up to Sean. "Which side of the road did you say the deer came from?"

"The right."

"The right."

He looked at me oddly. "Yes. Why?"

My heart was racing. I had one more question, and though I didn't want to ask it, I did. "How much did you have to drink that night, Sean?"

I could tell by his silence that he was reading all the subtext of my words, and for a long time he didn't speak. When he did, his voice had turned cold. "I only had two beers."

I hadn't replied. What could I say?

Whatever else Sean might have known about what happened that night, he kept to himself.

But things were different between us after that. He retreated into himself, and his normally infrequent outbursts of anger became more common, more pronounced. Everyone else believed it was from unnecessary guilt about the accident, but I'd always wondered if maybe the guilt was deserved.

Since then, the two decades of unwieldy silences had only deepened the rift in our relationship.

"Pat?" Amber said.

Her word jarred me back to the moment. "I'm sorry?"

She and Sean were staring at me.

"I was telling Sean how you might be teaching at the Academy again."

"Possibly," I said absently, still caught up somewhat in my thoughts. "Yes. I might."

We talked for a few minutes about the Academy and how the move to DC might affect Tessa, especially if we left Denver before the end of the school year.

"She tells me it doesn't matter, that she's cool with it if I want to go."

"She might be saying that just because she wants you to be happy," Sean observed.

"True," I admitted, a bit reluctantly. "You might be right."

At about ten minutes to 1:00, Jake interrupted by calling to tell me he was going into a meeting with Ellory and then had a phone interview with Director Wellington to brief her on what we knew. His press conference must have gone well; he sounded in high spirits. "I don't think I can make it to the sawmill by 2:00. Maybe 2:15, 2:30 at the earliest."

"Okay. I'll get a ride over there. See you when you get there."

After we hung up, Sean, who'd heard my side of the conversation, said, "No ride, huh?"

"I'm trying to get to the Pine Shadow Sawmill."

"Where Donnie worked." Again, past tense.

"Yes."

Amber spoke up. "I'll be heading that way. I can swing you by."

Okay, this was awkward.

"It's been awhile since I've been on a snowmobile," I hinted to Sean.

He thought for a moment. "Sure, I can give you a ride over there, introduce you to the guys. Sometimes people around here . . . Well, let's just say you'll make more progress if they know you're the brother of someone local."

"I'd appreciate that."

"Randy's watching the shop this afternoon. I just need to give him a call, let him know where I'm gonna be."

"Give him my cell number," I suggested, but before I could hand Sean my phone, Amber gave him hers. I jotted down my number on one of the napkins sitting on the table. Slid it to Sean so he could pass it along.

While he turned aside to talk to Randy, Amber turned to me. "I should give you my number too. In case you need to get ahold of me."

"Okay." She'd texted me earlier, but I confirmed that the number I had was correct, then Sean said good-bye to Randy and gave his wife back her cell. "We're all set."

We stood; I reached for my wallet, but Sean held up his hand. "I got it."

Although I had the urge to argue, I accepted. "Thanks."

"My sled's right outside. I don't have an extra helmet, but—"

"I've got one in my trunk," Amber offered. "It might smell like a girl, but you're welcome to use it."

Sean laid some bills on the table. "All right. Let's go. I just need to fill up on gas and we can take off."

As we walked outside, a few isolated snowflakes drifted through the wind and found their way to the ground.

Though still in its infancy, the snowstorm had arrived.

23

Alexei arrived at the Schoenberg Inn for his meeting with the Eco-Tech activists and went to the lower level on the south wing.

He found the door marked "Authorized Service Personnel Only," knocked twice, and was greeted by a meaty-fisted heap of a man whose nose had apparently been broken at some time in the past and never set right. Six inches taller than Alexei, he easily outweighed him by a hundred pounds.

From the videos and facial recognition that Alexei had taken last night, he knew this man was named Clifton White. He'd been a left tackle for the Patriots before getting kicked off the team for physically assaulting a Dallas Cowboys tight end in a barroom brawl, and then, soon afterward, served forty-four months for sexually molesting a teenage girl. Alexei suspected his involvement with Eco-Tech was motivated more by dollar signs than by ideology.

"I'm Alexei," he told him.

Clifton grunted, and Alexei calculated how many moves it would take to disable the enormous man if necessary. Four.

Three, if he was quick.

And he was quick.

He let Clifton frisk him. He had no weapons with him, save the bone gun.

"What's this?" Clifton asked.

"A medical instrument. It's used by paramedics," Alexei responded, "for administering medication. In stressful situations I sometimes need it."

After a moment's deliberation, Clifton said, "I'll hang on to it until we're done." A smile. "If you don't mind."

Alexei watched him slide it into the left breast pocket of his jacket. "Of course."

Clifton led him into an adjoining room, pine-paneled and dimly lit, where two men and one woman stood waiting. Alexei scanned the shadowy corners of the room, saw no one else. By posture and build he identified the three people as the ones he'd seen the night before, although today they were all wearing dark-colored ski masks over their faces.

Unwise.

In a fight, your adversary can simply pull the fabric to the side, thereby moving the eye holes and impairing your ability to see. It puts you at a severe disadvantage in hand-to-hand combat.

Never wear anything that covers or obscures part of your face.

Alexei ran down their identities: the man with the black ponytail snaking from beneath the back of his ski mask was named Becker Hahn, the slim man beside him, Ted Rusk, and the blue-eyed woman was named Millicent Alman.

All Eco-Tech activists, none with military experience.

No one spoke.

Alexei placed the duffel bag on a poker table that had been shoved against the wall.

"The money's in the bag?" Becker said.

Alexei reached for the zipper, but Becker held up his hand. "Hold on." He nodded toward Ted, who opened the bag and pulled out a thick stack of one hundred dollar bills. Slowly, he flipped through them.

"Don't worry, they're unmarked," Alexei said to Becker.

"Count it," Becker told Ted.

Three dozen more stacks lay in the bag.

Counting the money at a time like this was another sign of inexperience. It showed a lack of trust, and in these types of transactions, telegraphing a lack of trust was the kind of thing that breaks down relationships.

Amateurs were unpredictable.

"My name is Alexei Chekov." He gazed around the room. "What do you want me to call you?"

"Call me Cane," the ponytailed man replied.

Strike three. Always assume the person with whom you are doing business is a professional. Honesty is a form of respect. And respect is essential.

So, time for a little honesty. "How about I call you Becker?"

Alexei watched as Becker froze.

He pointed to each person in turn as he addressed them: "And I'll call you Ted, and you Millicent. I already met Mr. White in the hall."

Becker stared at Clifton. "You told him our names?"

Clifton's face reddened. "No."

"How do you know our names?"

"Research," Alexei said simply.

But the mood of the room had gone sour. Instinct told him that things were spinning off badly.

And they were.

He saw an almost imperceptible nod from Becker to Clifton, and Alexei prepared himself. Clifton made the first move, but as the huge man reached for him, Alexei stepped deftly aside, then grabbed Clifton's right wrist and, twisting it smoothly behind the man's back, drove him to his knees. He had the bone gun out of Clifton's pocket and pressed against his shoulder blade before the ex-football player could even throw a punch.

Clifton tried to wrestle free, but Alexei cranked his arm almost to the breaking point, and he cringed and submitted. Alexei took in the room. No one had moved. It appeared that they weren't prepared for this.

The whole thing might be a setup.

"I wanted this meeting to be civil," Alexei said.

They didn't reply.

"Can we kindly move things in that direction?"

Becker glanced across the shadows in the corner of the room. At last he nodded. "Okay. Of course. Yes."

Clifton was still straining to be free. Alexei said to him, "I'm going to let you go, Clifton, but I need you to behave."

He wasn't surprised when Clifton cussed at him, threatened him. It showed just how little self-control the man had.

Then Alexei felt tension in the man's arm and correctly anticipated that he was going to make a move.

Clifton lurched sideways, trying to break free, and reached for a knife that Alexei now saw was hidden in a sheath strapped to his leg just above his ankle.

Alexei depressed the bone gun before Clifton could raise the weapon. With a moist but solid crunch, Clifton White's left clavicle shattered and his arm went limp and useless by his side. His blade pinged to the floor.

Alexei let go of Clifton's wrist and the man collapsed, moaning.

He'd used his bone gun in this way before, and he knew that in the six weeks it would take the clavicle to heal, Clifton would be able to move his arm but not without a bundle of tight pain.

Earlier, when Clifton had frisked him, Alexei had noticed that his dominant hand was his right one. Now he said, "You still have your good arm, but if you stand up before I leave this room I'll need to shatter your other clavicle too."

Clifton cursed at him again but made no offensive move, just placed his right hand tenderly on his injured shoulder.

Alexei carefully surveyed the room again. No one else had gone for a weapon. He wasn't even sure why Clifton had made a move on him, but now he was wary.

And displeased.

He retrieved the knife, and then brought it down hard, blade first, embedding it into the table, burying it more than an inch into the wood. From all appearances Clifton was the only one in the room strong enough to wrench it free, and it wouldn't be an easy task even for him.

"Now, Mr. Hahn," Alexei said to Becker, slipping the bone gun into his jacket pocket, "could we kindly continue?"

Becker remained silent. Ted, who'd stopped counting the money in order to watch the confrontation between Clifton and Alexei, quietly and somewhat nervously resumed his task.

"The person financing this operation," Alexei said, "would like my reassurance that everything is in order and on schedule."

"Tell Valkyrie it's all on schedule." Becker emphasized Valkyrie's name, perhaps to prove he was better informed than Alexei might have guessed. For a moment he observed his associate finishing his cash count. "Do you have the access codes?"

Alexei told them what they needed to know.

Ted set down the last stack of bills, backed away from Alexei. "It's all here."

Alexei thought of Kirk Tyler and the mess he'd had to clean up. "My employer is not happy when people let him down."

"You just let Valkyrie know there's no need to worry," Becker said. "It'll all be taken care of. My team has stopped logging efforts in Oregon, long-line shark fishermen in the Galapagos Islands . . ."

As he listened, Alexei kept a close eye on the room.

Millicent still hadn't spoken.

Clifton was staring viciously at Alexei.

Ted looked troubled, his submissive body language telegraphing his unease.

None of them seemed interested in making a move on him, and Alexei was glad, especially with Millicent present. He was not at all keen on the idea of injuring a woman.

Alexei waited while Becker recounted his achievements of thwarting whaling efforts by the Japanese, disrupting mountaintop removal projects in West Virginia, and blocking a proposed nuclear waste dump site in Nevada, but none of these victories seemed overly impressive to Alexei, and he wondered again why Valkyrie had chosen to do business with this group.

What was Valkyrie's ultimate agenda here? Alexei was usually pretty good at discerning things like that, but so far, in this case, the reasons behind the reasons eluded him.

When Becker finally finished listing Eco-Tech's accomplishments, he said, "Give us until 9:00 tomorrow night. Be ready for my call. The timing matters. Not a minute before, not a minute after."

"I'll deliver the rest of the money when I have confirmation from my employer."

And then the meeting was over.

Alexei studied the group one more time to make sure no one was going to pull a gun, planned how he would deal with that eventuality if it occurred, then silently headed for the door.

But as he left, he noticed someone else, someone he had not seen earlier, standing in the deep shadows recessed at the far end of the room. No doors had opened during their meeting, so somehow this person had managed to slip from view earlier when he'd scanned the room upon his arrival.

Considering frame and posture, he guessed a woman, though in the halted light it was impossible to be certain. He could just make out that she wasn't wearing a ski mask like the other three people who'd been waiting for him, and that told him she was more confident and more experienced than they were.

He hadn't seen anyone with her build arrive last night, and that intrigued him. Either she'd been here already or had managed to enter this morning.

Maybe she was really the one in charge rather than Becker. It's how he would have played it.

Becker had looked toward that corner of the room before he agreed to proceed with the meeting.

Had this all been a ruse? A ploy?

Is that why these four were careless last night, allowing their faces to be illuminated by the Inn's entrance lights?

Evaluate, adapt, and respond.

Alexei arrived at the door. From now on he would be careful not to underestimate this group.

As he left, out of the corner of his eye he saw the woman step back as the darkness swallowed her.

Silent.

And whole.

And thirty seconds later, had he remained near the door, he would have heard the brief sound of a strangled cry coming from inside the room as the man who'd been on the business end of the bone gun fought uselessly to draw in a breath, and then dropped into a heavy, motionless mound on the floor.

24

The line at the pump took forever.

"Everyone's getting ready for the storm," Sean said, one eye on the cloud-blanketed sky. Flakes swirled around us.

Finally, after we paid for the gas, I asked Sean if he minded if I drove the sled.

"You still remember how to handle one of these things?"

"Let's find out."

As I took my seat I reviewed where everything on the snowmobile was located: the choke, the kill switch, the brake, the throttle.

Dad's instructions from my childhood came to me, words still clear after all these years: *When you're going down a hill, just let the sled do all the work . . . Stay right in traffic like you would on your bike and watch for warning signs for bridges, road crossings, driveways . . . Remember, you can't back up on a sled and they have a wide turning radius, so don't miss your turn or you're gonna have to get off, grab the back end, and swing it around. It's a pain and it's a telltale sign you're new at this.*

Amber's helmet was a little small and held her fragrance so I was glad it wasn't a long ride to the sawmill. Sean took a seat behind me. I slipped on the gloves I'd worn last night on my short walk beneath the stars, pulled the choke, revved the engine, and took off.

Sean had an older model Yamaha whose speedometer only went to 90 mph, but I anticipated that he'd pushed it up a lot higher. On this ride I had no intention of running it out all the way, but it might be fun to take it to the limit later if I had some free time.

Regardless of the snow whipping around me, rainbowed splinters of light shone in the plexiglass shield of the helmet, and it made the day seem bright and hopeful. For a moment I forgot why I was here in northern Wisconsin, why I was on this snowmobile in the first place.

But then I remembered.

Death.

Encountering the real.

25 mph.

Even at this moderate speed I could feel the wind rushing in the edges of the faceplate and through the small adjustable slits designed to let air in by the rider's mouth. I squeezed the throttle.

As we passed 35, there wasn't much of a difference in the feel of the machine, but as I accelerated to 40 a tight vibration began riding through the sled, especially as I swung around the curves on the trail.

45 mph.

Speed called to me.

Edging past 50, the ride remained pretty much the same, but then the trail straightened out, and once I hit 60 I could tell we were really starting to move. The sled's tracks skidded to the side whenever we hit a patch of packed snow, and the sled felt like it was ready to whip out from under me if I tried to make the slightest turn.

70 mph.

We raced past a field populated with half a dozen white tail deer, and in the moment that they caught my attention, the snowmobile began to fishtail; I let up on the throttle, took us down to 50, and as we neared a sharp descent, dropped us to 35.

With the noise of the engine, even though Sean was sitting right behind me, it was impossible to talk to each other, so now he patted my arm and pointed to the right. I took us across Highway K and then cruised to a stop at the entrance to the Pine Shadow Sawmill.

25

In his car, Alexei tracked the movement of the bag of money as the Eco-Tech activists left the Schoenberg Inn and headed along a country road that led to the west entrance of the Chequamegon-Nicolet National Forest.

The most direct route for him to follow was along Highway K just north of town.

He guided his car toward it.

We left the snowmobile by the other sleds and pickup trucks on the edge of the property and headed for the admin building.

Logs stood piled in pyramids nearly five meters high on each side of us. Parked throughout the yard, half a dozen backhoes, log loaders, and lumber haulers waited to roll, lift, reposition, or pile the logs. A cabbed snowmobile trail groomer with enormous treads for getting through deep snowbanks sat idle near the office building.

Even now, here in the yard, three men were driving specially outfitted forklifts, maneuvering around the stacks, hoisting and removing logs.

I could only imagine how muddy this place would be in the spring, but this winter the ground was frozen in deep, looping tire ruts and covered by a layer of dirty, hard-packed snow.

The sawmill's main building sat about fifty meters to my right, near a towering stack of massive white pine logs. The facility still had a sheet-metal roof and faded red barn boards on the side facing me. Evidently it had been a barn at one time before being called into commission as a sawmill. A thick log, two feet in diameter, lay on a conveyor belt and was riding into the mill where the blades waited.

Despite the weather, four men stood clustered outside the east entrance: two of them smoking, the other two digging through paper bags, apparently finishing late lunches before getting back to work.

"I know those guys," Sean said. "Come on."

He introduced me around. Though the men didn't seem antagonistic, they greeted me with a visible air of suspicion.

Sean explained that I was a member of the investigative team looking into Donnie's disappearance and the shootings at his house.

"Ardis and Lizzie," one of them said.

"Yes," I replied.

"You a cop?" he asked me.

It struck me that, just as I hadn't told Margaret about my brother, Sean hadn't told his buddies about me. "I'm with the FBI," I said.

The two men who were pecking through their lunches stopped. Stared at me.

I went through the standard questions: Do you know anyone who might have wanted to hurt Donnie or his family? Did he have any enemies? Had he indicated to any of you that he was upset with his wife or daughter?

The answers came quick and blunt: no, of course nobody wanted to hurt him; he didn't have any enemies; he loved his family. In fact, he and Ardis had tried for years to have kids and finally adopted Lizzie.

"How long has he worked here?"

"I don't know. Seven, eight years."

The door opened, and a looming, broad-shouldered Native American introduced himself to me as the foreman. He told me his nearly indecipherable Ojibwa name, then added that I could just call him Windwalker. "What do you need? We've already talked to Deputy Ellory."

I gestured toward the sawmill building. "I'd like a quick tour, then a look at Donnie's personnel files."

Windwalker didn't seem thrilled by the idea, but he agreed and led me into the sawmill while Sean stayed behind to catch up with his friends.

As we entered, Windwalker handed me a pair of industrial-grade headphone-style hearing protectors. "You'll need these."

Both of us slipped on a pair, and I took in the room.

Sawdust lay everywhere, and the smell of freshly cut pine was sweet and damp and almost overwhelming.

The white pine log I'd seen earlier on the conveyor belt was halfway in the building. The belt carried it forward until its end nudged up against a wickedly edged saw blade nearly two meters in diameter.

One of the workers pressed a button on a control panel to my left, and a 200-horsepower diesel engine growled to life. The shrill whine of the now-spinning blade filled the air. Then the saw blade slid to the side, the conveyor belt carried the log forward, and then the blade swung back into place, biting into the wood.

For a moment it reminded me of one of the Edgar Allan Poe stories Tessa had convinced me to read—*The Pit and the Pendulum*.

A blade swinging.

Slicing toward a victim tied to a table.

He escaped just in time.

I watched the saw blade chew through the log, then I surveyed the rest of the mill, keeping an eye out for anything unusual. Unfortunately, my unfamiliarity with the site made that challenging, so, rather than try to pick up specific clues, I tried to get a sense of the place, a spatial understanding of the sawmill where Donnie Pickron, the main suspect in a double homicide, had worked until two hours before his family was slaughtered and he disappeared.

Different workstations were positioned throughout the mill. Five men and two women sorted boards into piles, graded lumber, or removed warped and knotted timber, then sent the unusable pieces to the far end of the mill on a second conveyor belt to be ground into pulp for easier transport to the paper mills.

The wood shredder for grinding the logs into pulp was like nothing I'd ever seen before. The reticulated gears spun at an astonishing speed, powering through the boards and logs in seconds.

Hardly anything was left after the logs were shredded.

Hardly anything was left.

Donnie disappeared.

Unlikely, but not impossible, not out of—

A hand on my arm caught my attention, and Windwalker motioned toward the door. I took one more look around the sawmill and then we dropped off our hearing protectors by the door and he led me toward the admin building.

A rush of snowflakes slanted around us.

"Can you tell me about Donnie's job?" I asked.

"Transported the logs. Piled 'em here in the yard, sometimes drove 'em to Hayward."

"Was he hourly or on salary?"

"Hourly."

"And yesterday?"

"He was on a run. Left at noon. That's all I know."

"I need to see his time cards and a record of his arrival times."

"Time cards are just inside." His voice was curt. It was clear he was not enthusiastic about helping me here today.

We entered the building and found a receptionist's office. He mentioned briefly that he had "let the girl go" recently, and I could see that he'd taken over the office himself.

The room was arranged haphazardly with used, mismatched furniture, two old filing cabinets, a desk strewn with invoices and a decade-old computer. A small bookcase filled with three-ring maintenance and construction binders sat in the corner. A photo of Windwalker standing beside a waterfall with a man I had not yet met was propped on the corner of the desk. The window on the south wall overlooked the yard.

My phone vibrated and I took a call from Jake. He informed me that the Lab's handwriting analysts had confirmed "with a high degree of certainty" that Donnie Pickron had written the name on the helmet. Also, an unidentifiable set of prints were found on Ardis Pickron's cell. "They're not hers. Nothing came up in AFIS."

"Thanks," I told him.

"Press conference went well," he said, reiterating what I'd gathered from our earlier conversation.

"I'm sure it did."

"I'm still hoping to make it by 2:30."

"All right."

End call.

As it turned out, the time punch cards weren't in the office but down the hall in a makeshift employee break room.

When Windwalker and I entered, I was surprised to see a set of old gym lockers rather than the open-faced shelves I'd expected. It explained why most of the guys had left their helmets on their snowmobiles outside even though it was snowing—there wouldn't have been room for them in the narrow lockers. Just beyond the last one, a stairway led down to a basement.

Each locker was labeled with a strip of white tape containing the handwritten name of an employee.

Donnie Pickron's locker sat on the far right and had a padlock hanging from it.

"I have no idea what the combo is," Windwalker told me.

Even though I had my lock pick set with me, it wouldn't do me a whole lot of good with a combination lock. "Could you dig up a hacksaw or some bolt cutters for me?"

"Yeah, sure," he said grudgingly.

"I'll wait here."

The tracking signal in the bag that Alexei had left with the Eco-Tech activists disappeared.

He was driving on Highway K when it happened, and he slowed to a stop by the side of the road to check his equipment for a malfunction.

Moments later he'd assured himself that there was nothing wrong with his GPS tracking device.

Someone must have found the transmitter and disabled it, but with the thread-sized wires and a nearly untraceable signal it seemed remarkable that any of the amateurs he had met would have located it.

But maybe they were not all amateurs.

Alexei pulled out his phone.

Now that he'd delivered the money and the access codes, a status call to Valkyrie would be in order. A few strategic questions could give him the answers he needed, but as Alexei was tapping in this assignment's alphanumeric pass code for Valkyrie—Queen 27:21:9—he noticed movement in his rearview mirror.

A state trooper's cruiser had turned onto the road and flipped on its blue lights.

Alexei stopped his call.

There were any number of reasons for the lights, but he had a feeling he knew what the real reason was.

Someone who was not an amateur.

You left the knife there, left your prints with them.

But had enough time passed for that to make a difference?

Well, whether it was the prints or not, something was up.

They turned you in.

Maybe.

Probably.

The car rolled up behind him, kept its overheads on. Parked.

Alexei set down his cell. He would call Valkyrie after he'd taken care of this situation.

In his rearview mirror he watched the officer talking into his radio. Alexei gauged what he would need to do but then had another thought. He pulled up a GPS lock on his car and searched for any nearby businesses or parking lots where he could acquire a different vehicle.

■

Using the bolt cutters Windwalker had retrieved, I managed to cut through the combination lock and clicked open Donnie Pickron's locker.

Inside, I found a change of clothes, photos of Donnie's wife and daughter, an extra pair of brown leather gloves, a pair of the same type of headphone-style hearing protectors I'd used to protect my hearing from the grind of the motors and saw blades. All to be expected.

I was feeling the pockets of his Carhartt work pants when I found what I did not expect: a federally issued biometric ID card.

Windwalker was lurking behind me. I held up the card. "Any idea what this might open?"

He shook his head.

"Could you bring me Donnie's personnel file?"

A slight pause. "Yeah, sure."

I searched the locker more thoroughly but didn't come up with anything else.

I studied the ID card.

It'd been issued by the Navy. Above top secret, Sensitive Compartmented Information (SCI) access. I saw that he was a commissioned officer, a lieutenant commander. And he was most certainly not retired.

I had no idea what the card might have given him access to. As far as I knew there were no military bases nearby.

Windwalker returned with Donnie's personnel files. I collected the time punch cards I'd come in the room to retrieve. "Is there a place I could look these over?"

He gestured down the hall. "You can use the office. Long as you don't disturb anything."

■

The trooper still had not left the vehicle.

Alexei figured that if he'd stopped simply to help a stranded motorist he would have certainly gotten out by now to see if the person was okay.

In lieu of that, Alexei ran down what he knew about American law enforcement felony stops. The trooper would give instructions through his cruiser's PA system but wait until he had backup, a cover officer, before exiting his vehicle.

The language might vary, but the standard operating procedures were similar for law enforcement agencies throughout the United

States: single commands to ensure that the driver's hands were visible and that he was not going for a weapon: "*Driver, put both hands on the ceiling . . . With your right hand remove the keys to your car . . . Place your right hand on the ceiling . . . Open the window of your door with your left hand . . . Place your left hand on the ceiling . . . Throw the keys out the window . . . With your left hand open the door . . . Exit the vehicle . . . Face away from me . . .*"

Then he would tell him to interlock his hands behind his head and walk backward toward his voice until he told him to stop.

Then kneel and cross his ankles.

Now, as Alexei expected, the trooper's voice came through his vehicle's PA, but what he said was surprising. "Step out of the vehicle with your hands away from your body."

Not protocol.

Either this state trooper was a rookie or he knew that backup wasn't going to be arriving anytime soon. And either of those scenarios played in Alexei's favor.

The order came again: "Driver, step out of the vehicle."

Even before Alexei opened the door he had decided what he was going to do.

26

Alexei stood with his hands up, facing the officer, the bone gun slipped down into his right sleeve.

Weapon drawn, the state trooper approached him.

Alexei ran through what a typical civilian might say, how he or she might respond. "Is there a problem, officer?"

"No problem," he replied tersely. "As long as you keep your arms outstretched."

Windblown snow sliced through the air between the two men.

How would Neil Kreger, a used furniture salesman from Des Moines, Iowa, respond?

"I don't think I was speeding or anything. It's fifty-five along here, right? I was even taking it slow because of the—"

"Turn around and place your hands on the vehicle."

Okay.

So.

"Officer, I—"

"Turn around." The officer leveled his gun. "Now!"

Alexei silently complied.

The trooper approached him from behind.

Typically, you don't want your gun in your hand when you're patting down a suspect because it's too easy for him to knock it away or disarm you and acquire the weapon himself, so Alexei waited for the soft swish of the gun being holstered so that the officer could frisk him.

And he heard it.

Even though Alexei did not want to do it, he had to respond appropriately to the situation.

Three moves—rotating while bringing his arm down to knock

the officer's hand away, a round kick to the knee, and, as he collapsed, a straight, direct punch to the temple, sending him reeling to the ground. It only took Alexei a second to disarm the officer and use the bone gun on each of his wrists.

The man went instinctively for his radio, but as he did he cringed and cried out in pain.

"I'm sorry about that." Alexei tossed the officer's Glock into the woods. "A little surgery, a couple months of physical therapy, and you'll be able to feed yourself again."

"What?" Desperation quavered in his voice.

The shattered scaphoids wouldn't heal on their own, and until reconstructive surgery the officer wouldn't be able to grasp anything without debilitating pain. As long as he didn't try to move his fingers he would be okay.

But even now he was trying to move them and was crying out in a helpless, childish way.

"Just don't flex your fingers. Wait for the paramedics to arrive."

Alexei didn't bother to cuff him, really, there was no need, but he did place the man in the back of the cruiser. Not wanting him to go hypothermic in this weather while he waited for help to arrive, Alexei started the engine and dialed up the heat.

Since this man had called in his location, Alexei knew that additional state troopers would undoubtably be arriving any time. He needed to change vehicles as soon as possible.

At first he thought of using his rental car to get to a place where he could switch vehicles but immediately realized that since law enforcement was aware of the make and model, that wouldn't be wise.

His attention returned to the cruiser. A police cruiser always draws attention, even from people obeying the law. So that had its drawbacks as well.

However, in this case, taking into account the condition of the roads, the cruiser had better traction, more power, and he could monitor the radio while he drove.

So, the cruiser.

To take care of his electronic equipment in his car, he initiated the countdown of the small explosive device he'd brought with him, positioned it beneath the dashboard, and set the timer for two minutes. A nominal loss, considering everything.

He climbed into the front of the cruiser. The sawmill was less than five minutes down the road. He figured he could find another car there, or even better, a snowmobile, and disappear into the national forest.

Ignoring the groans of the man in the backseat, he ran down his priorities.

First, elude the authorities.

Second, contact Valkyrie.

Third, deal accordingly with the environmentalists.

There was nothing in Donnie's personnel files that indicated why he would have a government-issued biometric ID card with above top secret clearance.

Using my phone I clicked onto the Federal Digital Database and came up dry there as well.

But there was one person I knew who could give me some answers.

I tapped in Margaret's number.

"Director Wellington," she answered, even though I knew my name would've come up on her screen.

"Margaret, Pat. Listen, I need you to look up Donnie Pickron's military service records."

She responded promptly, "He didn't kill them, did he?"

Her words surprised me. "Why do you say that?"

"Jake filled me in on what we know. I've been doing some checking. Donnie was a Navy information warfare officer."

"Was or is?"

"What do you mean?"

"He's still active duty." I told her about the ID.

"I have no record of that information." Her tone held a nuanced threat, and I knew I wouldn't want to be the person who'd kept that information from her.

Although I was familiar with some jobs in the Navy, I'd never served in the military myself. "What is an information warfare officer, exactly?"

"Mainly they're involved with cryptology and intel evaluation or dissemination. Some of them work in deployment."

"Can you find out conclusively if Donnie Pickron is still active duty, still involved in either cryptology or deployment?"

I waited while she typed. It didn't take long.

"Not officially."

"In other words, yes."

"Yes."

"So what was a covertly commissioned Navy information warfare officer with a biometric ID card that gives him Sensitive Compartmented Information access doing here in the middle of northern Wisconsin working at a sawmill?"

The blank silence I got was not encouraging.

"Help me out here, Margaret. Is there anything more you know? Is there a regional information processing facility or cryptology center? A missile deployment base that hasn't been disclosed to the public?"

"None of those."

"Then what?"

"I need to check on something."

"We have at least two people dead and a third—"

"I know that, Agent Bowers. But I'm not going to make unfounded inferences here."

Margaret, as pernicious as she could sometimes be, was thorough, there was no question about that, and I did respect her for it. So although I was impatient, I knew that for the moment I had everything I was going to get. "Call me as soon as you find out anything."

"I will."

We hung up and I looked over Donnie's arrival times at work.

If, as his emails had indicated, he checked his messages just before he left home every Monday and Friday, then it apparently took him nearly two hours longer to clock in at the sawmill on those days than it needed to.

He might just take a scenic route.

Or, he might have another stop to make.

I pictured the trails in my mind, evaluating the most likely routes he might have chosen and their relationship to his house.

My thoughts raced back to the Navy and their interest in this case. Why here?

Why now, this week?

I needed to take a closer look at a topographic map of the region to see what areas the trails from his house might have passed en route to the sawmill.

While I was pulling them up on my cell, Deputy Ellory phoned.

"Pat here," I said, "what's up?"

"We have a suspect in the Pickron slayings."

27

"It's not Donnie," Ellory told me.

"Talk to me." Holding my cell against my ear with one hand, I collected the time cards and personnel files with the other.

"Twenty minutes ago we got an anonymous call to look for prints on a knife at the Pickron residence, and that it would point to a man named Neil Kreger—but that 'Neil' was just a name he was going under. They gave us the tag numbers for his rental—"

"Hold on. An anonymous caller told you all this?"

"Yes. Natasha was in the area. She checked the knife, found the prints, and apparently this guy's real name is Alexei Chekov."

"Who is he?"

"A ghost. No one really knows. She said the Bureau has a name, but no photo, no background. But he's a person of interest in half a dozen murder investigations worldwide."

I was on my way to the door. My next course of action clear: *call Quantico, get Angela Knight in Cybercrime on it. She can find out anything about any—*

"And," Ellory went on, "we have a location on his rental car."

"What? Where is he?"

"That's the thing. A state trooper pulled him over, then we lost radio contact with him. I sent a car and I'm on my way myself. The GPS signal on the officer's cruiser just went off the grid."

I stepped outside. Snow shot crazily past me into the room. The storm was picking up. I was really glad Tessa wasn't on the roads.

"Where exactly was the cruiser's last known location?"

"Two miles south of the river."

About six miles away.

"I'm at the sawmill," I said. "Where are you?"

"Close. Only a couple minutes out. Just south of you."

"Where's Jake?"

"Still at the sheriff's department in Woodborough."

A quick calculation. "All right. Swing by. Pick me up. Put out an APB on the rental car and the cruiser."

"Already done."

End call.

In the white fury of the storm I could just make out the snow-mobiles across the yard, near the entrance to the sawmill. I contacted Angela to get her started pulling everything she could on Chekov, then jogged through the stinging curls of snow toward the sleds.

28

Three minutes ago, in order to avoid drawing attention to himself, Alexei had parked the cruiser at a pull-off a few hundred yards down the road from the entrance to the Pine Shadow Sawmill, then he'd disappeared into the woods so that he could approach the property undetected.

Now, he neared the edge of the lumberyard. In a moment he would emerge, grab a sled, and be gone. Once he hit the trails that led to the national forest there was no way they'd be able to track him, not with this snowstorm covering his snowmobile tracks.

My thoughts scampered forward, backward, studying the case from a myriad of angles.

The shooter at the house used one of Donnie's rifles. Removed the spent cartridges.

I could feel my heartbeat quicken.

Timing. Location.

The lights in the study were off when the officers arrived.

Web pages had been accessed.

But the rest of the residence's lights were on.

All of them were on.

I put an immediate call through to Natasha and asked her to check for prints on the light switch in the study. "He may have unconsciously turned off the lights when he left the room." If I was right, the prints wouldn't match Alexei's but would match the real killer's.

I heard a siren close on the road and figured it was Ellory.

Hurried to the road.

Alexei peered between two thickly bristled white pine trees. A man stood about fifty yards away near one of the log piles in the lumberyard, but he appeared to be watching the road rather than observing the sleds.

After a quick review of the snowmobiles, Alexei decided on a sled, a newer-model Yamaha with the key still in the ignition, left the forest, and headed toward it.

Ellory swung to a stop at the entrance to the sawmill not far from me and leapt out of his cruiser.

"He's close," he hollered. "I found Wayland's cruiser just down the road. Wayland was . . ." Ellory's voice trailed off. "His hands. I don't know, this whack job Chekov. He attacked him."

"Where?"

"His hands, like I—"

"Where is the car!"

He pointed south. "About a quarter mile down the road."

I considered the typical flight patterns of suspects fleeing on foot. *No, not on foot. Not in this weather.*

My eyes landed on the line of snowmobiles.

A man was striding toward them. Jeans, a dark blue parka, a black stocking cap and gloves. I ran through the clothing of the men I'd seen at the sawmill, didn't recognize him as any of the employees I'd seen so far. Caucasian. Stocky frame. Six feet tall. Gait and posture indicated early to mid-forties.

"Hey," I yelled to him. "Hang on."

Alexei heard the man near the road call to him.

Time to go.

He snagged the helmet that was hanging by its strap on the back of the snowmobile, put it on, took a seat, squeezed the throttle, and hit the trail.

"Stop!" I ran toward him, but he disappeared across the road.

By the time I'd made it to the line of snowmobiles, Ellory had already found one and was firing it up. "That's him. Fits the description of our suspect!" Sean was on his way toward the sleds as well. Ellory took off.

"Stay here," I called to Sean, hopping onto his snowmobile. I gave him the files, grabbed his helmet rather than Amber's, and tossed him my phone. "Call for backup."

I envisioned the labyrinth of snowmobile trails that I'd memorized last night. Analyzed them. Played them out in my mind.

"What are these?" He was staring at the manila folders.

I didn't have time to explain. "Hang on to them and don't read 'em. I'll get them from you later."

He pointed at the sled. "I know how to handle a sled at high speeds. I know these trails."

"So do I."

I tugged on the helmet, cranked the ignition, and headed into the storm.

29

The suspect rode directly toward Tomahawk Lake.

Ellory was still ahead of me, and I wished I had a way to radio in our position because with the snow falling as thickly as it was, it would be hard to follow our trail.

I hit the ice and felt the engine whine as I squeezed the grip and leaned into the wind.

On the flat surface of the lake, throttling all the way, it didn't take me long to hit 70.

But I wasn't gaining on Ellory or the suspect.

Then 80.

It'd been years since I'd pushed a sled to these speeds, and I could feel a thread of apprehension run through me as I passed 85. I tried not to think about what wiping out on the sled at a speed like this would feel like.

The speedometer fluttered to the maximum speed of 90, then edged past it.

The far end of the lake was approaching fast, and the suspect aimed his sled for the flowage that led to the Chippewa River. Ellory looked like he was gaining on him.

They disappeared into the marsh.

Slowing to make the turn, I let go of the throttle but still nearly flipped as I cornered around a tree and swung back onto the trail that wound into the frozen marsh.

I tried to evaluate, with each of Alexei's turns, his most likely destination.

The national forest.

Maybe the Chippewa River.

The swirling snow decreased the visibility, but I could see the taillights of the sled that Ellory was riding a couple hundred meters ahead of me on the trail that led into the national forest.

Marsh grass flicked under the sled, whipped past me.

With the limited visibility and the number of trails in the national forest, if Alexei made it to the forest surrounding the Chippewa River, we might never catch him.

No longer worrying about the speed, I kept my eyes on the taillights in front of me and whipped along the serpentine trail through the frozen marsh.

And then they were at the woods.

A moment later, so was I.

I hopped onto a well-used trail. Positioning my snowmobile into the tracks, I felt the ride smooth out.

Ahead of me Ellory slowed, then disappeared around a sharp downhill bend.

I followed, but only too late did I see the fallen tree that blocked half of the trail, thick branches bristling across the path.

I swerved to the left to avoid it and felt a branch snap across my neck and shoulder, almost throwing me from the sled. My neck stung, and the snowmobile thrashed and fishtailed, but I held on.

Straightened out.

Sped up.

Alexei was heading for the Chippewa River.

A stand of pines rose in front of me, and though I saw the taillights flicker through the trees on the far side, I couldn't tell if Ellory and Alexei had gone right or left around the trees.

I chose right.

Chose poorly.

For a moment I lost the trail, and as I swept into a small meadow, I saw an eight-foot drop-off just ahead of me.

There is no good way to stop a snowmobile.

Speed up and jump it, or swerve and roll the sled!

Speed up or swerve.

Swerve—

No.

I sped up.

You do not want to do this!

But I did it.

I squeezed the accelerator and was going 60 when I left the edge of the drop-off.

The snowmobile took to the air, giving me a strange sense of weightlessness even though I had six hundred pounds of machine humming beneath me.

But in a fraction of a second I realized the skis hadn't been positioned squarely when I left the ground, and I wasn't going to land on the trail but smash into a looming oak to my right. I dove off the sled, tumbled violently through the snow, and heard the deafening sound of impact even before I turned and saw the snowmobile, smoking and crumpled at the base of the tree.

In real life, crashed vehicles don't typically explode like they do in movies, but I didn't want to chance it. Bruised, sore, and more than a little disoriented from the fall, I managed to scramble to my feet and get away from the wrecked machine.

Great, now you owe Sean a snowmobile.

Tossing my helmet to the side, I whipped out my SIG. Scanned the area for Ellory and Chekov.

At the top of the hill a hundred meters away I could just barely make out the two stationary snowmobiles. I ran in the direction of the sleds as fast as I could, but the forest was blanketed with nearly two feet of dense snow, beneath another rapidly forming layer of fresh powder, making any kind of progress exhausting.

Neither Ellory nor the suspect was in sight.

No gunshots. Good news.

As I crested the hill I saw the Chippewa River sixty meters below me, frozen except for a stretch of open water on our side of the river. It was along the shoreline's outer bend where the current would have been fastest and deepest. From my college river rafting days I knew that swift water never freezes, even when it's supercooled in weather like this. A ghost of frigid fog hovered above the churning waves.

The suspect and Ellory stood on the edge of the riverbank. Ellory appeared dazed and wasn't resisting Alexei, who was standing beside him, grasping the collar of his coat and somehow supporting him with only one arm.

But Alexei Chekov wasn't looking at Ellory. He was staring up the hill, directly at me.

30

"Stop!" I had to shout to be heard over the storm. "Step away from the river and let go of him." I leveled my gun and descended the hill through the thick snow.

Chekov didn't move.

As I got closer I could see that Ellory's face was a smear of blood, but he was conscious. Ellory was missing his weapon, and I had to assume Alexei was armed.

"I'm with the FBI." I approached them carefully. "Hands away from your body."

"Drop your gun, Agent Bowers," the suspect called, keeping his voice calm.

How does he know your name?

Maybe Ellory told him.

It doesn't matter. Deal with that later.

"I need you to drop your gun," he repeated. Surprisingly, he didn't sound out of breath despite the fact he'd just come down this hill, running through knee-deep snow—and then fought and subdued a police officer. "Or I will throw him in."

That was a direct threat on a law enforcement officer's life. I could take the shot. I could—

No.

Too close to the water, they're too close—

"Help me!" Ellory yelled.

By now I was close enough to see why he wasn't standing on his own: his left leg was buckled, bent sideways at the knee. With the strength of the current, if Alexei did throw him in, I doubted Ellory would be able to regain his balance on his own. He'd be dragged under the ice downstream.

However, if I shot Alexei, both he and Ellory would end up in the river, and from this distance I'd never be able to get to Ellory in time to pull him out before the current swept him toward the ice. The only way to save him was to buy time, play Alexei, and hope backup arrived quickly.

But in the storm, how'll they find you?

I had no phone or radio with me, no GPS signal for the state patrol to track. Alexei had been attentive enough earlier to disable the police cruiser's GPS, so I anticipated he would've also taken care of Ellory's cell phone and radio by now—probably tossed them into the river. If that were the case, there was no way for backup to find us in time to do any good.

The strip of oil-black water roiled behind them as it rushed downstream.

"I need you to put down your gun, Agent Bowers," Alexei called again.

Think, Pat. Think.

Fierce snow gusted through the air between me and the other men, blurring everything, making it all seem like a wicked water-color dream.

I eyed down the barrel of my SIG, evaluating if I could get the shot off without sending Ellory into the water, and I decided to give Chekov one more warning. "Step away from the river, Alexei. I won't tell you again. Pull the deputy away from the water and hold out your hands. I'm a federal agent and I will shoot you if I have to."

"Then Ellory will drown," Alexei replied. He didn't sound rattled at all.

We both stood our ground.

"I did not kill the Pickrons," he called unexpectedly.

"I know."

A pause. "How?"

"You're a professional—you wouldn't have used a rifle in the close quarters of the house or wasted any shots. Now step away from the water."

He didn't move, just said, "I have no quarrel with you." Most of his words held a generic Midwestern dialect, but when he said the word *quarrel*, I caught the faintest hint of a carefully buried Russian accent.

Time, buy more time.

"Who killed the Pickrons, Alexei?"

Rather than replying, he dragged Ellory even closer to the riverbank. "Drop the gun," he repeated. "Or Deputy Ellory is going in." Everything this man said was matter-of-fact. No sadism or malice in his voice. All calm. Controlled. Business as usual. "His left kneecap is shattered. The current will take him under. Do it now, Agent Bowers."

"Don't let him!" Ellory cried. His eyes had flicked toward the water and the ice that stretched past a bridge over the river a hundred meters downstream. I believed Chekov was telling the truth, that he would not hesitate to kill Bryan Ellory if he thought it would increase his chances of getting away.

Alexei glanced toward the river. "Time's up."

"Wait!"

Hastily, I calculated my options, but there weren't any good ways to play this.

I noted a tree beside me, its girth, its height, memorized the branch pattern and location on the hillside so I'd be able to find it again, then I tossed my SIG toward its base and held up my hands, hoping Alexei wouldn't shoot me.

"All right," I said. "Now walk away from the river and let him go."

"Step away from the gun. Come closer."

I did, until I was less than ten meters away from him and at least fifteen meters downhill from my SIG.

"There's no need to hurt him. My gun's up the hill. Listen"—I gestured toward Ellory—"he's hurt. Let me help him."

Alexei ignored me, edged closer to the water. "I'm sorry to have to do this—"

"No!"

"—but you'll have to believe me when I tell you it's necessary—"

"Don't!"

Get there, Pat. Now!

I sprinted forward.

But before I'd even taken three steps, Alexei had yanked Ellory's jacket backward, sending him flying into the raging black water of the Chippewa River.

31

Ellory disappeared beneath the waves.

I rushed through the snow toward the river's edge as Alexei ran for the bridge downstream. Out of the corner of my eye I could see a semi approaching, but my attention was on Ellory, who bobbed to the surface gasping for breath, flailing his arms. Then the water swallowed him again.

Go, go!

I fought my way through the trees, through the thick snow, scrambling to stay ahead of him, all the while looking for a branch I could use to fish him out.

Nothing.

The angry current was not going to bring him closer to shore.

You have to—

He surfaced again, his eyes wide with terror. He sputtered for air, gave a strangled call for help.

"I'm coming!" I yelled.

He went under again. There was no other choice. None.

I took a deep breath, braced myself, and leaped into the river.

Shock.

Frozen knives stabbed at me everywhere. The current immediately cut my feet out from under me, tugged me under. Breath escaped me.

I strained for the surface, instinctively gulped for air, swallowed water.

Planting my feet on the bottom, I pushed off and splashed to the surface, spit out the water. I struggled for breath, my chest clutched tight from the cold. Paralyzing. Terrifying. I couldn't see Ellory

157

and guessed the current had almost certainly taken him past me by now. I swam forward to catch up with him.

The bank of ice was less than twenty meters away.

I groped through the water, trying to find him, shouting his name. Desperately I pressed off a rock with my left foot, but the rock spun, trapping my ankle. The current dragged me forward, twisting my ankle free, sending a sharp streak of pain up my leg. I lost my footing and fell forward, sweeping my hands through the swirling water, trying to find an arm, a leg, Ellory's jacket, anything, but came up empty.

Every second it was harder to breathe, harder to move, as my body tried to conserve heat by sending blood to my vital organs— my heart, my lungs. The things that matter most. Fingers, toes, limbs—all expendable. But not the heart. Not the lungs. Survival trumps everything.

But I wouldn't survive unless I could move; unless I could get out of the river.

Once again I found my footing, and pain shot up my leg as I inadvertently put pressure on my injured ankle—sprained, maybe broken. But none of that mattered. I launched myself downstream again, daring to believe I'd find Ellory.

Ten meters from the ice.

I searched the water.

Nothing.

Get out, Pat, you're not gonna make it!

I grabbed a breath and dove under one last time, swam into deeper water, and felt something bump against my leg.

I thrust my hand down.

Snagged Ellory's armpit.

Kicking hard and stroking with my free hand, I went for the surface. My head broke through the water, and I drew in a desperate, uncontrolled breath.

The current tried to yank Ellory from me, but I wrapped my arm tight around him and squeezed. Scissors-kicked toward shore.

Five meters to the ice.

But at least that far from shore.

Options: a few branches stretched across the water, but they were still out of reach. A root system slithered out from the base of a tree and disappeared into the ice, but I could only grab its roots if I were under the ice.

Get out, you have to get out!

Muscles weak. Failing.

A dark and terrible thought grabbed me: I was not going to be able to save Bryan Ellory.

Two lives lost.

Two or one—

I fought the current, trying to—

Two meters.

Decide!

Now!

The edge looks thick.

Thick enough.

It'll hold.

One meter.

Clinging to Ellory, I threw up my free hand, took a deep breath, and then ducked my head to avoid smashing my face into the edge of the ice.

And I went under.

32

What happened next seemed to happen all at once and yet in slow motion, frame by frame, time condensing in on itself. Collapsing.

Expanding.

My forearm slammed into the edge of the ice as the current tugged at me; my arm slid down the ice to my hand, just as I'd hoped, and I was able to clutch the lip of the ice.

Don't break, please don't break!

The ice broke.

The current swept me farther under, but I snagged one of the roots, clenching it with finger-strength earned from years of rock climbing.

But it was moss-covered and slippery and I wouldn't be able to hold on for long.

Oxygen escaping me, I strained to pull toward freedom, but with Ellory's weight and the force of the current I couldn't do it. I'd never be able to get him to the surface.

No!

Dark water.

Death.

The real.

Two lives or one.

I let out my last gulp of air.

Please no!

I cried out in my heart, *God, don't let him die. Please don't let him die!*

But no help came.

There was nothing else to do.

I let go of Bryan Ellory.

The river took him from me, and I threw my other arm up so I could cling to the root with both hands.

No air in my lungs.

You let him go, Pat.

You let him die.

As quickly as I could, I worked my way up the root system, hand-over-hand, until finally, gaining leverage, I managed to grasp the edge of the ice. This time it held. One more tug and I was able to slide my elbow up, over the lip of ice, allowing me to get my mouth to the surface.

Quick breaths.

Life.

I breathed, breathed, breathed, both numb and weak, and realized I wasn't shivering—a bad sign. My body was already shutting down. I had to get to shore. Now.

I twisted so I could keep my mouth above the surface. Then, with one arm hooked over the ice, I slid my other hand along the ice's edge to pull my way toward the branches jutting out from shore.

It took all my strength to keep my head above the surface.

Though my body was numb and cold, somehow my left ankle still seared with pain. I swung my other leg down, planted my foot against one of the roots, and stretched for a large branch hanging above me.

But as I did, the ice cracked beneath my weight.

Lunging for a closer branch, I caught hold of it.

It sagged and dropped clumps of snow on my head and all around me in the water, but it did not break.

Thank God, it did not break.

One hand at a time I pulled my way toward shore.

You let Ellory go.

You let him die.

Finally, the river was shallow enough to stand, but I was too fatigued to do it; I crawled ashore, the wind-whipped snow lashing my face, the arctic cold immediately making its way through my drenched clothes.

Backup, they're coming.

No, not without a GPS lock they're not.

My frozen fingers felt useless, but I fumbled through my pocket in search of my phone, only to remember that I'd given it to Sean before I took off on his snowmobile.

Thoughts blurry.

Lost in a fog.

I tried to stand but couldn't even push myself to my knees. No shivering meant my pulmonary system was bypassing my limbs to keep my core warm enough to survive.

But it was failing.

I collapsed, able only to draw in shallow, quick breaths.

Then I felt my stomach clench, and I vomited a mouthful of water.

As best I could, I dried my face with my gloved hands to forestall frostbite. My thoughts bumped into each other, piled, buried themselves beneath the moment. I was both aware of where I was, and not aware, all the world unraveling like a thin, warped dream.

You let him go.

White merged with black, then somehow blurred with the pain riding up my leg.

Alexei got away. You let him get away.

And Ellory is dead.

Grief struck me, but so did the cold, and it seemed to be a living thing with a will and a goal—to swiftly and resolutely take my life.

I fought off the dawning realization, but it was stark and undeniable: unless I could get dried off, warmed up, I had only minutes to live.

Clouds and snow and water and death.

The driving snow was letting up, at least for the moment, and I scanned the area, didn't see Alexei anywhere. My breathing became rapid, shallow, quick, quick, quick, and then the world turned into a sea of white.

One last time I tried to stand, but couldn't. Dropping to the snow, I was vaguely aware of the river snaking along beside me, a stretch of white marred with a gash of black where the water refused to freeze. The water that'd taken Ellory beneath the ice.

He's dead.

And you let it happen.

I looked toward the bridge and saw that the semi had pulled to a stop.

The world became dim in a sweep of gray, then the moment enveloped me and became threaded with images of winter trails winding through a forest—the snow cruelly dotted with the blood of a mother and her four-year-old daughter.

Images.

A dream.

Of dark water rushing through the trees and flooding the trail, carrying the body of Bryan Ellory, dead and bloated, toward me. I'm up to my chest in the waves, and as I try to move away, he bumps into me, his arms wrap around me, and his flaccid lips press against my cheek in a cold, cruel kiss.

And then, all is black.

33

Alexei would have preferred letting the truck driver live, but when the man pulled a compact 9mm Beretta while he was taking possession of the semi, Alexei was forced to disarm him and, as he resisted physically, to deliver an immobilizing jab to the man's throat, crushing his windpipe.

One strike was all it took.

The man fell to the ground, gasped, and clutched at his throat. Alexei turned away, heard soft garbling behind him, then thankfully, before long, it was over. Just a brief, weak struggle against the inevitable. A quick and quiet transition.

Returning to the body, Alexei saw that the man wore a wedding ring, and he hoped that there would only be a wife mourning his passing—that no children would now be growing up without a father.

In order to slow down the discovery of the missing truck, Alexei carried the driver's body to the edge of the bridge near the shore. There was no open water here, but he tipped the body over the guardrail, sending it smacking onto a snowbank beside the river far below. Within minutes the falling snow would cover the corpse and, looking like just another mound of snow on the riverbank, it would be weeks, maybe months, before anyone would find him.

He returned to the still-idling semi.

Repositioning the mirrors, he saw a photo on the dashboard—the driver standing beside a slightly obese woman and a dark-haired boy of about seven or eight. All were smiling. A family.

He flipped the picture down so that he wouldn't have to look at it, then glanced toward the river where he'd thrown the deputy in.

Through the blizzard he could just barely make out a body on shore. The clothes told him it was the federal agent.

But there was only one body, which meant that the agent—the

one Ellory had, under slight coercion, informed him was named Bowers—had failed to save the deputy.

Alexei saw that Bowers lay motionless. If he wasn't dead already, in this weather it wouldn't be long at all before death took him.

Just a brief, weak struggle against the inevitable.

A quick and quiet transition.

Alexei gripped the steering wheel.

Paused.

It was impressive that this agent had tried to save Ellory, had actually jumped into the water to go after him. Not many people would do that, especially with an ice floe just downstream.

And now he was going to die for his courage, if he hadn't already.

Alexei's eyes found the photo he'd tipped upside down. He had a job to do, and there would always be casualties and consequences in this line of work, yes, of course, but he'd killed two people in the last five minutes, and that was more than enough.

A federal agent brave enough to rush into an icy river to save a drowning man deserved to live.

Alexei pulled out his cell.

For a moment he watched the snow pelt the windshield and waited to see if Bowers was moving.

He was not.

Alexei made his decision, tapped in 911, and told the dispatcher the location of the agent.

He found a tarp in the back of the cab, took it to the river, and wrapped it snugly around Bowers's body to at least afford him some protection from the wind. Then he carried him closer to the bridge, and jammed a tall stick into the snow beside him so EMS would be able to find the agent if the snow covered him before they arrived.

It might not be enough, but it was something.

Then he returned to the vehicle, released the air brakes, and took to the road to put some distance between himself and the river.

It was time to find out who was really leading Eco-Tech, and what exactly they were up to.

Cell phone in hand, he punched in Valkyrie's number and access code.

34

Alexei waited twelve rings, but Valkyrie did not answer.

He lowered the phone.

Nothing about this felt right on any level.

Maybe it'd all been a setup from the start, from that very first conversation with his mysterious employer last spring. But why? Just to make him look guilty for the death of a woman and her child? Could that be all? There had to be more.

He'd never had any trouble with Valkyrie before.

Yesterday, when Alexei had first heard about the Pickron murders, he'd tried to let the news of their deaths slide off him, tried not to let it distract him, but it'd crawled around in the back of his mind ever since. Bothering him.

You do not kill children.

And you do not kill women.

Alexei had eliminated his share of targets over the years, but it was not in his nature to take the lives of those he felt the need to protect.

And now as he thought about the woman and her daughter dying yesterday, a fresh gust of anger swept through him.

You do not kill women.

You do not.

He remembered the day he found Tatiana in their apartment in Moscow.

The argument they'd had earlier in the afternoon. Telling her that he never wanted to see her again. Words he didn't mean. Words he would always regret.

And then discovering her body.

The bullet wound in her forehead.

The blood still spreading out, soaking into the creamy white cotton sheets.

His frantic and fruitless search for her killer.

After his wife's murder, Alexei had vowed that when he found the person who'd killed her, he would return the favor, but her killer's passing would not be as quick as hers. At first Alexei would make that person beg for his life, but he was confident that there would come a time when the murderer would beg for the opposite. Alexei planned to make death the most desirable outcome of all, and then, to withhold that from his captive for as long as possible.

And Alexei had skills. The process would go on for a while.

But now, shaking those thoughts loose, he tried to direct his attention to the matters at hand.

The wise move at this point would be to leave the area, but before he did that, he wanted some answers.

He doubted that Valkyrie would have left the remaining $1,000,000 at the dead drop, and it didn't look like he would be delivering the money to Eco-Tech after all.

But he could put it to other use—if he could retrieve it.

He phoned Nikolai Demidenko again and said, "I need whatever you can get me on this number." He passed along the phone number and the alphanumeric pass code for reaching Valkyrie. "Trust me when I tell you that if you can lead me to Valkyrie, I will make it worth your while." He also told him the information he'd gotten from Rear Admiral Colberg the day before.

"All right, my brother. I will find this Valkyrie for you. You have my word."

Alexei had an idea of where to go from here, but it meant switching vehicles and then returning to the house where he'd left his equipment—after picking up the remaining $1,000,000 from Valkyrie's prearranged drop site.

If it was even going to be there waiting for him at all.

Tessa was having a hard time.

The roads were a mess.

She'd passed a small roadside motel about a half hour ago but had figured she should press on. Now, she wasn't so sure that'd been a good idea.

She didn't even know where she was, but at this rate she guessed it would still be another couple hours to Woodborough, where she was gonna meet up with Patrick. To make matters worse, the rental car hadn't been handling the cold or the roads very well, stalling out twice and not grabbing the pavement like it should. Three times in the last twenty minutes she'd slid precariously close to the ditch when she hit patches of ice.

So, status report: in the middle of nowhere, not making good time on roads that were becoming more and more impassable.

Brilliant.

Though she wasn't looking forward to his reaction, she decided she needed to call Patrick, tell him what was up. But when she tried his number, Sean answered.

After a quick greeting she asked if she could talk with her stepdad.

"He's working on the case," Sean said simply. "Where are you?"

"I have no idea." She explained her situation, that she was on her way and caught in the middle of the storm.

"Did you get to Hayward yet?"

All these little towns ran together in her mind. Besides, the snow was distracting and the visibility horrible. "I don't think so. I'm not sure."

"What kind of car are you driving?"

Okay, odd question.

"Some kind of Chevy sedan thing."

"All right, that's all right. Are you good with gas?" She could sense an underlying urgency in his questions, though it seemed like he was trying his best to downplay it.

She'd been so focused on the roads that she hadn't even been keeping an eye on the gas gauge and now saw that she had less than a quarter tank. She told Sean, and a moment later passed a sign that announced it was ten miles to Hayward. She relayed her location to her stepuncle.

"Tessa, in about five miles you should come to a bar called Lindberg's; just explain that you're my niece and that I told you to wait there for me, and Larry will let you in. It'll be on the right. I'm coming to get you."

"It's okay, I—"

"You don't need to be out in this weather, not in that car. Pat would never forgive me if I let you drive the rest of the way."

"No, seriously, I'll be—"

"I'm coming to get you." His voice rang with the same resolve and assurance that Patrick's so often held, and in a way it comforted her. "Go to Lindberg's. Get a burger. Wait for me. I'll be there as soon as I can."

Ew. A burger.

Not.

But this wasn't exactly the time to tell Sean she was a vegan.

"In this weather it'll take me at least an hour," he told her. "I don't want you on the roads. Be careful. I'll see you soon. I'll be driving a blue Ford pickup."

Honestly, she didn't want to be driving in this weather or this car anyway. At last she gave in. "Thanks. Seriously."

"I'm on my way out the door. I'll keep Pat's phone with me. Call me if you run into any trouble. And let me know when you get to Lindberg's."

"Okay."

She hung up and stared out the windshield at the blinding snow. Five miles to go.

At this speed, fifteen minutes. Maybe twenty.

As long as the stupid car didn't stall out along the way.

35

The Schoenberg Inn
Elk Ridge, Wisconsin
Lower level, north wing

Cassandra Lillo had almost missed locating the radio transmission wires in the duffel bag that Alexei Chekov had dropped off with her team, the bag she'd had Becker drive toward the base in order to lead Chekov away from the hotel. The transmitter was very high end. Chekov obviously knew his stuff.

And now.

Now.

She knew from monitoring the police dispatch frequency that the sheriff's department had found the knife with Chekov's prints, the one she'd had Ted deposit in the snow beside the Pickrons' house immediately following their meeting with Alexei.

And they already had the helmet that Becker had left in the water this morning before daybreak. On the police radios one of the officers had mentioned that the strap was buckled. *How could Becker be so stupid? How could he make a mistake like that!* He might be good at stopping loggers and whaling ships, but he was not proving to be especially gifted in this current line of work. Cassandra could only guess that, if the cops were thinking at all, the buckled strap would be enough to tip them off.

And now a deputy, Bryan Ellory, was unaccounted for, and even more fascinating, an FBI agent who was investigating the Pickron killings had been found beside the Chippewa River.

He'd been pulseless and unresponsive when the EMTs found him; however, from her scuba diving days, she knew the old adage that "you're not dead until you're warm and dead" was buttressed by an awful lot of medical research. Cold water immersion, as well as extreme hypothermia, slow the body's metabolism, and in numerous cases, clinical death had been reversed thirty, forty, even up to eighty minutes after it had occurred.

But whether or not this man would survive, she was intrigued by his presence here because she actually knew him. Patrick Bowers was the federal agent she'd met last year in San Diego—in fact, he was the one who'd caught her when she was working on an earlier project.

But her stay in prison had been relatively short-lived, and she had nothing against Bowers personally. He'd just been doing his job and she'd just been doing hers, but she knew that he typically worked serial homicides, so she found it informative that he'd been assigned to the Pickron murders.

Agent Bowers might recover, he might not, but in the meantime, the FBI's involvement was something to keep an eye on.

And use to her advantage, if possible.

Law enforcement is like a bull with a ring through its snout. You can lead them wherever you want, if you know the kinds of things they look for.

Which she did.

Her father had taught her all about that.

The original plan had been to keep the police focused on Donnie and only later direct the investigators' attention to Chekov. Admittedly, however, law enforcement had moved a little faster than she anticipated. Prudently, she'd been prepared for that contingency. An international assassin in the area was just too big a carrot to pass up.

At first, she'd intended for Clifton to disable Alexei but keep him alive so they could time his subsequent "suicide" appropriately. But when Alexei showed some skills and so easily overpowered Clifton White, she'd decided it would be more profitable to let Chekov go free, and then direct law enforcement toward him while he was on the run. It would be less work for her, less of a distraction. This way it would make for a good old-fashioned manhunt and galvanize law enforcement officers, keep them occupied longer.

Let Chekov lead the bulls around for her.

With only one good arm left, Clifton hadn't been of any further use to her.

She'd had to put him down.

Something else her father had taught her to do well.

And now it was time to move forward.

Cassandra's partner had explained it all to her last month. "To hack into a computer system with a USB stick you just insert code that'll automatically execute when it's plugged into a computer. Two approaches. One: leave a Trojan horse that'll spread to any additional USB memory device that's connected to the computer, and from there—"

"Spread computer to computer every time a memory stick is inserted."

"That's right. And have them transmit back information. That's why the military has banned USB jump drives from use on all its networks—but the computers still have USB ports. In this case, we'll do option two: a self-replicating algorithm that'll move through the system at the root level until it finds the files we need. We'll just need one USB device, strategically placed."

She already knew that computers respond differently to external hard drives than they do to portable USB devices. Every hard drive has a different individualized code, a sui generis fingerprint that allows programmers to identify when and where a drive is used. But, if you know the fingerprint of another drive, it allows hackers to mask the true identity of a drive by overlaying the original code on top of its own.

So you can stay hidden.

Even in plain sight.

And there was no better person to do that than her partner.

While she listened to the police dispatch channel, she studied her computer monitor, looking over the submarine information Becker had accessed and downloaded from Donnie Pickron's home computer.

Clicking to the Department of Defense's Joint Worldwide Intelligence Communication System, or JWICS, Cassandra confirmed that the USS *Louisiana* would be ideally positioned in the Gulf of Oman at just the right time, 03:00 GMT.

That's when her partner's algorithm was set to register the signal. That's when they had to send the transmission—not a minute earlier, not a minute later. No hack goes unnoticed forever, and the sub's computers would eventually notice the discrepancies in the code and respond with countermeasures.

Yes, countermeasures in some areas, but carelessness in others.

After all, the United States military doesn't just subcontract weapons systems to civilian contractors, but also hires private security firms and civilian companies for less mission-sensitive services.

Logistics.

Food service.

Custodial services.

No one in the Navy is excited about cleaning the heads or emptying the leftover raw sewage that hadn't been deposited in the ocean from a 150-crewmen sub after three months at sea.

And so, the US Naval Forces Central Command in the Persian Gulf used a private firm, Khdmāt Tjāryh at-Tnẓyf al-Bḥryn, the Commercial Cleaning Service of Bahrain, to clean their heads and drain their waste storage tanks. Since those areas were located in the sections of Ohio Class submarines that were designed to allow for civilian access, it wasn't a security threat. Besides, the cleaning crews were carefully vetted.

They would need to pass through the galley to get to one of the heads.

The computers in the galley were used primarily for meal planning and inventorying supplies, but of course, they were networked to the other computers on the sub—if you knew how to access the passwords and authentication codes—something a Navy cryptologist would be able to do, given the right kind of access to the system.

She put the call through to Bahrain, to her man who was assigned to the cleaning crew of the USS *Louisiana* while it was in port tomorrow.

Allighiero Avellino, an Italian expatriate and Eco-Tech loyalist who'd moved to the Middle East two years ago, assured her that everything was still in place.

"We will finish at the sub," Allighiero stated in his somewhat stilted English, "tomorrow afternoon at 3:00." Cassandra knew that was Arabia Standard Time; so here in Wisconsin that would be 6:00 tomorrow morning.

Yes, good.

She hung up.

Checked her watch.

5:41 p.m.

She would give it a little more time, then check on her captive in the next room and see how the project was coming along.

36

I dreamt.

And here was my dream.

Ellory sways in a pool of rippling water spreading out all around me. He's staring at me from a foot beneath the surface, his eyes open, his face grayish-blue, the color of death.

He's mouthing something, trying to speak to me.

I lift him and he's heavy and limp, the way only dead people are.

His face emerges and the water flows, drips off his skin, and he murmurs to me with a voice wet and thick, "It's cold." Water gurgles from his mouth. "So cold."

I'm repulsed, but I want to tell him that things will be all right, that I'll get him to shore, that I'll save him, but he's sinking and I can't support him any longer and there's no shore in sight, just vacant sky and lonely water in every direction—

"So cold."

Then I hear a woman's voice and she's whispering my name: "Patrick . . ." The word comes from another place and collides with the nightmare.

"Patrick . . ."

Suddenly I'm spinning free of my dream, watching Ellory's face disappear into the water, within the blurry fog of sleep.

"Cold, so cold."

Then the voice again. "Pat, are you okay?"

It's Amber and I want to reply, but I can't seem to open my eyes, move, speak. Anything. A thick weight is pressing on me.

I struggle to speak, and at last I manage to whisper her name. "Amber."

"He's waking up!" The words are liquid, floating and shimmering around me as if they were real things that could be touched, held, squeezed.

At last I work my eyes open and see her leaning over me, her face backlit by the sharp, white hospital room light, which forces me to shut them again.

"Oh, is it good to see you, Pat. Thank God."

The soft warmth of her hand rested on mine. She squeezed and it felt both right and wrong to have her touch me in this tender way. Skin on skin, as I awoke from my dream.

Thinking of my current relationship with Lien-hua, I slipped my hand away from my sister-in-law's.

Groggy.

Still groggy.

I shifted slightly, worked my eyes open again. It looked like I was in an ICU, although it was small and not as modern as I've seen, so I guessed I was at the hospital in Woodborough. An IV plugged into my left arm. A cardiac monitor.

A woman stood beside Amber. Gray hair, medium build, early fifties, a nurse.

"Dr. Bowers," the nurse said firmly, "you are a fortunate man."

"Fortunate?" The word was hoarse, didn't even sound like my voice.

"That tarp probably saved your life."

Tarp?

"Ellory." I tried to collect my thoughts. "He was there. The suspect threw him in the river. Did they find Ellory?"

Neither of them spoke.

"He went under the ice," I said.

"Just rest, Pat—" Amber began, her voice soft, palliative, but I cut her off.

"Where's Jake?"

"He stepped out of the room to get some coffee. He'll be back."

"I need to talk to Tessa, tell her what happened, can I borrow . . ."

But then, a realization.

When Tessa's father had died last summer, she'd become more

emotionally reliant on me, and if I spoke with her right now, she would certainly hear the weakness in my voice. And finding out I was in a hospital would only make her worry more—especially when she learned that I'd narrowly escaped drowning, not to mention freezing to death. Being stuck in the Cities and unable to see me wouldn't help matters at all. Right now the last thing I wanted to do was upset her.

Call her later, check in when you're not so queasy.

"What time is it?" My eyes flicked around the room, found no clock.

"Just past 6:00," Amber said.

No! That's too long!

I tried to prop myself up but was too weak to do it. "Tell me, did they catch Chekov?"

"Who?" She shook her head. "I'm not sure who that is." Then she thought for a moment. "I did overhear Jake on the phone, though, telling someone that the UNSUB was still at large. Is that him?"

That term *UNSUB* always annoys me. Unlike on TV crime shows, almost no one in the Bureau actually uses the term. Besides in this case, Alexei wasn't an unknown subject of the investigation, he was known, identified, there was no doubt he was the man who'd killed Bryan Ellory. Amber went on, "They were lucky to find you when they did."

I felt myself slipping away again, the thick dreamy darkness sweeping over me. "How did they? How did they find me?"

"Anonymous call."

"Anonymous call," I echoed softly. There was only one person who knew I was lying beside that river, but why Alexei Chekov would have contacted emergency services to tell them about me, to save my life, was beyond me.

The sense of weariness was overpowering. "Did you give me anything?" I said to the nurse, who had just finished adjusting my IV.

"No. Do you know your condition when we brought you in?"

So sleepy.

"I need to go." I fumbled with the IV to pull it out of my arm. Failed.

"It's okay," Amber said, her hand on mine again. "Relax, Pat."

"Listen, there was a semitrailer." I was in a fog. "You have to tell Jake. I only saw it for a few seconds . . ."

Focus, Pat!

"Peterbilt extended cab." My voice sounded faint, as if it were coming from someone else. "Maroon. Silver trailer. No distinctive markings, heading west."

Faintly, I heard the nurse: "He remembers that after seeing it for a few seconds?"

"Yes," Amber said.

"Have him call it in," I mumbled just before I felt myself slip away again into a thick and timeless dream.

37

Tessa could feel her stomach churning at the smell of the bar's greasy, fried meat. Just knowing that those animals had been ruthlessly imprisoned and then barbarously slaughtered just so they could be chopped up, fried, and eaten was disturbing enough, and now she was caught smelling the evidence of all that brutality.

But it was too cold to wait for Sean outside, and Larry had been generously bringing her free root beer and french fries, and he was so nice that she would've felt way rude complaining about the meat smell, so she kept quiet.

He started telling her stories about turkey hunting with "that lucky-shot uncle of yours," and the hunting stories didn't exactly serve to settle her stomach. She held back from sharing her views about sport hunting.

Tessa was halfway through her second platter of fries when the front door opened and Sean appeared amidst an angry swirl of snow.

He looked her way. "Hey, I'm sorry I was so long."

"I'm glad you made it." She stood.

After a quick hello and thanks to Larry, who still refused to let them pay for anything, Sean led her to the truck. "I need to tell you something important about Patrick."

A tremor of uneasiness. "What is it?"

"Climb in. I'll explain on the way."

━━━━━━━━━━━━ ■ ━━━━━━━━━━━━

The money had been at the dead drop, a fact that was a bit perplexing to Alexei, considering the fact that he was evidently being set up. Now he was on the road in a new vehicle, and the duffel bag containing the cash was carefully tucked in the corner of the trunk to make room for the person he was transporting.

He was nearly to the house when he received word from Nikolai.

"The phone number you gave me, it was used to phone the American consulate in Moscow to report that . . ." But then Nikolai paused and seemed to rethink his decision to share the information with Alexei.

"To report what?"

A blank silence. "The death of your wife."

"What? How do you know this?"

"We each have our methods, Alexei. But you must trust me. The number, I confirmed it with my sources."

Alexei let that sink in. *Valkyrie reported Tatiana's murder?*

That meant that, even if Valkyrie wasn't the one to pull the trigger, he—or she—was somehow complicit in the crime.

Alexei felt his anger, his thoughts, spiral in pin-tight. "Anything else?"

"I will let you know if there is."

"I'll give you an additional $250,000 if you can get me a name within twenty-four hours." After offering to transfer half of the amount now, as a sign of good faith, it didn't take a lot of convincing before Alexei's contact agreed.

Alexei ended the call. Electronically transferred the funds.

On Wednesday Valkyrie had mentioned his Tanfoglio. Mentioned Italy. Why even bring it up? How had Valkyrie found out about it, anyway? And why leave the remaining $1,000,000 at the dead drop?

Alexei didn't know, but he couldn't help but think that Valkyrie had been playing him ever since Tatiana's murder.

Okay, change of plans.

Becker Hahn had told him to expect a call at 9:00 tomorrow night: "Not a minute before, not a minute after." Alexei was aware that plans change, but 9:00 was also the time Valkyrie had told him earlier, so it appeared that he had a window of opportunity until then.

Alexei was confident that even if Nikolai came up short, Becker, who'd been so bold as to mention Valkyrie in the meeting earlier today, would have information leading to the intelligencer's identification or whereabouts. Eco-Tech had something planned, but even more importantly, they were still in this area and they were connected with Valkyrie.

Alexei arrived at the cabin, gently transferred the woman from the car's trunk to the room at the end of the hall, secured her, then pulled out his computer to review his notes about Becker Hahn and his team.

He was going to find the people who had set him up, and then go through them one by one until they told him who Valkyrie was.

I awoke.

No one else in the hospital room.

Looking around, I found my watch on a small dresser beside the bed and checked the time.

8:02 p.m.

I rubbed my head.

From the time I'd tried to save Bryan Ellory—apart from awakening briefly just after six o'clock—I'd been out more than six hours. I was off the cardiac monitor now, but still had the IV.

I felt bleary and weak and ached all over, either from the aftermath of the hypothermia or from some type of medication they were giving me. Whichever it was, it didn't matter, my energy was gone.

Knowing that my face had been exposed to subzero temperature for an indeterminate period of time, I apprehensively slid my hand across my nose, felt my earlobes. They still stung from frostnip, but thankfully, all seemed fine, frostbite hadn't ravaged my face. I checked my hands, my fingers, wiggled my toes. All good—but when I tried to move my ankle, I felt a jolt of pain.

I thought again of the river, of what had happened.

Ellory is dead. You let him die.

I'd barely known the man, and yet now I felt a wash of stark sadness and loss as if we'd been friends for years. He might not have been as thorough as he could've been in his police reports, but he was forward-thinking enough to send the Lab the tread patterns that led to the open water on Tomahawk Lake. And he was dedicated: he'd done all he knew to do at each scene, pursued the suspect through the snowstorm, and died trying to apprehend a killer.

No, he died when you let him drown.

You let him go.

Ellory was a hero, and I was the one who'd let him die.

Another voice tried to reassure me, but it was faint and distant: *No, Pat, you were the one who tried to save him.*

Any negative thoughts I'd had earlier about Ellory now vanished, and I felt armed with fresh fire and a deep sense of purpose to catch his killer. I was going to get the man who did this and I was going to bring him in or put him down.

Needles make me queasy, but I sat up, steeled myself, and tugged out my IV, then slid the piece of tape over the needle hole to stop any seepage.

My clothes were piled on a chair in the corner of the room. Surprisingly, all of them, even the camo coat, looked dry, and I was thankful for whoever had taken care of that little detail.

I swung my legs out of bed, paused to catch my breath and calm my dizziness, and noticed a note beside the phone in Amber's looping handwriting: "Good news from the X-rays. The ankle's not broken! I'll be right back. You're supposed to call Margaret.—A."

The last I'd heard, Margaret was checking on Donnie Pickron to see why he had Sensitive Compartmented Information access.

Since Sean still had my cell, I dialed Margaret's number from the room phone. She picked up.

"Margaret, it's Pat."

"Jake told me about the river."

"I'm all right. But—"

"Agent Bowers, do you have any idea how serious your condition was?"

"Listen, I'm not on a secure line here. Can you have security reroute the call through our proxy server and call me back?"

A pause. "Just a moment."

I hung up and only a few seconds later the phone rang and I answered. She spoke first: "I understand the suspect got away."

"He did."

"And we still have no confirmation that Donnie Pickron is dead?"

"That's right."

"How did you fall into the river?"

"I jumped in to try and save Bryan Ellory." It felt like a stone was lodged in my throat. "But I couldn't do it. I couldn't get him to shore. He's gone."

Another pause. "Yes, I heard. I'm very sorry. I've sent condolences to his wife Mia on behalf of you and the Bureau."

Just hearing his widow's name seemed to make things worse.

"You put your life on the line for him," Margaret said. "I'll recommend you for a citation of—"

"None of that matters." I didn't want to talk about the river. "Did you find out anything more about Donnie? Why he was in the area?"

A moment passed. "Yes. He used to lead an information warfare team at an old Navy communication base nearby." Her tone shifted slightly and indicated to me that, at least for the time being, she was willing to leave behind the conversation concerning what'd happened at the river. "I'll send you the files, everything I have on it. But the station was closed in 2004."

"According to the Navy."

"Yes." A small pause. "According to the Navy."

The recently issued biometric ID card came to mind. "Tell me about the station. Where is it?"

"In the center of the Chequamegon-Nicolet National Forest."

Hmm. Yes—the area Donnie would have passed on his snowmobile on the way to the sawmill.

I tried to stand on my swollen, discolored ankle. Couldn't. Dropped back onto the bed. "I'm going over there."

"Not tonight you're not. We have no idea what we're dealing with here. And you need to rest."

I would never admit it to her, but I really was exhausted right now and I couldn't even imagine fighting my way through a blizzard with this ankle in the pitch black looking for a communication station that might not even exist.

"Besides," she said, "for all we know, this Alexei Chekov is halfway across the state by now."

For all we know, he hasn't gone anywhere, I thought.

But she was right as well, he might be gone.

"Is there an APB on Chekov?"

"Well, that's the problem," she told me. "We don't have a photo."

"State patrol found the rental car he was driving and we have the plate numbers. The anonymous caller said he was using the alias Neil Kreger. Check with the rental car companies and airport security at all the airports within a day's drive. We should be able to pull a photo of him from airport surveillance cameras, get it to law enforcement across the state."

"Yes. Good. I'll get some agents on it."

"I assume there's an APB on the semi?"

"There is."

Maybe it was too obvious, but I felt like the next few words needed to be said: "This is a lot bigger than just the Pickron murders. I don't think he committed them."

"Then who did?"

"I don't know. An associate. An accomplice maybe. At the river he told me he didn't kill Ardis or Lizzie."

"And you believed him?"

"I did."

She thought about that for a moment. "You need a couple days of rest; however, if you're up to it, I'd like you to brief Jake, Natasha, and Sheriff Tait in the morning. I told them 9:00." I hadn't yet met Tait, who'd been down with the flu yesterday, but with Deputy Ellory gone it made sense that Tait would get involved even if he was still sick.

There was no way I was going to sit around resting for a couple days. "Nine isn't a problem."

"I'll have Tait send some state troopers to check on the site of the old ELF station as soon as it's light." Even though the sheriff's department was lead on this, I knew that in remote rural areas, they work closely with the state patrol, as it appeared Tait was in the position to do here.

"ELF?"

"Extremely Low Frequency, that's the kind of electromagnetic waves the communication system used."

"All right. I'll go with the officers."

"Don't be ridiculous. Do you realize you were not breathing when they found you?"

"That's probably overstating things."

"Not to mention your ankle. I need you to take care of yourself." She actually sounded concerned for me.

How does she know about my ankle?

"I'm fine, Margaret."

"I believe the word is stubborn. If the officers find anything, we'll get you and the rest of the team over there as soon as possible to have a look around."

With that, she ended the conversation.

Stubborn?

That wasn't very nice.

I put a quick call through to Lien-hua. She was in the middle of a meeting and sounded very rushed, so when she asked how I was, I simply told her that it'd been a long day, and that the weather had gotten the best of me. "I'll fill you in later," I said, "when we have a little more time to talk."

Before ending the call, she made a point of assuring me that my surprise was still coming. "You'll find it later tonight in your room."

"At the Moonbeam?"

"Yes." A slight pause. "Pat, I have to go. It's not that I don't want to talk. It's just—"

"No problem. Don't worry about it."

"Okay. Talk to you soon."

I was ready to get out of this hospital but didn't know where Jake or our car might be so I punched in his number and caught up with him at the sheriff's department in Woodborough. After I convinced him I didn't need to stay here, he agreed to pick me up in fifteen minutes to take me back to the motel. The doctors and nurses might not be happy that I was leaving, but I could deal with that.

———————◼———————

Tessa was annoyed that Sean hadn't called her while she was at Lindberg's to inform her that Patrick was in the hospital. "I waited because I thought I should tell you in person," he explained. "I didn't want you to worry."

"You sound like your brother."

He was quiet and she wondered if he had taken that to somehow be an insult.

"Seriously, though," she said, "he's okay?" She was uptight enough, and the pickup's gun rack right behind her head with two guns for killing wildlife wasn't helping her calm down any.

"From what everyone's telling me, yes."

She pulled out her cell phone, but Sean warned her, "I'm not sure we should wake him up. Before I picked you up, they told me he was sleeping."

She hesitated.

Then set it down.

Both of her parents were gone, and she couldn't even imagine the thought of losing Patrick too. If he died, that would totally put her over the edge. No question about it.

Death. Too much death.

She found her thoughts returning to her dad's funeral in June up in the mountains of Wyoming.

After everyone else had left, she and Patrick had stood alone and silent by the graveside. After a while she'd whispered to him, "They say we're never really gone as long as there's someone to remember us."

A moment passed. "Maybe that's what makes us human. What makes us unique from animals."

"What's that? Remembering the dead?" Figuring out what

separates humans from other animals had been sort of a big question she was dealing with at the time.

"No, loving them enough to remember them."

She'd stared at the gravestone and considered his words. The broad sky stretched above her, clouds covering the sun.

"I'll always remember him," she said.

"So will I."

Then Patrick put his arm around her shoulder and they stood there together quietly for a long time as the sun cut through a cloud and caught hold of a mountain range on the horizon.

And then despite herself she'd cried, and Patrick had wiped her tears away.

"Tessa?" It was Sean. "Are you all right?"

It took her a couple seconds to mentally refocus. "How far is it? I need to talk to him."

"Another thirty miles."

"Well, just get us there, then." Yes, her voice was sharp with impatience but it was mostly filled with concern. She hoped Sean could tell the difference.

"Don't worry." He stared determinedly at the road ahead of them. "I will."

38

CIA Detainment Facility 17
Cairo, Egypt
4:24 a.m. Eastern European Time

Terry Manoji sat in his wheelchair in the hospital room in which he'd been confined since the CIA transferred him to this location sometime last year.

Because of the coma he'd been in for eight months, time was a blur, but for the last few months he'd managed to get a handle on the passage of days, because nine weeks ago one of the nurses carelessly brought her Blackberry into his room. He was in bed when he saw it poking out of her pocket, so he sat up, swung his legs from the bed as if he were going to get into his chair, but then forced himself to lose his balance and topple to the floor.

She'd helped him back into bed.

And hadn't noticed what he had hidden in his hand.

She left soon afterward without realizing that she didn't have her phone with her.

Although flush toilets weren't common in the Middle East, because of his condition it was a necessity for him to have one.

There were no surveillance cameras in his bathroom.

Which worked in his favor.

Once in the bathroom, he used the phone to get online.

To get into the phone company's site he used a little port redirection and quickly gained administrator privileges, then created a back channel so it'd be quicker getting in again later if he lost the connection or when the nurse cancelled her contract after discovering her phone was gone.

Once in their system, he blocked the ability to trace future calls made to and from this number and climbed through the company's primitive firewalls to get to the central processing facility. After tracing the GPS signal to find out where exactly he was, he put a stop on the GPS tracking. If the nurse or agents tried to trace it, as they undoubtably would, the phone would simply appear to be turned off.

He was online.

Invisible and untraceable.

He was home.

The internet is one big playground, and wherever there's WiFi or a cell phone connection, a good hacker can jump on the wire, and once he's in, he's in. And he can go anywhere.

An hour later, when his interrogators came to search the room for the phone, he'd already hidden it. They meticulously scoured both his room and the attached bathroom but found nothing because before they'd arrived he'd used two discarded latex gloves, tied off, to create a double-layer waterproof bag, and then placed the cell phone in the toilet bowl, shoved back in the pipe so that it wasn't visible.

He knew he was taking a risk that someone might flush while they were searching the room, but thankfully they hadn't been that thorough or that careless.

Conserving the phone's batteries had been a concern at first. The electrical current in Egypt would be 220 VAC, which would fry the phone. However, by the make and model of the two video cameras monitoring his room he knew that they were not infrared.

So he could work at night.

An LED lamp that he didn't use beside his bed had a DC converter at the plug and, by scraping off the wire's insulation, he'd managed to create a crude way of recharging the phone by splicing the cord and using a bandage from his arm to hold the battery in place against the exposed wires.

It wasn't ideal by any means, and he had to be careful how much time he spent in the bathroom on the cell, but he found that charging the phone two to three times a week during the night was enough to get him through.

Then, on November 18, through his online correspondence, he'd arranged everything with his partner after helping clear the way for her escape from prison. Then he'd contacted Abdul Razzaq Muhammad to put his own escape plan into motion.

Since he was surveilled so closely, Terry was limited in what he could do from this room, but during his visits to the bathroom, he'd sent his partner detailed instructions on how to access the back doors he'd left in the military's top secret JWICS network back when he was still in the employ of the NSA.

And yes, also in the employ of the Chinese government.

Which was actually the reason why, according to his interrogators, the CIA had pressured the San Diego Police Department to announce that he'd died while in custody.

"As far as the rest of the world is concerned, you're dead and buried," the man had told him. "So we have nothing to lose keeping you here as long as we want." Then he'd leaned forward. "Or shortening your stay if it comes to that."

And so, Terry fed the interrogators just enough information each week about Chinese hacking protocols to keep them coming back.

Now he reviewed his plan.

A distraction layered inside a distraction.

The deal with Abdul Razzaq Muhammad had been simple— Terry would take out the target of Abdul's choice and Abdul would transfer a rather sizable amount of money to an offshore account and send a team of militants to free him.

According to Air Force Doctrine Document 3-12, or AFDD 3-12, released back on October 26, 2010, there are millions of attempts to hack into the US military's computers every day. And, as Terry knew all too well, that number had only continued to rise since then.

But a much earlier hack was the one that was going to make all the difference in his case—and was the one that, indirectly, was going to help set him free.

On October 1, 2003, at 03:25, Chinese hackers broke into the

Naval Ocean Systems Center in San Diego, California, and downloaded more than four terabytes of data.

It gave them just the information they needed to hop onto the Department of Defense's Joint Worldwide Intelligence Communication System.

When the Bush Administration first became aware of the malware placed onto the JWICS by the Chinese in early 2004, they responded quickly and took steps to protect the one means of communication with nuclear weapons systems that was not connected to or dependent on the internet in any way, the only viable nonsatellite, non-web-based means of contacting submarines: extremely low frequency electromagnetic signals, emitted from a small base in northern Wisconsin—or more specifically, from the part of the base that had never been made public.

And now, that very safety net that the military had put into place to guard against hackers was the one Terry was going to exploit to get out of this detainment facility and away from the reach of the CIA.

And back together with Cassandra.

Calculating the time, Terry knew that it was almost 8:30 p.m. in Wisconsin.

Okay.

He wheeled to the bathroom to make a call to his partner to verify that all was in place for tomorrow.

39

After signing out and leaving my irate nurse behind, I met Jake in the lobby of the hospital.

Reluctantly, but out of necessity, I used a pair of crutches to get to the car, then as we headed into the blizzard he filled me in: state patrol had found the Peterbilt truck that I'd seen crossing the bridge above the Chippewa River. It was parked at a restaurant about twenty miles west of Woodborough, but there were no other cars or snowmobiles missing at the restaurant and no one matching Alexei's description had been seen entering the premises.

"It's like he just disappeared," Jake said.

"No. He's smart. He abducted someone else in the parking lot and left with 'em in their vehicle so there wouldn't be any immediate suspicion."

"How do you know that?"

"Because it's what I would've done."

Jake was quiet.

"Any sign of the driver of the semi?"

"No. Still unaccounted for."

It was possible that the suspect had left the driver alive, perhaps to use as leverage like he'd done with Ellory, but even though I tried to hold out hope, I couldn't help but think of the truck driver only in the past tense.

Anger.

This guy Chekov was mine.

Jake went on, "No sign of Ellory, but if he drowned in that river like you said, that's no surprise."

"What do you mean if he drowned?"

"I was just noting that they haven't found his body yet."

"He went under, Jake. He didn't come up."

A moment. "Okay." Then, "The divers never made it down from Ashland, and with this storm it doesn't look like they will."

No surprise there.

"Where's Natasha?"

"With Linnaman at the hospital. Last I heard, she was assisting him with the autopsies of Ardis and Lizzie Pickron."

The snowfall illuminated by our headlights wasn't letting up, and the road we were on hadn't been plowed recently. Drifts, some nearly three feet high, were forming, jutting out perpendicular to the shoulders. I'd let Jake drive, and he was doing his best to avoid the drifts, but it didn't seem like he was used to driving in this kind of weather.

The going was slow.

"I also talked with Torres," he said. "They discovered Reiser's body near the trailer park. And get this: his lungs are gone."

Basque.

"He must have found out how close we were to catching Reiser and decided he was a liability," Jake speculated.

Analyze and investigate; don't assume.

"Time of death?"

"They're not sure yet. Still working on that. I haven't heard from the ERT, but I'm expecting we'll find souvenirs hidden somewhere in the trailer. Probably press clippings too."

Most serial killers keep tokens or emblems of their crimes—body parts of the victims, fingernails, hair, or jewelry, clothing, or accessories, so Jake's words didn't surprise me. I thought again of the profile he had drawn up on Reiser. "You're still thinking he followed coverage of his crimes? Documented them?"

"Yeah, if I'm calling this right, I'd say our guy is a scrapbooker for sure."

I told Jake about Alexei's claim that he wasn't responsible for killing the Pickron family. "It seemed important to him that I not associate him with the murder of Ardis and Lizzie."

"Typical assassin mentality," he said, profiling on the spot. "They have their own unique, individualized set of moral values and convictions. Often they see violence that isn't mission-oriented as immoral, but violence committed in the context of their professional life as simply necessary. Mental compartmentalization."

Jake was right.

But he was also wrong. It's not just assassins who do that, we all do. Freud once said that rationalization makes the world go round, and whatever else he got wrong, he nailed that one.

Everyone rationalizes their own immorality—people have affairs and yet look their spouses in the eye, they cheat on their taxes and then get mad at corruption on Wall Street, they lie outright to their bosses to get ahead and still manage to feel good about themselves, to have high self-esteem.

Mental compartmentalization.

Rationalization.

Without it we'd have to live in the daily recognition of who we really are, what we're really capable of. And that's something most people avoid at all costs.

As Lien-hua had told me once, "We run from the past and it chases us; we dive into urgency, but nothing deep is ultimately healed."

Despite my reticence to trust Jake's profiles and observations, I had to admit that he was iterating some of the same thoughts I'd had since my confrontation with Alexei at the river. If we were right about the assassin's state of mind, I wondered if there might be a way to use his skewed moral grounding against him. To trap him. To bring him in.

The conversation faded into silence, and about ten minutes later we arrived at the motel. I tried to stand on my own, but my ankle screamed at me and I had to lean against the car. I hid the gesture from Jake as much as I could.

He went on ahead, and after crutching my way inside, I used my room phone to call my own cell number, to find out where Sean was.

Tessa picked up. "Hey."

At first I thought maybe I'd inadvertently dialed the wrong number. "Tessa?"

She got right to the point: "You fell in a *river*? Seriously?"

"Why do you have my phone, Tessa? Where are you?"

"I'm with Sean. I decided to drive over and see you. He picked me up at—"

"You what!"

"Decided to come see you. And then I hear you, like—"

"Tessa, I was clear that I didn't want you driving today!"

"I thought you wanted to show me around. Spend time with me."

"I do, but that's not the point. You were supposed to stay there."

"Noted," she said. "So what happened at the river?"

"Tessa—"

"Tell me about the river, Dad."

Oh, she said that last word on purpose. Very sly.

Very.

Sly.

And despite myself, as I contemplated a reply, I found that her tactic just might be working.

Even though I was frustrated that she hadn't listened to me, I was also thankful she was safe, and right now, more quickly than I ever would have guessed, that relief was overtaking my irritation. "It's a long story." I laid the crutches against the wall and propped my leg up on the bed. "We'll talk about it later. Where are you two?"

"You almost drowned. You could have died."

Margaret did say you weren't breathing . . .

"Well, I'm up and at it again."

"You're always doing this to me," Tessa said softly.

"Always doing what to you?"

"Almost dying."

"How am I doing that to you?"

"I'm your daughter. You're the one . . . ." She hesitated until the silence became uncomfortable. "It's just, you can't go and get killed—or almost killed, or whatever. Not when you have someone that you have to, well, you know."

Take care of, yes, I know.

"I'll be careful."

"Yeah, I've heard that before."

"I mean it this time."

"That's what you said last time. When you got shot."

"That time was different."

"And the time before that, when—"

"Listen, are you two almost here?"

Faintly, I heard her speak off the phone to Sean before returning to the line. "Sean says we're like ten minutes from his house, about twenty-five from the hospital. Maybe a little more."

"Actually, I left the hospital. I'm at the motel." I'd reserved a room for Tessa earlier this morning, and in the rush of the day's events I'd forgotten about it.

But—

"Hang on, that'll take you even longer. Let me talk to him a sec."

A short pause as she handed Sean the phone. "You doing all right?" he asked.

"I'm good. Listen, just take Tessa to your place for the night. Don't chance the roads, there's no reason to. We'll connect in the morning."

"I was thinking the same thing."

"Great. And just hang on to those papers that I gave you at the sawmill. I'll get them tomorrow." I paused. "Oh, and did you hear about your sled?"

"I was there with the paramedics when they picked you up at the river. I saw what was left of it."

"Yeah. Sorry about that. I didn't really expect that tree to jump out at me like that."

"Didn't really shock me. You can be impulsive sometimes."

He had me there. "I'll get you a new one." A lightness that hadn't been present between us for years had entered the conversation, and it felt good. "Maybe I can even get the Bureau to chip in since I was chasing a suspect in a federal investigation when I commandeered it."

"Finally some tax dollars put to good use."

"Exactly."

"I'm just glad you're all right. Amber's snowmobile is in the shed.

I can use that if I need to get around." His words held forgiveness, and it made me wish my apology had been a little more forthright and comprehensive.

We said our good-byes, hung up, and then I headed to the front desk to borrow a couple five-gallon buckets.

Time to take care of that ankle.

40

Simon Weatherford, the manager of the Schoenberg Inn, hadn't given Cassandra Lillo's associate Ted Rusk any trouble on Wednesday when Ted offered him $50,000 of Valkyrie's money for exclusive use of the two basement sections of the hotel for the week. Weatherford vowed that they wouldn't be interrupted for anything, and so far he'd held unswervingly to his promise.

The hotel had been named a National Historic Landmark in 2004, and a federal grant had allowed the place to be restored and refurbished to its 1930s decor and even some of the little-used rooms in the lower level had benefited.

The two sections of the basement were on opposite wings of the building and weren't connected. She'd chosen a room at the other end of the hotel yesterday for their meeting with Alexei Chekov. A small precaution, but if he were as good as she was beginning to suspect he might be, a wise one. Now, even if he came looking for them, he would be looking in the wrong place.

She traversed the hallway toward the room where Dillinger had once stayed for five days in 1934, waiting for federal agents to give up their search and go home. As she did, she passed the rarely used guest rooms that now housed the seven members of her team she hadn't allowed Chekov to meet.

So, Bowers, the FBI agent, had survived—or been brought back to life, depending on the definition of death you wanted to use. In either case, even though it would probably take him time to recover, he was still around, and she would have to make sure the FBI didn't poke too closely into her team's affairs.

A brawny man who was standing sentry at the room at the end of the hall acknowledged her with an informal salute. She'd moved him into this role after she'd strangled Clifton White—who'd let her down when he encountered Chekov—and had her people deposit his body outside and cover it with snow.

She pressed the door open, and inside the room she found two more of her people on guard, as well as the man who'd been the reason for so many of the events this week.

Donnie Pickron.

Alive and well.

He sat at a desk with three flat-screen computer monitors arranged in front of him and now looked up from his work. Sweaty. Nervous. His bald head appeared shiny and polished in the blue-tinged light of the computer screens. "I want proof my wife and daughter are still alive." He spoke with a surprising amount of determination. "Or I'm not going to do any more work for you."

His words were not unexpected. Cassandra unpocketed her cell and walked toward him in silence. His right ankle was chained to the leg of the metal table.

"If I let you speak to your wife on the phone, will that be sufficient?"

He seemed shocked by the offer. "Yes."

She excused the two guards, tapped in a number, handed Donnie her cell.

He waited for an answer, then said anxiously, "Hello? Ardis?"

Cassandra watched him closely. Getting the electronic voiceprint earlier in the week from his wife hadn't been difficult. It simply meant stopping by their house to ask for directions and then recording Ardis's reply and the short conversation that followed. With some of the software these days, you don't need much audio at all to make a near-perfect match. To pull off the overlay, after you have the sample you just speak into a microphone hooked up to the computer, and the program does the rest.

However, there were always glitches in these types of operations, always—

"Is Lizzie there?" Donnie said into the phone. "Is she okay?"

Hmm . . . Good. Millicent Alman, one of the three people who'd met with Alexei Chekov in the basement of the Schoenberg Inn, was making it work.

"*She's okay.*" Cassandra ran through the words in her mind, as if she herself were part of the conversation. "*She's right here, but she's sleeping. They have guns. Oh, Donnie, please! Do what they say. They threatened to hurt Lizzie!*"

"You're going to be okay," Donnie said, as if on cue. "Don't worry."

Cassandra had been careful to brief Millicent on what to say and what not to say. "If he tries to ask you anything personal, perhaps about where you met or went on your honeymoon, or if he mentions a specific name, location, secret item, don't answer him. Stick to the threats you're under: tell him they're watching you. That they know everything. That they're listening to every word. End by pleading for his help."

Her operative had nodded. "I've done this before. I'll be all right."

After a few more moments of conversation, Cassandra took the phone from Donnie.

The look on his face made it clear that Millicent really did know what she was doing—he appeared convinced that he'd been speaking with his wife.

Now he looked at Cassandra. "And when this is over, you'll let them go? Let us all go?"

Though she didn't like to lie there were bigger things at stake here than her pointless sensibilities. She reassured him that he and his family would be fine.

"Okay," he said at last.

She gestured toward the keyboard. "How long?"

"Two of the authorization codes won't even be online until the sub leaves Bahrain tomorrow afternoon." That made her think of another lie she'd told this man. She'd convinced him—as well as her Eco-Tech team—that they were going to take the nuclear weapons that were aboard an Ohio Class submarine offline to send a message to the world about the importance of nuclear disarmament.

However, in truth, that wasn't quite the plan.

"And so," she said, "give me a timeline."

He glanced at the computer screen. "I'll need several hours to hash the encryption and get past the authentication protocols, but I'll need data from the station."

"You'll have it."

"How?"

"Don't worry, you'll have it. You have a simple job: monitor the frequencies, access the deactivation codes, send the signal. And if we don't get what we need, Ardis and Lizzie will die. I am not a woman who makes idle threats. Do you understand?"

For a moment he looked like he might challenge her, then said, "Yes."

"No one needs to get hurt."

He didn't reply.

Mentally, she reviewed her schedule for tomorrow: after briefing her team at 11:30, three of her people would travel to the eastern entrance to the national forest to take out the telephone lines, then she and the rest of the team would head to the maintenance building that had been left at the site of the now-leveled ELF base.

And from there they would access the facility.

When she left the room, she found Becker waiting for her in the hall. "Well?" he said. "How long?"

"After he gets the data from the station, a couple hours."

"But we have to have the uplink before 9:00—"

"I know. We will."

Becker looked at his watch again.

"We'll be in the base by 6:00," she reassured him. "It'll give us enough time. Don't worry."

"What did you tell him about his wife and daughter?"

She was tired of hearing about this. "You're still upset about that."

He was quiet.

"It was only two lives. There'll likely be—"

"I know, Dana, but—"

"Don't interrupt me, Becker." He'd used the name he knew her by: Dana Murkowski. One of her aliases. "We needed the videos of them to make our threat credible when the time comes."

"But you killed a little girl. Shot her mother in the—"

"It was necessary. Just like with Clifton."

"Necessary? Couldn't you have—"

"It was necessary." She let each word fall like a stone: *We are not going to discuss this anymore.*

He didn't reply, and she turned to leave but then felt his hand on her arm, gentle. An invitation. She paused.

"I'm sorry. I know you had to do it. Your conviction, your fearlessness, that's one of the reasons I fell in love with you." Well, his remorse over the death of the Pickrons must not have been as deep as he'd been letting on.

She faced him and said with a smile, "That's two reasons."

"Two reasons, then." He seemed to have already put the Pickron slayings out of his mind. "Twenty minutes ago I had a conversation with Valkyrie. Everything is in place."

"I'm glad to hear that."

"Alexei has the rest of the money. Picked it up from the dead drop."

"That shouldn't matter now."

He was caressing her with his eyes and she didn't discourage him.

He'd been an easy man to seduce.

One of her gifts was getting men to fall in love with her. And so, to solidify his loyalty, she had made sure that he was smitten; that he would do anything for her. She couldn't help but think of him as a gullible little puppet. After all, he still believed they were going to be disarming the weapons on the sub to make a statement to the world.

She let him take her in his arms.

Oh yes, they were going to make a statement.

She said nothing as he bent toward her.

And when he kissed her she did not close her eyes.

Sean led Tessa into his living room and she froze. The tragic remains of two deer heads and a four-foot-long muskie hung on the wall.

All right, that was just plain troubling. She turned away. "Is Amber here?"

"Last I heard, she was at the hospital with Pat. She's probably on her way home."

Although Tessa didn't know the details, from a few uncharacteristic moments of self-revelation from Patrick over the last year, she did know that before Patrick met her mom, he and Amber had had some sort of thing together.

Probably before she met Sean.

All ancient history.

Sean didn't seem to give a second thought to Amber visiting with Patrick tonight.

As he was walking toward the kitchen, the house lights flickered briefly and he made a comment about how, this far in the country, the electricity goes out all the time. Now that she thought about it, she realized that on the way to the house she hadn't seen neighbors anywhere close.

Sean motioned toward a pile of wood by the living room fire-place. "I'll get a fire going just in case." Then he caught himself. "Are you hungry?"

"I'm all right."

"You want some juice or something?"

No sense fighting it. You're not gonna fall asleep anyway.

"How about some coffee?"

"At this time of night?"

"I expect to be up for a while," she said simply.

41

Alternating ice baths—fifteen minutes in ice-cube-filled water, then a soak in the other bucket for ten, in water as hot as I could stand.

Repeat.

Again.

The chilled water takes the swelling down, the heat rushes blood flow to the area, helping circulation.

It's one of the best ways I've found to treat a sprain, but admittedly it isn't exactly nirvana in the moment you switch your foot from the steaming water to the ice bath.

I'd been at it for nearly an hour, my computer on my lap, working on the case as I soaked my ankle.

We knew Donnie drove his Jeep to work on Thursday, left at noon with the sawmill's truck, but where was it now? If he'd returned to the house and then left on the snowmobile, what did he do with the truck?

Obviously, if he was abducted, his captors could have hidden it somewhere, but I was a bit surprised it was still missing.

It hadn't been overcast yesterday afternoon or this morning, so now I checked the Defense Department's Routine Orbital Satellite Database, or ROSD, to see if I could get a glimpse of anyone driving to or from the Pickron home around the time of the crimes.

Since this is a remote, sparsely populated region, I wasn't surprised to find gaps in the footage between satellite passes, but it was informative to note that one of those coincided exactly with the time someone would have needed to access the house immediately preceding the crime, then again ten minutes later when they might have exited the scene.

The killers knew the precise times the Defense Department's satellites would and would not be passing overhead.

I had footage from 1:54 to 1:58, could even see the cracks appear in the glass from the gunshots.

Shots fired through the living room window. Why?

I considered the time: 1:54 p.m. . . . the date: January 8 . . . the orientation of the window to the sun . . . the longitude and latitu—

Hang on.

Going back to the satellite images, I saw that—

Yes.

Oh yes.

At that time of day, with the position of the house, the sun, the satellite, there was no glare on the house's northern exposure living room window.

The interior house lights were on when the police arrived, remember? Only the study's lights were off.

I don't believe in coincidences.

No, I don't.

The cracks in the glass obscured the view of the house's interior; however, it wasn't a person outside in the marsh that might have peered in and seen the killers at work, it was a satellite.

I zoomed in on the image of the window. Looking at the house, first without the cracks in the glass, then with them, I realized that with the carefully placed shots causing the networked pattern of cracks, I could not see clearly inside the house.

Then there was the phone call, then the final shot—

Was someone watching a live feed through the ROSD? Is that the reason for the call, to let the killer know another shot was needed? A status report on the satellites? A warning? A signal?

It was impossible, of course, to discern what the caller or killer might have been thinking at that moment, but the precise timing and location of the shots told me that whoever was coordinating this thought like me.

No. he's smarter than you.

You almost missed this.

Frustratingly, this line of thinking brought up more questions than it answered: How could someone have accessed the DoD's Routine Orbital Satellite Database in the first place? Were we looking for a federal employee? Obviously there was a team of people involved, but how many?

You would need a world-class hacker to pull off something like that.

It was impressive as well as unsettling.

Researching further, I found that the cloud cover earlier today hid any view the satellites might've had of Chekov's movements. And if someone did place the helmet in the open water on Tomahawk Lake, they must have done so during the night when there wasn't enough light for the satellites to image the area.

Based on crime scene photos and lab analysis, I confirmed that one set of boot prints from a men's size 9, LaCrosse 400 G pac boot matched prints approaching the open water on Tomahawk Lake and the prints exiting the Pickron residence.

Donnie Pickron wore size eleven.

Nothing solid pointed toward him as the shooter, absolutely nothing.

I felt strangely encouraged, however. Taking into account all the effort someone had gone through to make it look like he was dead, I began holding out hope that he was still alive.

I wouldn't be able to do much tonight to track Chekov, so I did the next best thing and took some time to study the ELF files Margaret had sent me concerning the now-closed Navy communication base.

Here's what I learned:

The Extremely Low Frequency electromagnetic transmission technology was developed during the Cold War and was used to communicate with US and British Trident nuclear submarines. At the time, it was the only communication system that was able to contact subs while they were at stealth depths and running speed.

The signals were nearly impossible to jam or decipher, which provided a perfect way to get messages to subs while they remained submerged.

Radio signals can travel through water, but their ability to spread out is reduced as the frequency of the signal is increased: lower frequency, longer distance under the water. To get the messages to subs, the signals would need to travel hundreds of feet below the surface, thus the extremely low frequency of 76 Hertz or less, allowing the signals to travel down a thousand feet or more.

There were two locations for the ELF stations, one in the Chequamegon-Nicolet National Forest, the other about 150 miles away in Republic, Michigan. The sites were chosen because of the efficient low conductivity of the underlying bedrock, which helped transmit the signals, not through the earth's crust as I would have expected, but up into the atmosphere. Apparently, the ionosphere and the curvature of the earth served to diffract the electromagnetic waves into the oceans around the world. Every ocean that the subs patrolled was covered by the signals.

Every ocean.

Every route.

Every sub.

I found it impressive that this technology was developed in the eighties, but when I read on I saw that it had actually been pioneered in the 1950s, which was even more astonishing. The original proposal was to build a deep underground system in Wisconsin called SHELF—Super Hard ELF.

The Navy had given the development of this original extremely low frequency system the name Project Sanguine and had debated using dozens of underground bunkers with buried electrical wires running thousands of square miles, but in the end decided it was more feasible and cost effective to use the aboveground wires, and Project Sanguine had been scrapped.

However, according to some reports, they'd actually started work on Project Sanguine, constructing more than two dozen miles of tunnels and even an underground bunker in the years before the environmentalists caught wind of what they were doing.

I could see where this might be going, and I hoped my hypothesis was wrong.

I read on.

The Wisconsin ELF station officially began operating on October 1, 1989, but even a decade before that there was vigorous debate about the environmental effects of the program and the resultant magnetic fields created by the station. Environmentalists claimed there would be wide-ranging and disastrous consequences—that the signals would cause leukemia in humans and all sorts of maladies to the wildlife of the region.

At the time, the Navy studied the problem and concluded that the risk of any adverse effects was minimal.

But in the 1984 case of *Wisconsin v. Weinberger*, the Seventh District Court disagreed—stating that there was substantial evidence of serious health hazards—and halted construction, but in the end the national security threat posed by Russia superseded the ruling, and the station was completed and commissioned.

Despite numerous subsequent studies over the next decade, no conclusive evidence was found to substantiate the activists' claims.

But the environmentalists hadn't given up.

Over the ELF station's operational years, socially progressive and environmentally conscious groups held regular protests at the base, cut down the telephone poles that supported the electrical lines, and filed relentless federal lawsuits to close the Wisconsin station. State senators Herb Kohl and Russ Feingold even got into the act, demanding that the ELF site be shut down.

So.

A few threads came together.

All Ohio Class subs are equipped with antennas to receive the extremely low frequency waves and have onboard instruments that decode the ELF signals. However, since the subs don't have miles of radio transmission wires, the communication between the station and the subs was one-way.

For that reason, the ELF orders were typically requests for the sub to surface to receive further communication, or to remain at depth and at immediate battle readiness.

Typically.

In 2004, the Navy, without warning, announced that they were closing the stations because they were outdated and no longer needed. The Michigan site was completely razed. Then, the military dismantled the communications array here in Wisconsin, taking down all the telephone poles as well as more than twenty-eight miles of transmission wires that had surrounded the station.

Naval personnel had bulldozed the station, removed all the rubble, and reseeded the field so that now all that remained was a looming maintenance building that was apparently left for the forest service to use.

I found myself wondering if the Navy would really invest nearly a quarter of a billion dollars and fifty years of research and then abandon a project just because it seemed dated.

Actually, they might.

But still, why then? Why 2004?

As all of this was circling through my head, I scrolled to the final PDF file and found a footnote that gave me pause.

According to some protestors, the ELF signal could be used to issue first-strike orders, although the Navy maintained that the signals could never be used in that way.

But in the 1996 case of *Wisconsin v. Donna and Tom Howard*, a former commander of a US nuclear submarine, Captain James Bush, testified that the primary purpose of ELF signals was to give go-codes to launch kinetic attacks against foreign adversaries.

In other words, to initiate nuclear war.

I felt a palpable chill.

A biometric ID card.

Above top secret access.

The preliminary Project Sanguine work was done in Wisconsin, possibly including tunnels being constructed.

Though I'm hesitant to make investigative assumptions, it was looking more and more likely that something still remained out there in the middle of the national forest.

Using my laptop, I pulled up the topo maps of the area and

overlaid the snowmobile trails Donnie Pickron might have used to get to the sawmill.

The GPS coordinates showed that the site of the old ELF station lay just off the Birch Trail, one of the three routes that would've made sense for him to use. The Schoenberg Inn and the sawmill lie in northeasterly and southeasterly directions, respectively. Although much farther by road, the site was geographically relatively close to them both—a little over five miles as the crow flies.

As I was considering the implications, I heard a knock at the door. After drying my foot, I hobbled across the room and peered through the peephole, a habit formed from too many years of tracking people who want to kill you. Amber stood outside the room.

I cracked it open, letting in a gust of arctic air. "Hey, is everything all right?"

"Can I come in?"

"Um, well, that might not be—"

"Please."

After a moment's hesitation, I stepped aside, and she entered my motel room and shut the door softly behind her.

42

"How are you feeling?" she asked.

"Good. I'm doing good."

"Your ankle?" She was eyeing the two buckets.

"Well," I said, repositioning myself so I was putting less weight on it. "It's okay."

Amber looked at my swollen foot but refrained from comment.

Being alone in a motel room with her like this brought back memories, sharp, vivid. The three nights we'd spent together talking, sharing—a fire of intimacy born of common interests, goals, dreams. The memories made me uneasy, and I waited anxiously for her to explain her visit, all the while, the information I'd read about the ELF station kept itching away at my attention.

Quietly, and before I realized what she was doing, Amber approached me, then brushed her hand across my arm. "I was so worried about you when they brought you in to the hospital."

I took a faltering step backward. "Don't be concerned. Really, I'm all right."

"When you were lying there unconscious, it made me think . . ." She took in a small breath. "I realized some things."

I couldn't see any way that this conversation was a good one for us to be having. Especially not here. Not now. "Amber, maybe you should go."

"I came here to talk to you about me and Sean."

"Amber, I'm not sure—"

"You know we've had our ups and downs."

Actually, I hadn't known about any problems the two of them were having, which was just further evidence of how superficially I knew my brother. And from past experience I was all too aware that when people use the phrase "we've had our ups and downs" it's just a euphemistic way of saying "we've had our downs."

"Things haven't been good between us," she said candidly.

I moved toward the door. "It's not my place to hear this, Amber."

Rather than reply, she abruptly changed the direction of the conversation. "Why did you end things, Pat?"

"Please, I'm not—"

"You never told me."

"It wouldn't have been right for us to keep going."

"Just when things were . . ." She paused, searched for the right words. "Moving forward."

"You were engaged to my brother."

"You can't tell me you didn't feel it, though."

"I'm with Lien-hua now."

"Yes."

"And you're with Sean."

A small pause. "Yes."

"What we had, Amber, it's over."

She turned her back to me, and I wished she hadn't. I wanted to see her face so I could try to read her, decipher what she might be thinking.

"I know there's more, Pat. All this time I've known. Was it something I did? I just need to know."

Her intuition was right. There was more, but it wouldn't be wise to get into all that. I needed to do something to end this conversation, to rescue what little rapport I had left with my brother, to help, at least in a small way, salvage his relationship with Amber. Over the years I've found that sometimes when a lie serves a greater good it can be a gift.

A lie.

A gift.

"I never cared for you like you did for me," I said as convincingly as I could.

She turned and looked at me, into me. "That's not true."

No, it isn't.

No, it isn't.

You're not a good liar, Pat.

Telling the lie troubled me.

The truth.

The greater gift.

Before I could edit them, rein them in, the words slipped out: "I ended things because Sean loved you." Yes, it was true, but it wasn't the whole truth. "And I didn't want to hurt him, to—"

"But so did you, right? You were in love with me too?"

She seemed distraught, almost desperate to hear me say it, but I avoided answering her. "Amber, really, I think you need to leave."

"Just tell me if I was wrong all this time. Just tell me the truth." She'd always been a woman unafraid to show her feelings, and her eyes were beginning to glisten. "Please."

"Yes, I did. I loved you." With every question, every answer, I was digging myself deeper into a conversation I didn't need to be in. I decided to try and wrap this up quickly. "I didn't want Sean to get hurt. You either."

"You broke things off to protect me?"

"Both of you."

She was crying now, and my heart broke to see it. If only I'd pulled away sooner five years ago, not let my feelings tug me farther than I needed to go.

"Amber, please."

"Are you doing it again?"

"What?"

"Trying to protect me?"

"We can't—"

"You left me because you loved me, because you wanted to protect me? Both me and Sean? That's what you just said."

You did this to yourself, Pat. You shouldn't have said anything!

"I never stopped caring, Pat." Her voice had become soft, broken. "Seeing you now . . . it's . . ." Her words trailed off, and she turned to hide her tears. As a man I couldn't just stand there and watch her hurt, watch her cry.

You hurt her, Pat.

You shouldn't have told her any of this.

"Come here." So I took her in my arms, and she leaned into my embrace and she held me the way she used to, and as I was brushing a tear from her eye I heard a quick double-knock at the door, and just as I was pulling away from her, it swung open, and Lien-hua, the woman I loved, the one I was hoping to marry, appeared.

43

The moment blistered apart.

"Lien-hua?" I quickly stepped back from Amber.

She's supposed to be in Cincinnati. Why is she here?

She told you she was sending up a surprise.

She told you—

Oh man.

"Pat." Lien-hua was looking from Amber to me and back to Amber. She entered the room, let the door close out the howling night behind her.

"This isn't what . . ." I started apologizing, wanted to apologize, but I couldn't quite pinpoint what to apologize for. "This is Amber." I took another step back so I could see both women at the same time. "Sean's wife."

"Sean's wife," Lien-hua echoed softly.

Turning to Amber, I said, "And this is Lien—my friend Lien-hua Jiang."

Your friend?!

Amber slid away a stray tear that remained on her cheek. "I'll go. I'm sorry." She told Lien-hua, "I just came to talk. That was all. He was just trying to help."

"Okay," Lien-hua replied, in a tone that was impossible to read.

Amber collected her purse and headed for the door. Lien-hua stepped aside to let her through, but before Amber passed her, I realized it wouldn't be safe for her to leave. "Wait. The roads."

"I made it over here." Amber's voice was strained with deep emotion. "I'll be fine."

I fished out the key to the room I'd reserved for Tessa earlier in the day. "Tessa's staying at your place. Take her room." I hated having this conversation in front of Lien-hua.

She shook her head. "I'll be all right."

"No, they closed the county roads," Lien-hua said. "State Patrol did. I had to ride with a trooper just to get over here." Despite the awkwardness of the situation, I heard genuine concern for Amber's welfare in her words.

"If the county roads are closed," I said, "you won't make it home."

"I'm used to—"

I held out the key to her. "Amber. For your own safety. Please."

After one final objection, she accepted it. "Room 104," I told her. I left off mentioning the obvious: that it was the room right next door.

She passed quietly out the door, into the storm, and then I was alone with Lien-hua, who stood by the bed and appraised me.

And I, her.

Asian elegance. Black hair with two curling strands that gracefully framed her face. A posture and grace that came from years of tai chi and competition kickboxing. A woman who was not only gorgeous and athletic but also had swift intelligence and deep perception, I'd fallen for her the first time I met her fifteen months ago. Since then we'd dated, faded apart, reconnected. Tried to make things work.

Ups and downs.

"How did you get a key to the room?" I asked lamely.

"The manager gave me one when I told him I was your girlfriend and that I'd come to surprise you."

This was just not good.

"The FBI credentials sealed the deal," she added.

I wanted to ask her about Cincinnati, how she got up here today, but a flight to Madison, St. Paul, or even Rhinelander would have been easy enough to arrange this morning. However, none of that mattered at the moment. She was here and so was I, and she'd walked in on me while I was in the arms of another woman.

"Really," I said, "you have to believe me, this wasn't what it looked like, here with Amber."

Lien-hua chose not to reply.

"She came to check on me."

And to ask you why you broke things off with—

"Margaret told me about everything that happened today. Now, honestly. Tell me. Are you all right? You're on your feet, so you must be feeling—are you feeling better?"

"I am, except my ankle is having a little bit of a rough time."

"You can sit down if you like."

"I'm all right."

"Really, Pat—"

"I'm all right."

"You almost drowned. You could have died of hypothermia."

"I just need you to know that I'm okay and that nothing was happening in here, a minute ago." Truthfully, my ankle was throbbing, and I did want to sit down, but I forced myself to stand.

A small silence. "Why was Amber crying?"

Not the question I wanted to answer.

"Because . . ."

Sometimes a lie is a gift.

Always the truth is.

All right. Everything out in the open.

"Five years ago"—I finally did take a seat on the bed—"I met her when she was engaged to Sean. We connected. Neither Amber or I set out to, neither of us wanted to, but we . . ."

"You had an affair?"

"It didn't end up going that far." I hesitated, then added, "But it went farther than it should've."

She was quiet.

This was even harder than I'd thought.

"I couldn't stand the thought of hurting my brother, so I broke things off, stopped seeing Amber, stopped calling her. I still feel terrible that the relationship ever got started in the first place. It was five years ago."

"You mentioned that."

I could think of nothing else to say.

"Were you in love?"

I gave her a tiny nod.

"And is that what you told her tonight? That you still loved her?"

"No. I told her I was with you. That whatever we had was over."

Profiler that she was, Lien-hua watched me, no doubt discerning as much from my pauses, body language, tone as she did from the words themselves.

"Are you still in love with her, Pat?"

"No," I said, but even I could hear the tiny hitch in my voice, and I hated that it was there. I'd chosen Lien-hua. Chosen *her*! Words rang in my head, from some TV show or movie I might have seen sometime: *Being in love with more than one person doesn't mean you're being unfaithful, choosing to pursue more than one person does.*

And I was pursuing Lien-hua.

Lien-hua.

A silence broad and deep. At last she said, "So that's why she was crying? That's it?"

"She's had problems with Sean."

"I see."

I stood once again, approached her. "I didn't even know that they—"

She held up a gentle hand to stop me. "She drove through a blizzard to meet you in your motel room to tell you this—that she and her husband are having problems?"

"You have to believe me, Lien-hua—"

"Please, Pat. Don't tell me what I have to do."

I felt helpless. "Let me explain."

"I don't think it's me you need to explain things to. I think it's your brother." Her words were sharp but filled with a delicate kind of pain.

Once again I started to respond, but she shook her head and said, "Pat, when you're seeing someone, you set boundaries. You keep yourself from situations where you're alone in a motel room at night with one of your former lovers."

She was right. Everything she'd just said was true.

She opened the door to leave, letting a sharp blast of winter wind into the room. "I'm staying in 124 with Natasha." Now her tone had taken on a remote and disheartening professionalism, just as it had in the days last spring when we'd drifted apart. The pain of hearing the coolness in her words struck me even more starkly than the chilled air rushing past her. "She told me that she was meeting with you and Jake in the lobby at 9:00 for a briefing. I'll be there. Good night, Pat."

Come on, figure this out!

But then she was leaving.

"We can talk about this more tomorrow, okay?" I said. "Straighten everything out?"

A small nod was the only response she gave me.

And then she was gone.

As I watched the door close, my initial thought was to go after her, but then I realized that pressing things at the moment would do more harm than good.

I sank onto my bed.

I tried to process what had just happened—the stirring of old feelings for Amber, our admissions of affection for each other, the look of pain in Lien-hua's eyes when she found us in each other's arms.

Man, I'd screwed things up.

I couldn't help but think of the diamond engagement ring in the box in Denver, waiting to be offered to Lien-hua.

What a mess.

Regret swept over me, and for a while I just sat there and listened to the storm rage against the window, a frigid and angry wind pulsing through the night.

Not only had Chekov escaped, not only had our one link to Basque gotten murdered, not only had Ellory and at least two members of the Pickron family been killed, but now two of the people who mattered most to me were hurting and it was all my fault.

The wind rattled my windows, but it didn't stop me from hearing, in the room next to me, Amber moving around, getting ready for bed.

And all I could manage to do was sit there trying not to think about what had just happened, waiting for the night to become quiet enough for me to be able to rest.

44

As Tessa was washing up, she realized she'd forgotten one of her bags, the one containing her pajamas and the pills she was using to help her sleep, in Sean's pickup.

Great.

For months she'd bugged Patrick to teach her how to pick locks until around Thanksgiving he finally gave in. Since then she'd gotten pretty good with residential doors and even handcuffs, but cars were not her specialty, and she definitely remembered Sean locking the truck before they came inside.

So now, as quietly as she could, she eased downstairs, donned her jacket and boots, grabbed Sean's truck keys from the keyboard beside the door, and went outside.

The snow slashed at her, and she had to use one arm to shield her face as she trudged along the path to the driveway. Although the walkway had been shoveled earlier and was bordered by piles of snow nearly six feet deep, in the light from the porch she could see that the storm had formed deep drifts crisscrossing the pathway in front of her.

She picked her way through them.

Despite the ferocity of the storm, everything around her looked so white, so pure, and in a sense, remarkably innocent.

A stark contrast to how she felt inside.

Seven months ago, on the night it happened, she'd watched a man outside the back window of the home where she and Patrick were staying get shot and drop in the moonlight. Detective Cheyenne Warren, the woman who'd just fired the three shots at him, eased out the door, gun in hand, to see if he was alive or dead.

Tessa remembered how terribly her heart was beating.

Beating.

Deep and chilled.

Moments later, she'd heard another shot outside, then the wisp of a door opening and a swish of soft movement behind her. She turned, saw a man's outline silhouetted against the moonlight seeping through the window behind him; his hand was raised high, something long and narrow in it.

Before she could call out, he brought the object down, hard, against her forehead, sending her spinning to the floor. The world went filtering, black on black.

A buzz inside her head.

Then she was on the carpet and everything was fuzzy and spinning and alive with colors that weren't colors at all.

And then the man was pressing a knee against her chest and stuffing a gag into her mouth.

Terror rising.

The world became blurry as the ache in her forehead pounded through her, but she was aware of this much: the man dragging her down the hallway toward her room. And then, only a few moments later, she heard the porch door pound open and Patrick calling her name. She struggled to get free but couldn't. The intruder yanked her to her feet and pressed a gun against her head. With his other hand he clung to a fistful of her hair.

Patrick called again and she tried to shout to him, but beneath her gag she barely managed to make a sound.

Then he was in the hallway, coming toward her, to help her, to save her.

The man jerked her backward into a room, closed the thick oak door, and took off the gag.

He demanded that Patrick tell her who was lying dead outside, threatening to kill her if he refused.

Patrick had tried to buy time, but in the end he'd told her.

Her father.

It was her father who'd been shot.

And when she heard the words, she screamed and Patrick used

the moment to shoot at the lock and kick open the door, but the man was behind her, the gun against her temple once again. This time he held his finger over hers, which was pressed against the trigger.

She knew she was going to die. She knew it, knew it, knew it, and reached across her chest, grabbed her elbow, and swung the gun backward.

And squeezed the trigger just as Patrick fired at the man's forehead. She felt the wet blowback of blood against the back of her neck as the bullets both found their mark and the man behind her died.

Crumpled to the carpet.

Then her ear was ringing and she was trembling, terrified, and Patrick was helping her outside and away from that house filled with so much darkness and death.

The hearing in her ear that was only inches from the gun never came back, and since that night Patrick had tried to reassure her that he was the one who'd killed the man; that it wasn't her fault, that the gun in her hand had fired accidentally.

He had tried to convince her of that.

And had failed.

Because she knew she'd pulled that trigger, had willed it, had planned it, had done it.

And in the end she was glad she did.

She'd lost her father that day, and somewhere between tilting the gun and shooting a man in the face, she'd lost herself.

The snow whirlwinded around her, forcing her to turn up her collar all the way even before she reached the truck. As she tried to unlock the door she fumbled with the keys and ended up dropping them into the slope of snow at her feet.

The wind bit at her.

With her bare hands she began digging through the powder, looking for the keys.

Remembering.

Of course she'd mourned the loss of her father, but since she'd hardly known him, it was almost like mourning a stranger—someone you hear about on the news: a body was found in the park and you feel a wash of loss and concern, and then end up with only a vague sense of guilt that you don't feel worse than you do.

In the seven months since that night, she'd learned to forgive the woman who'd accidentally killed her dad.

And over time, life had gone on.

In a way.

Because even as the sting of her father's death had healed, the reality of what she'd done, the fact that she'd pulled the trigger and killed a person, weighed on her now more heavily than ever.

She finally found the keys, unlocked the door, and went for her bag. As soon as she had it, she left the truck and started for the house again.

She had them.

The pills that would help her sleep.

45

Tessa reentered the house. Stomped the snow from her boots.

Patrick didn't know about the secret wound she carried.

Almost immediately after the shooting she'd decided it was something she needed to work through on her own, but that hadn't gone so well. She'd even tried seeing a psychiatrist a few times on Thursday afternoons, skipping her seventh-hour study period, bugging out of school and cruising over to the guy's office before heading home, using the money she'd inherited from her dad to pay for it.

But her shrink was a one-trick pony telling her over and over that getting her feelings out into the open was good for her, when in reality all it had done was churn up the pain and harsh memories and then leave them choppy and gray on the surface of her life when the fifty-minute sessions were over.

She'd stopped seeing him after three weeks.

She hung up the keys, shed the coat and boots, and then took her bag to her room.

Yes, that man she'd killed had a gun pressed against her head, yes, it was self-defense—she knew all of that intellectually and had tried to reassure herself that she wasn't guilty according to any law.

But reassuring her conscience was a different story.

"Tell me how you feel," the psychiatrist had said to her in their last session.

"Like I'm sinking."

"Into what?"

"Myself."

"And what does that mean? Sinking into yourself?"

It means I'm losing. It means it's getting harder and harder to breathe, to see a place where hope is real again. It means I'm sinking into a place I can't climb out of on my own.

She stared at him. "Is that what they teach you in graduate school? To just ask follow-up questions? Just active listening, reflecting back to me what I'm saying?"

Where were you on career day when they brought that little gem up?

He rolled his pen between his fingers. "It's okay to be angry," he said. "And it's okay to be disappointed." He paused and she waited. She wasn't going to make this easy for him. At last he said, "But you have to learn to forgive yourself."

"That again."

"Yes."

"Really. Forgive myself."

"That's right."

"What does that even mean?"

"To forgive yourself?"

"Yeah." She'd had enough of this. "And if you ask me what I think it means, this session is over."

He took a breath and then hesitated, and she could tell he really didn't know what to say.

Nice. He tells you to forgive yourself and then he can't even explain what he means.

"Obviously," she told him, "it's not just marginalizing the event or simply acknowledging the pain and then doing your best to ignore it, it's gotta be more than that or 'self-forgiveness,' if there even is such a thing, would just be a casuistic form of denial."

He looked at her oddly, finally said, "You mentioned that your mother used to take you to church. Are you a religious person, Tessa?"

"My mom was."

"Don't you think God wants you to forgive yourself?"

"Well, I looked that up last week after you started in on all this. The Bible never says to forgive yourself. Not once. So apparently, it's not exactly on God's top ten list."

The guy seemed to be at a loss.

"Look"—she stood, put a foot on the glass coffee table beside him—"if I break this thing, you can forgive the debt I owe you if you want, or you can make me pay for it, but how can I forgive *myself* for the debt that I owe *you*?"

He rose abruptly. "Tessa, put your foot down. I mean, you need to put it—"

Enough. This guy's more clueless than you are.

"I am so done with this." She bypassed shattering the glass coffee table and lowered her foot to the floor.

"Tessa—"

Without a word she'd left the office and never gone back.

Tessa entered her bedroom, closed the door behind her, and emptied her bag.

She checked through her stuff three times and finally had to acknowledge the truth—the pills weren't here.

She replayed the morning in her mind. Packing, stressing, hurrying out the door . . .

Oh.

Leaving her pill bottle on the countertop beside the sink of that dorm room at the University of Minnesota.

She slumped into the chair by the desk.

Now what?

Amber's a pharmacist. You'd think she'd have . . .

Feeling slightly guilty, she eased into the hall and slipped into the bathroom. Then, as quietly as she could, she searched through Sean and Amber's medicine cabinet but couldn't find anything she could use to help her sleep. But to her surprise she did find some Abilify, Wellbutrin, and Lamictal. She wasn't an expert on medications, but she'd seen enough drug commercials about the first two to know they were antidepressants. All three drugs were prescribed to Amber.

Patrick had never told her that Amber was dealing with depression. If he even knew about it.

227

This is way uncool. You should so not be doing this, Tessa. Looking through their stuff.

Feeling worse than before, she silently returned to the bedroom and pulled out her notebook. She stared at the blank page for a long time, but nothing came to her.

When she went to draw the curtains across the window to keep out the darkness, she noticed the dusty corpses of two wasps on the windowsill.

Too many dead things in this house.

She imagined what it would have been like to see those wasps flying over and over again into the glass, thinking that they were heading toward freedom, when they were destined only for death.

Now they slept and would never wake up.

Words came to her: *Time is a strange beast that cannot be tamed. It devours all things, but it lets you play with its mane in the meantime.*

The distance and the days collapsed in her mind, and she went back to her notebook, wrote,

> dead wasps lie on the windowsill.
> yesterday they tried
> to fly through the glass.
> to freedom. to life.
> today they lie still in death; all their
> hopes sheathed in their dry, quiet bodies.
>> all their busy buzzings are over
>> now that they're dead
> and forgotten on this side
> of the glass.

She thought for a long time and then added two more words:

> with me.

PART II

- WIND -

46

Saturday, January 10
US Naval Forces Central Command
Bahrain, Persian Gulf
12:21 p.m. GMT

Allighiero Avellino took a step forward in line and showed his ID to the Master-at-Arms, the United States Navy's version of military police, standing sentry at the end of the gangplank to the USS *Louisiana*, then waited while the man used a handheld scanner to run his name through DBIDS, the Defense Biometric Identification Data System, to verify his identity.

It was the fourth and final security checkpoint that he and the fellow members of his cleaning party had to pass through before they would be allowed onto the sub to clean the urine-stained floors of the heads before setting things up to pump the solid waste receptacles into the tanker truck that was still being inspected at the entrance to the base.

Although today he had another small task to complete in addition to his official duties.

For years Allighiero had believed that the environmental activist groups that sprang up in the twentieth century — Greenpeace, Earth First!, and the rest — hadn't taken things far enough: small demonstrations, people chaining themselves to trees or railroad tracks, cutting down a few telephone poles, spiking old forest growth, unfurling banners on bridges or boats. Yes, all of it was good for a few minutes of publicity, but in the end it almost never swayed public opinion or changed the minds of policy makers. It mostly just made the activists feel good, as if they were doing *something*.

The MA studied Allighiero's identification card one last time, then handed it back to him and waved him through.

He pushed his cart of cleaning supplies forward onto the gangplank leading to the sub's conning tower.

Media flash points.

That was about it.

You get a little coverage, maybe you get arrested to make a statement, but then the next soccer game or celebrity publicity stunt or political scandal takes over the news cycle, and nothing important ever changes.

A few days later you're out of jail and no one hears your name again.

But with the present worldwide irreversible environmental devastation, the time for procrastination was over. The time for protests was over. The time for real action was here. For the sake of the planet, for the sake of the future.

The world needed a wake-up call that could not be ignored.

And that was why he'd joined Eco-Tech in the first place last year. But, of course, because of his job cleaning nuclear submarines, he'd always been careful to keep his involvement with the organization quiet.

One at a time his co-workers disappeared with their military chaperones into the sub. Descending into the ship with the carts wasn't as tricky as it might look since the carts had retractable wheels and specially designed handles to slide down the ladder's handrails. At last, Allighiero met his escort at the conning tower, and the man assisted him in getting his supplies down the ladder.

"Glad I don't have your job," the petty officer told him.

"Grazie," Allighiero said, thanking him generically in Italian rather than letting on that he knew English.

"Right." The seaman sounded slightly judgmental. "Follow me."

Allighiero trekked behind the petty officer across the steel mesh floor of the walkway. Surrounding them in the cramped corridor: caged-in lightbulbs and valves and gauges, rivets and swarms of cables and wires. And deep beneath them, twenty-four Trident ballistic missiles. A great steel beast carrying oblivion in its belly.

A beast that not only did not belong in the ocean but did not belong on the planet.

American weapons of mass destruction were forcing the world to bow to the whims of capitalism, industrial commercialism, and the free market exploitation of the poor and marginalized around the globe.

Put simply, the neoliberal economic ideology of the US and the UK subjugated developing nations and devastated the rest of the world's natural resources.

Humans are destined for so much more than consumption, materialism, and self-absorption. How could a world in which products that poison the environment and take centuries to deteriorate are endlessly produced, consumed, and discarded with no aim toward sustainability of the world's ecosystems, how could that kind of civilization, by any stretch of the imagination, be called advanced? How could it even be called sane?

Nearly 28 percent of the world's energy is consumed by Americans, who subsequently refuse to pay a fair climate debt to the rest of the world, while 30 percent of the people on the planet have no access to clean water, let alone electricity, medical care, or adequate housing. More than 79 percent of the world's population lives on less than $10 a day; 1.4 billion people are forced to survive on less than $1.25 a day. All this, while Americans complain that there isn't enough whipped cream on their mochas or enough leg room in their SUVs.

As philosopher Peter Kreeft wrote, and Allighiero had long ago memorized in the original English, "Anyone whose common sense has not been dulled by familiarity should be able to see the blindingly obvious truth that there is something radically wrong with a civilization in which millions devote their lives to pointless luxuries that do not even make them happy, while millions of others are starving; a civilization where no hand, voluntary or involuntary, moves money from luxury yachts to starving babies fast enough to save the babies."

A world of people pursuing yachts and ignoring the babies.

The fruit of corporate greed and imperialism run wild.

And perhaps most disturbing of all: the proliferation of nuclear weapons that would eventually and inevitably fall into the wrong hands and create an unprecedented environmental catastrophe that would exacerbate the effects of global climate change and potentially wipe out billions of earth's creatures—humans and other precious species alike.

Allighiero followed his escort toward the galley. Maneuvering the cart of cleaning supplies through the narrow corridors was not easy, but he had been doing this for two years and managed with little trouble.

He palmed the USB memory stick.

Today he would help clean each of the eight heads on the submarine. But now on the way to the first one he would pass through the galley.

Which was where he was going to place the device.

Allighiero's task was simple—just insert a USB 3.0 jump drive into the back of the computer in the galley, a place no one would ever notice, would never even think to check for foreign devices. He had not been told exactly what the software he was uploading would do, but he knew that the drive contained some type of code that would spread through the sub to help accomplish Eco-Tech's goal of disabling the submarine's capability of firing its nuclear warheads.

He was a small cog in a much bigger plan. He knew that as well, but he had a part to play and he was going to play it.

When the world saw what a small group of environmentalists could do—the annihilation they could have caused if they'd had another agenda—the governments of the world would see the dangers of nuclear weapons for what they truly were, with eyes unclouded by political agendas and posturing.

Turning the tide of history would begin by first turning the tide of public sentiment.

A move toward peace.

A move toward a nuke-free world.

While his escort was distracted for a moment unlocking a door in front of them, Allighiero slid the device into the back of the computer console on the galley counter.

And just that quickly, his job was done.

In a little over fourteen hours and thirty minutes the world would wake up once and for all to the dangers of inadequately secured ballistic missiles.

47

I slept through my alarm, and even though I knew I probably needed the rest, I was still annoyed at myself for not rising earlier.

When I finally did climb out of bed, I found that, despite the alternating hot and cold baths last night, my ankle was still swollen. Still stiff. Still sore. Maybe even more so than when I'd gone to bed. And I was exhausted, my experience at the river still taking a huge toll on me.

I didn't like the idea of using crutches, so after downing some Advil I showered and got dressed, choosing boots rather than shoes to add needed support to my ankle. I decided I would tape the ankle as soon as I could get my hands on some athletic tape, or even a roll of duct tape.

Before heading to the 9:00 briefing in the lobby, I wrote a note of condolence for Mia Ellory, the deceased deputy's wife. Finding the right words wasn't easy, and email wasn't ideal, but it was something. It was a start. After a few online searches I had her email address. I typed it in and, though praying doesn't come easily to me, I offered one up for her recovery from grief.

Pressed send.

My thoughts cycled back to last night. To Lien-hua. To Amber. What a mess.

But there were more important matters at hand than my relational issues.

(1) Trying to establish whether Donnie Pickron and the driver of the semitrailer, Bobby Clarke, were alive or dead.

(2) Finding Alexei Chekov.

(3) Visiting the site of the old ELF station.

I grabbed my laptop and was about to head to the meeting when I noticed a folded sheet of paper lying near the base of the door. My name was written on the top in Amber's handwriting.

I picked it up, considered whether or not to unfold it, then a little reluctantly, I did.

And read:

Pat,

I'm so sorry about last night. I hope it doesn't hurt things between you and Lynn-nva. (I hope I spelled that right.) The last thing I would ever want to do is hurt you. I won't bring any of this up again, but I needed you to know that I'm leaving Sean. That's what I came to tell you last night, to see if you could help me find the best way to tell him. Now I see what a bad idea it was. I'm sorry for all the trouble I caused.

—A

I stood there stunned.

She's leaving Sean?

Though my brother and I had never talked about it, I was pretty sure he loved Amber and was committed to her, just like he'd been to his first wife. I could only imagine how devastated he'd be when he learned that Amber was leaving him. Sean was far from perfect, but he was faithful and—

You don't know that, Pat. You barely know him. It might be all his fault.

Or it might be yours.

I stared at the note, overcome with a desire to call Sean and tell him what Amber had written, to get everything out in the open, but undoubtably he would wonder why she'd shared the news with me first rather than with him. And I would have to tell him about my history with his wife.

On the other hand, if he found out later that she'd come to me, he'd almost certainly feel betrayed and wonder what was going on between us, especially if Amber told him that we'd been in love while they were engaged—and that her feelings for me had never gone away.

And of course Amber's decision was only going to make things worse between me and Lien-hua, who would now see the encounter last night here in the motel room in a whole different light. Considering the rocky spots we'd had in the past, I wondered what it would take to salvage things with her this time around—but I wanted to do so much more than just salvage things. I wanted us to take the next step in our relationship. And how was that going to happen if she didn't trust me?

Sean. Amber. Lien-hua.

It was a lose-lose-lose situation any way you cut it.

I crumpled up the note and threw it toward the trash can beside the desk; it bounced against the wall instead and fell to the carpet as if it were mocking me.

For a moment I had the urge to knock on Amber's door and square things away with her, but honestly, what good could come from talking to her right now?

9:02.

Already late for the meeting.

Focus.

Be here, Pat.

It's all about the case. You have to put this personal stuff aside and think about the case.

I opted for my black North Face jacket instead of the camo one. Ditching the crutches but carrying my computer—and trying unsuccessfully not to limp—I headed out the door to meet with Sheriff Tait, Jake, Natasha, and Lien-hua, the woman I couldn't imagine living without.

The woman I feared I might've already lost because of choices I made four years before we ever met.

48

Lien-hua and Natasha were waiting for me in the lobby.

I tried to read Lien-hua, hoping to see if she was harboring any animosity about last night, but she kept her emotions well guarded. She greeted me cordially—neither overly friendly or noticeably distant.

On the walk from my room, I'd noticed that the snow was letting up, but now as I glanced out the north-facing window I saw that the wind was fiercer than ever and the windswept landscape looked arctic and boreal. Even on a snowmobile it wouldn't be easy to get to the site of the old ELF station this morning, let alone find anything useful.

Natasha went for some coffee, and when Lien-hua and I were alone she asked how I was doing. "Is the ankle feeling any better?"

"It's not bothering me nearly as much as I thought it would," I said truthfully.

"The hypothermia?"

"Quite honestly, the whole river incident seems like it happened a month ago instead of yesterday."

Lien-hua nodded.

We'd discussed this sort of thing in the past—the ways that the mind deals with tragedy or trauma: sometimes events that happened recently become recorded in the brain as if they happened weeks, months, or years ago, and conversely, distant memories can slide forward and obscure more recent ones. "Memory isn't as contiguous as time," she told me once. "It's the mind's way of dealing with pain and fear and heartache."

Fear.

Heartache.

Trying to bridge into the topic of last night, I asked, "So how are you?"

"Okay."

I waited, gave her the chance to say more, but she chose not to.

She excused herself to get some juice, and I awkwardly offered to join her.

"Okay."

We filled our glasses in silence, then she pulled out some granola bars she'd brought with her. I grabbed a couple doughnuts to get me through until I could get some real food, we found a quiet corner in a private room just off the lobby and waited for Tait, Natasha, and Jake to join us. Silence stretched between us, and even if it was the right time for words, it didn't seem like either of us could think of what they might be.

Alexei had no intention of killing the woman who lay tied up in the bedroom down the hall.

But he was ready to do so if need be.

Or at least he told himself he was.

Yesterday, after retrieving the remaining $1,000,000 from the drop point and switching vehicles, he'd returned to the cabin near the Schoenberg Inn and parked the woman's car in the garage and brought her inside. At the time, he hadn't wanted to know her name because he figured it would just make things harder, but this morning he realized maybe that's what he needed.

So now he was going through her purse.

Kayla Tatum.

Yes, he'd been right, knowing her name was going to make this harder.

He set down the purse.

Last night, after leaving her bound in the room, he'd gone to the Schoenberg to look for the Eco-Tech team and slipped, unnoticed, into the basement. But when he went to the area of the hotel where he'd had the confrontation with Clifton White, he found it vacant. Even when he wirelessly hacked into the hotel's registry he found no rooms listed under the four group member's names he'd been able to identify.

He'd thought about locating the manager and persuading him, by whatever means necessary, to tell him the location of the group, but then Alexei had another idea. Perhaps he could use the manager's cooperation in a slightly different way.

Using his phone, Alexei went online and, studying the maps of the area, discovered that the Navy used to have a small communication station in the area of the Chequamegon-Nicolet National Forest where the Eco-Tech team had traveled toward with the duffel bag of money before they'd disabled the signal. A little research apprised him that years ago, environmentalists had protested against the base while it was in operation.

On Wednesday when Valkyrie sent him to go speak with Rear Admiral Colberg, Valkyrie had said, "Tell him we need the access codes to the station. He'll know what you're talking about."

So.

Alexei's gaze went toward the room where he'd left Kayla.

Yesterday, Becker, the ponytailed Eco-Tech member, had told him that his team would be done at exactly 9:00 p.m. tonight. If he was telling the truth, that gave Alexei less than twelve hours to work things out. But he was also well aware that agendas can change, and he wasn't sure how his flight from the authorities might alter their timetable.

And then there was the matter of Valkyrie, who was quite possibly in the area, evidenced by the fact that the remaining $1,000,000 had been there at the dead drop.

Yes, evaluate, adapt, and respond.

Alexei looked around the cabin. After leaving it this morning, he had not anticipated coming back. He began to pack up his equipment.

His threefold agenda: (1) take care of Kayla Tatum; (2) locate the Eco-Tech team; (3) find Valkyrie and kill him—or her—slowly.

Though he usually worked alone, he had an idea that might move things along more quickly. He knew of one person in the area who could help him, a person he was confident would do whatever it took to find the Eco-Tech team and stop them.

But recruiting him was another story.

49

Natasha returned, and while we waited for Jake to join us, I borrowed Lien-hua's cell and phoned Sheriff Tait to find out when he would be arriving. He told me he wasn't going to be able to make it to the briefing because of the roads and the number of emergency calls his department was getting—people trapped on the roads, power outages, accidents. Apparently, with the wind, it was proving nearly impossible for the county to keep the roads cleared. "I'm probably gonna be tied up here for at least a couple hours." He still sounded sick. "And I wasn't able to get any officers over to the old ELF site. I'm sorry."

One step forward, two steps back.

"There's nothing out there anyway, Agent Bowers." Weariness in his voice. "I've been there myself, last fall—some poachers on forest service land. I'm telling you, the station is gone."

"I understand," I said.

If an underground bunker and tunnels for electromagnetic lines did exist, the Navy would've had to take herculean measures to keep it a secret—not just from the environmental activists and protestors, but also from the locals. And while that wouldn't have been an easy task, over the years I've learned that despite government bureaucracy, pork-barrel spending, and WikiLeaks, when the government puts its mind to keeping something a secret they can be surprisingly effective at it.

After all, there are currently six military detainment facilities on US soil that the media has never gotten wind of, not to mention the FBI's two domestic processing centers and the CIA's sub rosa facilities abroad.

I assured the sheriff that I would brief him on everything we covered in our meeting, then picked up a key from the clerk at the front desk so we could lock ourselves in the room beside the lobby and not worry about being disturbed. A few moments after our call ended, Jake arrived and we began.

"All right," I said. "We have a lot to cover." It was hard for me to broach the next subject. "First of all, do we know how Ellory's family is taking the news of his death?"

Natasha answered, "I talked with Linnaman last night and he said that until we have a body he can't officially pronounce Ellory deceased."

"You're kidding me."

"Ellory might have surfaced somewhere downstream," Jake said. "It's possible he's still alive."

"No." I shook my head. "There weren't any other stretches of open water in sight." This discussion only made Ellory's death weigh more heavily on me. "He didn't make it."

All three of them were quiet. Finally, Natasha said, "I think his wife is still holding out hope. Linnaman's probably just trying to help her deal with all of this."

I'd seen this type of thing before in other cases, and it wasn't helpful; in the end it would only exacerbate her pain. In addition, I'd already sent my condolences to her. I rubbed my head. "Okay, we'll tackle that later. Let's move on. Bobby Clarke, the truck driver. Any word?"

Everyone shook their heads.

"I heard from Torres," Jake said, switching to our other case. "He said Reiser's time of death was sometime late Tuesday, which would have given Basque plenty of time to clear out."

But Reiser was seen entering the trailer Wednesday evening . . . The killer returning to the scene?

Maybe, or maybe just an unreliable eyewitness.

"They also found newspaper clippings," he said, "about the murders with Basque fourteen years ago and the more recent ones over the last six months. And some recorded television news footage covering the crimes as well."

So, Jake's instincts had been right after all.

"Cable or local?" I said.

"Both."

"But only the crimes with Basque?"

"Yes."

Lien-hua spoke up. "I've been thinking about Basque. About the knives. Using them isn't just a way of prolonging the victim's death, but also, the penetration of the knife into her body has obvious sexual connotations. For him, this act represents coition."

If you buy into the psychosexual theories of criminal behavior, which I did not, Lien-hua's observation made sense. It occurred to me that Jake, who'd been working on this case for months, and who did share that perspective, hadn't made that connection.

"Yes." Jake nodded. "Reiser's psych profile is consistent with a tendency to associate violence and sexuality."

Lien-hua shook her head. "That's not exactly what I'm getting at. Basque's partner would be less dominant than him, more easily manipulated, have a lower sense of self-worth, and most likely have followed Basque's lead in the crimes and the documentation of them."

"So you're saying?" Jake sounded irritated.

"Considering his submissive role in the murders, the significance of the blades would likely be different for him, might not even be part of his signature—if he were to have committed crimes without Basque present."

"Which seems probable, given thirteen years apart," I noted.

"Yes."

My mind was spinning, trying to sort through all that had happened in the last two days—searching for Reiser in his trailer, getting called to Woodborough, visiting the scene of Ardis and Lizzie's murders, finding the helmet, chasing Chekov, nearly drowning . . .

Letting Ellory die.

Jake stared at Lien-hua coolly. "I'll have to share my notes with you. Show you what I've come up with."

"Yes, that will be helpful," she replied.

I flipped open my laptop. "I'm not sure yet how all this is

connected, but has everyone had a chance to review the files Margaret sent about the ELF station?"

Jake and Natasha nodded, but Lien-hua shook her head. "The ELF station?"

I filled her in and when I was done, Natasha took the floor and mentioned that she'd pulled prints from the light switch in the study of the Pickron home. "In addition to Ardis's and Donnie's, I found one set of unidentifiable prints. I sent them to the Lab to see if they can dig anything up, do a more integrated AFIS search. The only prints in the laundry room were of family members."

She consulted her notes. "I spent some time yesterday going through Donnie Pickron's computer and reviewing his deleted files. Whoever accessed the computer wasn't just looking up deployment records, but also searched through schematics of Ohio Class subs."

"Schematics?" Lien-hua said skeptically. "Those are available to the public?"

"Not in their entirety," she explained. "Obviously, there are restricted areas that weren't detailed, but the basic design of the submarines apparently isn't any secret. I mean, just watch the movie *The Hunt for Red October* or *Crimson Tide*. But there was more on his computer than there should have been."

I typed a few thoughts onto my computer.

(1) Above top secret clearance.
(2) One-way communication.
(3) Deployment routes.
(4) Schematics.
(5) First-strike orders.

"Track with me for a second," I said. "The deployment patterns for the subs would certainly have changed since the eighties as world powers and threat assessments have changed over time, but those subs are still in use. I'm guessing they would still have the capability to receive and decode ELF signals."

"If they were still able to be sent," Jake added.

"Yes," I acknowledged. "If they were. So maybe whoever was searching through these files wasn't just looking at where the subs were deployed but also—"

"How they were designed," Jake interrupted impatiently. "Yes. We've established that."

I was getting tired of his attitude and was about to tell him so when Lien-hua leaned forward. "What are you thinking, Pat?"

"By knowing the most likely targets and the routes the subs traveled in relation to those targets years ago, it might be possible to extrapolate, at least generally, where the subs would be deployed today, taking into consideration the location of countries that currently pose a threat to national security."

"It's worth a look," Lien-hua said.

I turned to Natasha. "As soon as we're done I want you to follow up on those schematics."

"I can also ask the DoD about any recent chatter regarding US subs."

"Good."

A thought. "Go ahead and see if their data analysts can review the most likely targets of the late eighties and early nineties and compare those to today's threats. Maybe it's possible to come up with an algorithm that might anticipate the current deployment routes. If the Defense Department's number crunchers can do it, someone else might have been able to as well."

"You think we're looking at an attack on one of the subs?" she asked.

Not an attack on one, I thought, *an attack from one.*

"I'm not sure, but Donnie Pickron is a Navy information warfare officer, and if he's still alive and he's gone rogue, I don't want him sending any messages to our subs. Any messages at all."

"Or if he hasn't gone rogue," Lien-hua said, "but is being held by someone, forced to work for them."

Silence spread through the room.

Natasha nodded slowly, jotted a note to herself on the legal pad in front of her.

I told them about what I'd discovered last night on the Routine Orbital Satellite Database and my theory about the shots through the Pickrons' living room window being intended to obscure the view into the house. "We're looking for a hacker, or a team of hackers, with the ability to access some of the DoD's most sensitive information."

For nearly an hour and a half we tackled various aspects of the case, each of us offering our analysis, input, findings.

Sean still had my cell, so at 11:00, as we were wrapping things up, I borrowed Lien-hua's phone and called Angela Knight in Cybercrime to see what she'd uncovered about Alexei Chekov. She informed me that she'd had to pass the project along to a woman on her team and hadn't heard back yet.

"This is a priority," I said.

"Everything we're working on is a priority." She didn't sound argumentative, just exhausted. "I'll follow up with Alyssa, let you know."

"Thanks."

End call.

I've never been one to put much stock in profiling, an ongoing point of contention between Lien-hua and me, but now I had two of the NCAVC's most experienced profilers sitting here with me and I knew that despite my reluctance to trust profiles it would've been negligent of me not to tap into their expertise.

"All right," I said. "Jake, I want you to fill in Lien-hua with regard to the profiles you've been working up for both the Reiser case and the Pickron family's killer."

"You think they're related?"

"I'm not sure how they would be, but I want all the puzzle pieces on the table before we dive headfirst into fitting them together. Talk through what you have on Basque as well. Broad strokes, see if anything overlaps. I know we're limited on time."

He looked like he was going to object but remained silent.

"There's plenty to do," I said. "I have an idea on how to solve the mystery of how a Ski-Doo 800 XL could travel on a straight course a hundred meters without a rider. Also, I'm going to try to find a way for us to visit the ELF site so we can see if there's anything there that might lead us to Donnie Pickron or Alexei Chekov. Let's break, get back together at noon, and see where we're at."

Everyone stood.

By now the Advil had kicked in, and although my ankle was still stiff, thankfully, it seemed like putting pressure on it wasn't going to be as big a deal today as I'd thought it would be when I woke up.

Lien-hua's phone rang.

At first I thought it might be Angela returning my call, but when Lien-hua answered it, she looked at me quizzically. "It's for you."

"Who is it?" I asked her.

She shook her head, held it out to me.

"I'll bring it by your room when I'm done," I said.

The three of them left and I spoke into the phone. "Hello?"

"I hope you're feeling better, Agent Bowers."

I recognized the faint Russian accent.

Alexei Chekov.

50

Quickly, I evaluated how to respond. From everything I'd seen, this man was a professional, and I doubted gimmicks and games would work with him. I decided on a direct approach: "Where's the truck driver, Alexei?"

Chekov's close, he has to be. How else would he know to call this phone just as we finished the meeting?

I looked out the window.

Nothing.

"I regret to tell you that he's dead."

My grip on the phone tightened. "I'm coming for you."

Outside. Maybe he's in the woods nearby.

Yanking on my coat, I headed for the front door.

"For what it's worth," he said, "I truly am sorry for what happened to both him and Ellory."

It bothered me that Chekov really did sound remorseful. I wanted him to be completely evil, fundamentally different from the rest of us, not a combination of mixed motives, of good and bad. It would have made things so much easier.

Outside now, I carefully studied the windswept landscape. Saw no one. Only the wrath of the storm.

"I have a proposal to make," he said.

Keep him on the line. Keep this conversation going.

"What proposal is that?" The livid wind cut through my jeans. I used the building to shield me as much as possible as I passed around the corner and scanned the other side of the parking lot. Nothing.

"I would like you to help me find some people. The ones who killed the Pickrons."

"Good idea. Let's meet. Have a little chat."

He pressed on. "In return for my help, you have something that I need."

First he asks for your help, now he's promising his?

It didn't follow, but for the moment I decided to play along. "What do I have that you need?"

"Resources," he answered vaguely.

I returned to the front of the building but stayed outside to keep the conversation private. "You're in no position to ask me for anything, Alexei. You killed two people yesterday—or was it three? Did you abduct someone else from the restaurant parking lot where you abandoned the truck?"

A small silence. "I'll be letting her go. I have no reason to hurt her."

Sharp anger flared again.

He said "her," that helps, we can—

"I think you owe me, Agent Bowers. If I hadn't called 911, you'd be dead."

"I'd only be dead because you threw Ellory in the river. I was just trying—"

"To save him. Yes. I know. I was impressed. That's why I called emergency services for you. But now I'm making you an offer. If you help me stop these people you can save Kayla's life."

"Kayla?"

"The woman I took from the restaurant."

"You just told me you'd let her go, that you had no reason to hurt her. Don't play me, Alexei. What do you really want here?"

"I don't kill children. And I don't kill women."

"But now you're threatening to kill Kayla."

He was quiet.

He's conflicted. It's not about the Pickrons or Kayla.

"Prove she's alive. Let me talk to her."

After a tight silence I heard a woman gasp, then cry out for help, her voice shrill, desperate. "Help me! He's—" Then the sounds became muffled, and I pictured him gagging her.

"Oh, I am going to find you, Alexei, and I'm going to—"

"You left your laptop inside. Check your email."

How is he watching me?!

Promptly returning to the room beside the lobby, I flipped out my laptop and clicked to the secure FBI email server, opened my account, and found a message from Alexei Chekov, identified by name. This guy was unbelievable.

As I opened the file I wondered if he'd sent me pictures of Kayla, but it turned out to be photos of four people I'd never seen.

"Who are they?"

"Members of a group called Eco-Tech."

"Eco-Tech?" That was the group that had lobbied to have the information about the SSBN sub routes released through the Freedom of Information Act. "People from Eco-Tech are involved in this? How do you know?"

"I met with them. They're working on a project with someone using the code name Valkyrie. I don't know who it is, but I want to find out. I have an access code and a phone number I haven't been able to trace."

He gave the number to me, and the code *Queen 27:21:9*. I typed them into a Word doc. "You told me you'd kill Kayla unless I helped you. What are you proposing? Just trace this phone number? Is that what you meant by resources?"

"Help me find Ardis and Lizzie's killers. Just you. If anyone else comes with you, I'll disappear and Kayla Tatum will die."

Of course I wanted to find the killers, but why he would want to find them was a myster—

They turned him in, Pat, remember? The anonymous call.

"When we find them I will need to deal with them appropriately. That's part of the deal."

"Appropriately?" I said.

"Yes."

"I won't let you kill them, Alexei. I bring them in. That's the only way."

A pause. "I'll tell you what: if you get to them first and find a way to stop me, then you deserve to win."

A game?

Is this all a game to him?

This guy wasn't like any killer I'd ever dealt with before. It didn't frighten me, but it did fine-tune my focus. Actually, that felt kind of good. "You know that when this is over I'm sending you to prison."

"I'm experienced at eluding investigators."

"I'm not your typical investigator."

A small pause. "I'll text you with the time and location where we'll meet. You can have the Bureau look for Valkyrie, but don't tell your on-site team we've spoken. I'll know if you do."

How?

How is he watching!

"Agent Bowers, though I do not believe in killing women, I will take Kayla Tatum's life if I need to. While I am a man of conviction, I am also a man of resolve."

Before I could reply, he ended the call. A power play.

I pocketed the phone and went directly to my room. After doing a back trace on the call and failing to find either his number or GPS location, I turned to my word processing program. I tend to be pretty good with details, and I typed up the conversation. Even if I didn't get it word-for-word, I was confident that I was close.

Then I googled Kayla Tatum's name and found 3,780,000 hits. Only one of the women near the top of the list lived in Wisconsin. I started with her, and after locating her cell number I put a call through to her. When she didn't answer I left a message for her to call me immediately.

Taking Alexei's warning to heart, I bypassed telling my team here what was going on but contacted HQ and asked a desk jockey buddy of mine named Barry Callaway to pursue any relevant leads concerning women named Kayla Tatum. "I can't tell you any more than that, I'm sorry. Trust me on this one."

"Got it."

Alexei had already proven that he was good at flying under our GPS radar, but it wouldn't hurt to check. "Go ahead and track the

GPS on their cell phones and, where possible, their cars," I said. "See if any of the women are in this part of the Midwest."

"I'll let you know what I find out."

We hung up and I forwarded the email with the attached photos, as well as both the access code and phone number that Alexei had given me, to Angela Knight, then gave her a quick call and asked her to see if she could trace the location from which the email had been sent and what she could dig up on Eco-Tech.

She surprised me by telling me she was familiar with them. "They're on one of our watch lists. Small-scale hackers, but they're flagrant. They like to be in the spotlight."

"I need your team to see what connections they might have with Alexei Chekov." I decided for the moment not to mention that we'd spoken on the phone. "Also, have Alyssa send me whatever we have on him as soon as possible. Any cases in which he's suspected of involvement with a crime or a terrorist act. And also any links to someone using the code name Valkyrie."

Environmentalists protested the ELF base.

Now Eco-Tech is in the area.

After the call, I went online and after a couple of searches found just the site I was looking for—one that would help me follow up on the unswerving Ski-Doo tracks to the water. I posted my offer and then went back to the transcript of my conversation with Alexei and scrutinized it for clues as to his whereabouts that I might have missed earlier.

Alexei had confessed to killing the truck driver, Bobby Clarke. Normally, local law enforcement would notify surviving family members, but false confessions aren't uncommon and it might have been a gambit, so, for the time being I made sure Tait put it off until the body was found.

It struck me that this whole thing just didn't jibe.

While I did believe Alexei had a woman with him, if he was going to kill her, why all the talk about not killing women and children?

I couldn't shake the thought that I was being played.

Still, whatever his motives—revenge, clearing his name, protecting the innocent, or all of the above—it didn't really matter. I had an opportunity here to catch him, to save a woman's life, and, potentially, to find the people who'd killed Lizzie and Ardis Pickron.

But of course there was also the matter of the call and the email themselves. Somehow Alexei had found out both my confidential email address and Lien-hua's personal cell number, and had apparently known that I was with her and that our meeting was just finishing when he called. He even knew I had my laptop with me.

I wondered if he'd somehow planted a bug in the motel. If so, he would've had to enter the building.

I called the front desk and found out they didn't use security cameras. "No real reason to," the guy at the front counter said. "People up here, we trust each other." I gave a quick description of Alexei to him; he didn't remember seeing anyone who fit that description.

Maybe Alexei . . .

Unless—

He would need a place to keep a victim.

Oh.

I hurried to Natasha and Lien-hua's room. When Natasha opened the door, I found Jake and Lien-hua with her, bent over their computers. "We need to search this motel." I was speaking just loud enough to be heard. "It's possible Alexei Chekov might be here in the building."

When Kayla refused to quit squirming and trying to cry out beneath her gag, Alexei was forced to sedate her. He used a mild dose of Propotol so she would fully recover within a couple hours. Then, once she was unconscious, he removed the gag so that it wouldn't restrict her breathing.

Finally, he surfed to an online map of the area and considered the best place to meet with Agent Bowers.

Cassandra received confirmation from Allighiero that he'd finished cleaning the sub and the USB device was in place.

Good.

She told Becker to gather the team. "We'll meet downstairs in the old billiards room. I want to have a few words with them before we take down the landlines."

He left, and she flipped open her laptop to review her notes.

Terry Manoji calculated the time in Bahrain and realized that if the sub had not set sail yet, it would within the hour.

He waited for the nurse to exit his room, then rolled into the bathroom, pulled out the cell phone, went online, accessed JWICS, and through the Trojan horses he'd placed there while still in the employ of the NSA, began to transfer the data that his algorithm would be needing later in the day, once Cassandra and her team had entered the base.

Valkyrie thought about the ELF station, the payment, the deadline.

Everything would tear apart at the seams if anyone found out about the involvement of Abdul Razzaq Muhammad.

Especially if that person were Alexei Chekov.

Or Special Agent Patrick Bowers.

Today it was vitally important for Valkyrie to remain undeterred.

Focused.

Careful.

Tonight everything would come together. Alexei would be out of the picture and the money would be transferred to the account that only two people in the world had access to.

Tessa stared at the ceiling, then glanced at the clock beside her bed.

Already after 11:00. The last time she'd checked, it was just before 6:00 a.m., so somehow she'd slept for over five hours, amazing, since she hadn't even had any pills at all last night.

She rubbed her eyes and heard Sean in the kitchen. Smelled sausage frying.

What is the deal up here? Do they eat anything other than meat?

She threw on some clothes and carefully avoided the living room and the dead deer and fish on her way to the kitchen to grab some fruit and toast.

"Morning," Sean said as she stepped into the room.

"Morning."

He slid the frying pan from the stove and dumped a stack of sausages onto a plate. "Made you some breakfast—well, brunch."

Oh man.

"Um, I was just gonna grab some toast or maybe a banana."

"I make a mean plate of venison sausage."

Tell him, or he's gonna keep trying to feed you meat.

"Actually, the thing is, I don't really eat meat or anything."

He hesitated. "You don't eat meat?"

"No. Or eat eggs or cheese. Or drink milk. I'm a vegan."

"A vegan."

"Yeah, don't worry about it. I'll grab something on my own."

"No." He seemed to be repressing his true feelings about her admission. "I'll get you something." He opened the fridge. "I think we've got some apples in here. And maybe . . ." He paused. "Looks like some leftover spaghetti. I can take out the meatballs."

Oh, yuck.

The meat sauce'll still be—

Tessa felt bad that Sean had cooked brunch for her and she had to pass on it—even though it was something she'd never have been able to stomach. "Sure, okay." She was forcing herself to say it. "That'll be good."

As she waited for him to scavenge her some other food, she turned toward the window and stared at the wind ravaging the nearby woodshed and the field bordering the house.

It didn't take Natasha, Jake, Lien-hua, and I long to search all the rooms of the Moonbeam Motel, but we found nothing suspicious. No sign of Alexei or Kayla Tatum or any other women in distress.

When we reconvened outside the front doors, Lien-hua said, somewhat irritated, "Pat, you still haven't told us why you thought Chekov might be here. Does it have to do with the call you got at the end of the meeting?"

Alexei's words flashed in my mind: *Don't tell your team we've spoken. I'll know if you do.*

If Kayla's life really was in danger, I couldn't take the chance of sharing too much information with my friends.

"Nothing's as effective as hiding in plain sight," I said vaguely.

They all waited for me to go on.

"Who was on the phone?" Lien-hua asked.

"Listen." I lowered my voice. "Something's going down, and I need to play this close to the chest. That's all I can say right now."

"If you know something, don't keep it from us," Jake challenged me. "We're a team here and we've got a job to do."

Think this through, Pat. Be careful.

"We can't talk here," I said. "Grab your things, meet in my room in ten minutes."

It wasn't a lot of time, but at least it gave me a small window of opportunity to try to think of something honest to tell them that wouldn't end up endangering Kayla's life.

I turned to the thing I knew best, geospatial analysis.

51

As Tessa waited for Sean to heat up the spaghetti, she walked into the living room to get away from the sausage smell.

Last night all she'd really noticed were the deer and muskie, but now she took in the room. A quilt lay on the back of the couch, and paintings of loons and sunsets over northern lakes hung on the walls. A Brett Favre–signed football sat in a glass case near the window, from back in the day when he was still a Packer, before he retired, unretired, and the Packers fans turned rabidly against him.

Sean didn't have any photos of himself, just of his family: his parents, his son in Phoenix, Amber, Patrick, and two pictures of their younger sister who'd died when Patrick was eight. A staph infection that went systemic took Emily's life when she was only five. Over the last couple years, Tessa had noticed that talking about Emily's death was hard for Patrick, so she almost never brought it up.

One painting near the window particularly caught her attention. It showed a rippling lake with a sailboat leaning elegantly into the wind. The horizon was marked with a string of golden clouds hiding a twilight sun.

The picture invited her in, made it feel like she was a part of it, as if she were watching from a small island as the sailor rode the waves that reflected the dusky sky.

She knew that over the years, tons of stories had been written about people who magically entered or left paintings.

Someone steps into paradise.

Someone slips into the abyss.

Fiction.

Fact.

Only a brushstroke away.

The water looked so alive, and the wind seemed to whisper from the painting and glance against her face, but she knew, of course, that this was all an illusion. Of course the water was still. Of course the soft breeze was only in her imagination. No one can step into a painting or sail free from one. No one can step from one eternity to another. We're locked in here, on this side of the canvas.

On this side of the glass with the dead wasps.

And the deer and—

"Ready," Sean called from the kitchen.

After one more lingering glance at the painting, she went to the table. "Amber here?"

He was pouring a glass of grape juice. "She ended up staying at the motel in Woodborough. It was a good thing Patrick reserved a room for you because I can't imagine there would've been any left last night after the roads were closed down."

He slid a plate with two cut-up apples, a steaming plate of spaghetti, and a thick piece of toast covered with a generous layer of strawberry jam in front of her, then took a seat beside her. "So are you a vegan for health reasons or philosophical ones?"

She let her gaze drift through the doorway to the living room, toward the muskie hanging on the wall. "I don't believe in senselessly killing animals."

He was quiet for a moment. "All native cultures hunted, fished, lived off the land."

She almost said it, almost did: *Yeah, but they respected the natural world, they didn't just shoot things or snag hooks in their mouths to get trophies,* but she caught herself. She didn't even want to be having this conversation with him, not since he'd been so nice to her.

"I'm all for living in harmony with the natural world," she said vaguely. "And of course I know that for one thing to live another must die." She had more to say but left it at that.

Death.

Why did they have to be talking about death again?

You're a killer yourself, Tessa.

You took a man's life.

Senselessly killing animals.

No, but it wasn't senseless, he was—

Sean saw her look toward the other room again. "It's not such a simple issue, dealing with the deer," he said. "The whitetail population."

She quietly ate her spaghetti.

"You probably already know this, but since wolves, the natural predators for whitetail, are so scarce these days—"

"Only because of human encroachment and habitat destruction. There aren't enough undeveloped woodlands left for pack displacement and repopulation."

Easy, Tessa. You don't need to be arguing with him.

Sean didn't seem surprised by her words. "Yes, but now, as things stand, without hunters, the deer herd in this state would get too large, and eventually disease would ravage their numbers. Is it more compassionate to let thousands of deer die slow and lingering deaths than to put some of them down quickly, preserving as much meat as possible for food?"

Despite her desire to bow out of the debate, she felt herself getting riled up. "Okay, but you don't have to mount their heads; celebrate their death."

"I celebrate their beauty, their majesty."

"Do me a favor and don't celebrate my beauty when I die."

Oh, that was just brilliant, Tessa. Way to go!

Sean was quiet for a long time.

At last he pointed to a framed photo that she hadn't seen before, propped on the countertop by the stove. It was a picture of her at her mom's wedding. She was laughing, free and easy, and it was hard for her to even remember what that felt like—to be lighthearted, to smile and mean it, to let something beautiful sweep her away.

"Amber and I already do," he said.

His words stunned her. She'd never even met her stepaunt, but the woman cared about her, celebrated her.

Sean walked to the stove, took the plateful of sausage he'd cooked, and tipped it into a Tupperware container. "This is venison sausage from a doe that ran in front of my truck last month. I didn't want her life to be wasted." His voice wasn't sharp, just authoritative. "Senselessly."

Tessa kept quiet. She'd said enough.

He gestured toward her plate. "Hey, be sure to get plenty to eat. It'll help keep you warm."

"Warm?"

"We're going snowmobiling."

"Where?"

"I know you wanted to see Pat. I'm going to make that happen."

52

Cassandra joined her team in the basement of the Schoenberg Inn.

Becker, Ted, and Millicent were there, along with the seven team members she'd kept hidden from Chekov.

"As you know," she began, "the facility has three levels, all underground . . ."

It was possible that Lien-hua's phone had been compromised, so after making sure the room phone wasn't bugged, I called Sheriff Tait, brought him up to speed concerning the team's 9:00 briefing. Then, I phoned Callaway, and right after he answered, Jake showed up at my door. I let him in, and he took a seat near the window.

Callaway hadn't been able to locate anyone in the area by the name of Kayla Tatum. "I did find out that a Kayla Tatum who lives in Eau Claire didn't come in for work at the hair salon this morning," he told me. "Her boss said Miss Tatum didn't call in sick, just never showed."

A deep sinking feeling. "Thanks."

Momentarily after I hung up, Lien-hua and Natasha arrived, and I asked Lien-hua if I could hang on to her phone for the time being. "Just until I get mine back from Sean."

And until I hear back from Alexei Chekov about a meeting time.

She looked at me oddly. "Sure."

"All right." I set her phone on the desk beside me. "What do we know?"

"You were going to tell us why we were searching the motel for Alexei Chekov," Jake said pointedly.

"In a sec." Although earlier, while I'd been speaking on the phone with Alexei and then typing up the conversation, there hadn't been much time for them to work, I said, "Quick update. Tell me what you found." Being evasive like this wasn't characteristic of me, and by the looks on their faces I could tell they were surprised, but for the time being they didn't challenge me.

Natasha went first. "There hasn't been any chatter regarding terrorist threats concerning our nuclear subs. The DoD is working on the deployment route analysis."

Jake spoke up. "The profile on Reiser and Basque doesn't overlap with what we know about Chekov. Lien-hua concurs. Two completely different behavioral and psychological makeups."

Admittedly the connection had been a long shot.

"We took another look at Reiser's background, though," Lien-hua said. "His work history, the locations of the victim residences." I already knew Reiser had lived in La Crosse, Oshkosh, Superior, and South Chicago before moving to Merrill; some of those locations were near where victims had lived, some were not. She went on, "One of the videos found at his trailer contained news coverage of the murder of Aleste Norkum from WKOW in Madison. But Reiser was living in La Crosse at the time."

"And we have newspaper clippings from the *Rockford Register Star* and the *Business Courier*," Jake added.

Hmm.

We discussed Reiser briefly, then, switching gears, Lien-hua asked, "Did you set up a visit to the ELF site?"

"Still a few details to nail down."

"So what about the motel search, Pat?" Natasha cut in. "C'mon. What's going on?"

It's time. Let's see how this goes . . .

"Okay. I analyzed the topography and road layout of the area, taking into account the known locations relative to Alexei's movements: the snowmobile trails he chose on the way to the Chippewa River, the roads that led from the bridge where he killed the truck driver to the parking lot where he left the semi, and—"

"It showed you his familiarity with the region," Natasha observed.

I nodded. "And it gives me an idea of the way he forms cognitive maps of his surroundings. I was also able to use the location on Highway K where State Trooper Wayland pulled him over."

All of this was true. However, the data I was working from was by no means comprehensive, and when I'd run the numbers I'd gotten a bimodal result of two likely hot spots. The motel was actually on the fringe of the northeastern one.

The only real hiccup here was that I'd done the data analysis after, not before, our motel search.

"Using the same journey-to-crime models I use when I'm tracking serial offenders, I worked backward to identify the most likely places Alexei might be using as his home base while he's in the region—"

"And this was one of them," Jake finished my thought.

"Yes, and—"

"Wait a minute, Pat." It was Lien-hua. "You mentioned a moment ago that Alexei killed the truck driver. That hasn't been established yet."

"I . . ." *Don't lie, but be careful with the truth.* "I was assuming he did."

"No," Jake said, leaning forward, elbows on his knees. "You're the only person I know who doesn't assume. Not during an investigation."

Lien-hua studied me with her dark, knowing eyes.

"Call it a working hypothesis," I said.

No one looked particularly satisfied with my answer.

I felt conflicted.

Of course I wanted to tell them about the phone call from Alexei, but I honestly believed that Kayla Tatum's life was on the line. Somehow Alexei was monitoring us, and I didn't feel I could take the chance that he would find out I'd told them and then kill her.

On the other hand, even though I wanted to buy time until I heard from Alexei about a meeting place, I couldn't risk progress on the investigation solely on the word of an internationally wanted assassin.

There was one option that would both give me a little time to see if he'd contact me again and also move the investigation forward.

"There's only so much we can do from here," I said. "We need to get out there to get eyes on the ground at the old ELF site."

"How do you propose we do that?" Jake asked me. "We don't have any snowmobiles, the roads are still closed, and I can guarantee the national forest service access roads haven't even been plowed out yet."

"When I was at the sawmill I noticed a snowmobile trail groomer. Those things are beasts and can plow through almost anything. There's probably only room in the cab for two or three of us, but it's a start. It'll get us to the site no matter how much snow has drifted across the roads and trails."

Nods around the room. "Good idea," Lien-hua said.

Natasha flagged my attention. "I still have plenty of work to do processing the physical evidence from the Pickron house and a lot to follow up on with the Lab. If there's only room for a couple people, I'll stay here."

"Perfect."

While it was true that the trail groomer was probably our best bet, it would likely take a while for Windwalker or one of his crew to deliver it here, especially if no one was at the sawmill today, and in this weather, I thought that was a real possibility.

Hopefully you'll hear from Alexei by then.

I looked at my watch. "It's close to noon. Get whatever you can round up to eat, it might be a long day—Lien-hua, I saw you had some granola bars, maybe we can dive into your supply."

"No problem. I brought plenty."

None of the people stuck here at the motel had access to food either, and the roads still weren't open to civilians. "Natasha," I said, "why don't you see if you can reach Tait, have him get a snowplow up here to deliver some food to the motel guests. Or at least someone on a snowmobile with a few bags of groceries."

"Got it."

"Good." I stood. "Jake, call the sawmill, get the foreman on the line. Just ask for Windwalker. If the place is closed—"

"Don't worry. I'll take care of it."

"Okay. Let us know as soon as you find out. In the meantime, let's see how much progress we can make from here."

53

Cassandra gazed at the ten people gathered with her around the dusty pool table in the basement of the Schoenberg Inn: four military-trained operatives, three hackers, and the three Eco-Tech ideologues she'd allowed Chekov to meet.

Donnie Pickron was still chained to the steel work table in the neighboring room.

Earlier, Becker, true to his Eco-Tech loyalties, had suggested that the team members choose environmental code names for this mission. It'd seemed a little sophomoric to Cassandra, but she'd finally acquiesced and allowed him to go ahead with the idea.

So now, she was Solstice, he was Hurricane—wait, Cane for short. Around the table were Tsunami, Eclipse, Cyclone, Equator, Typhoon, Squall, Cirrus, Gale, and Tempest. A little tough to keep straight, but manageable.

Solstice's computer sat in the middle of the billiards table.

She tapped her remote control, and a hologram appeared, hovering about two feet above the table. The light-blue, three-dimensional image showed a labyrinth of tunnels fingering out from a multilevel control center buried deep beneath the earth. Although she was familiar with the location of one entrance to the base, her sources told her that there were two others, miles away from the station itself, connected only through these extensive tunnels. Once inside the base, she would discern which was which. She planned to use one of those to escape when all this was over.

So far, as much as possible, she'd kept the specifics of the mission to a minimum, on a strict need-to-know basis, and only four members of her team had seen the schematics already.

"That thing's a fortress," one of her men said. He was the hacker who'd chosen to be called Equator. And based on his circumference it was a fitting name.

"It might look that way at first glance," Solstice acknowledged, "but as we've discussed, it's only manned by a skeleton crew: four technicians and four Masters-at-Arms, one of whom will be off-duty when we arrive." She drew her team's attention to the top level of the hologram, which lay twenty-seven meters below the surface. "One of them will be based here, probably waiting for us when we arrive. We neutralize him and move down. Tempest, he's yours."

"Got it." He was a former Marine Corps Special Ops unconventional warfare specialist built like a brick wall, and she believed him.

"The next level is the living quarters: a bunk area, a galley, recreation room, bathrooms, library, fitness center, weight room, showers, storage, conference area."

"How do you know all this?" Tsunami asked her. "How did you get these maps?"

"If I wasn't good at what I do, we wouldn't be here," she told him bluntly, then indicated toward the hologram again. "Lower level: the generator room, electromagnetic signal production facility, washroom, break room, and the control center. This is where it's all going to happen. Tsunami, Eclipse, Tempest, you'll take out the two MAs. Here." She pointed. "And here."

Tsunami slowly rotated the tip of his knife, a seven-inch CRKT Ultima, against the calloused palm of his left hand. "So take 'em out. You're talking about—"

"We've been over this."

Tsunami glanced toward the corner of the room, where the automatic weapons lay. Ordnance canisters containing triacetone triperoxide, or TATP, sat next to them—something she planned to use to destroy the base when everything was finished. Tsunami continued, "I know, I'm just saying—what are the weapons for if we're not gonna use 'em?"

"Can anyone please tell Tsunami why we don't want to kill the three Masters-at-Arms tonight?"

Eclipse spoke up, "We may need additional information. It'll be better to keep our options open. We keep people alive as long as they serve a useful purpose." She smiled, blew Tsunami a kiss.

He stopped spinning the tip of the knife and laid the blade flat against his hand. Gave her a leering smile. "I can think of a useful purpose for those little lips of yours."

"Dream on."

"All right," Solstice reined them in. "The off-duty MA is a wild card. I'm not sure if he'll be in the crew quarters or one of the tunnels. In either case, we move through the facility, find the men, Tase 'em, cuff 'em, then collect everyone in the rec room." She nodded toward Eclipse. "You'll be in charge of watching the hostages."

"Guarding a room full of tied-up sailors? I think I can handle that."

"Every girl's dream," Tsunami said.

Solstice turned to the woman on her left, the Eco-Tech operative whose real name was Millicent Alman. "Cyclone, are you all set to take out the radio communication?" Although Solstice didn't know what outside party the people inside the base might try to contact via RF, she did know that they had the capability.

Cyclone held up the portable tactical radio frequency, or RF, jamming device.

"You've tested it?"

"Ready to go." She indicated toward a sprawling coil of thick wire and an electronic relay device near a stack of videotaping equipment. "As far as the wireless signal that we'll need in order to post the video, I should be able to rig the line in the shaft on our way down. I don't see any trouble with us getting online to monitor JWICS."

"Okay." Solstice turned to address the group as a whole. "Sentries are most alert during the beginning and the end of their shifts. The MA on the top level will be fresh, as well as the one in the comm center. The other one should be in the middle of his rounds when we move in."

"Hang on," Tsunami said.

She assessed him coolly. "Yes?" She'd never liked this guy's attitude. Cane had been responsible for recruiting Tsunami, and now Solstice decided she'd made a mistake handing that responsibility over to him.

"Earlier you mentioned disabling the base's communication center, but we're talking about . . ." He ticked off on his fingers. "A radio base station, a satellite uplink, internet access, telephone landli—"

"Haven't you even been listening?" Cane interrupted. "They don't use the internet in there! That's the whole purpose behind the station—stay offline so it can't be hacked into by—"

"Okay," Tsunami said sharply. "I get that. But the crew will undoubtably have cell phones."

"No mobile devices are allowed at the base," Solstice told him. "It could give hackers a window to get in."

"I don't buy it," Tsunami countered.

"Buy it. I've looked into it."

"Besides," said Cane, "this thing was built to withstand a direct nuclear hit. It's encased in concrete, ninety feet underground. You think a cell phone's gonna work down there?" His gaze wandered toward Cyclone. "Without that equipment?"

A stony silence.

"And as far as satellite communication—" Cane began.

"I know," Tsunami cut in, "they need an aboveground antennae, but the power lines leading to the forest service maintenance building? Come on. Really? That's a stretch. I don't think any of this was thought through like it should've been."

Solstice calculated the necessity of having this man on the team. Jobs and resources could always be reallocated.

She waited until all the eyes in the room had gravitated back to her. "The plan has always been to take out the landlines first, then the sat comm, then jam the radio signals. Do you have an alternate proposal?"

"If the base loses communication with the outside world, won't that alert the Navy something is wrong?"

"I've got that covered."

He eyed her. "I think we should take out the sat comm first." There was a clear challenge in his voice.

Solstice rubbed her fingers together. She couldn't have one of her team members questioning her decisions. This man had to go. She stood. "Most people think that when you attack your enemy, you should take out his strongest defenses first."

"And you're saying we should attack where he's weakest?"

"No. We attack where he doesn't know he's being attacked. In this storm, people won't question the landlines going down. It buys us time."

"I see." He looked around the room. "One last thing, then. You still haven't told us when we get our money."

"Are you concerned that you might not get your share, Roderick?" She stepped toward him, and he watched her insouciantly.

"I'm just trying to get things clarified." He smiled out of the corner of his mouth, looked around the room. "I mean, we're talking about a quarter of a million dollars here. I need to let my accountant know when the funds are coming in."

Solstice positioned herself behind him, placed a hand on his shoulder, and then stroked his cheek with the back of her other hand. "I promise I'll let your accountant know you were concerned about him."

"What do you mean 'that I *was* concerned about him'?"

"In the moments before you no longer served a useful purpose."

And then with well-honed quickness and before he could pull away, she grasped his head firmly in both hands and in one swift, smooth motion, snapped his neck as easily as if she were unscrewing a bottle cap.

She let go of his head, and it landed with a dull thud onto the table. "It looks like the rest of you just received a raise."

She tapped the remote control, turned off the hologram. "Tempest, Eclipse, Typhoon, get your skis. I want those telephone lines down. The rest of us will leave as soon as Donnie has the authentication codes."

54

12:32 p.m.

I had Lien-hua's cell on my desk beside my laptop in anticipation of Alexei's text.

She sat on the bed, typing on her laptop.

We still hadn't had a chance to sort through everything from last night, but just like my near-drowning incident yesterday, Amber's visit to my motel room seemed to have become buried, at least for the time being, beneath the forward movement of the case and the pile of new problems that the passage of time inevitably brings.

As for Amber, I'd seen her briefly when I was searching the motel for Alexei and Kayla. I hadn't said anything and neither had she, but she looked subdued. Sad.

It was hard being this close to Lien-hua and yet feeling so distant from her. However, the fact that she'd chosen to work here in my room while Natasha and Jake had gone to their own respective rooms felt like at least a small reprieve. I had the sense that Lien-hua did believe me when I assured her that nothing had happened last night with Amber, or at least she was willing to look for a reason to trust what I said.

Regarding the ELF site, Windwalker was bringing the trail groomer over, but he'd been at home when Jake called and first had to ride his snowmobile to the sawmill to pick up the groomer before coming here. It didn't look like he'd arrive for another forty minutes or so.

I went online to see if we had a solution yet to the puzzling snowmobile tracks leading to the open stretch of water on Tomahawk Lake.

Lately, I'd been dabbling with the use of wiki-based approaches to gathering nonsensitive case information. It seems to me that it's going to be the next step in the evolution of criminology, and, if I'm right, it'll revolutionize law-enforcement and intelligence-based policing in the near future.

Rather than do all the research yourself, let the experts and enthusiasts do it.

When I pulled up the site, I saw that not only was it possible to get a Ski-Doo 800 XL to travel over one hundred meters without a rider, apparently it wasn't that difficult.

Since I'd posted my offer on the website forum for Ski-Doo fanatics at just past 11:30, offering $500 to the first person who could figure out a way to do it and send me a video of the process as well as of the sled traveling the distance, I had six replies.

Within thirty minutes of my posting, a snowmobiler in Marquette, Michigan, had figured out a way to crimp the throttle closed and jam the sleds straight by altering the support plates and readjusting the spindle calibration to the skis. On his video, the Ski-Doo went nearly two hundred meters, and I figured that on a smooth lake and without obstructions, it would have traveled in a relatively straight line pretty much until it ran out of gas.

Five other solutions from five other Ski-Doo lovers followed.

If, within one hour, six people could figure out a way to keep the snowmobile straight just in the hopes of earning $500, certainly a group of eco-terrorists framing someone for murder could come up with a way as well.

My friend Ralph was the head of NCAVC, so I sent him an invoice for $500 for "consultation fees," emailed my winner a note of congratulations, thanked the others for participating, removed the posting, and then returned to evaluating the map of our area. I was studying the most likely areas Alexei might be using as his home base—i.e., where he was keeping Kayla—when an email from Angela arrived detailing what we knew about him.

"I'm still investigating Valkyrie," she wrote at the top of her report. "Looks like some arrows point toward a specialty in communication technology and hacking. That's about it for now."

That would fit with Eco-Tech.

I read on: "Nothing on the back trace of the email Chekov sent you, but here's what Alyssa dug up on him."

Apparently, Ellory had been right yesterday when he told me that Chekov was a ghost—Prague, Johannesburg, Rome, Hong Kong—Alexei would materialize out of nowhere, do his work, and then disappear. But at least now, thanks to the video surveillance cameras at the Minneapolis–St. Paul International Airport, we had a photo of him.

I studied it.

Dark hair, knowing eyes, a haunted intensity about him.

It wasn't confirmed, but it was believed that he was a former member of the Russian Air Force. According to the dossier Alyssa had worked up, if he was the same man, he'd flown experimental aircraft for twelve years and then began working for the GRU, Russia's foreign military intelligence directorate, four years ago.

The GRU has always been responsible for many more assassinations than the KGB ever was, so I found the scenario believable. Their psych profile listed him as "of volatile and irregular temperament," in other words, slightly unstable. He seemed remarkably self-controlled to me so I was a little surprised to see that. But on the other hand, you probably would need to be a little disturbed to be an assassin. He'd disappeared unexpectedly in May after returning from an assignment in Dubai.

I clicked the chat icon at the bottom of the email, and Angela's picture popped up.

"Did he ever kill women or children?" I typed.

"Not as far as I can see," came the reply.

"Any affiliations? Accomplices? Causes?"

"He's a freelancer. Seems to prefer taking care of problems no one else wants to touch. His wife was killed last spring in Moscow. A head shot. Point-blank range. It looks like it might have been another assassin, unless he did it himself. After that he dropped off the radar screen."

I wondered if his wife's murder might help explain why he was so insistent that he didn't kill women or children.

That is, if he loved her. If he's ever really loved anyone.

I wrote, "Look closer for any connections he has with law enforcement or with our government. He has a source somewhere."

"Got it," she typed. Then, "Lacey's analyzing the Queen 27:21:9 alphanumeric sequence as well as the phone number you gave me." Lacey was the name Angela had lovingly given to her computer. To say they were close would be an understatement.

Despite the fact that Lacey was much more qualified to decode the cipher than I was, I found myself analyzing the numbers. *All divisible by 3, also, 27 is 6 higher than 21, which is 12 higher than 9—also all divisible by 3.*

But what does that mean?

I had no idea. Maybe it was just a random series of numbers.

I trusted that Angela and Lacey would figure it out.

"Thx," I typed.

At the end of the email, Angela had also included background on the Eco-Tech members whose photos I'd forwarded to her. Ted Rusk had the most extensive hacking experience of the group and had earned a Carnegie Mellon undergrad computer science degree. Other than that, two of the others were ideologues who'd participated in various protests and civil demonstrations, and one, Clifton White, was a felon who, based on his record, might have been working for Eco-Tech as security or maybe as a bodyguard.

After the chat, I recalled my conversation with Alexei and found myself staring into space, thinking of Eco-Tech's connection, the ROSD hack. After a moment I noticed Lien-hua looking my way. "Yes?" I said.

"Something's going on in that head of yours."

"What motivates professional hackers?"

"Professional hackers? Well, the same thing that motivates mountain climbers."

"Challenge. Wait . . ." It took me a moment to see where she was going with that. "Maybe telling them it's unclimbable. Newbies will walk away, but the pros will be more committed than ever to be the first one to scale it."

"You understand motives better than you like to admit."

"You must be rubbing off on me."

She accepted that with a kind nod. "Besides challenge, add in the rewards that come from accomplishing what no one else has. Why do you ask? What are you thinking?"

I tapped my computer knowingly. "There's more going on here than meets the eye."

"Really." There was a friendly touch of sarcasm in her voice. "And let me guess, Captain Cliché—you're going to find out what it is."

"Bingo."

"I think you've been reading too many pulp fiction novels."

"Nope. Thrillers. My favorites are the stories that have a good twist at the end."

"You mean like when someone who seems innocent for the whole book turns out to be the killer?"

"Sure. Or when everything you thought was true turns out to be an artifice, a giant house of cards."

"And the truth"—now she gave me a diminutive smile, and it lifted me more than anything else had in the last two days—"was something you never even saw coming."

"Exactly."

For a moment I thought of darker twists, those in the other direction, in which innocent people you think will survive don't, or hope that seemed guaranteed disappears in a final dramatic plunge, but I pushed those thoughts aside.

Lien-hua went back to work but a minute later rested her chin in her hands; it was her turn to be deep in thought. "The Reiser case, Pat. Some of the things Jake told me don't seem to fit."

"Those are?"

"If the autopsy is correct, Reiser would have already been dead when the eyewitness said she saw him enter his trailer. The date of the unopened mail in his trailer supports that." She leaned forward. "But if Basque did kill Reiser because we were getting too close, why linger in the area another day after killing Reiser? Or more specifically, why chance getting caught entering his trailer disguised as Reiser when that's not even where Reiser was killed?"

"Good point." I drummed my fingers on the desk for a moment. "Hang on. We're already assuming too much. We don't know that Basque killed Reiser and we don't know if it was Basque at the trailer. In the search for truth, it's only by chance that you can find the right answers without asking the right—"

"Questions," she inserted, then quoted directly what I'd been planning to say: "So it's always better to begin with inquiries rather than assertions." A slight smile. "Yes, I know."

"I've said that before."

"Once or twice." She stood, paced toward the window. "Okay, let's back up for a minute. Is it possible that Reiser wasn't even Basque's partner at all, that he was set up for the crimes from the beginning? After all, he was a drifter and an ex-con, the perfect kind of person to lay blame on for a series of crimes like this. He lived in half a dozen different places while those crimes were occurring."

"No," I said, "that doesn't work. Last summer his DNA was matched to that found at four of the original Basque crime scenes fourteen years ago. That's a long time to sustain framing someone."

"But the very thing that makes that unlikely also makes it unlikely that Reiser has been Basque's accomplice all along."

I looked at her curiously. "Why's that?"

"Time, Pat. Fourteen years? Could Reiser really have made it that long without leaving any DNA at any other crime scene? Even if Basque was the dominant partner, serial killers almost never go that long between crimes."

"You can't just turn it off," I reflected. She was right. Of all the hundreds of serial killers I've studied over the last fifteen years, unless they were incarcerated, only a handful had ever managed to stop committing crimes for more than a few years. A murder spree with Basque, then thirteen years of good behavior? It didn't fit. "It would be almost unheard of."

"Right. So think about it—all those years, no evidence left, and then suddenly he reconnects with Basque—who's smart and meticulous—and Reiser starts leaving his DNA behind again?"

And now we only find news clippings and news coverage footage of the crimes with Basque? Why? If he was a scrapbooker, why only follow Basque's crimes?

I let the implications sink in. Out the window I noticed a snowmobile approaching the motel. Two people on it, but at this distance I couldn't tell who they might be.

"But if Basque has a different partner," I observed, "it's unbelievable they would have planted another individual's DNA fourteen years ago and then picked up where they left off."

"But fourteen years ago when the state of Wisconsin first prosecuted the case, the DNA hadn't been identified. Could Basque or his partner have somehow recently switched the lab samples to point to Reiser now?"

"I don't see how anyone could have done that. I'm more involved with this case than anyone, and even I couldn't have pulled off something like that."

She went on, undeterred. "But what if the unidentified DNA was never entered into the court records? Or, even if it was, those were all digitized two years ago; if a person had access to the online case files, she could—"

Her phone vibrated on the desk.

"I'll get it," I said. With a small flutter of apprehension I picked it up.

A text: "One hour. Woodborough hospital. Lower level. Come alone."

The hospital? Why the hospital?

I noticed Lien-hua eyeing me inquisitively. "Who's it from?"

Beyond her, outside in the storm, I identified Sean and Tessa on the snowmobile. My stepdaughter wore a pink snowmobile suit that must have been Amber's. Pink was in no way Tessa's favorite color, and it might have been comical if everything else going on right now wasn't so serious.

"Pat?" Lien-hua indicated toward the phone. "What's up?"

"It's a source who might know something about the Pickron murders," I said honestly. I had until 1:45 to get to the basement of the Woodborough hospital, but the road in front of the motel hadn't been plowed in hours, and I didn't have time to wait around for the trail groomer. "I'm sorry, but that's all I can tell you right now."

Before she could follow up with another question, I grabbed my coat and left for the lobby to get the thing I would need if I was going to make it to that meeting with Alexei Chekov.

55

I met Sean and Tessa by the front door. Snowmobile helmet off, my stepdaughter's midnight-black hair swirled endearingly around her shoulders.

Though I was still a little upset that she'd left the Twin Cities against my will, I was relieved to see her, and when she came toward me, I held out my arm to her. "Tessa, I'm so glad you—"

Instead of an embrace, however, she smacked me hard in the arm. Not a friendly nudge at all.

I blinked. "What was that for?"

"Almost getting killed."

She could really pack a punch. "Keep that in your repertoire in case you need it for some guy sometime."

She looked at me incredulously. "I'm seriously upset and you're making light of everything?"

Sean stepped to the other side of the lobby to give us at least a modicum of privacy.

"Listen," I said to her. "I haven't seen you all week, and now you just walk in here and—"

"Hang on." A hand in the air, palm toward me. A teenage girl's stop sign. "You almost drown, you almost freeze." Her voice caught. "I have to drive through a complete blizzard . . ." As she struggled to get through her sentence, I could tell she truly was upset. It hadn't struck me so much yesterday, but she must have been terrified when she heard that I almost died. She falteringly picked up her thought where she'd left off, "And then everywhere I go, everybody's cooking animals."

She unzipped the pink snowmobile suit, and it looked like she was going to comment about that too, but instead her jaw quivered slightly and a wide tear formed in her right eye. I stepped forward, took her in my arms.

"Hey, it's okay."

"You seriously cannot die on me."

"I won't," I said, although I was aware I was promising something that was beyond my control.

As anxious as I was to get going, I could tell that right now I needed to be here for her, at least for a minute or two. "I didn't mean to make light of anything."

At last she stepped away and quickly brushed her hand across her face to dry her eyes. "Yeah, I know." She tweaked her hair back. Tried to smile.

"I'm serious."

"Yeah."

"Okay, because I just need you to—"

"Don't overdo it," she said. "It'll get weird."

"Right."

"I'm just . . . I'm glad you're still here."

"That makes two of us."

"But I have to say, jumping into a river in subzero weather? That is *way* off the screen. Even for you." Her gaze drifted toward my feet. "So, frostbite?" she said uneasily. "Any toes missing or anything?"

"Still intact."

"Good. 'Cause that would have totally creeped me out."

Pat, you need to get going.

I turned to Sean. "Thanks for bringing her over."

"No problem. It's good to see you on your feet." He handed me a bundle of manila envelopes. "The papers you gave me yesterday at the sawmill."

Donnie's personnel files and time cards. "I appreciate it."

A second passed.

How to do this.

I turned to Tessa again. "Listen, I'm really glad to see you, but—"

"I said that's enough." She spoke softly, and I noticed that she was eyeing the young man working behind the counter. I hadn't really noticed before, but he was in his midtwenties, with ruffled hair, dark, deep-set eyes, and a cute, sly sort of grin. He'd been checking her out too and abruptly averted eye contact when he saw me look at him.

Tessa always goes for the older guys and doesn't always show prudence when it comes to vetting dates, boyfriends, on-the-spot crushes.

"Come here." I led her to the room beside the lobby, and when we were alone and the guy at the counter was out of sight and wouldn't distract her, I said, "I need to go somewhere for a little bit. It's very important, but I'll be back as soon as I can."

She looked at me quizzically. "I just got here and—by the way, were you limping just now?"

"Yes."

"What happened?"

"I turned my ankle a little yesterday. It's no big deal. So, I'm just saying—"

"You're leaving."

"Yes. This isn't about us. This is—this was from before."

"Then why did I even come?" She didn't sound angry, just confused. "Why'd I have to go and ride a snowmobile all the way over here in this weather if you were just gonna leave as soon as I got here?"

Obviously I hadn't even known she was on her way, but that wasn't really something I needed to point out at the moment.

"I'll be back as soon as I can," I repeated. The words were true enough, but I was also aware that if I did head out with Alexei to look for the Pickron killers, I might be gone for hours.

"This has to do with the case?"

"Yes."

She scrutinized me. "Agent Vanderveld's here, right? So have him check it out." She knew I'd been working with Jake on the Reiser case in Merrill, so it wasn't a master feat of deduction to guess that he was here.

"This time it has to be me."

"Why?"

"It's complicated."

"Really." Ice had crept into her voice, and I was getting disoriented by our conversation's penduluming swing of emotions. "Just a minute ago you were telling me how glad you were to see me and now you're just taking off."

"This doesn't have to do with you."

"Oh. I see."

"Tessa—"

"You almost died and I would have been alone."

"I wish I could stay here, right now, with you, but I have to— look, we'll talk through everything later, okay?"

She started for the lobby. "Right."

"Hang on a sec."

She spun. "What? I just agreed with you."

"Trust me on this. Okay?"

"Trust you?"

"You can stay here with Sean and Amber."

"End of discussion, right? Is that it?"

"Don't be like this, Tessa."

She turned on her heels and swept out of the room, and I followed, ready to confront her again, but then I saw that Lien-hua had entered the lobby. Her eyes flicked from Tessa to me to Tessa.

"Hey, Tessa," she said.

"Lien-hua. I didn't know you were here."

"You okay?"

"Yeah." Tessa strode to the far side of the lobby and then stared, arms folded, out the window. The guy behind the counter looked toward her, then glanced my way and quickly went back to texting someone on his iPhone.

Oh, boy.

Salvage this and then get out of here.

Sean and Lien-hua said nothing, and I realized they'd never met. I quickly introduced them. "Sean, this is Lien-hua; Lien-hua, Sean."

They shook hands amiably, but their attention was obviously still on me and Tessa.

"Sean," I said, "I need to borrow your sled."

"It's Amber's," he told me needlessly.

"Right."

He must have been able to tell I was anxious to leave because he didn't argue, just handed me his helmet. "Nothing impulsive, okay? It's the only snowmobile we have left."

"I promise."

I gave Lien-hua the personnel files and time cards that Sean had brought with him. "Take a close look at the date Donnie started working at the sawmill," I said. "And check to see if and when he clocked out on the day of the murders and if he received any phone calls that day at the mill prior to leaving."

When I mentioned the phone calls, Sean reached into his pocket. "Oh yeah. Almost forgot."

He passed my cell to me, but I realized that Alexei had Lien-hua's number, not mine, so I would need to keep hers in case he texted me again.

I gave her my phone. "I'll get yours back to you as soon as I can."

"Where are you going?"

"I have an errand to run." Then I said to Sean, "Amber's in room 104. Can you guys keep an eye on Tessa?"

"Absolutely."

After reading Amber's note this morning, I wondered when she was going to tell Sean about leaving him. I hoped she'd have the good sense to wait until Tessa and I were out of town.

Go, Pat. You need to move.

"I have to go, Raven," I called. "I'll be back as soon as I can."

She was quiet.

"Tessa."

She didn't turn. "Sure."

Wonderful.

"Lien-hua." I motioned toward the door. "Can you come here a sec?"

We stepped outside, and I held out my hand. "I need your gun."

"What's going on here?"

"Mine's in a snowbank by the Chippewa—"

"That's not what I mean."

"I can't—"

Her hands went to her hips. "Are you going to the ELF site by yourself?"

"No, it's just . . . Please . . ." For the second time in two minutes I said it: "You have to trust me."

"Trust you."

"Yes. You trust me, don't you?"

The hesitation in her reply made me think of last night when she'd walked in on me and Amber, but then she took off her holster and her Glock and handed them to me. "Be careful and call me if you need me. Don't shut me out."

"That's the last thing I'd ever want to do."

I wanted so badly to hold her, feel her arms encircling me, gain strength from her embrace, the scent of her presence, but I knew things were still tenuous between us. Instead, I placed my hand gently on her arm. "You're the person who matters more to me than anyone else." As I said the words I realized they were true to an extent I'd never even been aware of before. Yes, I cared fiercely for Tessa, loved her in a protective, parental way, but with Lien-hua I had to acknowledge that my feelings were the deepest, most intimate kind. "You know that, right?"

"Yes." The answer didn't come as promptly as I would've hoped, but there was no uncertainty in it.

After a moment's debate I gave her a light kiss on the cheek and whispered, "I love you."

"You too," she said softly.

And in her words I found a shot of courage and a renewed sense of hope that we were going to work things out after all.

She turned and went back into the lobby, and as the door opened I heard Jake's voice. "Where's he going?"

"Out," she answered.

Then it swung shut, and I limped down the path to the snow-mobile to go meet Alexei Chekov in the basement of the hospital I'd been in yesterday, recovering from trying to save the man he'd thrown into the Chippewa River.

I only hoped I would be more successful saving Kayla than I'd been when I tried to save Bryan Ellory.

56

On the computer screen in front of her, Solstice monitored the progress of three of her mercenaries.

Forty minutes ago Tempest, Eclipse, and Typhoon had skied toward the east entrance to the national forest, where they were now preparing to take down the telephone lines that led into the Chequamegon-Nicolet National Forest.

Meanwhile, in the corner of the room, Cane and his two Eco-Tech hard-liners were reviewing the speech he was going to record after the team had taken over the station. Seated at a table beside them, Gale and Equator were online, keeping tabs on the JWICS chatter through Terry's back doors. Nothing so far on subs or the ELF station. Cirrus was analyzing the base schematics, calculating the most effective placement for the TATP ordnance.

Solstice had thought the team members might be troubled about Clifton White's or Tsunami's demise, but everyone seemed to accept that the mission took precedence over any personal attachments. In fact, Solstice had a feeling that seeing her decisive response to incompetence and insubordination had served a solidifying effect on their loyalty.

Or maybe it was all about the money to them after all. The best and most reliable motivator on earth—a bigger bottom line.

The three operatives in the forest all wore cameras attached to their headsets, and now, through the video signal relayed to her computer, Solstice saw that Tempest was ascending a telephone pole.

A few residential customers would be affected by the downed telephone lines, and she was confident that soon enough the scattered users would contact the phone company on their cell phones, and the disruption in service would be reasonably blamed on the storm.

The staff at the ELF base would no doubt use their satellite uplink to get an update on the disruption in landline service and have no immediate cause for concern.

With the roads as bad as they were, no phone companies would be able to send crews out until tomorrow at the earliest. And by then it wouldn't matter anyway.

Solstice felt her pocket, fondled the passport she was carrying for Ariose Heaton, another of her identities. Waiting out the storm wouldn't be difficult. Flying out of the regional airport in Rhinelander, an airport without facial recognition software, would be no trouble. And then, in two days, she would be reunited with Terry in Mali, a country without extradition treaties with the US, and they would have enough money to hide away for the rest of their lives.

Unless, of course, they decided to engage in a little mischief now and then along the way.

That thought brought a smile.

"How long?" she asked into her mic.

"We've run into a few issues," Eclipse replied. "Nothing serious. We should be done by three."

Perfect.

"All right. We'll meet you at the maintenance building at 3:30."

Tessa wasn't exactly into hanging out with Sean and Amber, but she'd never met her stepaunt before, and even though the circumstances were sort of awkward, she seemed nice enough and Tessa tried to concentrate on being here, talking with her, but she was still upset about her conversation with Patrick, and that was sort of swallowing up her attention.

She wasn't mad at him, more shaken by hearing he'd almost drowned. More this weird kind of loneliness and longing to connect. She even found herself wanting to tell him about the shrink, about how terrible she still felt about killing the man last summer, about the prescription for the sleeping pills—just lay everything out in the open, let Patrick listen, offer whatever help he could, be the dad he obviously wanted to be.

Later, when he gets back.

Now, she was in Amber's room—the one she would've had if she'd made it to the motel last night. Sean sat somewhat obtrusively in the corner and Amber was trying a little too hard to negotiate a conversation between the three of them, but with Sean being sorta quiet and Tessa being so distracted, it wasn't going too well, and finally Amber suggested a bit too brightly that they see if there was anything on TV.

"Okay," Tessa said, trying to sound enthusiastic.

Amber clicked on the remote, and their discussion, which had never really gotten off the ground in the first place, ended. A sports wrap-up show came on, and even though, as far as Tessa could tell, none of them really had any interest in it, they all sat quietly and stared at the screen.

I arrived at the hospital and parked the snowmobile beside the main entrance. Shed the helmet. Set it on the seat.

Seven minutes until my meeting with Alexei Chekov.

The road in front of the hospital had been plowed, and I figured that transportation to the only medical care facility for miles had to be one of the county's top priorities. Maybe that's why Alexei wanted to meet here—he knew it'd be the one place in the region that would have clear roads in front of it, guaranteed access.

It seemed like a good reason to me, one he would have thought of.

Before going inside I wanted as much information about Chekov as I could get, and as far as I knew, there was only one person alive in the area besides me who'd actually spoken with him: State Trooper Reggie Wayland, the man whose wrist bones Alexei had shattered yesterday afternoon.

I figured he'd be in the hospital himself, and though I could ask for him at the front desk, a dozen cars were parked in the windswept parking lot, so instead of walking in yet, I phoned the front desk and took the opportunity to walk the lot, memorizing the plates.

Surprisingly, the receptionist told me that Wayland had already checked out. When I called his home, his wife answered, and when I explained who I was, she told me that he still couldn't grip anything but that, yes, yes of course, she would hold the phone for him.

"Talk me through what happened," I said. "I don't have a lot of time."

Quickly and succinctly, Wayland detailed how Alexei had attacked him, even described the weapon he'd used. Wayland had a sharp memory, and I was glad.

We hung up and I tapped at my phone, going online to the Federal Digital Database. I entered the plate numbers for each of the cars in the parking lot, and seconds later found out that none of them were registered to Kayla Tatum.

Chekov might have switched vehicles again.

I returned to the hospital's entrance.

It seemed obvious that Alexei had abducted Kayla, but as I've learned in the past, things are not always what they appear to be. Once again I was reminded of what my mentor, Dr. Calvin Werjonic, used to say: "Truth often hides in the crevices of the evident." It was possible that Kayla wasn't Alexei's captive but his partner. He might not have killed the Pickrons, but I didn't want to discount—as unlikely as it was—the possibility that she might have.

As the automatic doors whooshed open in front of me, sucking in a double curl of twirling snow, I pulled up Kayla's DMV photo on Lien-hua's cell. A middle-aged receptionist sitting at a small booth in the lobby looked over the top of her glasses at me as I entered.

"Some weather we're havin' out there," she said with a strong Wisconsin accent.

"Yes. I'm looking for—"

"D'you drive?"

"Snowmobile." I held up my credentials. "Listen, I'm looking for the lower level."

She gave the ID only a cursory look. Her eyes jumped past me to the glass doors. "I hear the roads are gettin' worse."

"Please, the lower level?"

Finally, she gestured vaguely to her left. "Elevators are over there. By the bathrooms."

Elevators announce your arrival, and people can be ready for you when the doors slide open, but if you use the stairs, you retain, at least for a few extra seconds, the element of surprise.

"I'm looking for the stairwell."

With a somewhat disgruntled look, she motioned in the other direction. "End of the hall, past the chapel, turn left. Stairs'll be on your right."

"Thank you." I showed her the photo of Kayla Tatum. "Have you seen this woman come through here? Maybe with a man about six feet tall? A stocky guy, might have been wearing a blue parka?"

She shook her head. "Nope. Been here since 7:00." Then, looking toward the doors again, she added, "On the news they're saying more snow's coming tonight, but it's supposed to warm up and maybe hit ten degrees—a heat wave, y'know."

I couldn't tell if that was supposed to be a joke or not.

"Thanks." I turned to go.

"'Course with the windchill," she said still contemplating the weather, "it's gonna feel a lot colder."

As I left, I noticed her eyes following me all the way across the lobby until I was past the vending machines.

At the end of the hall, I unholstered Lien-hua's Glock, pressed open the door.

And entered the stairwell.

57

I descended the stairs.

My senses were dialed up the way I like it.

Sharp.

Focused.

At the base of the steps I slowly opened the door and saw a long, bone-white hallway stretching before me the length of the hospital where it ended in a T.

Nobody else in sight.

Gun ready, I eased the door shut behind me.

Alexei's text had only told me to meet him in the lower level of the hospital. No room number. No details. Although this wasn't a large facility I noted at least a dozen doors in this corridor.

Rather than call his name I decided to start searching for him in the rooms closest to me and systematically work my way to the far end of the hall.

The first door was to a radiology lab. I pressed it open, and as I was leaning to look inside, I heard a voice behind me in the hallway. "Patrick."

I spun, Glock raised. Alexei stood beside a door fifteen meters down the hall.

"Hands where I can see them, Alexei."

He lifted his hands, showed me they were empty.

"Where's Kayla?"

"I'd rather not talk here in the hall. We might get interrupted."

"Where is she?"

"She's safe."

Careful, Pat. This guy's the real deal. He killed two people yester-day. "Stay where you are." I approached him warily, scanning the hallway for other movement in case he wasn't alone and this was some kind of trap, but the hall appeared to be empty. "You're going to pay for what you did to Bryan Ellory and to Bobby Clarke."

"The truck driver."

"Yes."

"I have no doubt."

Just a few paces away now, I motioned for him to back up. "Into the room and don't make any sudden moves. I'm not having the best week, and shooting you would probably be good therapy." Not something I was planning to do, but he didn't know that and, honestly, it felt a little therapeutic just to say it.

We entered the nondescript administrative office: a desk with a flat-screen monitor, an overstuffed bookshelf, a few chairs, a filing cabinet. I closed the door. "Turn around."

He complied.

A common misconception among civilians, probably because of seeing too many cop movies and TV shows, is that you read someone his rights when you arrest him. That's not true. You read him his rights before you question him back at the station.

Mirandizing could wait for the moment.

After talking with Trooper Wayland, I knew that Alexei had turned his back on him as requested, then attacked him. I wanted to see if Alexei would try the same thing on me. "Hands against the wall."

He placed his hands against the paneling.

Attentive to the fact that he might go for my weapon, I holstered the Glock before frisking him. I found no knives, no guns, just a small handheld device that appeared to be a medical instrument, the very weapon Wayland had told me about.

As I was removing it from Chekov's pocket, he spun, lightning quick, leading with his left elbow and bringing his right arm over my shoulder to reach for the device, but I was ready. I shoved him backward, brought my forearm up, pinning his neck against the wall—with my other hand I swung the device up, planted the tip against the bone just below his left eye socket. "What's this, Alexei?"

It took him a moment to answer. "It's a spring-loaded bone injection gun." His Russian accent slipped into more of the sentence than usual, and I realized that might be his tell when he was under stress.

"Sounds like it might hurt."

"It does." He didn't struggle. I thought I saw a flicker of admiration in his eyes. "You have quick reflexes, Agent Bowers."

"Where's Kayla, Alexei?"

"As I said, she's safe."

I held him in place, locked eyes with him, didn't look away. "So where do we go from here?"

"You have the bone gun and a Glock, I have no weapons, so I suppose that's up to you."

That doesn't mean he's not dangerous, that he still couldn't take you out.

"I'm tempted to bring you in right now," I said.

"Would you risk a woman's life just to get an arrest?"

I didn't answer.

His gaze flicked to the bone gun, and I felt a sense of assurance that he wasn't going to chance moving abruptly and allowing it to engage. "I needed to know," he said. "That's why I went for it."

"The bone gun."

"Yes."

"You needed to know what?"

"If you were as good as my sources tell me."

"What sources?"

"I'm afraid I'm not at liberty to say."

"Of course you're not."

Somewhere down the hallway I heard footsteps approaching the room. I hoped we weren't going to be interrupted.

After a moment, I released his neck and stepped back, still jacked on adrenaline and ready, ready, ready to respond if he made another move.

Slipping the bone gun into my jacket pocket and gesturing toward the Glock, I said, "I'll drop you if you try anything like that again."

The steps in the hallway came closer.

Alexei rubbed his neck. "I believe you."

"Where are these people, the ones you say killed Ardis and—"

But before I could finish my sentence, the door behind me flew open and Jake Vanderveld burst into the room with his weapon drawn. "Don't move!" he shouted at Alexei. "Or you're a dead man!"

58

"Jake," I yelled, "lower your gun!"

He ignored me, hollered to Chekov, "Hands away from your body!"

"Easy, Jake," I said. "He's unarmed. Lower your weapon."

But Jake just leveled his gun at Alexei's chest. "Hands up!" He was wound way too tight. "Now!"

"Jake, stop." I stepped between him and Alexei so that now his gun was pointed at me. "Listen to me. He's got a woman. A hostage."

"What are you . . . ?" My words finally registered. "Where?"

"I don't know. Now lower your weapon."

Jake finally lowered his gun and yelled past me, at Alexei, "Where is she, you scumbag?"

More footsteps in the hall. Hurried.

"Who's that?" I asked him.

A small grin. "Backup."

No, no, no!

Two state troopers muscled their way through the doorway, guns drawn. "Step back!" the larger man yelled at me.

"I'm Agent Bowers. FBI!"

"He's with me," Jake said.

They accepted that and strode toward Alexei.

Jake spoke to me, "Who's this woman, Pat? Who are you talking about?"

I made the mistake of looking his direction. "Her name is Kayla Tat—"

But the two troopers must have recognized Alexei from the APB as the person who'd killed Deputy Ellory—a local man they undoubtably knew—because as soon as my back was turned, I heard the sound of someone being thrown to the floor. I spun and saw the two of them, expandable batons out, leaning over Alexei.

"No!" I rushed to stop them but they still managed to land half a dozen brutal blows and kick him twice in the face and abdomen before I was able to pull them off.

At last they both stood angrily by my side. Tense. Glowering.

"He was resisting arrest," the larger officer said to me. His badge read: H. Burlman. "You saw that, right?"

"You touch him again and your career is over." I turned to his partner. "Both of you. You understand?"

The air in the room went wire-tight.

Jake said nothing.

Alexei lay at my feet, his face bloodied, studying the two officers. He hadn't grunted or cried out in pain at all, and I imagined he was calculating what he might need to do to escape.

Yesterday by the riverbank I'd seen him single-handedly support Bryan Ellory's weight, and I guessed that if he'd wanted to, he could've made things a lot harder for these two state troopers just now.

Burlman pulled out his steel handcuffs, and I realized that at this point there was no defusing the situation without bringing Alexei in.

"I'll get him." I took the cuffs, then knelt beside Alexei and drew his hands back to restrain him. I whispered to him, "I didn't tell them. I came alone."

"I believe you," he said quietly.

"Alexei, where is Kayla?"

"Safe."

"And the people who killed Lizzie and Ardis?"

"Later."

"Is Donnie Pickron still alive?"

"I don't know."

And that was all.

Then the two troopers came forward and manhandled Alexei to his feet.

"Easy." I made it clear that I was not kidding around.

As they led him into the hall, I glared at Jake, then smacked the paneling. "What are you doing here? There's a woman's life at stake, and we might have had a lead on where the Pickron family killers are!"

"I didn't know that. You were keeping us in the dark. That's not right."

"In this case I didn't have a choice." I wanted to ask him how he'd found me, but I could deal with that later. "Alexei threatened to kill her if I told the team, and since he already murdered two people yesterday, I believed him."

Jake was quiet for a moment. "Is that how you knew Alexei'd killed the truck driver yesterday?"

"Yes, it's—"

Suddenly I realized something: Alexei didn't fight back when the troopers attacked him.

He tested you.

He tested you.

Maybe he was testing them.

I stepped away from Jake and caught up with the troopers in the hall, pulled aside Burlman, whose insignia told me he was a trooper first class, in this case the senior officer. "You need to really watch him."

"We got him." He didn't even look at me, and I could tell he was not attending to my words like he needed to.

I snapped my fingers in front of his face, directed his eyes toward me. "Listen to me. This man is dangerous like you've never seen. If you turn your back on him, he will not think twice about killing you."

"We got him," he said again.

"I'm not sure you're hearing what I'm saying."

"Like I said," Burlman replied, spittle hanging from his lip, "we got him."

The troopers waited impatiently for me to wave them on, and finally I did. They headed toward the elevator.

But almost immediately I began to have second thoughts.

Right now Alexei was our only link to finding Kayla Tatum and our best bet for tracking down the Pickron family killers.

She's safe; he told you she was safe.

Angela confirmed that Alexei doesn't kill women or children.

According to what he'd said, Alexei had been planning to search for the Pickron family killers with me, so if he was telling the truth that Kayla was safe and that he'd been willing to let her go, it seemed likely that he would've left her in a secure location where she could safely remain until he returned to free her or lead me to her.

But I also had to consider the grim possibility that he might've been lying—and that Kayla might already be dead. In that case, he would simply want to escape.

But then why would he have shown up here?

Why ask for your help?

I didn't care that Alexei was cuffed and without his bone gun. In the last eight months he'd killed and then eluded capture in countries all over the world, and, handcuffed though he was, if he wanted to take out these two men on the way to the station I doubted they would be able to stop him.

They were twenty meters from the elevator.

Don't leave him alone with them, Pat.

Jake had joined me in the hall. "I'm going with them," I told him. "We'll both go."

"No." I shook my head. "I need you to initiate the search for Kayla Tatum. I'll send one of the troopers back to help you." I took out Lien-hua's cell and emailed him Kayla's DMV photo. "Her car isn't here, so I'm wondering if Alexei stole someone else's vehicle, maybe left hers at that person's house. Follow up on every vehicle in the parking lot. Check all the trunks. Also, search this hospital room by room. Talk with Tait and get as many other officers as you can on this. Go to every house, every business within walking distance of the hospital. Work your way out from there."

"Okay."

"Fill in Natasha and Lien-hua. You know everything I do now."

The officers had made it to the elevator. "Hang on," I called to them. "I'll be right there." Then I said to Jake, "By the way, how'd you find me?"

"I tracked your location with the GPS from Lien-hua's phone."

Not bad.

"I didn't know there was a woman who was . . ." He sounded defeated. "I should've trusted you, Pat."

"It doesn't matter."

He was quiet.

"Shake it off. I need you on your A game. Are you good?"

A small nod. "Yeah."

"All right." I left for the elevator. "Get started looking for Kayla. I'm going to see what I can find out from Chekov."

59

After sending the lower-ranking trooper inside to assist Jake, I joined Burlman and Alexei beside his cruiser.

The rental car that Jake and I were using this week sat near Amber's snowmobile. I was surprised Jake had been able to navigate the drifted road in front of the motel, but if a snowplow had arrived with food, the timing would've just barely worked out for him to arrive when he did.

Burlman opened the door to the backseat, but as he grabbed Alexei's collar to shove him in, I noticed something and said, "Wait!"

I felt my left pocket.

Empty.

Unbelievable.

Going to Alexei, I patted him down again and found the bone gun concealed along the back waistline of his jeans, a narrow, barely noticeable bulge hidden by his belt.

I retrieved it. "It was when I cuffed you, wasn't it? I leaned a little too close?"

"You really are good, Agent Bowers."

So was he.

"Get in."

After starting the cruiser, Burlman said to Alexei, "Bryan Ellory was a friend of mine."

"I'm sorry for your loss."

Burlman's jaw tensed. "I'm gonna kill you, you son of a—"

"No, you're not," I corrected him. Then I faced Alexei, looking at him behind the police cage partition. It bothered me a little that I was about to ask him for his motive, but at the moment I was willing to try anything to get him talking. "I know you don't want to hurt Kayla, that she's your leverage for finding the other people. But why? What's at stake here, Alexei?"

"This isn't the time to talk."

As Burlman pulled onto the road, he eyed Alexei in the rearview mirror. "You'll have plenty of time to talk soon enough."

Alexei licked at some of the blood on his swollen lip.

Burlman grinned. "Yeah, I know you felt that one. Give me five minutes alone with you and you'll never forget it."

"I have no doubt," Alexei replied, his voice even. Measured.

"No more threats," I told Burlman unambiguously. I didn't even want to think about what Alexei Chekov could do to this guy if I left them alone for five minutes. "I won't tell you again."

He clenched the steering wheel. "He resisted back there."

All three of us knew that wasn't the case, but arguing right now wasn't going to serve any useful purpose. I called Lien-hua to get an update. She told me Jake had already contacted her and brought her up to speed about Alexei and Kayla.

"Windwalker just got here with the trail groomer." She sounded exasperated at the long wait. "We're on our way out the door now. You wanted me to check on Donnie—he's worked at the sawmill since 2004, when the base closed. He left work on Thursday at lunchtime, no phone calls to him that morning before he did; that's about all we know. I need to go. I'll call you if I find anything at the ELF site."

"Talk to you soon," I said.

After she hung up, I tilted the rearview mirror so I could keep an eye on Alexei. And I watched him watch me as Burlman maneuvered us through the storm toward the sheriff's department.

60

Tessa sighed.

A few minutes ago the sports wrap-up show had ended and a reality show about some people who investigated supposedly haunted libraries had come on.

How thrilling.

As the library program began, Sean had left with Lien-hua and this big Native American guy on a snowmobile-trail-groomer thing.

Amber was the one who'd suggested that Sean go along. "There's nothing for you to do here right now anyway," she'd told him. "And this'll give me and Tessa a chance to get to know each other. A little girl time. Besides, you know those trails out there better than anyone. It might be a good way for you to help out."

Lien-hua hadn't seemed too excited about the idea, but when Sean assured her that he did know the area and could help with whatever it was she was looking for, she finally gave in.

Before they left, Lien-hua mentioned to Tessa that she was staying at the motel with this other agent named Farraday. "But"—she handed Tessa a keycard—"if you need some privacy, here's the key to Patrick's room. He's in 106. I'm sure he wouldn't mind if you hung out in there."

Tessa knew things were pretty serious between the two of them; she even had the impression Patrick might be thinking about proposing. But she was a little surprised Lien-hua had a key to his room. She might need to have a little talk with this stepfather of hers.

Then they left.

Everything was sort of in limbo until they got back, or at least until Patrick did.

But it'd already been nearly two hours since he took off on the snowmobile, right after promising that he was gonna come back as soon as he could. Sure, Tessa knew he had a job to do, but still, she wished he would have at least touched base, sent her a text, something. A bunch of times she'd thought about calling or texting to see where he was, but then decided she didn't want to seem too needy or puerile.

Now she was alone with Amber in the motel room, and despite the time of day, she found herself eyeing the bed. Even after sleeping in until 11:00, for some reason she was already feeling drowsy.

A burst of ominous music interrupted her thoughts, and Tessa went back to staring unemotionally at the group of ghost hunters stalking through the reference section of a small county library in Connecticut.

A couple of minutes later the show cut to commercial, and Amber asked, "Did you ever play Guess the Plot?"

"What's that?"

"Well." She repositioned herself on the bed so she was sitting cross-legged. "We surf to a random show, give it thirty seconds, and see if we can guess the plot."

Oh joy.

"It's the opposite of watching a movie trailer from a Nicolas Cage flick," Amber explained. "You know, when there's no good reason to watch the film."

Tessa looked at her quizzically.

"With his trailers, you get the whole plot in thirty seconds. Here we guess it." A smile. "Wanna try?"

Um . . .

C'mon. She's just trying to be nice.

Tessa shrugged. "Sure."

Amber punched in channel 142, and a news show came on saying that the secretary of state's meetings in Tehran were moving forward despite the "strained diplomatic relations between the two nations."

She had to click up through three channels of commercials before she finally found a movie.

The scene: a hip, young guy in a suit speaking to a bunch of government officials seated around a large conference table. Within a couple of seconds it was clear that this person was supposed to be from another planet.

"So, okay," Amber said. "Aliens are testing the human race to see if we can learn to stop going to war with each other, and if we don't pass the test, they'll be forced to blow up our planet."

"Kill the people off before they can kill off each other," Tessa observed. "A perfectly natural response from peace-loving aliens."

"Nice." Amber handed her the remote. "You try."

After flipping through a few more channels, Tessa came to a scene of two bishops whispering to each other in a shadow-enshrouded Vatican hallway. Shifty eyes. Foreboding music. The whole nine.

"Okay," she said. "There's an Ancient Deleterious Manuscript that's been hidden in the Vatican archives For Thousands of Years and there's A Secret Organization That's Sworn To Protect It At All Costs so that the Church Can Retain Its Power."

"Wow. That's never been done before. How clever."

Tessa was beginning to like this woman.

Amber eyed her. "By the way, deleterious?"

"It means detrimental, injurious, nocuous."

"I figured something like that. I was just . . . surprised by your vocabulary. It's impressive."

Tessa was a little embarrassed. "Sorry, sometimes stuff just slips out."

Now she thinks you were trying to show off!

"No need to apologize. I like it."

They did a few more shows—a buddy cop movie, a zombie flick, and a romantic comedy that they actually ended up watching for a few minutes and saw that it really was about a guy who spent too much time at the office and ends up falling for a klutzy cat-owning librarian lady who *astonishingly* becomes a complete babe when she takes off her glasses and lets her hair down. What a plot twist that was.

Groundbreaking cinema this afternoon.

Finally, Amber shut off the TV and said, "So when you're not watching bad movies, what do you like to do?"

"I read. Mostly. Listen to music. Patrick's into all this outdoor stuff, like rock climbing and rafting and everything, but that's not really my thing."

"Those Bowers boys do like the outdoors."

"Yeah."

"So what do you like to read?" Amber sized her up. "I'm thinking fantasy, right?"

"More horror, actually. Gothic stuff. Poe, like that. Some of the French realists: Guy de Maupassant, Flaubert, Zola, you know. Poetry sometimes. I never got into fantasy. The authors just aren't creative enough."

A pause. "Fantasy writers aren't creative enough?"

"Yeah, I'm like, I get it, but could you please come up with a better way of creating your character names? Just add 'or,' 'en,' or 'ick' to any name and you get a fantasy novel name. Choose whichever one you prefer. I'd be probably be Tessaor. You'd be Amberen."

"Or Amberick. Hmm. Yeah. Or Amberor."

"See?"

"Patrickick doesn't quite flow," she said, "but Patricken works. Patrickor's not too bad. Nice."

"Yeah. And your husband would be Seanor or Seanen."

"Or Seanick."

"It doesn't quite work with everyone, though," Tessa admitted. "Patrick has this guy at the Bureau that he's friends with—Ralph Hawkins."

"So Ralphor, Ralphen—"

"Or Ralphick."

Amber grimaced. "Yeah, not as good as Patrick's."

"Or Sean's."

"Right."

For a moment the conversation pooled into silence, but it was more friendly than awkward.

"So, you're a pharmacist?" Tessa asked her, but it was one of those conversational pseudo-questions because she already knew the answer.

"Yes."

"Cool."

More silence.

Hmm. An idea.

"So then, if I had a prescription, you could fill it?" Another blatantly pseudo-question.

"You're from out of state so I'd need a paper script, but sure. Is there one you need?"

"I take these pills to help me sleep. I forgot 'em in Minneapolis."

"Well, do you have the prescription with you?"

"Uh-uh. It's in Denver."

"Well," Amber said reflectively, "I guess I could call your doctor, he could fax me your prescription, but it's a Saturday. Maybe your regular pharmacy would have a copy on file?"

Tessa wasn't excited about the idea of telling her that her doctor was a psychiatrist or that Patrick didn't know about the shrink or the pills. "Yeah, um, we'll see. Maybe I'll be okay without 'em."

Silence again, longer this time.

Finally, Amber said, "Tessa, how are you doing since your dad's death?"

Wow. That was a leap.

"Um . . ."

"I'm sorry if that's too personal, I was just . . ."

"No. It's okay," Tessa replied. She tried to think of what to say. "It was hard, you know, but it seems like it's getting better. With my mom it was worse. I was into this pretty intense self-inflicting stuff for a while. You know, cutting, that sort of thing." She paused. "This friend of mine, Anisette, she started in with bulimia after her parents divorced. That was just harsh. I'm glad I never ended up going there."

A brief pause. "I've been praying for you."

Her comment about prayer and the previous exchange about meds made Tessa think of her last session with the shrink—when he'd asked her if she thought God wanted her to forgive herself.

"So you pray a lot, then?"

"Probably not as much as I should."

"But you believe in God? Forgiveness? That sort of thing?"

"Yes."

"So did my mom."

Tessa remembered that after her mom was diagnosed with breast cancer, even though she seemed to take the news relatively well, Tessa had been devastated. Her mom had told her more than once that she needed to learn to believe in grace as much as she did in pain, in forgiveness as much as she did in shame.

Just ask her.

"So do you ever think about what it means to forgive yourself?"

"To forgive myself?"

"Yeah."

Amber considered the question for a long time. "Honestly, that sounds kind of arrogant to me."

"How is it arrogant?"

"Well, that someone could claim to have the power to cancel the debt that they owe God."

Tessa tried to let that sink in. She remembered her little object lesson with the glass coffee table in the shrink's office and understood where Amber was coming from with the debt idea but hadn't exactly thought of it in any kind of religious terms before.

"When you ask someone to forgive you," Amber said, "you're really asking the other person to sacrifice for the benefit of the relationship."

Duh. If you would've shattered the doctor's end table and he forgave you, he would've been the one to pay for it, the one to sacrifice.

"But what if you wrong yourself?" Tessa retorted. "I mean, can't you—oh, I get it. We're accountable to someone else besides ourselves. To God."

Amber said nothing, and it looked to Tessa like she was deep in thought.

Regardless of the theological ramifications, the idea that this whole forgiving yourself deal was an act of arrogance seemed kind of weird, and Tessa wasn't sure she bought it.

She stood. "You know, I'm gonna go to Patrick's room. Maybe lie down."

"You're welcome to stay in here."

"That's okay, I'll see you in a little bit. Hey, it was cool, though. Thanks for hanging out."

"Any time."

Patrick's motel room looked pretty much like Tessa expected— a clutter of papers on the desk, clothes strewn across the floor, sweaty workout stuff hanging up in the bathroom. Disgusting. A couple buckets of water on the floor—no idea what those were for. A brand-new camo jacket flung on the chair. Wow. How very Wisconsin of him.

She pulled the shades shut, grabbed the extra blanket from the closet, flopped onto the bed. Closed her eyes.

And thought of arrogance.

Was it really an act of arrogance to be haunted by guilt? Or was it an act of humility, admitting that you weren't living up to the standards you'd set for yourself?

Two ways to look at it.

Guess the plot, huh?

Yeah, well, she really didn't have any idea where this one was heading.

61

Sheriff Tait was waiting for us outside the building when we arrived.

He looked about sixty, was a little too round, but still had a formidable appearance. His face was chiseled with creases and shadows, and as we approached he snuffed out a cigarette against the wall and flicked the butt into the snow.

An observation of Tessa's came to mind: *Smoking is suicide. It just takes longer than a gun*, but I kept it to myself.

Alexei remained silent while he was processed and fingerprinted and then led to a cell. "You get one phone call," Burlman taunted. "You better make it a good one."

"I'll wait on that for now." He was looking at me.

I tried to think what to do.

How are you going to find Kayla without his help?

Once Alexei was out of earshot, I said to Tait, "I want two people watching his cell at all times. Rotate them in and out."

"No good. We're short on staff with this storm, with the search for Kayla, with everything."

"This man is an escape risk, Sheriff, and we cannot let him get away."

"We're stretched thin here, Agent Bowers, you know that."

"I'm not sure the cells here will hold him."

He eyed the wall beside me. "I can give you one officer. That's it."

"At all times then. But not Burlman. And Chekov stays cuffed, even in the cell."

"Sure. Okay." He tapped the edge of his lip with his tongue. "This guy, he killed my deputy."

"I know this is easier said than done, but you need to set that aside for right now. We just have to make sure Chekov doesn't slip out of here."

"Oh, he won't." His voice was filled with acid, and I had a feeling I knew what he was thinking.

"Sheriff Tait, two state troopers already beat him with their batons."

"Yeah, I heard. Kicked the living—" He caught himself, perhaps concerned he shouldn't be defending police brutality by cussing to an FBI agent. "He was resisting arrest."

"I know you don't buy that." I wasn't going to play this game. "I'll be filing a report dealing with their actions later. For now, Alexei stays in his cell, and no one goes in there with him. Mistreating him in any way isn't going to encourage him to give up anything on Kayla's location—or help us get a conviction against him for Ellory's murder."

A pause. "You gonna interrogate him, then?"

"I am."

Although I was planning to talk with Alexei, I honestly couldn't see him giving anything up unless he decided it was in his best interest—and even striking some sort of deal wouldn't make any substantial difference in the charges that were going to be brought against him.

I looked around.

In the next room over, the 911 dispatch call board was staffed by a bleary-eyed overweight man in his thirties. Some storage rooms, a few offices, two holding cells, restrooms, and a small conference room rounded out the place. The building wasn't equipped with anything close to a secure interrogation room, and I figured Alexei would do whatever it took to escape and would likely somehow use the transfer to any other room to his advantage, so I decided to leave him in the cell when I spoke with him.

Sheriff Tait was quiet for a moment. "So did he tell you why he killed the Pickrons? What he did with Donnie?"

"I don't believe he killed the Pickrons."

"Why's that?"

"The evidence points in another direction."

"Oh, I get it." His tone had turned snide. "Keeping an open mind, huh?"

"Would you suggest we do the opposite?"

"'Course not. It's just . . . what Burlman told me before he headed to the hospital, and Chekov . . . well, there are two sides to every story, Dr. Bowers."

"Yes. But there's only one truth."

And sometimes neither of the two sides is telling it.

He took a somewhat strained breath. "I'll make sure nothing happens to him."

Behind him I saw Alexei sitting placidly on his cot, examining the walls of his cell, his cuffed hands resting on his lap. I wished I could climb inside his head, unravel his thoughts, and study them one by one, not just to find out what he was pondering at the moment but to find out where Kayla was, to discover if she really was okay.

I checked Alexei's spring-loaded bone injection gun into evidence, then pulled over a chair and took a seat beside his cell.

62

Solstice drew her skis to a stop at the edge of the woods and scanned the barren field stretching before her.

Though not yet dusk, with the thick cloud cover, daylight was already beginning to fade. A bitter wind shrieked around her.

She'd heard the rolling whine of a motor as she approached the field, and now, at last, saw a snowmobile trail groomer about a quarter mile away. She had no idea how long it had been in the area, but it was pressing forward along one of the trails that skirted directly around the old ELF site.

Taking a trail groomer out in weather like this wouldn't be entirely unheard of, but the all-too-convenient fact that someone was doing it here, today, disturbed her.

At the moment, she and her team were still hidden in the forest, as well as dressed in Marine Corps Disruptive Overwhite snow camouflage so they wouldn't be visible to the people in the trail groomer, and she took a moment to orient herself and see if there might have been more than one machine out.

To her left, two wide swathes of forest were missing, lonely for the ELF lines that had been removed back in 2004. A few intermittent scraggly grass blades fingered through the snow, breaking up the otherwise pristine snowscape. Only one structure was visible: a windowless thirty-foot-tall sheet-metal maintenance building with six reinforced sliding garage doors.

That was her destination.

No other trail groomers or snowmobiles were visible.

Solstice knew that the forest rangers occasionally used the building to store old vehicles and trail upkeep equipment, but, though the rangers wouldn't have been privy to it, that wasn't the only purpose the building served.

Three power lines stretched from a telephone pole to the top of the building. One provided electricity to the building, another was the now-useless phone landline, the third served as the sat comm antennae for the base.

The trail groomer turned south, toward Solstice's team.

She borrowed Tempest's semiautomatic AR-15 and sighted through the scope. It took a few moments for her to get it dialed in, but at last she was able to identify three people in the cab. An Asian woman, a Native American man, and a male Cauca—

Wait.

She knew that Asian lady from a previous encounter, the same one in which she'd met Agent Bowers last year. Jiang. She was an FBI agent as well.

Solstice took a moment to let things sink in.

Agent Bowers is here. So is Jiang.

She peered through the scope again.

Solstice couldn't identify the two men with Jiang. One might be a civilian operator, but FBI agents usually work in teams so she went with the most likely assumption that at least one of them was a federal agent as well.

Somehow the FBI knew.

But why only send three or four agents? If they really had intel about what she was up to, they would have certainly sent a larger team—at least a second trail groomer.

They're just on a fishing expedition.

Immediately, she thought of Chekov. The Bureau had to be getting their information from somewhere, and he was the most likely link.

Perhaps she hadn't made the right choice in allowing him to live after all.

The only way she was going to get her money or see Terry again was if the mission was successful. This was not the time to make a misstep.

She considered aggressive action, but if these three went missing, it would only draw more attention to the site at a delicate time in her operation. Definitely not something she needed.

Option one: press forward, get her team to the building, deal decisively with the people in the trail groomer.

Option two: retreat to a safe location, monitor the situation, and move in as soon as night fell. Only respond with force if necessary.

Waiting it out in the cold wouldn't be ideal, but it would be manageable.

So, option two.

Solstice spoke into her mic, ordered everyone over the ridge to the west: "There's an old hiker's shelter. We'll wait there until they're gone."

"What about the MA patrol routes?" Cane asked through her earpiece. "The timing?"

"We still have forty minutes or so. If these people aren't gone by then, we'll put 'em down and make our move on the base."

The team skied over the ridge, and as they did the wind pursued them, sending snow quickly scurrying across their path, obscuring their tracks.

Forty minutes max.

Then, move on the base.

63

Alexei Chekov still hadn't told me anything about Kayla Tatum's location.

From my regular updates with Tait, I knew we still had no idea where she was. Jake and the officer with him had found no sign of Kayla at the hospital or in any of the surrounding homes. However, one of the cars in the hospital parking lot belonged to a nurse who they found tied up in her basement. Kayla's car was in the woman's garage, so at least we knew how Alexei had gotten to the hospital.

But that was about all we had.

Alexei still hadn't asked for a lawyer or made a phone call.

Over the years I've learned that during interrogations the best thing is usually just to get people talking, really about anything, and then move to the specific matter at hand. And almost always, the best way to get them to open up is to find out what they're interested in and then simply ask them about it.

So, over the last half hour, hoping to spark Alexei's interest, I'd tried mentioning some of the locations where he'd done his work. It hadn't been especially fruitful, and now, in my search for interests and commonalities, I said, "I heard that during the Cold War, Russians had a saying that the Kremlin was the tallest building in the world."

"Because you could see Siberia from the basement," he said, quoting the rest of the axiom. He gave me a wry smile. "Yes. Thankfully, I never had that experience."

I remembered his wife had been murdered last spring. "I lost my wife about two years ago," I said. "Breast cancer."

He told me a little about Tatiana, about arguing with her the day she was murdered and how he had regretted it ever since. After a moment he said, "I have someone to take out my vengeance on; you have only God to blame."

His words caught me a little off guard. I'd done just what he said for a long time and wasn't sure how to respond to his comment.

The conversation broke off, and I tried something a little less personal. "One of my friends in the US Air Force used to test our experimental planes. The new designs."

Alexei looked at me inquisitively. "Do you remember which planes he flew?"

"He wasn't allowed to tell me. But he mentioned something about aerostatic wing design."

"Active *aeroelastic* wing," Alexei corrected me. "Yes, for smoother roll maneuvering. Which years was he flying?"

"2006 to 2010."

"Probably the Boeing X-53. NASA worked with your Air Force and private contractors on that one."

"Did Russia have active aeroelastic wing planes too?"

He shook his head. "A few similar designs, but nothing as advanced." Then, slowly, he began to open up, telling me about some of the planes he'd flown: the Su-47 Berkut, a forward swept-wing supersonic jet. "The lift to drag ratio is higher," he explained. "It's more maneuverable and doesn't require as long of a runway for takeoff and landing." The MiG 1.44, which actually never ended up being developed, the Beriev A-60: "They're comparable to your Boeing YAL-1, equipped with megawatt-class chemical oxygen iodine lasers to shoot down missiles, other planes, potentially satellites."

That sounded like science fiction to me. "A laser-shooting plane that takes out satellites?"

"The laser heats the outer casing, causes structural failure. Given the right conditions, it can be accomplished from over five hundred kilometers away."

I remembered hearing about China shooting down one of its satellites a few years ago. "Does China have planes like this too?"

"It's likely, although it hasn't been confirmed. They're a bit more clandestine about their experimental aircraft than America is." He looked past me into the corner of the room. "My favorite plane was perhaps the Sukhoi PAK FA. It can cruise at over forty-five-thousand feet at speeds of over Mach 2. Very enjoyable to fly. I was in on the early development."

Then he gave a nostalgic sigh and shook his head. "Our two countries. Your president slashes NASA's budget in order to buy car companies and socialize your health care; mine sells our military secrets to Iran for money to build caviar-producing fish farms. America turns Marxist, Russia dabbles in capitalism. What has happened to us in the last thirty years?"

As interesting as all of this was, I was more concerned with getting him to feel at ease enough with me to share something actionable regarding Kayla.

Move to the case, Pat. Press him a bit.

"Earlier today," I said, "you were anxious to go look for the people who killed the Pickrons. What's changed? Do you think they left the area?"

He didn't answer me.

I didn't like how he was carefully appraising me, and I took my turn to look him over once again. He wore boots, jeans, a neatly pressed oxford, bloodied somewhat from when he was attacked. When Burlman processed him, he'd taken his belt so that he wouldn't have a way to kill himself—something that in this case I didn't think was very likely.

Alexei certainly didn't look threatening.

Looks can be deceiving.

I asked him one last time about Kayla, and when he didn't answer, I thought, *Enough of this. You need to get to your notes, find a way to locate her.*

My computer was back at the motel and so were Tessa and Natasha. In addition, Lien-hua would be returning there after searching the site of the old ELF station. Honestly, sitting here talking with Alexei was getting us nowhere.

"We'll talk more later." I rose. "Or I need you to tell me something specific related to Kayla's whereabouts now."

"Eco-Tech hasn't done what they came here to do, or else you would've heard about it and asked me about that instead of Kayla."

"And what did they come to do?"

"I'm not certain."

Getting very irritated now. "Alexei, I don't like these games. If you have something to tell me, tell me. Otherwise I'm leaving to find Kayla."

"You won't find her unless I inform you where she is."

I felt a surge of anger, partly because I believed him, but I tried not to telegraph my feelings. I waited for him to elaborate. When he didn't, I turned toward the door, then heard him say, "In 2009, Canadian scientists found that the Chinese had hacked into 1,300 computers at embassies around the world."

Now he had my attention. I faced him one last time.

"The malware they used would turn on the computer's camera and microphone without letting the user know that they were on, and then it would send the audio and video feeds back to China. The machines had been sending sensitive data back to China for twenty-two months before the researchers uncovered it."

"So that's how you did it?"

"Yes."

I held out Lien-hua's cell phone. "Both the mic and the camera?"

"Yes."

That means he had a computer or phone somewhere in the area, a way to receive and view the signal that was sent during the briefing at the motel.

I stepped closer to the bars. "How did you get my email address?"

"I have people that I know."

Another answer that didn't answer anything.

I could sense that this interchange was just becoming more and more of a power play to him.

"If you make your phone call in the next half hour," I said, "use

Agent Jiang's number. Otherwise, call my cell. Do you need the number?"

"No, I've got it."

"I thought you might." I headed for the door. "Good night, Alexei."

"I'll call you on my way out," he said.

His words gave me pause. After passing Burlman in the hall on his way to the dispatch room, I found Tait at his desk. "Have your officers keep a close eye on him."

"We will. He's not going anywhere."

"And I don't want Burlman watching him."

Silence. "Gotcha."

I had no idea when I would get a chance to go out to the river to retrieve my SIG from the snowbank, so before leaving the sheriff's department I signed out a Glock from the gun vault. I also stocked up on a few extra magazines for the gun, some plastic cuffs and requisitioned a GPS ankle bracelet. I had a feeling I might be needing them later in the evening.

Procuring one of the cruisers, I left the sheriff's department to return to the motel to get to my computer, regroup with my team, and evaluate what to do next.

Tessa's ringing phone woke her up. Lien-hua's ring tone.

She sat up and fished out her cell. "Hey."

"It's me. Patrick."

"Huh?" It took her a moment to shake the sleep from her head. "Where are you?"

"On my way back over there. Sorry things were rocky between us when I left earlier this afternoon. You doing all right?"

"Yeah." She held back a residual nap-yawn. "Did you find what you were looking for?"

"No." A pause. "I'll see you in a little bit, all right?"

"Sure."

The brief call ended, and she figured she'd go back to Amber's room to hang out until Patrick arrived. As she was straightening the bedsheets she noticed a crumpled-up sheet of paper next to the trash can beside the desk.

No surprise there—the room was pretty much a mess.

But the way the page was balled up allowed the girlish handwriting to be visible even from where Tessa stood.

Considering the fact that Agent Jiang had a key to Patrick's room, Tessa thought at first that the note was probably from her, maybe a love note? *But then why would he be throwing it away?*

No, Tessa had seen Agent Jiang's notes to Patrick lots of times, and even from where she stood she could tell this wasn't Lien-hua's handwriting.

Whatever. Don't worry about it. Just go see what's up with Amber.

She was halfway to the door when it struck her that while they were making up fantasy names, Amber kept mentioning Patrick first, instead of her husband.

Huh.

Naw. It couldn't be.

They have some sort of history together.

Tessa let her eyes linger on the note.

She picked it up.

Gazed at it.

At last, she dropped it in the trash can and went for the door.

But as she was about to leave the room, her curiosity got the best of her. She returned, snatched up the note, flattened it out on her hand. And read what it said.

64

Tessa stared incredulously at the words.

No way.

Amber was leaving Sean? And she came over to tell Patrick first? To ask a guy who barely knew his brother the best way to break the news to him?

Yeah, right.

Obviously, based on what Amber had written, something had happened between her and Patrick last night that might hurt Patrick's relationship with Lien-hua.

That was unbelievable, that was seriously—

Is Patrick cheating on Lien-hua with Amber?

No, that didn't work. Not at all.

From what the note said, Amber was the one apologizing, and whatever had happened seemed to have been her fault.

Besides, Tessa refused to believe that Patrick would mess around with his brother's wife. Not only was he in a serious relationship already, she couldn't imagine him treating his brother—or any guy—like that.

But there was something between Patrick and Amber, wasn't there? Back in the past, before Amber and Sean got married?

And now she was leaving Sean?

Tessa flumped onto the bed.

This was for Patrick's eyes only. You were never supposed to see this.

She debated what to do. If she said anything to anyone—Sean, Amber, Patrick—it would probably only make things worse.

If you bring it up with Amber, she'll totally assume Patrick told you—which would not be cool.

And anyway, this wasn't really any of her business; whatever issues Sean and Amber were having, they needed to work them out on their own.

However, this also had to do with her dad, and, if she was reading things right about him and Lien-hua, her potential stepmom.

She stared at the note.

But you could at least feel things out, right? Amber brought it up to Patrick. Who's to say she won't bring it up to you too?

Yeah, that might work. Just feel things out.

But be subtle.

Tessa scrunched up the note.

Subtle. She could do subtle.

She tossed it into the trash can.

Then left to go find Amber.

For a little girl time.

I was in the cruiser en route to the motel.

The day was growing pale, slipping into night.

Both the sheriff's department and state patrol had their hands full with the electrical outages from the storm and stranded civilians who hadn't stayed off the roads, not to mention the search for Kayla and Donnie and the added security for Alexei. We could definitely use some more eyes up here.

I punched in SWAT Team Leader Antón Torres's number, and he picked up.

"Pat, good to hear your voice."

"Are you guys still in Merrill?"

"Yeah." He sounded irritated. "We're not making a lot of progress down here, though. Did you get word about the news footage? The press clippings?"

"Yes, but I haven't had a chance to review them yet."

"Yeah, well, the Evidence Response Team found some videos hidden in the trailer. We've got three DVDs recording the murders from the last six months, and get this: six VHS cassettes' worth of footage of the crimes fourteen years ago. The ERT's digitizing them now. I'll have 'em send you the files as soon as they're done."

"So, only videos of the crimes with Basque?"

"Yeah. Looks like it."

I thought again of the theory that Lien-hua and I had been probing that someone other than Reiser was the killer and had dabbled with the DNA evidence to make it look like Reiser was our man. The tapes and DVDs could have easily been planted in his trailer before we arrived.

Who had access to Basque's case files? Me. Jake. Ralph, who originally helped me track him down. Torres, who'd needed to prep his men for the mission in the trailer park. A number of lawyers, detectives, and agents over the year. Lien-hua—

"What are you thinking?" Antón asked me.

"I'm wondering if Reiser was set up, if he wasn't really Basque's partner at all. You arrived in Wisconsin before I did. Did your team have any other clues that might have led to someone other than Reiser?"

"No. Nothing."

"Listen, Antón, if you and your team aren't needed down there, I've got a job for you up here."

"What's that?"

"We've got two missing persons: Donnie Pickron—"

"The guy whose family was killed?"

"Yes, but it doesn't look like he's the shooter. We also have a missing woman named Kayla Tatum. Alexei Chekov is in custody."

"Chekov?"

"A cleaner. A freelancer. Local law enforcement is stretched thin, and between you and me, I don't trust them to contain Chekov."

"I should be able to come, but I'll have to clear it with the director."

"Call her. Put it into play and let me know."

"The roads are a mess, though. It might take us awhile to get there. Everything's closed down tight around here, and the snow's still coming down."

"Do what you can. I could really use your help."

A small pause. "So, did you ask her yet?"

"Who?"

"Lien-hua. I heard she's up there."

If nothing else, he was persistent. "Antón, the timing hasn't been quite right for popping a question like that."

"I'm telling you, Pat, the future's uncertain. You never know what might happen. You need to seize the day."

"I'll see you tonight."

"I'll be there. Bro."

While we'd been speaking, the day had continued to die. Now as I hung up, I realized that in their search for anything suspicious at the old ELF site, Lien-hua, Sean, and their driver no longer had daylight on their side.

65

Amber was gazing in the mirror above the sink, lightly touching up her lipstick. For the past few minutes, Tessa had done her best with the small-talk-understated-probing-question thing but hadn't really found out anything. She was anxious to get to the point, so finally she said, "So you and Patrick first met, when?"

"Back when Sean and I were engaged. A little over five years ago."

Feel her out, Tessa. Don't, like, accuse her of anything, just try to see what might have been going on. Subtle, remember?

"And you, what? You hit it off?"

Amber paused. Looked into the mirror not at herself but at the reflection of Tessa sitting on the bed behind her. "I guess you could put it like that."

"How would you put it?"

"How would I put it?"

"Yeah. You struck up a friendship? Had a lot in common? There was a good vibe going on?"

So, okay, screw subtle.

Amber seemed to be debating whether or not to reply. Finally, she turned and faced her. "What would you like to know, Tessa?" The words sounded flat and steely. A tone Amber had not used with her before.

"Are you leaving your husband to be with my dad?"

Almost instantly, Amber flushed, as if she'd just been caught red-handed shoplifting or lying to a friend. "You read the note."

Tessa nodded. "Well?"

"Patrick has nothing to do with why I'm leaving Sean."

Tessa wasn't sure she believed her. "Whatever happened between you and Patrick? Did you guys . . . well . . . you know?"

She half-expected Amber to evade the question or tell her in no uncertain terms that it really wasn't any of her business, but instead she said, "It's not what you think. It was . . . Mostly we just talked." Amber slowly put her makeup back in her purse. "There's nothing going on between us. Between me and Pat. You need to know that."

"What about when my mom was alive?"

"No," Amber said unequivocally. "Nothing. I swear. Pat and I didn't even speak for almost three years."

"Is this why you didn't come to the wedding?"

"I was in the hospital."

Oh yeah, now she remembered, Patrick had told her. "Food poisoning."

A long, unbalanced silence. "It wasn't food poisoning, Tessa. It wasn't that kind of hospital."

The depression meds?

"Oh."

"I was ashamed, so Sean and I never told Pat. Believe me, there's nothing going on between me and your father."

Tessa wanted to believe her, in a sense did believe her, but felt like she needed to hear Patrick's side of the story before she made up her mind about any of this.

"Okay." Tessa stood. "I think I'm gonna go wait for him in the lobby."

As Tessa passed her, Amber touched her arm gently. "I'm telling you the truth." Tessa could hear a tiny tremble of pain in Amber's voice, an unsettling fragility.

She's been dealing with this for a long time. It's not just seeing Patrick again.

"Okay." Tessa managed a half smile.

"Don't say anything to anyone, Tessa. Please. Especially to Sean. I'm the one who has to tell him."

Yes, you are.

"Okay."

Solstice watched the trail groomer's headlights disappear into the tenebrous, snowy night, turning north along the trail.

Since she and her team had arrived in the field, the trail groomer had systematically covered each of the main trails surrounding the old ELF site. Agent Jiang had stepped out a few times to look around, but that was all. Eventually, as the day grew dim and then gave way to night, they must have decided there was nothing here to see.

Now the forest was nearly pitch black.

After the trail groomer left, Solstice waited a few minutes to make sure they weren't coming back, then, with everyone using headlamps to find their way through the storm, she led her people to the maintenance building.

They buried their skis and poles in the snow, she picked the lock, everyone entered, and she snapped on the lights. Three lines of high fluorescents illuminated the vast, windowless building. She heard the sheet metal roof crinkle uncomfortably above her in the wind.

The air was thick with the smell of motor oil, grease, and dust.

A few chainsaws hung on the wall beside her, a cluttered tool bench lay just past them. Three forest service signs in need of repair leaned languidly against the wall in the southwest corner of the room.

The maintenance building had a concrete, oil-stained floor checkered with thick seams in large, neat rectangles, sectioned off almost like sidewalk partitions. An old John Deere tractor sat at the far end of the building. Beside it, a brown rusted Toyota sedan rested on cement blocks.

All in all, the building looked like someone's vision of how a maintenance building was supposed to look.

A caricature of the real thing.

It's a set.

Solstice studied the uniform grid of cracks in the concrete, each rectangular section about four feet wide and six feet long.

Typhoon and Eclipse grabbed their slings and cable cutters and headed outside. Solstice didn't expect that it would take them more than a few minutes to ascend the telephone pole and take out the power lines stretching to the building, but she ordered Tempest to cover them. "In case the Feds decide to come back and have another look around."

He swung his AR-15 assault rifle into his hands. "Absolutely."

As far as the rest of the crew, Cane stood guard beside Donnie, whom they'd forced to ski over here but now stood handcuffed near the disabled sedan. Cyclone and Gale were bent over the radio jamming device, checking the settings. Squall and Cirrus were carefully removing their backpacks that contained the triacetone triperoxide canisters and were placing the packs gently on the concrete. Equator, the rotund hacker, was looking vacantly around the room, awaiting further instructions.

"Everyone get ready," Solstice said into her headset mic so that the three people outside would hear her as well. "We move in five minutes."

66

I arrived at the Moonbeam Motel.

Just a few minutes ago Torres had called to let me know that Margaret was on board with the SWAT team coming up to help out. He and his men were just finishing packing and would be on their way shortly.

When I entered the lobby I saw Tessa waiting for me, half scoping out the guy behind the desk, half watching the front door. When she saw me, she made her way toward me, but the lobby was packed with ten people I hadn't seen before, not even when we searched the motel room by room. Two men were pleading with the clerk, trying to finagle a room. A cluster of young children clung to the pant legs of their mothers or moped around the lobby looking as exhausted and beleaguered as the adults did.

Tessa circumnavigated the crowd. "What's up?" she said.

"How are you?"

"Hungry."

One of the men at the counter pulled out his wallet. "We can all share one room," he offered. "And we'll pay you for two." But the dark-haired guy who'd caught Tessa's eye just shook his head apologetically. "There's nothing available. I'm sorry."

I nodded toward them. "What's the story here?"

"They were stranded in the storm, I guess. Agent Jiang said she wanted to talk to you about that. She just got back a little bit ago." Tessa looked at me expectantly. "Mostly I've been hanging out with Amber."

"So you two got a chance to get to know each other?"

"We seemed to hit it off. We talked for a while."

330

I sensed she was hinting at something. "And what did you talk about?"

"Movies. God. Drugs. Guys."

"You talked about drugs?"

"She's a pharmacist," Tessa explained, then added suggestively, "It was mostly guys. Relationships."

If this had anything to do with my past with Amber, it was not something I wanted to chat about. "Fair enough." I gazed around the lobby. "So where's Lien-hua?"

"Follow me."

Squall was staring at the building's cement floor. "You're sure they'll still have electricity down there?" he asked Solstice.

She could hardly believe she was hearing this. "Everything is run by the generators on the command level." She said into her mic, "Cyclone, Typhoon, Eclipse, on my mark."

"Roger that," came back the replies.

The people inside the building turned on their headlamps.

"Five," she began. "Four . . . Three . . . Two . . . One—"

The overhead lights cut off.

"Outgoing and incoming radio signals are jammed," Cyclone said beside her. "Once we're down the shaft, I'll take care of the unit-to-unit comm inside the base."

A moment later Tempest's voice came through Solstice's headset. "It's done." But since the interior of the building was already dark, it wasn't exactly a noteworthy announcement.

"Good," Solstice told him. "Come back inside and let's get ready to go down."

With the electricity out, the maintenance building was now illuminated only by the streaks of light shining from her team's headlamps.

Solstice aimed hers at the sedan.

Their means of getting into the base.

I stepped into Natasha and Lien-hua's room while Tessa waited for me in mine. Lien-hua was there, Natasha was gone.

"I had no idea that Jake was going to do that," Lien-hua said apologetically, "to follow you. When he left he just told us he needed to check on something."

"Honestly, I don't really blame him. If I was in his place, I probably would've done the same thing. I'm just glad Alexei's behind bars, but I hope it didn't harm our chances of finding Kayla."

For a moment neither of us spoke; it seemed to be a way of honoring Kayla's plight. Then I told Lien-hua about Torres and the SWAT guys, we exchanged cell phones so that we each had our own once again, and I returned her Glock to her. "What else do we know?" I asked.

She ticked off the items one by one on her fingers. "Natasha's with Linnaman at the morgue. Jake's in his room making some calls. I didn't see anything unusual out there by the ELF site." She sighed. "Doesn't surprise me, though. If there is anything there, it's not going to be sitting out in the open."

"True," I acknowledged, "but we needed to have a look."

"It's possible that the ELF connection is just a red herring."

Yes, it was possible, but the farther we moved into this case, the less likely that seemed. "I'd like to visit the area myself in the morning."

A nod. "Listen, some state troopers found two families of stranded tourists out on the highway. They brought 'em here to the motel."

"I saw them in the lobby. No rooms available."

"Right. So here's what I'm thinking. Tessa's things are all back at your brother's house; everyone's been cooped up here all day. Amber's been acting a little, I don't know . . . something's on her mind. I told her I wasn't upset about last night, that I really wasn't, but she seems rattled being here. I was anticipating that you'd want to go out to the ELF site tomorrow and . . . well, from here it's a haul but—"

"From Sean's house it's a lot closer."

"Yes. You and I could head out first thing in the morning. I talked to Sean, and he has cross-country skis we could borrow—if that would work with your ankle. Maybe if we taped it really well?"

Last night I'd downplayed to her how badly my ankle was bothering me. Honestly, I couldn't even imagine cross-country skiing on it, but I buried that thought for the moment. Lien-hua was right about one thing: the location of the Moonbeam really was working against us. It hadn't been a bad choice when we were investigating the Pickron residence and the site of the snowmobile's disappearance on Tomahawk Lake, but now the focus of the investigation was shifting toward the ELF site and the area surrounding Elk Ridge and the Schoenberg Inn.

If Natasha and Jake stayed at the Moonbeam while Lien-hua and I went to Sean's place, it would give us a strategic, two-pronged approach for searching the region both for the Eco-Tech people that Alexei had told me about and for Kayla Tatum and Donnie Pickron, who, as far as we knew, might both still be alive somewhere.

"That might not be a bad idea," I said. "We should all be able to cram inside the cruiser."

"Amber's car is here too."

"Okay."

Lien-hua went to tell the desk clerk that two rooms had just become available—mine and Amber's—and I went to touch base with Jake and then grab my things.

67

Solstice peered into the sedan. She envisioned something from a Get Smart or a James Bond movie, with a seat that would flip backward and then shoot the driver through a chute that led to a secret high-tech military base.

It wasn't quite like that.

Not quite.

"All right," Solstice said to Donnie. "You're on."

"I don't have my keycard," he said. "I've been telling you that—"

"There's an override. Right before the retinal scan." She told him the access code she'd gotten from Chekov, that he'd gotten from Rear Admiral Colberg. "Type it in."

"How did you . . . ?"

"We have your wife and daughter," she said irritably, "and we will not hesitate to kill them if we need to. Now get us into the base."

Still in handcuffs, Donnie climbed into the driver's seat and flipped down the windshield sun shade. A key dropped into his lap, and, though the car was on cement blocks, he slipped it into the ignition. When he turned the key, rather than the engine starting, the radio flipped around in the console, revealing a numbered keypad. He typed in the code, and the car's trunk clicked open.

Solstice studied the concrete. "Where is it?"

Donnie pointed to one of the uniform rectangles formed by the cracks near the front of the car.

"We go in two groups," she called. "Eclipse, Tempest, Cyclone, you're with me. Squall too. Tempest, bring Donnie over when he's done."

The crack that outlined the rectangle was nearly a centimeter wide. Solstice had been a little worried about the width, but it looked big enough to allow the web router's relay line to pass through. She was prepared to deal with things either way, but it would make everything a lot simpler, of course, if her team could remain online the whole time while they were in the base. She tested her weight on the section of concrete. It felt as solid and ungiving as the rest of the floor.

While she waited for the people she'd just called to gather, Donnie, guarded by Tempest, went to the car's trunk, rooted around beneath the carpet until he came out with another key, then returned to the driver's seat. When he inserted this one into the ignition, a small light came on in the lower corner of the dashboard, and he stared into it while a small laser scanner swept across his retinas.

Cyclone connected the comm line to one of the legs of the workbench, then unreeled it and brought the remaining coil of wire to the concrete slab beside the car.

When the retinal scan was down, Solstice heard the deep grinding sound of giant gears crunching against each other.

Slowly, the slab began to lower.

The initial incursion team packed in around her on the platform.

Tempest grabbed the keys and manhandled Donnie onto the platform, which was beginning its methodical, controlled descent through the maintenance building's floor.

As the slab lowered, rough cement walls appeared on each side of them, with one wall showing the reticulated steel track that supported whatever beam or cantilever rested beneath their concrete platform.

When Solstice tipped her light down the narrow slit between the edge of the slab and the shaft walls, she saw only uninterrupted darkness stretching into the earth.

The communication relay line trailed above them, snaking up through the opening. Squall, the slim man who'd counted the money that Chekov had brought to the meeting yesterday, watched it nervously. "Let's hope it doesn't get cut when the opening closes."

"It won't get cut," Cyclone assured him.

Solstice wasn't quite so sure.

After they'd descended about fifteen feet, she shone her light up and saw another concrete puncheon, identical in size to the one on which they stood, and supported on long, sturdy hydraulic arms, unfold from the side of the shaft and rise to cover the opening. The comm relay line was pressed to the side, but threaded comfortably through the crack between the second concrete barrier and the rest of the maintenance building's floor.

It appeared to be fine.

Cyclone checked her equipment. "Good to go."

"All right," Solstice said. "There'll be at least one Master-at-Arms waiting for us in the entry bay." She spoke rapidly, restating what she'd briefed them about earlier in the day. "The others should be down on the command level. But be ready. There's a small arms locker in the crew quarters, and it's possible the warfare information officers will be armed as well. And don't forget about the MA who's off-duty."

As they descended, Eclipse and Tempest readied their AR-15s. Everyone else pulled out Tasers or sidearms. Solstice unholstered her FN Five-SeveN single-action autoloading pistol—fifty-meter range, twenty-round magazine firing a 5.7x28 mm cartridge. A nice little package.

"Remember, I want them alive, if at all possible."

Cyclone recalibrated the portable tactical radio frequency jammer so that whoever they might encounter on the top level of the base would not be able to communicate with the other sentries throughout the facility.

They were now about fifty feet down, just over halfway.

A few moments later, a sliver of light emerged in the narrow space between one side of the slab and the wall. Solstice already knew that the other three walls would remain closed off, just like in a real elevator.

The thin strip of light grew brighter as they neared the bottom of the shaft.

"Donnie, you don't say a word," she warned. "We'll do the talking."

As they finally edged past the end of the shaft, light spread around them, and the cavernous room on the top level of the base came into view.

Solstice called out, "Set down your weapons, we have Lieutenant Commander Pickron!"

"Run!" Donnie yelled suddenly. "Get the—"

Solstice swung her sidearm violently at him, a harsh pistol-whip to the side of the head. He dropped to the concrete like a spent cartridge.

A sole Master-at-Arms stood twenty feet away with his sidearm drawn, a look of shock on his face. "Put down your weapons!" he yelled unconvincingly.

The slab settled onto the ground.

Whatever the MA might have been expecting, it was undoubtably not a team of people holding his friend at gunpoint. And it was almost certainly not having two assault rifles with laser sights aimed at his chest.

He looked at Donnie. "Commander." His voice cracked. "You all right?"

"He's fine," Solstice answered.

The MA turned his gaze to the semiautomatic in Tempest's hands. "Let him go," he managed to say, but his voice was faltering, uncertain. Solstice wondered how someone this easily rattled had ever gotten this assignment.

"Set down your weapon," she told him firmly. Donnie had pushed himself to his knees, and now she pressed the barrel of her FN Five-SeveN to his forehead. "Or I'll make you watch him die. I'll give you five seconds."

Donnie squeezed his eyes shut. Trembled in fear.

While Solstice waited for the MA to comply, she took in the cavernous room.

It was an octagonal Spartan chamber twelve feet high, sixty feet across. Lit by fluorescent lights and supported by a dozen thick concrete columns, the space reminded her of the lower level of a parking garage. The eight tunnels containing the electromagnetic transmission nodes merged with the entry bay, fingering out in all directions, one from each wall. Thick cables snaked down each of the tunnels.

Solstice noted narrow gauge railroad tracks in two of the tunnels, and based on the orientation to the elevator shaft, she calculated that the one on the left would be her escape route. In addition to the tunnels, a stairwell to her right led to the second level of the base. A nearby utility closet housed the hydraulic lines and machinery override for the concrete freight elevator and power supply relay station for the transmission nodes.

Bypassing a countdown and not really wanting to let on that she was bluffing about killing Donnie right now, she nodded toward the MA and told Tempest, "Take him."

The former Marine slipped his AR-15 around his back on its shoulder sling and moved unflinchingly toward the MA. "Set down your weapon and you won't get hurt."

The man wore a radio on his belt, but it had an attachment with the speaker mic clipped to the front of his shirt collar beside his chin. As Tempest approached him, the guy went for his radio. Tempest kicked the gun from his hand, then spun and smashed his face with the heel of his other foot. The MA went down hard. Only then did Tempest tase him.

He let it go on for a while.

At last he cuffed the dazed man.

"Why didn't you tase him first?" Squall asked.

"What's the fun in that?"

Solstice was really beginning to like this guy and realized she should have used him against Chekov rather than that useless thug Clifton White.

Well. Live and learn.

She turned to Donnie Pickron, who was still on the ground, a deep gash seeping blood down his forehead.

"Pick him up," she told Eclipse, who brusquely yanked Donnie to his feet, held him in front of her in an iron grip.

"I told you not to cry out," Solstice said to Donnie. "Not to try to alert them." She raised her sidearm, held it to his head for a long satisfying moment, then lowered it and pulled out her phone. "You just killed your wife."

"No!" Donnie struggled to get free, but Eclipse held him fast. "Don't!"

"Gag him." Squall stepped forward and obeyed. Solstice gestured toward the MA. "Him as well."

Squall pulled out another gag.

"Cover the passageways," Solstice ordered. "Tempest, get the stairwell. Cyclone, set up the comm relay so we can call out on our cell phones." Cyclone looked at her curiously, but after a wink from Solstice, she bent over the dials and a moment later nodded toward her.

Donnie was staring desperately at the phone, shaking his head, trying in vain to pull free from Eclipse.

While everyone took their positions, Solstice tapped at the cell's screen. Of course she wasn't really calling out, but Donnie either didn't realize that or wasn't thinking clearly.

"I told you earlier that I am not a woman of idle threats."

He was trying to cry out beneath his gag.

She spoke into her phone, to the empty air, "Do it. Yes. The wife." She held the phone to Donnie's ear so he could hear the recorded gunshot, and when he did, his eyes went wide with terror. Then she turned the screen so he could see the video she'd taken on Thursday of Ardis's body lying dead on the steps. Donnie's strength failed him and his legs gave way. He would've dropped to the ground if Eclipse hadn't been supporting him.

"Lizzie will also die unless you do what we brought you here to do. Now, do you understand?"

Distraught, grief-stricken, broken, he nodded. He closed his eyes.

She glanced toward the MA, who now lay gagged with his hands bound behind him with plastic ties. She relieved him of his radio, then had Cyclone go to the override panel and release the cover platform above the shaft and send the elevator back up for the rest of the team.

Although the base itself wasn't large, she knew that the tunnels surrounding her stretched for miles to accommodate the 1,100 four-foot long, graphene-based ultra-capacitors driven into the bedrock to produce the electromagnetic signal that the twenty-eight-miles' worth of aboveground lines had delivered until they were removed back in 2004.

A few moments later the other team members arrived in the entry bay.

Stepped out of the shaft.

"Squall, Cane," said Solstice, "get the two prisoners. Most likely, the other MAs will reconvene in the control room when they don't hear from their buddy. I don't want to have to wander around looking for them. We wait until they try to radio him, then we move. Cyclone, readjust the RF jammer so we can hear when they try to contact him." She indicated toward the stairwell. "Tempest, Eclipse, you're on lead."

The team members posted themselves where they could cover all the entrances to the tunnels and waited for the green light from their leader. She didn't realize it, but part of the reason for their unswerving loyalty was the news Squall had secretly shared with them earlier that afternoon: that in truth Dana Murkowski was not just their leader, she was the one who had planned everything from the beginning.

Valkyrie.

A person who would not put up with things being mishandled.

We pulled into the driveway and parked beside Sean's pickup truck.

I reviewed—Amber's snowmobile was still at the hospital, Lienhua's rental was out of the picture, Tessa's rental was at Lindberg's Bar near Hayward.

Well, at least we still had the cruiser, Sean's pickup, and Amber's Subaru here at the house in case we needed them.

We trekked through the snow to the door.

Sean and Amber had two spare bedrooms, one of which Sean's son Andy used when he visited in the summers. I chose that room, and Tessa and Lien-hua agreed to share the other one, which was also the room where Tessa had slept last night.

They trooped down the hall, and I went to put my things away.

68

Not a shot fired.

And although Solstice didn't mind violence when it served a necessary purpose, she was glad for the lack of fatalities, because keeping all the hostages alive for the time being gave her more options as things moved toward the 9:00 deadline when the sub would finally be in position.

Tempest and Eclipse found the other two on-duty MAs waiting for them in the control room, almost as if the men had attended Solstice's meeting earlier in the day and positioned themselves precisely where she needed them to be in order to make it easiest for her team to subdue them.

After a brief standoff, her people disarmed and restrained them, located the off-duty MA waiting to ambush them in the crew quarters, and took him down as well.

The four Navy information warfare officers who were manning the base had raided their small arms locker but hadn't had the opportunity to use their weapons once.

And now they weren't going to get the chance.

All eight naval personnel had been herded into the recreation room, where they now lay, gagged and securely bound.

Solstice posted Eclipse with a semiautomatic rifle to keep an eye on them, just as she'd planned, and then, to slow down any potential law enforcement or Bureau response, she sent Cirrus and Squall to disable the rudimentary freight elevator they'd ridden down. She made it clear she wanted the slab covering the top, barring entry to the shaft.

"How will we get out when we're done?" Squall asked her.

"I've got that covered," she assured him. "There's a room beside the elevator, all the machinery is in there. Do what you have to do."

As a testament to their belief in her, the two men obeyed without any further questions or need for explanation.

Now on the lower level, she gazed around the control room at the display boards, computers, HDTV and plasma monitors, stylish glass desks, and holographic cryptogram decoding stations. Yes, this was more like it—a stark contrast to the austere Cold War appearance of the upper level. That place had reminded her of a concrete crypt; this room looked a lot more like a twenty-first-century military communication center.

She sat Donnie down at one of the keyboards, flipped open her laptop, connected it to their system. He looked like he was in shock at the death of his wife, still completely unaware that she'd already been dead more than forty-eight hours.

When Solstice removed his gag, he didn't resist, pull away, respond. She bent and spoke softly into his ear. "All right. Let's get started."

Tessa, Lien-hua, and I finished getting situated in our respective rooms while Sean removed his two deer heads and mounted muskie from the living room wall and put them in the garage so Tessa wouldn't be freaked out. Amber threw together some leftovers, and we all gathered in the kitchen and ate in a somewhat subdued silence.

When we were done, Tessa migrated downstairs to the TV room, carrying a book that at first appeared to be a Gideon Bible from the motel, but I realized I had to be mistaken; I couldn't imagine her reading a Holy Bible, let alone taking one from the Moonbeam. Amber and Sean went to work on the dishes, Lien-hua disappeared into her room to work on her profiles and follow up on Natasha and Jake's progress, and I set up a workstation in Andy's room.

Outside my window, in the light migrating around the corner of the house from the porch, I could see that the falling snow was coming down in a frenzy again. As the wind writhed over the roof, some snow ascended in updrafts, while other flakes rushed sideways in the storm, not so much falling as skirting parallel to the ground. It was as if the storm had caught its breath and was panting forward into the night with a renewed sense of purpose and urgency.

As I flipped open my computer, Amber showed up at my door, holding two bottles of medication and a roll of athletic tape. I'd learned my lesson last night, and this time, rather than end up alone with her in the room, I met her in the hall.

She handed me the tape and one of the bottles, which I now saw was Advil. "For your ankle," she said.

"Thanks." I was eyeing the other bottle.

"Oh, this is for Tessa," Amber explained. "She left her meds at the dorm."

"Her meds?"

"She asked if I might be able to fill her prescription for her, but obviously I wasn't able to get to the pharmacy today." Amber handed me the bottle. "Anyway, these are mine. Over the counter. But they should help her sleep."

Sleeping pills?

I looked at her curiously.

"Oh." She realized what I was thinking. "You didn't know she was taking anything."

"No, I didn't."

"I'm sorry, I wouldn't have . . . She didn't tell me."

I accepted the bottle. "It's okay."

Tessa had never claimed that she *wasn't* taking prescription meds, so she hadn't technically lied to me, but still, in a way, I felt deceived.

"I'll make sure she gets them." I didn't really know what else to say. "Thanks."

Amber didn't leave immediately. "I'm really sorry about last night. The note. Everything."

"Don't worry about it. It's all in the past." There was obviously a lot more we could talk about, but I just offered her the words that were foremost on my mind: "Maybe you could reconsider with Sean, though? Try working things out? Give it one more chance?"

She looked as if she were going to object, then said softly, "We'll have to see." Quietly, she stepped away.

It wasn't much, but maybe it was a start.

Before sitting down at my computer, I took some Advil to deal with the sharp pain returning to my ankle, then wrapped it tightly with the athletic tape.

I decided to deliver the sleeping pills to Tessa later, when it was a little closer to bedtime—and after I'd had a chance to process the fact that she was taking prescription medication that she hadn't told me about.

Over the last few months I'd thought we were becoming closer, beginning to confide in each other more. I wondered if I'd done or said something that had betrayed her trust.

She's old enough. It's legal.

Yes, but that wasn't exactly the issue.

Putting personal matters aside for the time being, I directed my attention back to the case.

There was a lot to cover:

(1) Follow up with Margaret about the ELF station, specifically get those base schematics or details on how to access the facility.

(2) Narrow down the search parameters and try to deduce where Alexei might have left Kayla Tatum.

(3) Touch base with Angela about her team's progress in identifying Valkyrie and deciphering the "Queen 27:21:9" sequence.

(4) Evaluate the newspaper clippings and news footage, and watch the videos that the ERT had found in Reiser's trailer.

First I tried contacting Margaret, but, unable to reach her by phone, I left a vm and then, to cover my bases, also sent an email requesting the ELF schematics.

I moved on to the search for Kayla.

Even though I'd analyzed Chekov's travel patterns earlier, I decided to start over and take a fresh look at the data, hoping to do so as quickly and yet as thoroughly as I could.

After pulling up the geoprofile that I'd started at the motel, I went online and overlaid the findings against a satellite view of the area from two days ago, before the storm clouds had covered the sky.

And I began to study the map.

Donnie's eyes were bloodshot, his voice barely audible. "So what about Lizzie?"

"I have no intention of harming her," Solstice said truthfully.

"How can I know you're not going to . . ."

She tapped at the computer screen. "Just verify the deactivation codes and everything will be fine."

Leaving him under Cane's supervision, she found Cyclone and had her acquire a voice sample from one of their captives, Chief Warrant Officer Dickinson. It took a little convincing, but at last he unwittingly gave her enough of an audio sample for a voiceprint by answering a few harmless questions about the base's fitness room and the food prep area.

Utilizing the same software they'd employed yesterday to persuade Donnie Pickron that his wife was still alive, Solstice had Tempest call the Pentagon through the web-based router, and, pretending to be Chief Warrant Officer Dickinson, he assured the Navy that the sat comm lines had simply gone down in the storm and not to worry. "I came to the surface to let you know," he said, and then told them a reference number Donnie had looked up to verify his identity as that of the chief warrant officer.

It wouldn't hold off the Defense Department's suspicions forever, but at least it would help buy the team a little more time.

Then, Solstice returned to Donnie's side.

"When do you want to send the signal?" he asked her falteringly.

She looked at her watch. 5:44 p.m.

Three hours and sixteen minutes.

"It's going to be a little while. Just get everything set."

For now, sit low, monitor the JWICS, and wait for the USS *Louisiana* to sail into position in the Gulf of Oman for the 9:00 p.m. ELF transmission.

From the very start, Valkyrie had been aware that things could go either way.

After all, $100,000,000 is a lot of money, and when that kind of dollar figure gets put into play, people's allegiances have a tendency to become malleable.

So far, Valkyrie had been careful to remain invisible, undetectable while playing people's loyalties, their agendas against them.

Everything was a distraction layered inside a distraction.

Yes.

Wednesday night, Valkyrie, not Kirk Tyler's partner, had been the one to film Erin Collet leaving the mall in San Antonio while her father, Dashiell Collet, was being interrogated by Tyler.

Valkyrie had been the one to kill Tyler's cohort even before Erin Collet exited the back of the mall. Then Valkyrie was the one who'd taken the fresh corpse's button camera and worn it while following Erin to the car.

Valkyrie was the one who'd drugged her and left her in the vehicle before detonating the cell phone that took off Kirk Tyler's head.

And of course, Valkyrie was the one who'd sent Alexei Chekov to dispose of Tyler's body, and arranged for him to speak with Rear Admiral Colberg in Virginia.

And now, Valkyrie was the one making sure everything was going to come together at 9:00.

Tonight, the queen would go up in flames, the Eco-Tech ideologues would be out of the picture, and Valkyrie's future would be wide open and bold with possibilities.

With $100,000,000 to fund them.

PART III

- NIGHT -

69

The geoprofile pointed me toward the region east of Woodborough, and I sent word to Tait, who'd since left the sheriff's department and was now on patrol, to have his men begin searching homes as well as outbuildings and barns in the area. "Start with the ones that are heated. I don't think Alexei wants Kayla to die."

I checked my email and voicemail but still hadn't received any word from Margaret. I tried her number again, and it went directly to voicemail. Annoyed, I left another message for her to call me and to send those schematics as soon as possible.

Earlier in the day, Alexei had hacked into Lien-hua's cell phone and received, and then interpreted, the signal from somewhere. I knew a few hacking tricks myself, but I didn't know how to back trace a closed-route wireless loop to find where its receiver might have been.

I wasn't even sure there was a way to do it, but if there was, Angela Knight at Cybercrime would know how.

I tried her office and was thankful to catch her just as she was about to leave for the day. After a short greeting, she somewhat wearily agreed to a video chat. A quick tap of my mouse brought up the chat window. I hung up my cell and faced my laptop's camera.

Angela was seated at her workstation, two of Lacey's monitors to her right. Curly-haired and kindhearted, Angela wore conspicuous glasses and was no longer in the shape she'd been in eight years ago when she first became an agent. She'd been trying to address that issue lately, and instead of her typical can of Diet Coke and stash of Kit Kat bars, she had a bottle of Vitamin Water and a half-finished bowl of miniature carrots positioned prominently on her desk. As she situated herself in front of the camera, she gave me a smile, but it was marked with her typical look of irrepressible concern.

"The DoD sub route analysis didn't bring up anything," she began. "That looks like a dead end. Oh, it appears someone using the code name Valkyrie was present in Moscow when Tatiana Chekov was killed. As far as Alexei goes, we've learned that the GRU is very interested in finding him."

"I'm sure they are."

"The best Lacey could come up with for the 'Queen 27:21:9' cipher was Revelation 21:9."

"How is that Queen 27?"

"Revelation is the twenty-seventh book in the New Testament."

"But what does it have to do with a queen?"

"I'm not sure, but what troubles me is the reference to the last seven plagues. Here, look."

She tapped her keyboard, and the verse popped up in a text window at the bottom of my screen. I read: "And there came unto me one of the seven angels which had the seven vials full of the seven last plagues, and talked with me, saying, Come hither, I will shew thee the bride, the Lamb's wife."

I'd gone to Sunday school as a kid and knew enough to realize that the Lamb here referred to Jesus Christ.

"The King of kings," I whispered.

"What?"

"The Lamb is a reference to Christ, but somewhere else he's referred to as the King of kings, so—"

"The Lamb's bride would be a queen."

"Yes."

"And who is that?" she asked. "Who's the bride?" I couldn't tell if she was asking her question rhetorically or not; if she already knew the answer.

"Well, metaphorically, the church, I think, but . . ." I was no theologian by any stretch of the imagination. "We'll have to follow up on that."

Get to the cell phone call. Nail down that location. It's your best bet at finding Kayla.

"Listen, here's why I called. Let's say I wanted to hack into someone's cell phone, turn on their speaker or camera, and then send that feed back to another computer. What do you know about that?"

"Sure. We do it all the time." Then she added somewhat hastily, "Whenever we have a warrant."

"Of course. Well, someone did it with Lien-hua's phone. I need to back trace the signal, find out where the feed was sent to."

"A physical location or a device?"

"Physical location, if at all possible." I relayed Lien-hua's cell number to Angela, and she tapped it in, then glanced at one of her other computer screens, where a scrolling stream of computer code appeared.

She let her fingers dance across the keys, then gave the screen a fierce look and bit violently through a carrot. "Whoever did this is good. I can locate it, but it's going to take me some time."

It didn't surprise me that Alexei had done a thorough job of covering his tracks. "All right, while you work on that, let me ask you another question. Hypothetically, if I were going to hack into a nuclear submarine, what would I have to do?"

She stopped chewing the carrot, stared directly into her video chat camera at me. "A nuclear submarine?"

"Hypothetically."

"Whenever someone says 'hypothetically,' he's never talking about something hypothetical."

"Theoretically, then."

She looked rebukingly at me over the top of her glasses.

"Same difference, huh?" I said.

"Yes."

"Can you walk me through it?"

"Which do you want?" She glanced at the screen beside her. "The cell trace or the hacking seminar?"

"Well . . ."

"Let me guess. Both."

"And she's a mind reader too."

"Mm-hmm."

She took another carrot, rolled it between her fingers, then crunched into it. "Okay, go to the toolbar, scroll down the View menu, then click on Split Screen/Chalkboard."

I did as she instructed, and the video chat image on my computer folded in half and fluttered into two windows. The one on the left held Angela's picture, the one on the right did indeed look like a chalkboard. She picked up a stylus, and as she drew on a data pad beside her, a cloud appeared on the chalkboard window on my screen.

"Here's the internet." She added a small arrow pointing to the cloud, then extended a line from it toward the right side of the window and diagramed a series of four boxes separated by short lines. "Here we have external military servers and proxies . . ." She inserted more lines and boxes to represent additional machines. "And also these are your personal computers, workstations, and so on. At each place where they connect to one of the three Department of Defense intranets, they go through a router that's supposed to catch malware."

None of this was new to me, but I let her go on rather than interrupt her train of thought, which I thought might only eat up more time.

"At any point, in any one of these layers, it's possible to hack in, but it gets harder and harder the closer you move toward the top secret communication channels from the Non-classified Internet Protocol Router Network—"

"NIPRNET."

"Yes. Then on to the Secret Internet Protocol Router Network, or SIPRNET, and then to JWICS. Especially if . . ." She swiped her finger across her data pad, erasing the lines that connected the military's routers and their intranets of computers. "If the military were to find out about a threat, they'd sever the connection between the Cloud and their network."

"That's possible? I thought that was one of our biggest vulnerabilities, that our communication infrastructure was too dependent on the web?"

"Well," she admitted, "it's not easy, considering the whole purpose of the internet is interconnectivity. The very thing that makes the internet strong—decentralization—is the thing that makes it weak. But USCYBERCOM, the Navy's 10th Fleet, the Army's Cyber Command, and the 24th Air Force have been working on ways."

I already knew that the United States Cyber Command, an attempt within Homeland Security to assess, forestall, and intercept cyber threats to the military and the US infrastructure, was a bureaucratic nightmare and still woefully inefficient, but I wasn't sure about the military divisions she'd just listed. "Tell me about the 10th Fleet and the 24th."

"Well, as you know, there are nearly three dozen cyrberwarfare agencies in the US government, but the Air Force's 24th is probably the best, especially their Computer Emergency Response Team—AFCERT. They're in another league using algorithms to analyze worldwide trending."

"Trending?"

"The type and flow of information passing to and from servers worldwide. They work mainly in host-based intrusion prevention systems to locate and block malware or attempts to infiltrate military networks. Then they patch vulnerabilities for pilots and scour all air force networks for forward-facing internet presences."

That was a mouthful.

"Hackers," I said.

"Foreign ones. Yes. They also work in space-based comm systems, drones, full-spectrum network defense, and new architectures."

"So does the 24th track domestic intrusion too?"

"Yes, as does the Navy's 10th Fleet, USCYBERCOM, but if we're talking more cybercrime than cyrberwarfare, then it's me and Lacey. It all depends."

"On what?"

"Whichever agency happens to stumble onto the threat."

Her choice of the word *stumble* was not very reassuring.

"But getting back to your question—even if we cut the connection to the Cloud, we might still be in trouble."

"How?"

"If the hackers had gotten in before, left malware or back doors that would allow them persistent access. Once you inject the bad code in there, you're good to go." She thought for a moment. "Also, it's possible they could bypass the Cloud altogether and access JWICS physically at one of the computer stations around the world that's already connected to it. Some sophisticated malware can hop file shares in virtual machines. Or you could've implanted a physical transmitting device into the computer, say, before it was shipped out to the military."

"The more complex a system, the more vulnerable it is."

"Sure. You can gain access through a Trojan, counter-encrypting, port knocking. Use a covert channel. There are a dozen ways."

Perhaps what struck me the most was how unfazed she seemed by all this.

She downed some Vitamin Water, then her eyes ghosted toward the screen displaying the cell phone analysis. I could tell she didn't want to drop that project in the middle, and she must have noticed something pertinent because she silently bowed out of our conversation and went back to work completing the cell trace. Thousands of lines of indecipherable code streamed down the screen beside her. She reminded me of a code reader from one of the Matrix movies.

"Let's back up for a minute," I said, "and say we're trying to hack into that submarine, but that we had no access to the computers to physically plant a device before they were shipped out. Who could hack into JWICS?"

"Well, at least forty countries have military cyrberwarfare units."

"Forty!"

"In the next three years that number is likely to double."

"Doesn't that worry you, Angela? Doesn't any of this get to you?"

"Pat, this is my job. I deal with it every day. China has more honor students than we have students. Russia has four-year college degree programs on hacking. There are tens of millions of hacking attempts against the Department of Defense each *week*. It's the reality of the world we live in, and we just have to work with what we have and stop whatever we can."

I could see why she looked perpetually under the gun, and I empathized with her. "Sorry. So now, today, any ideas which countries have the technological savvy to get into JWICS?"

"Right now? Russia, Brazil, Israel, China—the US—North Korea. Maybe three or four others. Probably half a dozen citizen hacker groups in China could do it." She hesitated for a moment, then added, "As well as a handful of individuals who could pull it off."

I had a feeling she'd been a little uncomfortable noting that individuals could hack into JWICS because she knew I'd been friends with one of those people until last year, when I figured out he was involved in a biotech conspiracy. He'd been ready to kill Lien-hua, and when I stopped him, he was electrocuted and slipped into a coma. Terry had died not long after that, and even though he'd been a traitor and wanted to murder the woman I loved, he'd been my friend for a long time before all that, and his death had really bothered me. Actually, it still did.

"Once you pwn a system," she said, drawing me out of my thoughts, "you're home free."

"Pwn? You mean control it? Compromise it?"

She nodded her approval that I was familiar with the hacker term. "Once you own the source code or the rootkit, you can download or destroy data, overload circuits, transfer funds . . ." As she typed at her keyboard and eyed the computer code flickering in front of her, she continued rattling off her list: "Turn off air traffic control communication, shut down safety valves at power plants, blow up refineries, reroute trains, take hospitals offline . . ." Then she added offhandedly, "Basically, take down a country."

Wow. This was such an encouraging conversation.

Though I knew that Iraqi insurgents had hacked into our drones, the Chinese had gotten into our power grid, and at least one of the fatal airline crashes in the last few years was due to malware in the navigational system, I tried to reassure myself that Angela was almost certainly overstating things. "But aren't there firewalls in JWICS? Antivirus programs? Encryption software? User authentication, that sort of thing, throughout the network?"

"Forging the response to the DNS server can get you past a firewall. A skilled hacker can crack an LM hash algorithm in seconds, even NTLM hashes can be cracked quickly with pre-computed cryptanalytic tables. Getting past authentication protocols takes a little longer, but we're talking minutes not hours. Hacking 101: identify the system's countermeasures, probe for vulnerabilities, access the system, crack the passwords, gain privileged access, hide, exploit, transmit." She thought for a moment. "A morale computer would be a good attack vector on the sub."

"No good. Crewmen on a nuclear sub wouldn't be allowed to communicate with the outside world via the web because it might give away their location."

"Good point." She spoke softly as she scrolled through the lines of code on her right-hand screen. "Tell me more about this hypothetical question that isn't hypothetical."

"To put it bluntly, I want to know if it's possible for a hacker to remotely fire a ballistic missile from one of our nuclear submarines."

I thought she'd be rattled by my question, but she took it completely in stride. "Once you're at the root level and have administrator access to a weapons system, you're only one keystroke away from Armageddon."

"Now you're just being melodramatic."

She chose not to reply, and her silence seemed to buttress her point. "So are we talking a domestic or foreign threat?"

"Domestic." Then I thought of Eco-Tech's international ties. "But it might be internationally funded."

"Let me think about that." She typed quickly for a moment, then said, "I've got a GPS location for you."

"Fantastic."

She gave me the coordinates, and when I opened another tab on my web browser and punched them in, the Bureau's satellite mapping program brought up a cabin that lay less than a mile from the Schoenberg Inn. "Give me a sec to call this in, Angela. In the meantime, see if you can come up with a way to remotely fire that missile."

70

I phoned Tait and gave him the address. "Start there, move out. I think there's a good chance Kayla might be there." Then I called Natasha to see if she could go process the site.

"Do you want Jake to come with me?"

"Yes."

End call.

Good, good, good. A break.

Back to Angela.

"Do you have actionable intel here, Pat?" she asked.

"Not yet. No."

"But you're thinking there's someone who might try this? Try to hack into a nuclear sub? This Eco-Tech group?"

Everything I had so far was circumstantial, a loose network of clues all pointing in one direction, held together merely by assumption and hypothesis rather than conclusive facts: the word of an assassin, speculation about the involvement of an environmental activist group, an uncertain agenda.

"Yes." I tried to sound more confident than I was. "That's what I'm thinking."

"But Eco-Tech is anti-nuke, Pat. Why would they try to detonate a nuclear weapon?"

"I have no idea."

"Well, even if they wanted to, I just don't think they have the resources or personnel."

"They might have a Navy information warfare officer with them."

She was quiet. "No, I still don't see it happening."

"You just told me 'one keystroke away from Armageddon.' Right?"

"I was probably overreaching. When you're talking about firing a nuclear weapon, there are just too many redundant systems. Don't you need to have, what, two, three people turn keys at the same time?"

"I'd say at least that many."

"There you go. Plus authentication codes, scripted orders, verification protocols. Even if you were able to somehow get the launch codes, one person can't set off a nuclear device by himself. You cannot physically be in two places at the same time to turn the keys."

"But could you bypass those two people and their keys altogether, just like bypassing the Cloud?"

Angela looked at me quizzically.

This was one time I did not want to be playing devil's advocate. "Turning the keys doesn't actually fire the weapon, the computer does that. The keys simply tell the computer what to do. What if you could insert the code that would tell it what to do—"

"You mean without the keys turning."

"Yes. One person can't be in two places to simultaneously turn two keys from different parts of a room or a sub, but one person could turn them simultaneously—"

"From inside the computer." Her voice was soft and frangible.

"Theoretically, yes, once you pwn the system."

"You just said theoretically, Angela."

The look of worry on her face deepened. "I'll contact USCYBER-COM and the Pentagon. Ask them to raise the DEFCON level on the fleet of nuclear submarines, but they're going to ask for a threat assessment, and you know how long that can take, especially without actionable intel."

Unfortunately, I did. "Tell them it has to do with Eco-Tech and the ELF station in Wisconsin. I'll send you all my notes. I think we should have enough to get their attention, and they can call me if they need anything else."

"How is this related to ELF?"

For anyone else it might have surprised me that they were familiar with the extremely low frequency technology, but not with Angela. "They'll know. Just get them the word and keep me up to speed."

"All right."

"I don't know what kind of time frame we're looking at here," I said, "but I don't like how quickly everything is happening here, so fast-track this."

"I'll make that clear."

"And could you do me one more favor?"

Angela looked at me somewhat suspiciously. "What's that?"

"I can't seem to get ahold of Margaret and she was supposed to send me the schematics to the ELF station. Can you look them up?"

"That station has been closed down for years."

"Wait till I send you the files."

A pause. "If the schematics are on the Federal Digital Database, I can get them for you."

"It might only be on the JWICS. And you're probably going to need above top secret security clearance."

A long thin silence. I could tell that she was evaluating my request in lieu of the conversation we'd just finished regarding the hacking scenarios. "I think Director Wellington is still in the building. I'll track her down, ask her."

"And if you can't find her?"

"I'll see what I can do."

I'd worked with Angela enough to know that pressuring her any more right now was not going to help. "Thanks. I owe you one."

"If you're right about any of this, you don't owe me anything." She signed off.

I closed the chat window, forwarded all of my notes to her and to USCYBERCOM, then, as I was finishing up, I thought about the GPS location Angela had uncovered and that I'd relayed to Tait. It wasn't far from from the Schoenberg Inn. Earlier in the day I'd had my team search the Moonbeam because of the possibility that Alexei was keeping Kayla there.

So the Schoenberg? Just get a room, knock Kayla out, lock her in there? It would keep her safe, warm, out of the picture.

I called Tait back and told him to have his men search every room of the Schoenberg while they were in the area after they'd inspected the cabin.

Then I ran down where things were at: Angela was pursuing raising the threat level and looking for Margaret, USCYBERCOM had all the data I did, Tait was having officers search the most likely locations for Kayla, and Alexei Chekov was behind bars. I had the sense that right now just about everything I could put into play on this case was in play.

Dealing with more than one investigation at a time isn't easy, but more often than not, it's the default setting for my life. So now, as I reviewed the objectives I'd noted earlier, I realized it was time to review the videos Torres had sent me, the ones found in Reiser's trailer.

Still at my computer, I braced myself and then pulled up the footage that the ERT had digitized from the VHS cassette documenting Lana Gerriksen's murder more than a decade ago.

And I pressed play.

71

CIA Detainment Facility 17
Cairo, Egypt
2:29 a.m. Eastern European Time
2 hours 31 minutes until the transmission

After wheeling into the bathroom, Terry used the cell phone to contact Abdul Razzaq Muhammad.

"Two and a half hours," Terry said. "Your team will be here?"

"They are already in the area. Have the numbers changed?"

"No. They keep a steady rotation here. There'll be eight to ten agents present."

"We'll wait until we have confirmation that the event has occurred, then we will—"

"No. Simultaneous," Terry said. "That was our agreement. Don't forget, I can still call this off."

No reply.

"Do you understand what I'm saying?" Terry pressed him. "It all happens at 03:00 GMT."

"My men will move in when the missile hits, not when it is fired. Sub-launched missiles are slower than ICBMs, not as accurate. It might miss the target, or it might be disarmed prior to impact."

"It won't miss, and once a Trident missile is in the air, it can't be disarmed, redirected, or recalled."

"I don't believe you."

"Some of the newer missiles, maybe, yes. But not the older ones. Not the ones on the USS *Louisiana*."

Abdul was unyielding. "We move on impact. Not before."

After a short internal debate, Terry decided that at this point it wasn't worth fighting about; a few more minutes wouldn't matter in the end, not after all these months of captivity. "All right. It'll be in the air eleven minutes. So, exactly 03:11 GMT."

"I do not deal well with betrayal. If you don't deliver, we will kill you, find your female friend, and she will join you in eternity, but only after my men and I have taken our turns with her."

Spoken like a true religious fanatic.

Terry wasn't intimidated. "I would expect nothing less." *From you*, he thought. "And the money?"

"It will be transferred at 03:11 GMT. Exactly."

The road to this moment had all begun the day Terry acquired the phone.

China's growing weapons and economic ties to Pakistan had given him the perfect in. After he'd stolen the phone, he'd contacted his old handler from China to find out who to be in touch with in Pakistan. He bypassed the Taliban and went directly to Al Qaeda sympathizers in the Pakistani government and made Abdul Razzaq Muhammad the offer: "I will acquire a nuclear weapon from one of the United States's Ohio Class Submarines. I will fire it at the target of your choice if you will provide two things for me in return."

"What are those?"

"Free me from a CIA detainment facility in Egypt and wire $100,000,000 to the bank account number I provide you."

Yes, the dollar figure was significant, but so were Abdul Razzaq Muhammad's contacts.

Terry calculated that some of the money would come from oil, but, considering the people he was working with, he knew that most of it would come from the United States government itself, siphoned from the $2.4 billion of annual aid that the US gives to Pakistan, officially "to help the citizens of the country democratically grow their economy," unofficially, to combat the rampant anti-American sentiment: "A core component in the worldwide fight against global terrorism."

In other words, spend billions of American taxpayer dollars to help grow the economy of a country where nearly 70 percent of the people still think the US is their enemy, while American unemployment hovers at 10 percent.

A plan like that could only come from Capitol Hill.

After making the offer, Terry had given Abdul the information he would need to confirm his identity and qualifications, and it took the Al Qaeda operative less than a day to verify that Terry Manoji, a man who'd worked undetected as a spy for two years while employed at the NSA, was the person he claimed to be and could deliver what he said he could.

So Abdul took the proposal to his people.

Terry thought they would come back to him with an American target, perhaps one of the usual suspects: Washington DC, New York City, LA, or maybe an American embassy or military installation abroad.

But Abdul's associates chose someplace else.

The city of Jerusalem.

"We will bring down the Zionists," Abdul told him, "while also putting the Great Satan in its proper place of humiliation in the eyes of the world."

Orchestrating it so that the US rather than an Islamic nation wiped out Jerusalem was brilliant in a twisted sort of way. As far as Terry could see, in one fell swoop it accomplished nearly every goal Al Qaeda ever had—humiliating America, killing millions of Jews, devastating the US economy, and effecting all of this by turning the weapons of the world's greatest superpower against one of its closest allies.

"What about the Muslims who live there?" Terry asked. "The Palestinians in East Jerusalem?"

"Allah will welcome any of the faithful who are martyred in his name."

Martyred.

That was an interesting way to put it.

"And the Dome of the Rock?"

"Unwavering devotion to Allah is more important than the veneration of a shrine."

Truthfully, Terry didn't care about either Al Qaeda's target or their reasons for choosing it. He cared about only two things—his freedom and his reunion with Cassandra. But he needed to know how committed Abdul would be to fulfilling his part of the bargain, so he asked him, "Your own clerics have called Islam a peaceful religion. Are you sure you're ready to go through with something like this?"

"Anyone who calls my religion one of peace mocks it," Abdul stated firmly. "Just as anyone who claims it is about war. Islam is not about peace or about war; it is about surrender. The name *Muslim* means 'submission to God.' Our religion is one of total submission to Allah—it is not about tolerance, it is not about appeasing others or compromising to make sinners happy. It is about devotion. We celebrate all that is in submission to the Creator, we fight all that is in opposition to Islam. You misunderstand if you think Muslims are for peace or for war. We are instead wholeheartedly surrendered to the spread of Islam because it is the will of Allah."

"And your target threatens that?"

"Rejects it." Now Abdul Razzaq Muhammad's tone had turned cold and spiteful, and Terry could hear the man's venomous hatred for Jews coming through loud and clear. "There is no greater calling than spreading the will of God to those who would scorn it or mock it or fight against it! Allahu Akbar!"

The rhetoric didn't impress Terry, nor did the reasoning persuade him. As far as he was concerned, Islam was a religion of violence and totalitarianism. How else could you explain the deafening silence of the majority of its adherents to the daily suicide bomb attacks against civilians that their fellow Muslims carried out? How else could you make sense of the international outrage, protests, and deadly riots when someone drew a caricature of Muhammad or threatened to burn a Qur'an?

Even to Terry Manoji, for a religious person to place books and cartoons above human life was unfathomable. Sharia law? That wasn't surrender to God; that was fascism.

But as long as he got his money, as long as he got his freedom,

Terry didn't care about their warped reasoning or their sophomoric and fustian ways of justifying violence in the name of religion.

And then, there was the matter of Israel's response. Over the last few years, Israel had not been at all shy about their right to preemptively attack Iran if they thought Iran had nuclear weapons.

And of course, if there was a nuclear missile heading straight for the heart of Jerusalem, Israeli leaders would not hold cabinet meetings and forums, they would assume it was fired from the country that had repeatedly threatened their very existence.

Iran.

Even if the US claimed the missile had been fired by hackers or terrorists, Israel would presume who was responsible.

And they would retaliate.

Terry could only imagine how much damage they would do to that country in the eleven minutes between the time the *Louisiana*'s missile was fired and when it actually struck the heart of their capital.

It would certainly be a memorable day, that much was for sure.

"It's a deal," Terry had said simply.

Now, with less than 150 minutes left before the ignition sequence would begin, Terry said to Abdul, "All right. You told me the consequences if I don't deliver what I promised, now I'm going to tell you the consequences if you don't."

"And what are those, my friend?" Abdul's voice did not sound friendly.

"Jerusalem will not be the only city lying in ruins. Mecca will become one giant crater and Allah will welcome 1.7 million more 'martyrs' home. Do we have a clear understanding here?"

"Yes, Mr. Manoji. It is quite clear indeed."

Solstice was pleased.

The hydraulic lines that powered the lift in the concrete shaft had been disabled. All was set. The base was secure. No one would be coming down to interrupt them.

Although Equator had identified increasing chatter on JWICS about US nuclear subs, nothing specifically related to her mission or the ELF station had come up, which, given the obvious FBI interest in the site, did surprise Solstice a bit.

Since taking over the base, her team had carefully and strategically placed nearly half of the TATP ordnance, leaving, of course, one of the tunnels free of explosives so that no one would be trapped down here when they detonated.

Well, that's what they thought, but in reality only one person was going to be leaving this base. Solstice had decided it would just be too inconvenient leaving any survivors to tell the story or to point the finger in her direction.

"Finish with the TATP," she said into her handheld radio. "And then I want Cane, Gale, and Squall back down here so we can film that video."

72

1 hour 36 minutes until the transmission

The murder videos were viscerally disturbing.

When you watch things like this, knowing that they really happened, that the images weren't created by computer graphics or by using special effects, it's terrifying and unnerving.

I'd been at it for over an hour, but I knew that tonight I wouldn't have time to watch all the videos in their entirety, so I played some parts but fast-forwarded through others. I recognized each of the victims' faces from the cases I'd worked over the years as I'd tracked Basque—either while I was a detective in Milwaukee or during the last six months when he reemerged and started right where he'd left off, torturing, slaughtering, eating.

Basque was visible in all of the videos, doing his work on the women. Occasionally, I could hear slight laughter from the person filming the crimes, but interestingly enough, Basque's partner never appeared on screen. The only indication that it might have been Reiser was the fact that we'd found the videos in his trailer home.

But that, of course, was merely circumstantial.

Reiser's lungs were gone when they found him this week.

Gone.

Basque only abducted women.

Careful, Pat. As far as you know, Basque only abducted women.

My ringing phone interrupted my thoughts, and I received word from Angela that the Defense Department had approved raising the threat level on our fleet of nuclear subs. "I can't find Director Wellington," she told me. "She must have left for the day and she's not answering her cell. But I sent an official expedited request through to the Pentagon for the schematics."

"How long will that take?"

"They assured me you would have them as soon as possible."

I cursed under my breath, hiding my frustration from Angela. I wanted a time frame—like maybe five minutes ago.

"I know, Pat," she said, reading my silence. "Believe me, I made sure they know how urgent it is."

"All right. Keep me posted."

Shortly after I hung up, Tait updated me that his officers had found nothing at the cabin, the Schoenberg Inn, or any of the residences or buildings in the area I'd suggested they focus their search; neither had Alexei shared any information or made his one phone call. To make matters worse, when I contacted Antón Torres for an update, he told me his SWAT team had gotten caught behind a truck accident on Highway 8 that shut down the road. Antón figured they were still at least two hours out.

I went back to the Reiser case. Bypassing the videos for now, I spent some time studying his residential history and comparing it to the locations of the crimes. I realized that, while he could have traveled to commit the murders and follow the news stories, the locations didn't overlap like I would have expected.

Reiser was killed Tuesday night . . .

DNA from two missing people was found on his knife—a man from Milwaukee, a woman from DC . . .

Clippings were found from the Rockford Register Star *newspaper . . .*

The facts revolved, spiraled through my mind, but I was mentally exhausted and couldn't seem to sort them out. I rubbed my head, stood, and stretched my back.

I hadn't noticed before, but now I overheard Lien-hua and Amber talking in the living room, and I found myself being thankful, since the more understanding there was between those two women, the better off everything between me and Lien-hua was going to be—at least that's what I hoped.

Sean was outside, shoveling the driveway so that we'd have our vehicles available in case we needed to get out of here. Earlier when he was getting his boots, I'd suggested he snowblow it, but he told me he didn't own a snowblower, and then added in no uncertain terms, "Three things real men don't do: they don't tweet, they don't wear Velcro shoes, and they don't snowblow their driveways."

Nope. No arguing with that.

As far as I knew, Tessa was still downstairs reading.

I tapped my spacebar and saw the frozen image of Basque, scalpel in hand, leaning over a dying woman in Monona, Wisconsin, and decided I needed a break from this, even if just for a few minutes.

It occurred to me that with so many things in play all day long, I hadn't really had much of a chance to talk with Tessa, and, to put it mildly, our short conversation at the motel before I went to meet Chekov hadn't ended especially well. I had a feeling things were only going to get more complicated from here on out tonight, and I might not even be around the house, especially if we located Kayla, so if I were going to get any chance to connect with my stepdaughter, now was the time to do it.

Besides, I still had the pills Amber had given me to pass along to her. I hadn't yet come up with a good way of broaching the topic of Tessa's undisclosed prescription—honestly, I hadn't thought about it at all in the last hour—but regardless, it was something I needed to at least address.

Going downstairs, I found her lounging on the couch, rereading Richard Brautigan's *Revenge of the Lawn*, a book she'd described to me once as "an underground, anti-establishment creative nonfiction classic." She looked like she was really into it.

"Hey," I said.

She looked up. "Hey."

"How's the book?"

"Sick."

"Sick."

"Yes."

"Isn't that supposed to mean gross?"

"It's a versatile word."

"Now it means, what, cool?"

"Sure. It's like stupid. If I say, 'That was just *stupid*,' it means it was awesome, righteous, wicked."

I looked at her curiously. "But if you say, 'That's stupid—'"

"I mean it's stupid."

"Oh. So, stupid means brilliant and sick means sweet."

"Pretty much."

"That's stupid."

A tiny smile. "Now you're catching on."

Tessa set down the book.

She was totally curious about what had gone down last night between Patrick, Amber, and Lien-hua, and she wanted quite badly to ask him about it but wasn't exactly sure how to bridge into the topic.

Patrick took a seat on a footstool across the room from her. "Are you still mad about earlier today, at the motel when I had to leave?"

"Naw. It's all good."

"So the winter session class at U of M, that was, what, kind of stupid—in the stupid sense of the word?"

"Yeah. But it was nice to see some of the spots Mom used to visit. Dad too."

Ask him about Amber.

No, start with Sean.

The lights in the house flicked off then on, and a moment later Amber's voice floated down from the top of the stairs. "Sean? We should really bring in some more firewood, in case the electricity goes out."

"He's still shoveling," Patrick called up to her. "But I can get some for you." Then he made eye contact with Tessa, and she realized that was probably not a good sign. "Tessa and I will get some."

"Seriously?" she said unenthusiastically.

"Seriously. Come on."

A few minutes later she was dressed for the weather and meeting him outside the patio door. He was wearing his snazzy new camo jacket. "Promise me you'll leave that here when we go back to Denver," she said.

"Deal."

He clicked on his flashlight, and they started trudging through the driving snow toward the woodshed.

After a few steps she said, "Patrick, what was it? Whatever happened between you and Sean?"

"What do you mean?"

"Something happened. It's always there, between you two. A wall. Was it an argument or something?"

He didn't answer right away. "It wasn't an argument."

"What then?"

"Life," he answered vaguely. "Schedules, work. His family and my career. Hey, I was really hoping we could talk about—"

"That's weak."

"Weak?"

"Every family has that stuff. You either choose to stay close through it all or you don't."

For a few moments he walked in silence through the night, holding his flashlight steady against the weather. "I guess we never did."

"So you're saying *you* never did, or that *you both* never did?"

"Tessa, this isn't really—"

"Okay, whatever." She waited. It wouldn't be long.

She started counting to herself to ten, made it to six before he said, "All right."

They reached the shed, and he muscled open the snow-sealed sliding door but didn't enter. "When I was seventeen, Sean and I were driving home from a party one night. The roads were icy and I was dozing off. He swerved. We hit another car and"—Patrick took a small breath—"tragically, Tessa, a woman was killed."

"Oh, my God."

———————————————◼———————————————

Her words weren't glib or impudent but filled with sympathy, and I wondered if maybe I shouldn't have told her the news.

On the other hand, it was probably time she knew what'd happened. I gestured for her to go inside the shed, then I followed her. "Sean always said he was trying to avoid a deer, but I, well . . . I wondered if maybe he'd had too much to drink."

"Did they do a Breathalyzer test?"

"I don't know. It would've made sense, but if they did, it didn't raise any red flags." There were no lights in the woodshed, so I handed Tessa the Maglite, then started scooping up split logs. "I'd seen him drinking at the party. When I asked him about it later, he told me he'd only had two beers."

"So not nearly enough to get drunk — not for a big guy like him, not over the course of a whole night of partying."

"No. Not if it was only two beers."

The way she held the light I could see her face, and she was looking at me questioningly. "What do you mean, 'if it was only two'? You didn't believe him?"

"I didn't see any deer tracks, Tessa."

"Deer tracks?"

"By the side of the road." Clutching the logs against my chest with my left arm, I used my right to add to the stack. "I looked for tracks, but I didn't —"

"Yeah, well, you just said it happened at night. How can you be sure you didn't just miss seeing 'em?"

"Tessa, it was —"

"He's your brother. You don't just distrust someone like that — unless, did he lie to you all the time?"

"No. Not at all." I finished gathering as many logs as I could. "Are you going to get any?"

"Well, there you go, that's it, then." She picked up a few logs, but instead of carrying them herself, she added them to the heap in my arms. "No wonder he pulled away from you. You were the only one who was with him that night; he probably needed you more than anyone else to believe him." She shook her head disparagingly. "Big surprise things didn't turn out so peachy for you guys."

I'd had similar thoughts at times over the years, but I'd never let myself articulate them as bluntly as she'd just done; however, that didn't mean I was particularly thankful to her for pointing all this out.

She grabbed a couple more logs, laid them on top of my stack so that now it reached my chin, then said, "Don't worry. I'll get the flashlight."

Then she picked up two small branches and left the shed.

Wow, great job there, girl. Way to blame him for all the problems he's ever had with his brother. Nicely done.

So, she'd royally screwed up this conversation, and they hadn't even gotten to the topic of Amber.

Tessa aimed the flashlight's beam onto the snowdrift-littered trail to the house.

As she thought about what Patrick had just told her, she couldn't even imagine what it would be like to accidentally kill someone like that. But then she realized that she shared something macabrely significant with Sean—both of them were responsible for taking the life of another human being.

But you shot a man on purpose; he killed a woman by accident. You shot a man on purpose.

She tried not to think of that night, of the warm spray of blood splattering the back of her neck, or the soft thud of the man's body landing on the floor behind her, or the worst part—the iniquitous satisfaction she'd felt squeezing the trigger.

Her answer to the psychiatrist rushed back to her: *"It feels like I'm sinking into a place I can't climb out of on my own . . . like it's getting harder and harder to breathe, to see a place where hope is real again."*

A place where hope is real again.

Yeah, that would be nice.

Even now as she remembered firing that gun, she sensed it again, savage instinct climbing up through the ages and spreading through her like fingers from an outstretched hand. Something primal, that unspeakable part of human nature that feels comfortable in the dark.

A shiver ran through her, and it was not because of the storm.

"Tessa." Patrick's voice disturbed her thoughts. "How did you sleep this week?"

"How did I sleep?"

"Yes."

Sean and Amber's house had been built half into a hillside with the basement and garage on the lower level. Since the fireplace was upstairs in the living room, she headed up the hill toward the patio door. "Pretty much like always."

"You've never gotten into a fight at school. Not once since I've known you."

A fight?

Oh, I get it. This is about Sean. He's mad you said that about Sean.

They reached the house, and she propped the door open. "No. I don't get into fights."

"But yet I can see you're really good at beating people up."

"I'm sorry, I wasn't trying to beat you up or anything, I was just—"

"No, Raven. It's not me I was talking about." With the wood in his arms, he had to turn sideways to make it through the doorway. "It's you."

For a moment she stood there, speechless, frozen in place by his words, paralyzed by her past.

Beating herself up?

Yes, yes, she was.

And for good reason too!

She entered, closed the door.

Sean was still shoveling the driveway out front, and Lien-hua and Amber were talking in Amber's bedroom, so Tessa quietly followed Patrick through the vacant living room to the fireplace.

He bent to deposit his logs. "I'm just saying, I think you're being too hard on yourself."

"You think I'm being too hard on myself."

"Yes."

"For killing someone?"

"I was the one who shot that man, Tessa. I was—"

"Don't do this, Patrick." She set her branches down and helped him unload his wood onto the pile that was already waiting by the fireplace. "I told you before I'm the one who pulled the trigger of the—"

"Tessa, he turned the gun on himself. He knew it was over for him. He knew he would spend the rest of his life in prison. So he—"

"Tried to put me into another kind of prison. So you've said." She let out a sigh. "Forget it."

"No, wait—"

"I said forget it. It doesn't matter." She gave him back his flashlight. "Is that gonna be enough wood?"

"We can get more later if we need to. And it *does* matter. This has been eating away at you for months, and it's something we need to deal with."

"I'm gonna get changed." Tessa knew that her words had barbs to them, but she didn't try to remove them at all.

As she left to stow her winter clothes, she did her best to shake off the thoughts of that night when she'd fired the gun and—whether it was really that guy's intention or not—had plunged out of reach into her own private little prison.

73

Tessa and I met downstairs again, sans jackets and boots.

I chose the footstool, she returned to the sofa.

Though she didn't seem like she wanted to talk about that night, now that we were into this, I wasn't ready to drop the conversation in the middle. "Let's say for a minute that I believed you, that it wasn't a suicide attempt, that, just as I shot him, you turned the gun on him and squeezed the trigger."

"Yeah, but you don't believe it, though."

"How would it change things if I did?"

She was wearing a gray hoodie and began unconsciously toying with the hood's string. "What do you mean?"

"Is that what it would take for you to leave this behind, to stop revisiting it?"

"For you to believe me?"

"Yeah."

"You mean like with Sean?"

"That's different."

"Oh. I see."

"But maybe," I backpedaled. "I don't know. Maybe, yes. Like that. Like if I would've believed Sean. Would things be different?"

She stood and walked across the room, pausing beside a framed cross-stitched picture of a whitetail deer hanging on the wall near Sean's minibar. "You remember that guy in San Diego like a year ago who tried to . . . well . . . force himself on me?"

Even now the memory burned hot and intense. "Of course."

"Well, what would it mean for me to forgive him? Do I have to be able to go up to him one day and chuck him on the shoulder and say, 'Hey, by the way, it was no big deal that you tried to rape me back there. How 'bout I friend you on Facebook?'"

"This is serious. Don't be flippant about it."

"I'm not being flippant. It's the same as what you were saying — what would be *different* if I forgave him? That's what we're talking about. What does forgiving someone even mean?"

"I think in some way you need to be willing to let go of what happened. Whenever you don't forgive someone—"

"Don't even say 'you end up hurting yourself.'"

I was quiet.

"Were you gonna say that?" She didn't sound spiteful, and I almost wished she had. More than anything she sounded lost. "Were you going to throw me an overworked cliché?"

She stared at me, waited for my response.

"My point is, it's not helping anything for you to live in the past."

"I'm not living in the past," she said sharply, "but I can't help being *affected* by it. Right?"

I didn't know what to tell her. Talking through issues like this, finding deep answers for a hurting teenage girl, I felt like I was way out of my league. "You're right," I agreed, "yes, the past affects us. It affects everyone."

"So is that what it means then? To forgive yourself—is that what you're saying? To just stop beating yourself up for the past, to stop hating yourself?"

"Or in this case, hating him, I don't know. But that's not exactly what we were discussing. Forgiving someone else is one thing, but we were talking about *you*, and I'm telling you, I don't think you need to forgive yourself for what happened that night in DC. That man was threatening to—"

"All right." Her tone was stiff and certain. "One last thing, then. That school shooting in Oklahoma last year, remember that?"

"What does that have to do with—"

"Just, do you remember it? Those two sophomores and the sixteen other kids they . . . well . . . ."

"Yes. I remember."

"Well, afterward I heard this guy being interviewed on Fox News; he was, like, some kind of youth motivational speaker or something—you know, who travels around telling kids at school assemblies not to use drugs and to have positive self-esteem, stuff like that. Anyway, on Fox News they asked him why he thought those two kids did it, why they killed those other students."

Of course I remembered the incident and the nationwide search for answers that followed it. "What did he say?"

When she'd mentioned self-esteem, it sent my thoughts flying to the videos I'd been watching earlier and made me think of Lien-hua's comments on the submissive role of Basque's partner: more easily dominated, lower self-worth.

The knives would hold different meaning to him—or none at all.

In the videos, Basque was—

"The guy"—Tessa said, crossing the room toward me again—"he was like, 'I can tell you this much, those two kids didn't have any answers. They were lost, they hated their classmates, hated themselves.' And the anchorwoman, she leans forward and says, 'But what is the answer?'"

"And did he have one?"

Only Basque was filmed. So who would stand behind the camera, the dominant partner or the submissive one? I wasn't certain, but my inclination was that the person behind the camera would be the one calling the shots.

Unless that's his signature, recording the murder of women—

"No." Tessa looked at me. "The youth speaker guy was, like, 'I don't really know, but I know kids oughta feel good about themselves.'"

"Self-esteem again," I said, still struggling to follow both her train of thought and my own.

The locations of the victims matter.

It's always about timing and location.

"So here's the thing: go to any auditorium full of teenagers and ask 'em if a coach, a teacher, a counselor has ever told them to feel good about themselves, how many hands do you think would go up?"

"All of them."

DNA from two victims was found on a knife in Reiser's trailer, but no videos of their deaths.

Torres arrived the day before you did. Lien-hua was in Cincinnati...

The psychosexual background would show a close association between sex and violence...

"Right." She tapped her finger against the edge of the couch. "So then, ask the kids if they already know that's not the answer. Guess how many hands go up then?"

"All of them," I conceded, still unsure where she was going with all this.

The videos were planted. That's why that person returned to Reiser's trailer Wednesday night...

"Exactly."

You need to follow up on any other cases with videos of people being killed during the years of Basque's imprisonment, see if the person who filmed him might have used a different partner in the intervening—

"Because," she went on, "they know they've done stuff they shouldn't feel good about. That's the thing—any idiot can see that just feeling good about yourself isn't the answer, and I'm tired of being told that it is. I'm tired of being lied to. Are you even listening to me?"

Her words scattered my thoughts of Reiser and his murderer. "Yes. Sorry, I am."

"You get it, right?"

I wished I had a quick fix for her, a way to heal her emotional scars, but I didn't. Honestly, I had the feeling that anything I said would only come out sounding trite or cavalier. "No one likes being lied to. Especially about something as important as dealing with a heavy conscience."

It wasn't a great reply, but she accepted it, then let out a soft breath. "You can't just make it go away, Patrick. It's there—guilt or shame or whatever. And trying to feel good about yourself isn't gonna solve it, not if you're trying to be honest with yourself at the same time—honest about what you're capable of. Denial is too cheap a cure for what I did."

Having her finally open up like this meant a lot to me, but also left me feeling awkward and ineffectual because I could hear her desperation and brokenness and I had no real answers for her. "Even if you did kill him, Tessa, wouldn't that be a sign of courage, not weakness?"

"How would it be courage?"

"He was unjustly threatening the life of an innocent human being, and you saved her; it's just that in this case the innocent person happened to be you."

She was quiet. "I didn't feel courageous. I felt terrified."

"Ralph once told me that fear is one of the key ingredients to courage. That if your life's in danger and you're not afraid, you're just a moron. And a liability."

"But it felt good to kill that man," she said softly, almost imperceptibly, and with fragile honesty. "I was glad I did it. That's different from just being afraid. I'm not sorry he's dead, I'm sorry it felt good when I shot him."

She was quiet, and the air seemed to beat with dark wings around us.

I knew this feeling personally, this one she'd articulated. More than once I'd flirted with the seductive lure of the forbidden. Just one example: when I was apprehending Basque, I needlessly broke his jaw, and the gratuitous violence excited a part of me I'm ashamed is even there.

"Tessa, I don't—"

"It's okay. I know there's not—"

"Hang on, let me finish. I'm no expert on any of this. And you're right, denial isn't the answer. Somehow forgiveness, or making amends, or some sort of penance, is—has to be, or else—"

"Or else you just gotta live with it, right? Let bygones be bygones, pick up the pieces and try to move on?"

"Well . . ." Even I could tell that wasn't really an answer, more of a metaphysical cop-out.

Lien-hua's observation came to mind: *"We run from the past and it chases us; we dive into urgency but nothing deep is ultimately healed."*

"They're good questions." I searched for something else, something more solid to offer her. "I need to think about all this some more." I was struck by how completely unsatisfying a response that was.

"Yeah, me too." Then after a pause that went on too long, she said quietly, "I read the note."

"The note?"

"The one from Amber. About last night. In the motel room."

"Oh, that note."

"Amber gave me her explanation this afternoon. I've been wondering if I could hear yours."

74

I fingered the prescription bottle in my pocket. I could confront Tessa about the meds or delve into the whole issue of my dubious relationship with Amber five years ago.

Great alternatives.

"What's the deal with you two?" Tessa pressed.

"It's complicated."

"Whenever people say something's complicated, they never mean complicated, they mean fractured, that somebody got hurt—and in this case it was both of you, wasn't it?"

I hate it when she does that.

"All right. Here's the edited version. Amber and I met when she was engaged to Sean. There was chemistry and—"

"Did you sleep with her?"

"No."

She waited. "But?"

"But we did fall in love," I admitted.

"And how did that happen?"

"What do you mean, how did it happen? We fell—"

"C'mon, no one just falls in love. You drift there purposely. You make choices in that direction or it never happens."

It took me a moment to reply. "You're right. Yes. We made choices in that direction."

Tessa was quiet. "What happened last night?"

"Nothing. I would never cheat on Lien-hua. And I would never do something like that to my brother."

"But yet you fell in love with his fiancée."

"Yes." This was not at all the conversation I wanted to be having. "I did."

I heard the garage door open. Sean must have finished shoveling.

"You were right," Tessa said. "That was highly edited."

The garage door rattled shut.

Hearing Sean enter the garage, I thought of what Tessa had just told me a few minutes ago about my not believing him ever since we were teenagers and how that had hurt things between us. And now, as I thought about the awkward issue of my past with Amber, it struck me that on all fronts I'd been the one, not Sean, who'd sabotaged our relationship.

Tessa seemed to be reading my mind. "Maybe you should go see how he's doing."

"Maybe I should."

Go on. Talk to him, then get back to those videos and follow up with Tait to see if there's been any progress on finding Kayla. And check for footage from other unsolved cases that might lead you to Reiser's killer.

I stood. Reached into my pocket and pulled out the bottle of pills.

Tessa watched Patrick unpocket a pill bottle.

"Amber couldn't get to the pharmacy," he said, "but she had these here. They're over-the-counter. She told me you were asking about getting a prescription filled? For sleeping pills?"

"Um . . ."

"I wish you would've told me."

"I was . . . I was trying to work some stuff out on my own."

"I would've helped. If you would have let me."

I was ashamed I needed it, she thought, but said nothing.

"Where did you get the prescription?"

"A psychiatrist."

"You're seeing a psychiatrist?"

"I was. I mean, I did. Just a few times."

He took a breath. "Look, I understand it's been rough, but . . . just keep me in the loop. I know I'm just your stepdad but—"

"No, you're more than that. I should've told you. Seriously. I'm sorry."

He put a reassuring hand on her shoulder, then held out the bottle to her, and she could see that he wasn't angry. Not really. "Amber said to just take one. They're supposed to be pretty strong."

She accepted the bottle. "Just one. Got it."

Then Patrick left to talk to his brother.

And Tessa took one of the pills.

75

There was no room for a car in Sean's garage.

Instead, the space was jammed full of tackle boxes, cross-country skis, fishing poles, tents, duck hunting decoys, and sleeping bags. A workbench rested against the far wall stacked with boxes of bird-shot, shotgun shells, and tools. One of his guns lay on the bench, a Mossberg 930 Tactical; it looked like he might've been interrupted in the middle of cleaning it. A small fridge sat beside the door, and I imagined it might be for his night crawlers in the summer, his beer and brats year-round.

The trophy deer heads and muskie that he'd removed from the living room for Tessa's benefit were propped against a huge card-board box stacked high with back issues of *Wisconsin Sportsman* magazines.

"So, did you get it all shoveled?" It was a lame conversation starter, I knew that. But that's the way things were between us.

"As much as I could. It's still blowing pretty hard." He stowed the snow shovel in the corner of the garage near the workbench. "At least we should be able to get out if we need to."

The garage was deeply chilled, and even though I'd grabbed my coat, I still caught myself shivering.

As I was trying to think of a way to transition into the topic of the accident twenty years ago, Sean said abruptly, "I thought there was a detective from Denver you were interested in?" His question took me off guard. I'd never told him about Cheyenne, and I was surprised he'd heard about the potential relationship that had never gotten off the ground.

"Cheyenne Warren."

"Yeah. That's it."

Cheyenne had been the one to fire the shots at the man who, as it turned out, was Tessa's father. Since that terrible night, her relationship with Tessa had remained visibly strained, although both of them claimed things were all right. In the disquieting wake of the shooting, Cheyenne had left law enforcement and gone back to ranching. Neither Tessa nor I had seen her in more than three months.

"I'm with Lien-hua now," I told my brother.

"I got to know her a little on the trail groomer. She's nice."

"Yes, she is."

Telling him that I was thinking of proposing to Lien-hua seemed like the sort of thing that might serve in some way to draw us closer together, but also a little too personal to share at this point.

He stamped the snow off his boots. "Well," he said ambiguously, then headed for the refrigerator. "Want a beer?"

"Naw."

"Can't drink while you're on duty?"

"Something like that."

He went to the fridge, pulled out a bottle of Leinenkugel's for himself, screwed open the top.

Absently, I picked up one of his ice-fishing poles. "Has it been a good year out on the ice?"

"Hasn't been bad." He watched me. "Oughta take you out before you leave. I know all the best spots in the area."

"I'm afraid ice fishing's never really been my thing."

"It's warm in the shanty. We have lawn chairs in there. A heater. Wieners. Some beer. Unless after what happened in the river . . . I mean, if you need to stay off the ice for a while."

I gave him a halfhearted smile. "I appreciate that. When things settle down with this case, I'll have to give it a shot." I leaned the pole against the wall again.

A small pool of silence.

The more we fumbled around in the quagmire of small talk, the more painfully obvious the shallowness of our relationship was.

I decided to just go for it.

"Sean, remember how things used to be between us?"

He took a long draught of his beer. "How do you mean?"

"When we were kids."

"When we were kids."

"Yeah. We'd go fishing with Dad all the time. Never seemed to catch much, but—"

"I remember."

"Trolled around the lake a lot."

"Lake Windemere."

"Yeah. We got to know that shoreline really well."

"I remember."

"I think the last time we went fishing together was that autumn before the accident."

He regarded me for a moment. "The accident."

"On New Year's Eve."

"I know which accident you meant."

"I'm sorry," I said.

"No." He took another drink. "Don't be."

"I mean, I'm sorry for the way things were after that. Between us."

"The way things were?"

"The way they are."

He lowered his beer, assessed me coolly. "Is that what you came out here to do? Go through that again? That night she died?"

"We've never really gone through it, Sean. Never really talked about—"

"Right. Okay." He moved toward the door. "Hey, what do you say we head inside, see how the women are getting along?"

"Sean, I'm saying I'm sorry I didn't believe you. About the deer. I know it hurt things between us."

For a moment I thought he might just walk away, but then he faced me and I searched his dark eyes for understanding, for some kind of reprieve, but it didn't come and I wondered if maybe our relationship was scarred in a way that would never heal. "I made things worse," I said.

"No."

"Yes," I protested. "I did."

"It was me."

I shook my head. "I should have—"

"No." He cut me off forcefully. "It was me. If we'd left that party earlier, if I'd let you drive, she never would have died. I don't want to talk about this."

"You can't blame yourself." I saw his hand tighten around the bottle. "It was an accident. You swerved to miss that—"

"You don't understand."

"No, I do understand. You—"

"There was no deer that night."

"What?"

He shifted his weight. "There was no deer."

"The ice? Is that what you're—"

All at once he turned from me and launched the beer bottle across the garage. It spun wickedly through the air, leaving a spray of suds in its wake until it smacked into the wall, sending an explosion of beer and glass splattering across the concrete.

The random movement above us in the living room stopped, and a moment later I heard purposeful footfalls moving across the room toward the stairs that led to the garage.

"I had too much to drink." Sean was staring in the general direction of the shattered beer bottle, but he seemed to be looking beyond it to another place. "I had . . . I shouldn't have been drinking."

Footsteps on the stairs.

"You just had two. That's not—"

"It was more than two. It was a lot more than two."

Every time he reiterated his guilt, the words struck me harder. In many states there's no statute of limitations on reckless vehicular homicide. If he really had been drunk that night, he could be—

The door to the stairs swung open, and Amber appeared. She peered at the foamy trail of beer extending the length of the garage, saw the smashed bottle, then fixed her gaze on Sean. Rather than asking what happened, she just shook her head slowly and then turned toward the stairs again.

"Wait," he called.

"No. I'm tired of your—"

"Amber, just give me—"

"No!" There was razor wire in her voice and I couldn't help but think of what she'd told me last night about her and Sean having their ups and downs. I could see this quickly moving into a major down.

"Don't walk away from me when I'm talking to you." Sean started after her, and I followed to see if I could defuse things before they spiraled off any further in the wrong direction.

76

"It was my fault, Amber," I said, entering the living room. "I brought up something that—"

"No, Pat." She was standing across the room from Sean and me, fiercely rooted beside Lien-hua. "You didn't lose your temper. Sean did. You didn't throw a beer bottle against the wall. Sean did. And this was not the first time."

"Okay, but the reason he was angry was—"

"Do you know what it's like being afraid of the person you're supposed to feel safest being around?" The words blistered through the air, and no one moved. Immediately, I knew that this was not the right time for Amber to be confronting Sean like this, not when he was already so upset thinking about his culpability in Mrs. Everson's death.

Still, the idea that Amber feared for her safety around my brother struck me deeply.

That's why she's leaving him. That's why—

"You're afraid of me?" Sean asked her. "Since when are you afraid of me?"

"You'll have to forgive us," Amber said to Lien-hua. There was a tremor in her voice. "Sean and I . . . we've had some . . . rough times. Lately."

Sean repeated more forcefully, "Since when are you afraid of me?"

There was no hesitation in her reply, no holding back: "Since drinking became more important to you than spending time with me." Even though her words were on fire, her eyes were beginning to glisten.

"Oh. Really."

"Listen—" I began.

Amber looked at me. "He needs to know."

No, please don't . . .

"I need to know what?" Sean exclaimed.

"Back when you and I were engaged, when I first met Patrick. We—"

Lien-hua put an arm out toward Amber. "Maybe we can find a better time to—"

"We were in love," Amber said softly but firmly. "We fell in love."

Oh, not good, not good at all.

Lien-hua lowered her arm.

"What?" Sean looked from me to Amber to me. "What do you mean you fell in love?"

"It's not what you think, Sean," I said.

"Really?" He glared at me. "Then why did my wife just say the two of you were in love?"

"We talked," Amber tried to explain. "But it was never—"

Ignoring her, Sean fired another question at me. "Did you sleep with her, Pat?"

"No."

"What then?"

"We talked and—"

"Talked. You talked. Well, were you in bed while you were talking? Were you holding her, hugging her, kissing her? Did—"

"That's enough," Lien-hua stepped in. "Let's just—"

"We did," I confessed to Sean. "Kiss. Twice. Yes. While you were engaged."

"You son of a—"

My phone rang.

"We never slept together," Amber reiterated.

"I'm speaking to Pat," he said gruffly.

For the moment I ignored the phone and came to her defense. "Don't take it out on her." Lien-hua gave me a cautionary look: *Standing up for Amber at a time like this is not going to help things!*

I added, "I take full responsibility for what happened."

"Yeah? And what does that mean, exactly? Full responsibility?"

The cell buzzed again. "This probably isn't the best time to talk about this." I drew the phone out of my pocket, and the caller ID told me the number belonged to Hank Burlman.

Burlman? Did they find Kayla?

Sean came closer until he was within arm's reach. His eyes were narrow, his jaw set.

Amber pleaded, "Please—"

"Quiet!" he hollered.

"I said"—my voice was firm, resolute—"don't take it out on her." Regardless of whether or not it was wise to intervene, I was not going to let him yell at Amber.

Return the call in a minute. Settle things here first.

I silenced the phone and placed it on the end table.

"Guys," Lien-hua said authoritatively. "Just, everybody, take a breath and calm down."

But things were not just going to calm down. When men get jacked up like this, they don't just decide the issue wasn't such a big deal after all, give each other a big hug, and sit down to a cup of tea. Something has to happen.

And it did.

Sean shoved me, not hard enough to send me flying, but assertively enough to let me know he was not joking around.

"See, this is the reason!" Amber shouted. "How you lose your—"

That stopped him. "The reason? The reason you and my brother were—"

"No! The reason we can't make things work, you and me!" By now she wasn't even trying to hold back her tears. "Why I can't stay with you anymore!"

"You're leaving?" His eyes shifted toward me. "To what? To be with Pat?"

"No," I said.

Lien-hua stepped forward, valiantly, one last time. "If we could all—"

Sean lunged at me, two hands against my chest, thudding me into the wall. With my injured ankle it was a struggle to keep from toppling to the floor. "We broke things off," I said, "before they went too—"

"Kissing her wasn't going too far?"

"No, you're right, it—"

"Maybe you wouldn't mind if Lien-hua and I took a little time to—"

I positioned myself in front of him. "That's enough."

"Stop it!" Amber implored. "Both of you!"

Sean clenched his hands into fists, and I braced myself. This was something he needed to do, and, honestly, I felt like I deserved it. I could have ducked, could have blocked the punch or stepped aside, but I didn't. I just said, "I'm sorry that things—"

Then it came, fierce and hard, a haymaker to the jaw. The force of impact whipped me around, and I slammed into the wall. A sailboat painting a couple feet away crashed to the floor corner-first and sent a shower of glass shards spraying across the carpet.

A moment later I heard Tessa's footsteps on the stairs.

"I never meant to hurt you," I said to Sean and I meant it. Facing him, I wiped some of the blood from my lip. He was a powerful man and he hadn't held anything back. I felt dizzy from the blow. "I'm very sorry."

"You kept this from me all this time." Now the anger in his voice had turned into something harsher, deeper—a sense of betrayal.

It's your fault, Pat. This is all your fault!

Amber's eyes were wide with tears, and she had her hand over her mouth. She took a step toward us but paused as Tessa appeared at the doorway.

"What's going on? I heard—" She saw my bloody, already-swollen lip. "What happened to you?" Her eyes tipped toward the shattered picture. "Oh . . ."

Sean cut into me with his eyes. "What you did wasn't right." Just those five final words, and that was all. It was as if he'd forgotten that Amber was even in the room with us.

"I wish it'd never happened. Believe me. I knew it wasn't right."

"This is . . ." Tessa said, putting two and two together. "Oh man."

Sean brushed past me and headed for the stairs that led to the garage.

"Where are you going?" Amber's voice was slight and uneven.

He didn't reply, just snatched his truck keys from the peg board at the bottom of the steps, and then he was out the door. He could have slammed it, but instead he let the door drift closed slowly, and that seemed to accentuate his anger even more forcefully than if he'd banged it shut.

Amber retreated to her bedroom, and even from this end of the hallway I could hear her sobbing. Lien-hua left to console her.

You did this, Pat.

Five years ago you set this all into motion!

My cell phone sat on the end table beside me. I picked it up to redial Burlman.

"Are you okay?" Tessa said.

"Oh, I'm on the brink of perfection."

I tapped at the screen to get to the missed calls.

"I mean your face." She sounded quite concerned.

Frankly, I felt like I'd been blindsided with a two-by-four. I touched my split lip gently. "I'm fine."

Sean's truck roared to life in the driveway.

"Well, go after him."

"This isn't the time, Tessa."

"Are you kidding?" She pushed my arm, lowering my hand holding the phone. "This is *so* the time. Go make things right."

"Tessa, there's nothing I could say right now that would make things right."

"Tell him you'll do whatever it takes. Because you love him. Because he's your brother. Quick, do it. Before he drives off."

Our conversation earlier about forgiveness and denial and guilt seemed to be fueling her admonition for me to make amends.

She was staring at me beseechingly, waiting for my reply. "Well?"

If there's any way to fix this, Pat, you should at least try.

I processed everything for a second. "Okay."

I retrieved the keys to the cruiser and redialed the last incoming number, then grabbed my jacket and jogged as quickly as I could manage on my taped ankle down the steps.

A man answered the phone, but it was not Hank Burlman; it was Alexei Chekov. "Agent Bowers, I'm going to tell you where Kayla Tatum is."

"I'm listening." I threw open the door. "Talk to me."

77

"Kayla is at the Schoenberg Inn."

"No." I stepped into the frigid night. "We already looked there."

"There are rooms that would not have been searched."

"Where?"

"The basement."

"I don't believe you."

I fought my way through the seething snow toward the police cruiser. *Why is he using Burlman's phone and not the phone from the station?*

"The Eco-Tech team paid the manager for exclusive use of certain rooms," he told me. "I offered him substantially more than they did. When you get there, ask about the rooms in the south end of the basement."

Wouldn't the officers who searched the hotel have known about them?

Maybe, maybe not.

Cranking open the car door to the cruiser, I climbed inside. "Is she all right?"

"I anticipate that she should be fine."

Key in the ignition. "How did you get Burlman's phone?"

"The laces in my boots have metal-tipped ends."

I froze.

He picked the cuffs, the cell's lock. Tait didn't listen to me. He let Burlman stand guard!

"What did you do to him?"

"I spent a few minutes with him. I didn't need five."

My teeth clenched. "You killed him?"

"No. But I'm not sure he'll walk again. Both of his tibias are quite severely fractured."

The bone gun. He got into the evidence locker!

I knew that Tait had left the station earlier, but the man working in the dispatch room would've still been there. "What about the dispatcher?"

"He'll be all right. The dispatch system, though, I'm afraid that will be down for a bit."

The taillights from Sean's pickup were a quarter mile down the road already. Once again I thought that even if I did catch up with him, I was the last person on earth he would want to see right now.

Unsure what to do, I let the engine idle.

"Why are you telling me all this?"

"I want you to find Kayla. I never wanted to harm her. I'm sorry we won't have the chance to work together."

I could tell he was about to wrap up the call. "Alexei, what room is she—"

"Good-bye, Agent Bowers."

The line went dead.

I redialed the number.

Nothing.

Tried 911.

No signal.

I smacked the steering wheel, then punched in Tait's cell number. "Where are you?" I said.

"Just south of Woodborough."

"Alexei called me."

"What!"

"We need an ambulance at the station ASAP. He's free and there are two men down—Burlman and the dispatcher. It's serious, but I don't think their injuries are critical. Alexei also took out the EMS dispatch channel. And we'll need to get some officers to the Schoenberg. Kayla's there."

"We looked—"

"No. The basement. Alexei said she's in a room on the south end."

"All my men left the Schoenberg when we came up dry an hour ago. What did he do to the guys at the station?"

"Burlman's legs are broken, I'm not sure what he did to the dispatcher. How long till you can get someone back out to the Schoenberg?"

"Twenty minutes. Maybe fifteen."

No!

I calculated the distance to the hotel from where I was.

It'd be a long shot, even if I hurried, but if it took the officers twenty minutes, I might be able to beat them there.

As long as the roads haven't drifted shut.

Get there, Pat.

Now. Go.

"I'm heading over there," I told him. "If your officers arrive first, tell them to have the manager take 'em to those rooms in the basement. And they need to keep an eye on him; Alexei said he bribed him, but the manager might be more involved than that."

Bring Lien-hua. She's better at interviewing victims and suspects than you are. Kayla might open up to her; give us an idea of where to look for Alexei.

Hanging up with Tait, I left the car and hastened toward the house.

Get the GPS ankle bracelet and the biometric ID card. This doesn't end with finding Kayla.

I burst through the door. "Lien-hua," I called, "grab your coat." Then I was on my way up the stairs. "We need to go."

78

"Why didn't you go after him?" Tessa asked as I stepped into the living room.

I could still hear Amber crying at the end of the hall. Even though I felt like I needed Lien-hua with me, considering how rough the week had been on both Amber and Tessa, I wasn't excited about leaving the two of them here alone. However, at the moment it didn't seem like I had a choice.

"Patrick?" Tessa must have sensed my urgency. "What's going on?"

Time was of the essence, so I cut straight to the point. "Listen, there's a woman who was taken, kidnapped. We might finally know where she is. Are you all right staying here with Amber?"

She looked at me anxiously. "Who is it?"

"Her name is Kayla. Will you and Amber be okay?"

"Yeah, no, totally. We're fine. We'll be fine." A line of worry scribbled across her face. "I didn't know someone was kidnapped."

"Call me if you need to."

She was staring uneasily at me.

"What?"

"He hit you really hard."

I translated that to mean that my face was really a mess.

Turning to the side, I drew my sleeve across my chin, leaving a long smear of dark blood on my jacket. I managed to keep from wincing from the pressure against my lip. "Lien-hua!"

"I'm coming."

Back in my room I grabbed my computer, as well as Donnie's biometric ID card, additional magazines for the Glock, my folding knife—a Randall King black automatic TSAVO-Wraith—the extra plastic handcuffs, and the GPS ankle bracelet. After encouraging Amber to call Lien-hua's cell if there was anything we could do or if she needed to talk, I said an awkward and rushed good-bye. On my way through the living room I discreetly asked Tessa to text me as soon as Sean came back, then I left to meet Lien-hua by the cruiser.

Sliding into the driver's seat, I handed her my computer.

"I can drive if you like," she offered.

"Sometimes I process things better when I'm behind the wheel."

I took us down the driveway, sliding momentarily on the ice. Wind-driven snow sliced at our headlights.

"So the Schoenberg Inn," Lien-hua said. "Alexei left Kayla right under everyone's nose?"

"If he's telling the truth, yes. And if Kayla is there, I want you to talk with her first."

"Sure. Of course."

On the road I hit another patch of ice and we fishtailed precariously close to a snowbank, then straightened out again.

"You sure you don't want me to drive?"

"I'm all right. See if you can trace the GPS location for Hank Burlman's cell."

It only took Lien-hua a few seconds to put the trace through, but Alexei knew how to operate off the grid and not surprisingly she came up empty.

A dozen puzzle pieces were cycling through my head. Too many things to keep straight. "Okay," I said. "Check my email. There should be a file from Angela or Margaret containing the schematics for the ELF base."

Lien-hua clicked to my email. "No. Nothing."

"What's taking them so long?" I muttered. "Send them both a message that we need that ELF info now."

Lien-hua did as I asked, then said, "Next."

"Two things. First, see if the Navy has had any communication problems tonight with the ELF base. Any alerts, anything at all."

"Who should I contact?"

"Admiral Winchester is the one who put this case in Margaret's lap. Try him. I'm not sure how to get in touch with him."

"I'll figure it out. What's the second thing?"

"Check the statute of limitations for vehicular reckless homicide in Wisconsin. I need to know what they were twenty years ago."

A moment of silence. "What's that about?"

"When I was in high school there was an accident. Sean lost control of our car, there was a collision, a woman was killed."

"Oh, Pat."

"No charges were brought against him, but when we were in the garage just now he told me he'd had too much to drink that night before getting behind the wheel." I didn't want to add this last part, but I wasn't sure if Lien-hua knew that my brother was only two years older than me. "Sean was underage at the time."

She quietly tapped at the keyboard. "I'll see what I can find out."

79

Tessa knocked on Amber's bedroom door. "Hey, can I come in?"

"Sure." She could tell that Amber was trying to stifle her crying.

Tessa opened the door somewhat haltingly and found Amber seated on the bed, a box of tissues on one side of her, a pile of crumpled tissues on the other. She was blowing her nose, doing her best to make it sound soft and insignificant.

Whatever confidence Tessa had displayed a few minutes ago when she was reassuring Patrick that everything would be fine had now evaporated.

"It's gonna be okay," she told Amber inaptly.

Amber patted the bed. "Come here."

Tessa crossed the room and took a seat beside her.

She's taking depression meds, this must be totally weirding her out.

"I'm sorry," Amber said.

"No, you don't need to be sorry."

But Tessa wasn't sure if that was true or not.

Overall, Sean seemed like a nice enough guy, so on the one hand she was upset at Amber for wanting to leave him, but Sean *had* punched Patrick—which, actually, Patrick probably had coming—and Amber had told her earlier that Patrick wasn't the reason she was leaving her husband, and apparently Sean did drink a lot, so it was hard to know what to think.

Tessa wanted to remind Amber of the stuff they'd talked about at the motel about canceling debts and sacrificing for the benefit of the relationship and all that, but she wasn't really sure if Amber needed to forgive Sean or divorce him. Obviously, Amber had issues too; however, as far as forgiving yourself, Amber had told her that she thought that sort of talk seemed arrogant, so in the end Tessa ended up saying nothing rather than chance saying the wrong thing.

Instead, she just reached out and took Amber's hand.

And Amber let her hold on.

———————◼———————

"Okay," Lien-hua said, "sat comm with the ELF station broke off a couple hours ago, but the Navy received a web-based encrypted audio message that everything is okay." She paused then added, "Yeah, unlikely. I know."

I'd heard Lien-hua's side of the conversation with the admiral's aide but hadn't been able to decipher all the specifics. "Who was the message from?"

"A chief warrant officer named Dickinson. He said the storm took out the satellite communication and landlines and that he'd come to the surface to check in. Because of your suspicions, though, the Department of Defense did a voiceprint analysis on the audio, and it was him. It's confirmed."

Could he be working with someone? With Eco-Tech?

"That's not enough to convince me."

"Me either. But it seemed to reassure them for the time being." Her voice stiffened. "They're closely monitoring the situation."

"Closely monitoring it."

"Their words, not mine."

That phrase "closely monitoring a situation" really means "not taking any immediate action," and that was the last thing I wanted to hear right now. I wished Torres and the SWAT team were here. I could sure use their help, especially if there was something going down at the base.

"Pat, I'll look up those statutes in a sec, but I never told you what I was working on at Sean and Amber's house earlier—doing research, trying to pull together a preliminary profile on Valkyrie."

"What'd you find out?"

"Unfortunately, not a whole lot. Valkyries are found in Norse mythology and were originally goddesses who flew over battlefields and determined who would be slaughtered and who would survive. Basically, angels of death. Eventually, the myths turned them into beautiful, alluring spirits who waited on slain heroes in Valhalla."

"Quite a transformation."

"Well, beauty and death are central themes of nearly all mythic systems. Very Jungian—if you buy into that. Anyway, psychologically, the code name draws from images of death, eternity, beauty, marriage. Maybe even judgment or eternal rewards." She paused slightly. "Code names by high-level operatives are rarely chosen indiscriminately."

I thought of the Bible reference to the bride of the Lamb and the seven last plagues: images of death, eternity, beauty, marriage.

It seemed like more than a fluke to me. "Anything else?"

"Our guy will be experienced in law enforcement or involved in the intelligence community. Midforties. Computer science training. High intelligence. A history of international travel. Multilingual. Male. Nationality at this point is still too hard to call."

"But a Valkyrie is a goddess. Why are you thinking we're looking for a male?"

"Female criminal masterminds might make good villains on the big screen, but they're almost unheard of in real life. For the most part, spying is a man's game. We should also look for possible religious idealism or mission-oriented terrorist affiliations. Possible motives: revenge, monetary gain, ideology."

"Or challenge."

She considered that. "Yes. Or challenge."

"So in essence, we need to discern what Valkyrie wants? Is that what you're saying the key is here?"

"Well, to nail down motive, yes. To glimpse personality, no."

I was no expert on profiling, but her comment took me by surprise. "No?"

"To find out what lies at the core of someone's personality, you need to know more than what he wants."

"What he loves?"

"No."

"Dreams of?"

"Uh-uh."

"Fears?"

She shook her head.

"Then what?"

"What he regrets. Only when you know what someone most deeply regrets will you know what matters to him most."

I took a moment to reflect on that, recalling my thoughts from my conversation with Jake yesterday about assassin mentality: *Without rationalization we'd have to live in the daily recognition of who we really are, what we're really capable of. And that's something most people avoid at all costs.*

Tessa's observation: *Denial is too cheap a cure.*

"What happens," I said, "when you're not able to rationalize or justify your deviant thoughts or behavior? When you're left with regret but no hope of forgiveness or resolution?"

"The mind has to deal with guilt somehow. When it's overwhelming, escaping reality is sometimes the only choice."

We run from the past and it chases us; we dive into urgency but nothing deep is ultimately healed.

"So, some kind of psychotic break? A split personality?"

She shook her head. "I see where you're going with this, but that's incredibly rare. Usually people just find a way to diminish the wrong or justify themselves in some way. Assassins, terrorists, espionage agents are experts at that." She sighed in disappointment. "I'm sorry, I know at this point all of this is sketchy, just unfounded conjecture."

"No, it's more than that. It's your instinct based on experience."

"Pat, you don't trust instincts."

"I trust you."

A long moment. "Thanks." She regrouped at the keyboard. "How much farther to the Inn?"

"Just a couple minutes."

"Let me see what I can find out about those criminal statutes."

One hour and four minutes left.

Solstice had thought they should just use a small, handheld camera, but Cane had wanted to go all out, so they'd brought a Sony HVR-HD1000U digital high definition HDV camcorder along.

"Go ahead and set it up," Solstice told Gale. "Let's get this statement filmed."

He flipped open the tripod and began to pull out the equipment.

"I made a real mess of things," Amber said, her voice quavering in a delicate, broken way. "Sean—he's not really that bad of a man. He never hurt me. Never hit me. He's never . . . I love him. I think I was just looking for a reason . . ."

To justify leaving him . . . Tessa thought, filling in the blanks.

"It's all gonna work out," she told Amber. "Don't worry."

Cliché, cliché, cliché.

Lame, lame, lame!

In the unsettling silence following her words, Tessa remembered the broken glass from the sailboat painting in the living room. "Maybe we should clean up that glass? From the picture, in the other room?" Okay, it was a little pathetic, but at least it might help distract Amber for a little bit.

Amber took a breath that was obviously an attempt to compose herself. "Yes."

The lights flickered briefly as the two of them traipsed down the hallway.

"There should be some flashlights in the kitchen," Amber suggested, obviously in anticipation of a power outage. "And we should probably get that fire started. Just in case."

"All set," Gale announced as he finished tightening the height adjustment on the tripod.

Solstice nodded.

Right now, three members of her team were carefully setting the remaining TATP ordnance in the tunnels on the top level of the base; Eclipse was guarding the hostages on the second level. Cyclone had taken Donnie up to the crew quarters for the time being so he wouldn't disturb the filming. The remaining team members were here with Solstice in the control room.

She eyed the remote control detonator on the desk next to her keyboard. A simple five-step plan: (1) send the transmission, (2) get to the tunnel that wasn't rigged to explode, (3) shoot anyone who tried to stop her, (4) blow the base, (5) disappear.

No more Eco-Tech team.

No more ELF base.

No loose ends.

Cane and Squall donned their ski masks and positioned themselves in front of the camera. Behind them hung a flag with a picture of the earth taken from outer space, as well as Eco-Tech's logo and their boldly lettered motto: A New Breed of Green—Dialogue When Possible, Action When Necessary.

"Ready?" Gale asked.

Cane nodded, Gale moved behind the camera.

The light went on.

And the filming began.

80

Lien-hua and I were less than a mile from the Schoenberg Inn.

Ever since starting in law enforcement sixteen years ago, I've always prided myself on my commitment to uncovering the truth and then seeing justice carried out, but now in this situation with my brother, I was sorry I knew the truth and I wasn't sure I wanted justice carried out at all.

"All right, Pat." Lien-hua took a small breath. "I've got something. In Wisconsin there's a fifteen-year statute of limitation on prosecutions for second-degree reckless homicide. It was in place at the time of the accident."

"But, let me guess: for first-degree reckless homicide there isn't one."

A pause. "That's right."

"We could be talking about a twenty-year sentence for—"

"Pat, it doesn't do any good jumping to conclusions like that."

"How do the statutes define the difference between second- and first-degree homicide?"

She consulted the computer. "First-degree reckless homicide—whoever recklessly causes the death of another human being under circumstances which show utter disregard for human life. It's a Class B felony." She scrolled to the next part of the law code. "Second degree—whoever recklessly causes the death of another human being. It's a Class D felony."

Utter disregard for human life. What does that mean exactly?

I already knew the answer to that: it would be up to a jury to decide.

The Schoenberg's parking lot lay a quarter mile ahead of us, and I could see its parking lights glowing blearily in the snow-strewn night. "Are there any statutes that specifically address vehicular homicide?"

"Yes, but that's not as clear-cut. According to Statute 940.09 1(c) it looks like a Class D felony. Unless . . ."

"The person was legally intoxicated."

"Let me see." She gazed at the computer screen, but I had a feeling she was stalling, that she already knew the answer. "Yes, there's another statute that determines if it's a Class B or Class D felony, 340.01 (46m). And yes, you're right, it has to do with blood alcohol content."

There were so many factors that we didn't know, would never know—Sean's alcohol concentration, Mrs. Everson's, whether or not she was driving too fast for conditions, whether or not he was—

Utter disregard for human life.

A skilled prosecutor could probably make the case for the first-degree reckless homicide charge, but the only way he'd be able to make it stick would be with proof of Sean's intoxication. And after all these years, the only evidence he would have of that was—

"Does that help?" Lien-hua asked.

"Yes," I said unenthusiastically. "Thanks."

—Sean's confession in court—

—Or the testimony of a federal agent to whom he had personally confessed.

We arrived at the Schoenberg Inn, and as I parked the cruiser, I tried to put thoughts of my brother and what he'd told me aside.

I tugged out my phone and pulled up the security camera photo of Alexei Chekov from the Minneapolis–St. Paul International Airport, but even as Lien-hua and I hurried inside to see if Kayla Tatum was all right, my disquieting fears for my brother's future wouldn't leave me alone.

And neither would the nagging question of where Alexei had gone after he'd left the sheriff's department.

81

It took us only a few moments to locate the hotel manager, Simon Weatherford, a gaunt-faced lanky man in his early forties. His shaved head and slightly graying goatee made him look more like an avant-garde artist in LA than the manager of a historic hotel in northern Wisconsin.

"You have rooms you did not show the officers earlier," I told him firmly. "I want to see them. Now. The rooms on the south end of the basement."

"I don't know what you're talking—"

I held up my phone and showed him Alexei's photo. "This man paid you for the use of a room and he left a woman there. She was kidnapped and right now you're facing charges as an accessory. Take us to her *now*."

Weatherford's face flushed. "He said she was hungover when he brought her in, he—"

I grabbed his arm and directed him toward the hall. "Let's go." I didn't even try to hide how furious I was that he hadn't shown the officers earlier where Kayla was.

Reckless homicide.

Utter disregard for human life.

Weatherford took the lead and hurried us through a network of corridors and past a series of plaques that celebrated the history of the Inn and its inclusion in the list of National Historic Landmarks in 2004. When I questioned him about Alexei, he admitted that Chekov had given him $200,000 cash with the promise of another

413

$300,000 in twenty-four hours if he didn't tell anyone about the woman.

A stunning amount of money. No wonder Weatherford hadn't led the officers here. Half a million dollars can buy an awful lot of silence.

We came to a dusty, wood-paneled lounge. Weatherford went directly to the far wall and pressed open a doorway that had been cleverly and imperceptibly hidden in the paneling.

A set of steps descended to a lower level. Lien-hua and I drew our weapons.

I passed Weatherford and jogged down the stairs, slightly off-kilter as I tried to keep pressure off my ankle, then proceeded through a door that read "Authorized Service Personnel Only" and entered a dim hallway with rooms on either side.

"Which room?"

Weatherford produced a key card and approached the second door on the left.

Secure the scene, Pat. Then assist the victim.

I motioned for Lien-hua to take the key, and as soon as she'd unlocked the door I flung it open and swept inside, leading with my Glock.

Kayla Tatum lay tied up on the king-sized bed and appeared only semi-conscious. Lien-hua rushed to her side while I quickly scanned the room for Alexei or any accomplices.

Saw no one.

Weatherford gasped when he saw Kayla. I didn't want to take any chances; I pointed to the floor. "Get down. On your knees."

"I didn't know—"

"Down."

He knelt, and I holstered my gun and quickly patted him down, found no weapons.

Protocol called for me to handcuff him to something in the room. I chose one of the sturdy chairs near the wall.

I doubted I would get cell reception this far underground, but I pulled out my phone and was surprised to see two bars. Good enough. My initial thought was to call 911, but then I remembered that Alexei had taken out the EMS dispatch line.

Try anyway!

Flicking open my knife, I slit the ropes that bound Kayla's ankles while Lien-hua bent over her wrists. I dialed 911 but got nothing but dead air, so I put a call through to Tait. "When are your officers going to be here?"

Lien-hua finished freeing Kayla, helped her sit up.

"Julianne's on her way; should be there shortly. Jake said he'd come over too, but that'll take longer. He's on the other side of Woodborough."

"What about an ambulance? How long till you can get one here?"

A pause. "All of 'em are on call. After the dispatch line went down, people started phoning the hospital directly, asking for help. It's been a nightmare trying to sort out what the real emergencies are."

Natasha's close; she's in the cabin Alexei used. She could—

No. She needs to stay there in case he returns to retrieve or destroy evidence.

"All right," I said, my thoughts swirling. "Maybe Julianne can take Kayla to the hospital to get her checked over. Any news on Alexei?"

"No. Nothing. Burlman and Marty Lane—he's the dispatcher—they're on their way to the hospital. They'll both survive. But 911's gonna be out for a while. Chekov fried the system."

The conversation ended, and I saw that Lien-hua had an arm around Kayla's shoulder, supporting her, comforting her.

Kayla had a slim build, light brown hair, delicate features. She was in her late twenties and wore black jeans and a blue long-sleeved sweater, but the sleeves weren't long enough to cover the bruises on her wrists where she'd evidently struggled against the ropes that had bound her.

I felt a renewed sense of anger rising against Alexei Chekov.

But he called you, Pat. He wanted you to find her. He didn't want to hurt her—

Maybe, maybe not. Right now I was caught in a thick coil of lies, and I thought it best to work from worst-case scenarios.

I put a call through to Natasha, and when she didn't answer I left an urgent message for her to get in touch with me immediately. "We found Kayla at the Schoenberg. She's all right. Be on your guard. Alexei might return to the house."

End call.

Lien-hua was talking softly, reassuringly, to Kayla. "My name is Lien-hua Jiang." She gestured toward me. "This is Patrick Bowers. We're FBI agents. You're safe now."

Kayla didn't reply. Just nodded, wide-eyed.

"How are you feeling, physically?" Lien-hua asked her.

Kayla's eyes were red, and obviously she'd been crying, but she appeared to be regrouping, gathering her senses. "I'm okay." Her voice was delicate. Words of glass.

"The man who took you," Lien-hua said, "did he hurt you?" The slight pause that she added before the word *hurt* lent a deeper meaning to the sentence, and I took it to mean "Did he assault you?" or perhaps "Did he rape you?"

Kayla shook her head. "He actually seemed . . . I don't know. It was almost like he didn't want me to be afraid." She looked around distractedly. "I didn't know what to do."

"Do you know where you are now?"

Kayla shook her head.

"We're in a hotel. The Schoenberg Inn. Does that ring a bell?"

"No."

"Okay. Do you have any idea where he might have gone? The man who abducted you?"

She shook her head.

"Can you remember," I asked, "did he bring you here right away or stop someplace first?"

Kayla thought about it. "We were in a cabin. I remember that. I don't know exactly where. The walls were these really thick logs. He gave me something that made me sleepy. Some kind of shot. I don't really remember anything else."

Lien-hua placed a gentle hand on her arm. "You're going to be all right."

Considering what she'd been through, Kayla seemed to be doing remarkably well, and I was thankful, but this conversation didn't look like it was going to lead us any closer to Alexei or the Eco-Tech team he'd told me about.

My thoughts shifted to the ELF station.

See if those schematics have arrived.

I had my phone with me, and although I could access my email with it, my laptop would be better for analyzing data. It was still in the cruiser.

"Lien-hua, are you good here?"

"Yes."

"I'm gonna grab my computer. I'll be right back."

"We'll find the man who took you," Lien-hua said to Kayla. "I promise."

Kayla gave a weak smile. "Thank you."

I freed Weatherford, hauled him to his feet. "You, come with me."

Even though I was walking with a hitch because of my ankle, I was in a hurry and he struggled to keep up. As we returned up the stairs, I asked him, "The man who bribed you, did he give you any indication where he might be going?"

"No."

"What about the other people who paid you to use the basement? The Eco-Tech members? Where are they?"

"They were in the other part of the basement. But they're gone."

"Don't lie to me."

"I swear they're not here. I don't know where they might be."

"How many of them were there?"

"Ten. Maybe eleven."

We passed through the paneled lounge containing the hidden doorway, and I thought of the ELF station, of how we might get there.

The Navy would need to staff it, transfer people into and out of the base, deliver supplies, remove waste.

Forest service roads?

Maybe. But then how would they do it during the long Wisconsin winters with those roads closed?

What about Project Sanguine, the buried cables? The underground bunkers? Is it possible there are still tunnels leading to the base?

As we neared the lobby, Natasha phoned me. "I got your message," she said. "So, Kayla's safe?"

"Yes."

"There's no sign of Alexei here. Did you get my email?"

"I'm on my way to check my messages now."

Donnie has worked at the sawmill since 2004.

What about his Monday and Friday trips to work? Why did it take him so long to get to the sawmill from home?

She went on, "The Lab finally identified the prints on the light switch in the Pickrons' study. I sent you the report."

"Whose prints are they?"

"Becker Hahn's."

That made sense; he was one of the Eco-Tech members whose photos Alexei had forwarded to me, but I couldn't understand why the Lab had taken so long to identify the prints. *Maybe someone's been tinkering around on AFIS, deleting data? The same person who got into the ROSD?*

"But," she said, "here's the big news. Angela found he was on the same flight last week to Milwaukee as Dana Murkowski, an alias used by Cassandra Lillo. She and Becker traveled up here together."

"Cassandra Lillo?" I was stunned. "What? Are you sure?"

"It's confirmed."

Why wouldn't her alias's name have been on a watch list!

Weatherford and I arrived at the lobby and I hustled him toward the front door.

Last winter I'd tracked a team of—for lack of a better term—domestic terrorists who were trying to steal a classified military device that could be used to cause a stroke or a catastrophic cerebral event in another person. Cassandra Lillo was a scientist who'd partnered with her father and my NSA friend Terry Manoji to steal the device and sell it to the Chinese. Right before she was taken into custody Cassandra had said to me, "You have no idea what we have planned."

I'd thought she was talking about the device.

Was she talking about this? About something now?

Cuffing Weatherford again, this time to a table near the hotel entrance where I could keep an eye on him, I exited the building to get my computer from the cruiser.

A tirade of thoughts, of puzzle pieces.

I remembered Cassandra's escape in November: a transfer order to send her to another detention facility had come through, and during transport she'd strangled one guard and overpowered another, permanently disabling him, before making her escape. Later, the request for transfer was found to have been caused by a computer glitch. I'd never believed that, and now, in light of everything that was going on, I was even more convinced it was not a random processing error.

At the car, I grabbed my laptop.

At least the submarines are on alert. At least that's covered.

"Pat? Are you still there?" Natasha asked.

"Yes, sorry." *Cassandra's father and Terry are both dead, both out of the picture.* I turned back toward the hotel. "Is there anything else in the report that I need to know?"

"Not that I can think of."

"Stay where you are. Watch out for Alexei. And find out where Jake is."

"I will."

Terry was a spy for the Chinese government.

Eco-Tech consulted with foreign governments. We knew about Brazil and Afghanistan, but it was possible—

Truth often hides in the crevices of the evident.

Secretary of State Nielson was in Tehran this week in bilateral talks with Iran about their nuclear program.

As soon as I entered the lobby I pulled up Margaret Wellington's cell number and punched it in.

———————————◼———————————

Tessa and Amber had just finished cleaning up the glass from the shattered painting and were putting the garbage can and vacuum cleaner away in the kitchen when the electricity went out.

This far out in the country with no street lamps or city lights, the house was immediately swallowed in a deep, corporeal darkness. The two women each had a flashlight that Amber had scavenged. Tessa flicked hers on. A moment later so did Amber.

The beams of light slit the kitchen's black air like long, narrow knives. Tessa saw the flash of her own face as her flashlight beam danced across the framed photo that Sean had shown her earlier of her at her mother's wedding, the picture in which she was smiling, lighthearted, a photograph that seemed like it must have been taken in another life.

"Are you any good with starting fires?" Amber asked. "I'll give you first dibs."

Tessa had seen Patrick start fires a bunch of times on the camping trips he'd managed to drag her along on. "Sure. I'll give it a shot."

82

I found a chair on the far side of the lobby, away from Weatherford and the three guests who were chatting near the front desk. Just as I'd finished opening up my email program on my laptop, Director Wellington answered: "Pat."

"We found Kayla," I said promptly. "It looks like she's all right. We're going to get her to a hospital as soon as possible. Alexei escaped."

"Leads?"

"No, listen, a couple things: first, we need to see if Eco-Tech has any ties to Iran. The timing of Nielson's visit there this week with all of this going down, it can't be a coincidence."

"I'll talk with him." Brisk answers. Everything right now was forthright and down-to-business.

"What about the schematics to the ELF station. Why haven't you sent them?"

"I did send them. An hour ago."

"I'm looking at my email right now. There's nothing here."

No email from Natasha either.

And nothing from Angela.

"Agent Bowers. The email was sent."

"No . . ."

Oh.

Wait.

This morning Alexei hacked into your account.

No!

421

"Chekov might have gotten into my account, downloaded the file."

"How could he get access to your email?"

"He has a source. An inside man. I don't know who."

Valkyrie?

Is Valkyrie someone in our government?

I told Margaret the address of a gmail account I keep so I don't have to give credit card companies my Bureau address. "Resend the file. I'll download it from there."

"I'm not at my desk." I noted the change in her tone that you hear when someone you're talking with on the phone starts moving around. "It'll take me a minute to log into my office computer."

"Did you know Cassandra Lillo traveled up here with Becker Hahn, one of the Eco-Tech activists?"

A pause. "I hadn't heard that."

"Her father was—"

"I know who her father was. Sebastian Taylor."

"An assassin."

"Yes."

"And he trained her to kill, just like—"

"Yes." Impatience in her voice. "I've read the files."

"After you send me the schematics, can you get in touch with the CIA and see if Taylor was ever on an assignment at a location where Chekov might have been present?"

"You think they're related?"

"Taylor and Chekov—both assassins—then Taylor's daughter shows up here while Chekov is in the area? It seems like too much of a coincidence for them not to be connected somehow."

I remembered my conversation with Angela and her list of who she thought might be able to hack into a nuclear sub, and, taking everything I knew about this case and the one in San Diego into account, I tried to process the implications.

Cassandra Lillo? Could she be Valkyrie?

Someone hacked into the California Department of Corrections and Rehabilitation computers to help her escape . . . Someone called

Ardis's phone from Egypt, accessed the DoD's Routine Orbital Satellite Database . . . The name Dana Murkowski didn't raise any red flags at the airport . . .

You'd need a world-class hacker to do all that.

A world-class hacker.

It felt like the puzzle pieces should have been interlocking before my eyes, but I still couldn't see the big picture.

Truth often hides in the crevices of the evident.

"One more thing. This is going to sound crazy, but Terry Manoji. Find out from the CIA if he's still alive. I'm wondering if—"

"He is."

"What?"

"He awoke from the coma four months ago."

I pounded the arm of the chair I was sitting in. "How come you never told me!" The people near the front desk looked my way, offered me judgmental looks, then returned to their conversation.

"Do not raise your voice at me, Agent Bowers." Margaret's tone was cold and censorious. "It was not your concern. Terry Manoji's contacts in China have close ties to three terrorist groups in Pakistan, one of which is Al Qaeda. The CIA concluded it would be in the best interests of national security to keep his existence and his whereabouts a secret."

"All right." This was unbelievable. "I hear what you're saying, but where is he?"

"Don't worry, he's at a secure loca—"

"Don't give me that, Margaret, you know—"

"Enough, Patrick."

Through the window I saw the blue-red-blue flicker of overhead lights from an approaching cruiser.

Julianne. Finally.

"He was in a coma," I said. "Is he still in a hospital? Still recovering? Because if he is, nearly every one of their systems would be connected to the internet, and anything that's connected to the internet can be hacked into. Given enough time he would find a way to get in—"

I caught myself in the middle of my thought.

Anything that's connected to the internet can be hacked.

Hacked into.

One keystroke away from Armageddon.

"Margaret, all the indicators are pointing toward someone sending an ELF signal to one of our subs. We have to assume it's—"

"That's covered," she replied. "The DoD raised the alert level to DEFCON 2."

"Have 'em raise it again."

"Patrick," she responded curtly. "The military needs evidence not just conjecture to make an escalatory decision like that."

I wanted Julianne to help me clear the other part of the basement, make sure no one from Eco-Tech was still lurking downstairs. I started toward the door.

Becker has no history of violence, but Cassandra does. There were two sets of boot prints outside the laundry room of Donnie's house. She was there.

"This guy Becker Hahn was at the Pickron home, and Cassandra, Terry's old partner, is working with him." The clues were like filaments, narrow, encircling each other, dancing, flirting, never quite touching. "The call to Ardis's phone following the murders on Thursday came from Egypt. If that's where Terry's being held, I'd say that's enough evidence to move forward."

Margaret didn't reply immediately. "I'll get the schematics to you and track down Terry Manoji. You—find a way to get to that base."

Julianne arrived, and after we'd confirmed that the other section of the basement was unoccupied, I took Weatherford to her car and had her lock him in the backseat so we wouldn't have to keep an eye on him when we went to get Kayla Tatum.

While Tessa worked at the fire, Amber sat beside her in chilly silence. It made Tessa uneasy and she knew she needed to do something, say something to help her. But she had no idea what in the world that might be.

———————————◼———————————

Three armed CIA agents burst into Terry Manoji's room, strapped his wrists to the arms of his wheelchair, and began methodically searching the room.

Despite himself, Terry felt a tiny wisp of concern.

Without consulting his phone he didn't know exactly what time it was, but he did know that in less than forty-five minutes Cassandra would be sending the ELF signal and eleven minutes after that Jerusalem would cease to exist and he would be free—but someone had obviously tipped off the CIA that something was up.

Terry's phone was tucked beneath one of his useless thighs. As long as the men kept him restrained in the wheelchair he would be all right.

But if they decided to move him to the bed, it would be another story.

As he watched the CIA agents scour the room, he began to quietly formulate an appropriate response in the event that they tried to transfer him out of the chair.

83

Julianne Doerr and I arrived in the room where Alexei had left Kayla.

Officer Doerr, a sturdy, serious-looking woman in her early forties, reassured Kayla, "I'm going to take you to the hospital so we can make sure you're all right."

But even as she said that I realized that in the spate of phone calls over the last few minutes, I hadn't been thinking clearly. You never let a victim ride in a police car with a suspect and you never let a civilian ride in the front of a cruiser, so if Julianne took Kayla to the hospital, Weatherford would need to stay here with Lien-hua and me—but that wouldn't work, since Margaret had been clear that she wanted us to find a way to get to the ELF base.

Quickly, I called Natasha again, arranged for her to come over and transport Kayla to the hospital. Officer Doerr agreed to take Weatherford to the sheriff's department for questioning, since he was already in her car, then she and Lien-hua helped Kayla, who was still somewhat groggy, to her feet.

On the way up the stairs, I thought about Becker Hahn, Alexei, Cassandra, Terry; the loose, tangential web of associations that seemed to tie them all together.

And Valkyrie? Where did Valkyrie fit in? Was there psychological significance to the code name after all, as Lien-hua had postulated?

I like cases in which facts are solid, verifiable; you lock them into place and move on; you discover a truth that you can't disprove and it gives you a basis on which to build your investigation. However, this week I felt out of my element, forced to deal with facts that didn't quite mesh and hypotheses that squirmed out of my grasp as soon as I tried to pin them down.

Maybe I did need to trust my instincts more.

When we hit the lobby, Lien-hua and Julianne waited with Kayla for Natasha to arrive, and I flipped open my laptop to check my gmail account to see if the information from Margaret had come.

It had.

She'd sent a short text message with an attached, password-protected PDF file. In her note she mentioned that the CIA's analysts hadn't found any evidence of instances in which Taylor and Chekov's paths might have crossed. Also, they were sending their interrogators to Terry's room "to confirm that he has had no access to the internet."

I unlocked the PDF file, and though only moments earlier I'd been optimistic that the schematics would help us, now that I was finally able to examine them, I found their thoroughness and attention to detail frustratingly disappointing.

There were three levels to the underground base, that much was clear: an entry bay for some kind of freight elevator that led to the surface, a middle level of crew quarters, and a command center and power generation facility below that. Eight tunnels led from the facility, but there was no clear indication of where—if anywhere—they might be accessed.

These can't be the most detailed or up-to-date files.

Why would Margaret send me these?

As I studied the diagrams, Natasha arrived. Julianne led Kayla to her and Lien-hua strode toward me.

The underground ELF base was located near the coordinates in the center of the Chequamegon-Nicolet National Forest where the aboveground station had been. *The forest service roads haven't been plowed, we'll never be able to get there by—*

"Well?" Lien-hua stood beside me, and I tilted my laptop so she could see the screen. She studied it. "Is that the only entrance?"

"It's the only one visible on this set of maps." I pointed to the tunnels that spread away from the station. "But I find it hard to believe that there would only be one way into the base."

"Always leave an escape route."

"Right."

"Where do the tunnels terminate?"

I shook my head. "There's no way to tell."

Unless—

"Hang on." I closed my eyes and visualized the topography of the area surrounding the old ELF site, evaluating the terrain and comparing it to the snowmobile trail map I'd studied my first night up here. Carefully, I rotated both maps in my mind, overlaying the features.

Donnie took longer than he needed to when getting to work on Mondays and Fridays . . .

"They would have to staff the station . . ." I said, thinking aloud. "That means getting people into and out of the base undetected. But in such a small, close-knit community, how could you do that?"

Opening my eyes I studied the schematics again, scrutinizing the precise geographic orientation of the tunnels. "Where could strangers regularly arrive and leave from without raising any red flags?" I mumbled, but even as I said the words I realized where one of the tunnels, if it were long enough, would lead.

"Oh, Lien-hua, that's it."

"What? What are you thinking?"

"Renovations in 2004. It would have been the perfect time to—"

She gave me a sudden look of comprehension. "What? You mean here? The hotel?"

"A National Historic Landmark can't be torn down. The government was protecting its investment." I was on my way to the door, laptop in hand.

"Where are you going?" She quickened her pace to catch up with me.

"Weatherford. He knows more than he's been letting on."

‎◼

The fire was slowly growing large enough to warm Tessa and Amber, and they'd pulled a couch close and now sat together, silently watching the flames. Amber had lit some candles, and the room smelled of sweet vanilla and crackling, burning pine. Just a few feet away, the storm churned outside the window.

Amber drew out her cell, called the bait shop. "Sean, the electricity went out." Tessa could tell she was leaving a message. "Pat and Lien-hua had to leave. I'm here with Tessa." A long pause. It seemed like Amber might start crying again. "I'm sorry about everything tonight. About things with Patrick back . . . I love you . . . um . . . if you get this, call me. Okay?"

After she hung up, Tessa tried to reassure her. "I'm sure he'll be back soon. You guys'll figure things out, okay?"

"Okay."

Even in the dim, flickering light Tessa could see a storm of loneliness burdening Amber's face, but before she could say anything else to try and cheer her up, Amber said, "Did Pat give you some sleeping pills earlier tonight?"

"Yeah, they're in my room."

"I think maybe I could use one to calm down."

"Okay. Sure. They're on my dresser. On the left." Tessa scootched forward to retrieve them, but Amber stood first. "That's all right. I've got it."

From the edge of the couch Tessa watched her stepaunt head toward the hallway, and then disappear into the shadows lingering just beyond the fire's light.

84

I stared at the door.

Rusted, located at the back of the Schoenberg Inn near the dumpsters beside the food service loading bay. Though the door had a keycard reader and a numbered touch pad, since it was just an unobtrusive exterior door around the back of the building, I imagined it wouldn't draw much attention from anyone.

That's how they could transfer staff and supplies into and out of the base without being noticed. The thought gave me hope that there would be a motorized way to get to the base after all.

Julianne, Lien-hua, and Weatherford stood beside me. He'd taken bribes, wasted our time, endangered lives. I was so angry with him, but I kept my mouth shut. I was on the brink of saying something I would seriously regret.

"How much did the Navy pay you?" Lien-hua asked him irritably.

"They don't pay me, it's just a condition of my employment." He sounded rattled but also slightly defiant. "All I know is that the door is here. People come. They leave. I almost never even see 'em." He gestured toward the flat surface of the door where a doorknob or handle should have been. "I don't even know how to get in."

I do.

"Get him to the sheriff's department," I said, pulling out the biometric ID card.

Julianne began to escort Weatherford back to her cruiser, but as they reached a strip of ice just past the dumpster, he kicked at her leg and she went down hard.

"Hey!" I yelled. I started for him, but he rabbited toward the woods, and with my ankle slowing me down, Lien-hua was able to pass me and get to him first. She tackled him with authority.

I was moving toward her, but she shook her head. "Get that door open, Pat. We'll take care of him. I'll be right back."

She and Julianne hustled Weatherford out of sight around the edge of the building, and I went back to insert Donnie's biometric ID card into the scanner.

◼

Tessa heard the water running in the bathroom sink.

"Did you need one?" Amber called.

"Naw, I actually took one earlier. Thanks." Now that the topic had come up, Tessa realized she *was* starting to feel a little mellow, the medication-induced drowsiness catching up with her.

"I'll leave them here in the medicine cabinet." Amber's voice sounded more muted than it should have, as if the hungry darkness in the hallway were swallowing some of the sound.

But Tessa did manage to hear the faint click as the medicine cabinet opened, and then another as Amber shut it again. And for some reason she thought of Patrick, of his mission to find that kidnapped woman. Though it was a little uncharacteristic of her, Tessa said a brief prayer for his success. And a short prayer too, for Amber, that she would be able to find the rest and peace that she needed tonight.

◼

The keycard didn't open the lock.

Instead, on the screen just above the number pad, a prompt came up asking me to enter a password, and I had no idea what that might be.

Remembering the cipher I'd passed along to Angela and Lacey, I tried 27219.

Nope.

I entered Donnie's work ID, the phone number we were tracking related to Valkyrie, even alphanumeric ways of spelling Queen, all to no avail.

The clues circled around, sliding into place, then dislodging again. Squirming away.

Revelation 21:9.

What did it say again? Seven plagues? Seven vials?

Maybe there's something in that verse. Something you can use.

Having left my computer in Julianne's cruiser, I used my phone to pull up an online Bible: "And there came unto me one of the seven angels which had the seven vials full of the seven last plagues, and talked with me, saying, Come hither, I will shew thee the bride, the Lamb's wife."

Seven angels. Seven vials. Seven plagues.

I tried 777.

No.

As I scanned the next few lines I felt my heart plummet: "And he carried me away in the spirit to a great and high mountain, and shewed me that great city, the holy Jerusalem, descending out of heaven from God."

Jerusalem?

Is Jerusalem the bride? The queen?

Pulse racing, I read the verses again, hoping to establish if that's what the apostle John was referring to. It seemed to be, but I wasn't certain of the interpretation, there might be more to—

Secretary of State Nielson is in Tehran this week . . .

Iran and Israel? Is this something to do with Jerusalem and Tehran?

Alexei had mentioned that Russia sold its military secrets to Iran.

Jerusalem.

The bride. The queen.

What else had Alexei said? *The Beriev A-60 can shoot down a satellite, even from hundreds of kilometers away . . . It heats the outer casing, causes structural damage.*

It was the Russian version of the Boeing YAL-1.

None of this was certain, but if Alexei was right, it played in our favor. I called Margaret again and asked her to check on any Boeing YAL-1s we might have stationed in the Persian Gulf.

She didn't even question why I was asking this but took a minute to make a call on another line, then said, "No. That aircraft was only experimental. The program was scrapped. There are only a couple left at Edwards Air Force Base."

That was in California. "Hang on a sec."

A quick online search told me that the Vahdati Air Base was the closest Iranian Air Force base to Israel.

That would be the most likely one.

If you're right, Pat—yes—

Timing . . . location . . .

I told Margaret what I was thinking about Jerusalem, and she listened intently. "If anything happens," I said, "Israel is going to strike back at the most likely country to fire a nuclear missile at them. Get in touch with Secretary of State Nielson. He needs to call his counterpart in Israel, get them to put up whatever missile defense shields they have around Jerusalem. And we're going to need Iran to scramble some planes."

When I mentioned the Beriev A-60s Margaret scoffed at first but finally committed to calling Nielson. Before we hung up I remembered the web-based encrypted message from the base, realized there was a way to communicate with the outside world, and informed her I'd follow up as soon as I could. "Keep this line open."

She hung up and I saw Lien-hua jogging toward me, her sable hair whipping wildly behind her in the wind. "No luck?" she called, pointing to the door.

"No. Any ideas?"

She studied it. "Step back." I was surprised to see her crouch into a ready position for kickboxing.

"It's a metal door."

"Step back, Pat."

"Lien-hua—"

I saw the intensity in her eyes and I stepped back.

She took a calming breath and then burst forward with a fierce front kick, landing her left foot against the door right beside the key-card reader. The impact didn't appear to do any damage to the lock.

"We need to find another way—"

"Quiet."

I was quiet.

She went at the door again, aiming for the lock itself, and when she kicked it, the door shuddered, but still the lock didn't give. She backed up a third time, took a deep breath, then flew forward with a brutal spinning side kick, and this time when her foot smacked against the door I heard a pop inside the lock.

Nice.

If Eco-Tech used this entrance, they might have left someone to guard the entryway. I drew my weapon and pressed against the door to test it, but it wouldn't give.

"One more shot," she said softly.

I moved aside, and she exploded toward the door—another care-fully placed spinning side kick—and the lock finally shattered. Im-mediately, the door snapped open. She had her weapon out now too.

"I never doubted you for an instant," I said.

"Uh-huh."

I signaled that I'd go first; she covered me.

"FBI!" I shouted into the darkness. "On the ground. Arms outstretched!"

No verbal response. I drew out my Maglite and clicked it on, held it between my middle and ring fingers of my left hand, cap end against my palm so I could use a standard two-handed grip on my weapon.

Swung through the doorway.

Empty. Nothing, except a downward-sloping tunnel of hard-packed earth.

So they could roll supplies in, I thought, once again hopeful that there'd be some means of transport to the base. *It's at least five miles. Surely they don't just walk the whole way . . .*

Before going any farther I contacted Tait to get backup on the way, but in this weather I knew that'd take awhile and I wasn't about to stand around here waiting for them.

"Let's go," I told Lien-hua.

Weapons drawn and ready, we entered the tunnel.

◼

One of the interrogators searching Terry's room discovered the spliced section of cord from the lamp beside his bed, the wires Terry had used to charge the cell phone.

"He's got something here," he announced. "And I want it found. Now!"

Terry watched the three men carefully, noting which of them appeared least vigilant about keeping his weapon protected.

The youngest agent, a guy Terry had heard the others refer to as Riley, seemed to fit the bill.

It wouldn't be easy, Terry decided, and he might not be able to kill all three men before they could get a shot off at him, but if it came down to it, he was willing to take that chance rather than risk having them move him out of here before Abdul's militants arrived.

◼

"We do this," Cane said into the camera, wrapping up the video, "to show the world that time is running out and that action, swift and decisive, must be taken to assure the survival of our species, the survival of our planet. If a small group of activists can break into and disarm one of the most secure weapons systems in the world, someone else could break in as well and use the weapons to cause apocalyptic harm. There is no sure and certain way to secure nuclear weapons. They must be dismantled. They must be destroyed. The time in human history has come for us to rise above our base instincts of survival and self-preservation and move toward a more peaceful, nuke-free world for the sake of our children and the future of our race."

Solstice heard the spiel but wasn't really listening to it. Instead, she was thinking about the launch that would occur in just over thirty minutes.

Threats in today's cyberworld aren't often identified until the last minute, so the military's decision cycle of observe-orient-decide-act, or OODA, is infinitely compressed and has to happen almost simultaneously. There are no "T-minus ten . . . nine . . . eight" countdowns, like in the movies. Not these days.

In real life, nuclear weapon launches are immediate and rather anticlimactic things. A couple of keys are turned, a couple of buttons are pressed—a bit of computer code flits through a system—and the silo or submarine door opens and the missile is on its way.

And so, tonight, the ELF signal carrying the launch codes would arrive at the sub, the malware would initiate the launch sequence, and the missile would fire.

Simple.

Immediate.

Irreversible.

Cane concluded his talk, Gale stepped away from the camera, and Solstice assessed the room. "Start up the electromagnetic generator. And get Pickron back down here. Let's send this message of peace to the world."

85

Passing beneath the hotel, Lien-hua and I found ourselves in a tunnel that reminded me of the abandoned gold mine I'd been in last year on a case in which I'd been chasing a killer in the mountains west of Denver. Eventually I'd stopped him, but not before he tried to bury me alive in the mine.

Not the best memory at the moment.

The air smelled damp and earthy, but the ground underfoot was hard and dry. The windchill outside the hotel had been below zero, but in here the temperature hovered in the midfifties, but because it would be too cumbersome to carry our jackets, we kept them on.

Our flashlights allowed us to see about twenty-five meters. All looked clear.

Given the distance we were from the ELF site in the Chequamegon-Nicolet National Forest, I'd never be able to walk the whole way on this ankle. Even if the tunnel went directly to—

"There, Pat, look." Lien-hua pointed. A narrow-gauge railroad track was just barely visible at the far edge of our light.

I quickened my pace. "That's it."

As we moved forward, I shared my speculation about Jerusalem being the queen, and Lien-hua listened intently. I could see that the track disappeared around a gentle bend in the tunnel. Still no one in sight. She said to me softly, "I need to know something: did Amber tell you she was planning to leave Sean?"

"She left me a note this morning."

There has to be a cart or something. There has to be.

"A note."

"Yes."

We were beginning to make our way around the tunnel's curve. Still no sign of anyone from Eco-Tech. "She was testing the waters," Lien-hua observed, "coming to you last night, seeing if there was anything still there, any possibility of making things work with you."

"There isn't any possibility. You're the one I love. You're the one I want to be with. You believe me, don't you?"

"Honestly, Pat, I do."

I wasn't certain how this night was going to play out, and I couldn't shake Antón's words that the future is uncertain, that you never know what might happen, that you need to seize the day. So as we approached the tracks, I whispered, "Lien-hua, if for some reason I don't make it out of here tonight, I want you to know—"

"Don't talk like that."

"Seriously, there's something I was—"

"Pat. Stop."

"Listen, I know this is a bad time, but I was gonna ask you if—"

"Patrick. You know I don't like talk about finality and failure." Her words were unequivocal. "Whatever it is, tell me later. When this is over."

I recalled our conversation at the motel about twists at the end of the story, when everything you thought was true turns out to be a giant house of cards, when hope that seemed guaranteed disappears in a final dramatic plunge.

No, she's right, Pat. This isn't the time. Make it special. Make it right.

"Okay. Later, then," I consented at last. "When this is over."

We finished rounding the bend, and I saw what I'd been hoping to find: resting on the track twenty meters away was a small motorized platform built to transport people or supplies.

The railcar was simple—four steel wheels attached to a metal base about two meters square. A handrail rested on narrow supports that skirted the perimeter of the platform. On the left, a control panel sat above a small but powerful-looking motor. Two operating lights hung from the railing, one on the front of the cart, the other on the back, to light the way when traveling in either direction on the track.

Stretching beyond the railcar, the tunnel disappeared in a straight southeasterly direction. "It must go under the Chippewa River," I muttered.

Lien-hua climbed onto the platform and approached the control panel. "I'll drive."

I stepped up beside her. "That's good by me."

It took her only seconds to figure out how to start the motor. When she did, the two electric running lights flicked on and a yellowish glow appeared in front of and behind us.

"How fast do you think this thing can go?" I asked.

"Let's find out." She throttled forward, and the sound of the motor filled the passageway. It wasn't as loud as I expected, but it was noisy enough that it'd make it difficult to talk during the trip.

Flicking off our flashlights, we both kept our guns out and ready.

And we accelerated toward the ELF station.

———◼———

Amber had completely stopped crying, and for some reason that made Tessa uneasy. The fire flicked, danced before them.

She believes in God, Tessa thought, *in forgiveness, in all that.*

"So I read some of the Bible tonight," Tessa said tentatively.

"Really?"

"Yeah, I sorta stole one from the motel."

"You stole a Bible?"

"Pathetic, huh?"

A slight grin. "Well, I'm sure that's one thing you can be forgiven for."

"Actually, that's what I was reading about. Forgiveness."

"Oh, and is that why you mentioned you stole it?" Amber sounded amused, and that heartened Tessa. "To transition to the topic?"

Busted.

"Um. Maybe."

The fire flickered. Snapped. "What were you reading?"

"A story about this woman who crashed a party where Jesus was eating supper. Everyone thought she was a terrible sinner, I guess, I don't know, a prostitute. And she was weeping on his feet and drying them with her hair."

"I know it. That's a powerful story."

"So yeah, and Jesus starts talking about how those who've been forgiven much love much, right? But that those who haven't been forgiven much—or *don't realize* that they have—don't end up expressing much love."

Amber listened, watched the flames devour the wood Patrick had carried in from the shed.

"Here's the part I don't get. Jesus says that the woman was forgiven because she loved much. But given the context, it should've been the other way around—that she loved much because she'd been forgiven much, because that's what he'd just explained." She waited to see if Amber would comment. When she didn't, Tessa continued, "So which comes first, forgiveness or love?"

Amber sat for a long time, and the silence unsettled Tessa.

"I'm sorry," Tessa said. "I mean . . . I wasn't trying to be disrespectful, like questioning the Bible or anything, I just—"

"No, it's okay. Maybe I just need a glass of water." Amber's voice sounded wavery, uncertain. "I'll be right back."

She rose.

And returned to the bathroom.

The USS *Louisiana*
International waters, Gulf of Oman

"*Louisiana* full stop," Captain Reaves said, then heard the ensign echo his command.

He felt the forward momentum of the submarine change, but after twenty-two years at sea it didn't affect his balance at all, and he stared unflinchingly at the emergency action message that had just printed out.

Though it still needed authentication by his executive officer, the EAM was properly formatted.

He studied it silently, picked up the mic. "Lieutenant Commander," he said, "to the con."

The reply came back through the intercom. "Aye, sir."

The message told Reaves to move to DEFCON 1, known in the military as "cocked pistol." Maximum readiness.

Something big was up. And he and his crew were right in the middle of it.

86

The cool air of the tunnel whipped past my face.

It was hard to calculate the cart's speed, but I would have guessed we were moving at twenty-five, maybe thirty miles per hour, which meant that if it was five miles to the base, we should've arrived by now. Unfortunately, however, I didn't see any indication that we were nearing the end of our route. Instead, all I saw was the perpetual purple-black darkness pressing in against the forward operating light's meager beam.

It's possible this doesn't end at the base. It's possible you were wrong.

No, these tracks have to lead somewhere.

As we traveled, we passed a series of cylindrical nodes buried partway into the earth, placed uniformly about thirty meters apart, all connected by a thick bundle of wires.

The extremely low frequency electromagnetic transmitters.

I reviewed what we knew—or at least what I *thought* we knew: we would arrive at the top level of the station. From there, a stairwell in the east corner accessed the base's second level and another stairwell at the far end of the crew quarters led down to the command level, where the control room would be.

Weatherford had told me there were ten or eleven Eco-Tech members, but of course, it was possible there were more.

What's their agenda? If they're anti-nuke, why try to fire a nuclear missile? Are Cassandra and Terry just using them as pawns?

Even if SWAT or local law enforcement had arrived at the Inn the very moment we'd left it, without another cart on that end of the tunnel, they wouldn't be able to—

A light.

Faint, distant, but there was definitely something ahead of us. I motioned for Lien-hua to let up on the throttle, but she must've noticed it as well because we were already slowing.

"What do you think, Pat?" she called.

"Take us up there. As close as you can."

"They might hear the motor."

"If there're people there, they've heard it already."

We closed the distance until I could see that the light was indeed coming from the upper level of the base where all eight tunnels converged. Lien-hua brought the motorized cart to a stop about twenty-five meters from the portal.

We stepped down. A steady, audible hum was coming from the long line of electromagnetic nodes.

"They're powered on," Lien-hua said.

Not good.

The noise wasn't overwhelming and I doubted it would've masked the sound of our railcar.

Flashlights off and guns unholstered, as quickly as we dared, Lien-hua and I approached the base's entry bay.

87

Solstice asked Donnie, "Are we ready to send the signal?"

"Yes."

She handed him a copy of the coded message. He stared at the indecipherable sequence of numbers and letters. "What are these?"

"Deactivation codes," she lied. "Enter them in but wait with the signal. Eight minutes. We send it at nine o'clock."

"Why?"

Because that's when the Louisiana *is in position*, she thought.

"Our agenda doesn't concern you," she said.

"And if I do this, Lizzie—you'll let her go?"

"No one will lay a hand on her."

"Tell me. Swear it!"

"I swear it to you. No harm will come to her."

Obviously still distressed about the death of his wife, but finally compliant, he turned to the keyboard.

She spoke into her headset radio to get an update from her team and make sure the explosives were all in place. Eclipse told her the hostages were secure. Everyone else confirmed that they were on their way to the control room, except for Cyclone, who did not respond.

"Cyclone?" Solstice repeated into her mic, but once again there was no reply. "Millicent, where are you?"

Nothing.

She turned to Typhoon. "Check on her. Sweep the crew quarters first, then go take a look in the tunnels."

With a heavy nod, the thickly muscled ape picked up one of the AR-15s and stalked through the hall toward the stairs.

We entered the upper level of the base and I saw the concrete-encased elevator shaft to my right. It appeared to be just over a meter wide and nearly two meters across and reminded me of an extremely runout and exhausting crack I'd climbed in Yosemite a few years ago. An electrical line stretched up from a relay control module and disappeared out of sight in the shaft.

That's how they sent the web-based message earlier that everything was fine.

I made note of it. I could use that to contact Margaret.

After we'd stopped Cassandra Lillo.

Twelve stout concrete pillars supported the ceiling of the room. Seven other tunnels spidered out in all directions. The second opening to our left contained a cart that looked like the one Lien-hua and I had just ridden here.

I pictured the topography of the terrain above us, evaluated that tunnel's direction in relation to the one we'd emerged from, and had an idea of where it might lead. Silently, I gestured toward the stairwell, but before we could reach it I heard movement in the tunnel containing the other railcar.

Swift, cat-like, Lien-hua leapt against one of the support columns to cover me. I raised my gun and my flashlight, approached the tunnel's entrance. "FBI! Put your hands in the air!" Sweeping the beam before me, I saw Alexei Chekov standing about twenty meters away.

A woman lay at his feet.

She wasn't moving, and from here I couldn't tell if she was alive or dead.

88

8:54 p.m.
6 minutes until the transmission

"Hands away from your body, Alexei!"

He held up his empty hands. "We need to hurry. We only have until 9:00."

I motioned with the barrel of my gun for him to step away from the woman. "On the ground. On your knees. Do it."

"We have six minutes."

"Down!"

He stepped to the side, went to one knee, then the other.

"Six minutes until what? They send the signal?"

"Yes."

I punched at my watch so the timer would go off in five. Alexei gestured toward the radio hanging from the injured woman's belt. "They're sending someone to look for her."

Keeping my gun trained on him, I signaled for Lien-hua to check the woman's pulse, then I walked around Alexei so I'd be able to monitor the tunnel's entrance while I frisked him.

Cautiously, Lien-hua approached the woman, no doubt aware, as I was, that all of this might be an elaborate trap.

I had the plastic cuffs with me, and though I doubted cuffing Alexei would do much good, I did it anyway. At least it might slow him down if he tried to make a move on me or Lien-hua.

From where I stood now, I could see the woman's face and recognized her as one of the the Eco-Tech operatives whose photos Alexei had sent to my email account. "Her name is Millicent Alman," I told Lien-hua.

"She was setting explosives." Alexei nodded toward the dirt wall of the tunnel. "Triacetone triperoxide." A strip of TATP with a wireless detonation package had been implanted into the tunnel's wall with two narrow spikes.

Oh, this was just getting better and better.

Lien-hua bent beside Millicent, checked her pulse, her airway. "She's alive."

I patted Alexei down. "What did you do to her?"

He was clean.

"It's Propotol." He was eyeing the tunnel's opening carefully. "She'll be all right, but she's going to be out for a couple hours. We should really get out of the line of fire."

I thought again of the geographic alignment of this tunnel.

Donnie's biometric ID was at the sawmill . . . In their break room there was a stairwell to the basement . . . With a second tunnel, that would explain—

"You came from the sawmill, didn't you?"

"Yes."

"You hacked into my email, read the schematics, that's how you found it." It was more of an observation than a question.

"Yes."

I helped him to his feet. "Where's the bone gun?"

"I don't have it on me."

"What about Burlman's sidearm?"

"I don't use guns."

A person in his profession?

"Because of your wife? Because she was shot?"

He stared at me. "Yes. Because of my wife."

Millicent had a handgun, a radio, and two sets of plastic hand-cuffs, all of which Lien-hua helped herself to.

When Alexei had first asked me to help him, he'd told me he wanted to deal "appropriately" with the people who killed the Pickrons, and he'd wanted my help finding Valkyrie . . . "It was Valkyrie, wasn't it?" I said. "That's who killed Tatiana?"

He chose not to reply, but I took his silence as a yes.

At the sheriff's department when the topic of our wives' deaths had come up, he'd said that he had someone to take out his vengeance on, that I had only God to blame.

That's why he's here. To kill Valkyrie. "Did Millicent tell you who Valkyrie was before you drugged her?"

"Yes."

"Dana Murkowski?" I said, referring to the alias Cassandra Lillo was apparently using for this mission.

Alexei looked at me stiffly. "That's right."

But why would Cassandra have killed Alexei's wife?

"Pat," said Lien-hua urgently, "we need to get—"

Abruptly, Alexei held out both hands, palms up, dropping the spent cuffs to the ground. I aimed the Glock at him, but he wasn't coming at me. He'd freed himself even faster than I'd guessed he would.

"If you fire," he said, "it'll give away our location."

I looked at the time on my watch: 8:55.

Move, Pat. Go.

Dragging Millicent across the ground wasn't ideal, and with my bum ankle and Lien-hua's slim frame, we weren't well-suited to move her. Gesturing toward Millicent and then the railcar, I told Alexei, "Carry her over there." He lifted her, brought her to the cart, gently set her down. Lien-hua tested one of the bars supporting the metal runners to make sure it was sturdy, then cuffed Millicent's left wrist to it.

You can't leave Alexei here.

And you can't take him with you.

"Stick out your leg," I told him. "Quickly."

Giving me a curious look, he obeyed. While Lien-hua kept her gun trained on Alexei, I secured the GPS ankle bracelet that I'd brought with me around his left ankle.

"You knew we'd meet up with him?" Lien-hua sounded amazed.

"I had my suspicions."

Lien-hua asked Alexei, "Did Millicent say anything about Jerusal—"

"Get down!" I'd seen movement near the stairwell.

We ducked, flashlights off.

The three of us slid behind the railcar.

A dump-truck-sized man came into view and turned toward our tunnel, an assault rifle in his hands.

He was less than thirty meters away.

"Cyclone?" he yelled.

If you call to him he'll pin you down, but you can't fire first, not without—

"You in there?"

Alexei tossed a rock ahead of us, and it clanged on the metal track. The man with the rifle raised his light, saw Millicent unconscious, and immediately sprayed a burst of bullets at us, hitting the cart. Lien-hua and I returned fire. I hit him in the chest, she might have as well, but he was wearing body armor and he didn't go down, but instead lurched awkwardly back into the stairwell out of the line of fire.

"You threw that stone so he'd shoot at us," Lien-hua said to Alexei.

"Law enforcement protocol," he replied. "You have rules. I realize that. It was the best way to get him to—"

The radio we'd acquired from Millicent came to life. The guy was calling for his team.

This was going down.

Now.

89

8:56 p.m.
4 minutes until the transmission

Solstice heard Typhoon radio for help.

"Spread out," she barked into her radio. "Cover the hallways. No one gets to the control room."

Then she ordered Donnie, "Finish with the code now or I swear I'll have my people shoot your little girl where she stands!"

I recognized the voice on the radio. Cassandra Lillo.

"We have to move. Lien-hua, cover me. Alexei, you stay here." I angled toward the entry bay and waited for any glimpse of the shooter edging around the corner of the stairwell.

Nothing.

Heart slamming against my chest, I made my way toward the end of the tunnel.

Amber didn't come out of the bathroom.

Tessa reassured herself that Amber was just using the toilet or maybe cleaning up after having her tears smear her mascara so much, but beneath those thoughts was a dark inkling, a tiny, discomfiting suspicion that barely even registered to her on a conscious level.

But then it did.

The toilet had not flushed. The water in the sink had not been turned on. No sound at all was coming from the room at the end of the hall.

With a deepening sense of apprehension, Tessa picked up her flashlight and went to check on her stepaunt.

———————◼———————

"Pat!" I heard Lien-hua whisper harshly behind me, but I'd already seen what she was warning me about—Alexei, streaking toward me through the tunnel, flipping something out of his right sleeve.

The bone gun.

How?

You had him carry Millicent. Maybe he'd hidden it under—

I almost squeezed the trigger, but he wasn't coming for me. He reached the room, and as Lien-hua and I went after him, he disappeared into the stairwell.

Two rapid shots.

The sound of a body tumbling down the stairs.

By the time Lien-hua and I got to the stairwell, Cassandra's voice was cutting through the radio we'd taken from Millicent: "Kill the hostages."

The metal stairs twisted out of sight before us.

No one visible. Not Alexei, not the shooter.

Lien-hua and I flew down the steps, taking them two at a time.

———————◼———————

Tessa rapped on the bathroom door. "Amber? Everything okay?"

Nothing.

She tried the doorknob.

Locked.

"Amber. Open the door."

Only silence in reply.

"Amber," Tessa cried louder, trying the doorknob again. "Open up the door!"

———————◼———————

We reached the bottom of the stairs.

The shooter lay at our feet. His neck was broken, his head

contorted at a hideous angle. He was breathing hoarsely, wide-eyed and afraid.

The AR-15 semiautomatic rifle he'd fired at us lay on the ground—Alexei had left it—but a large sheath on the man's belt was missing its knife. "Help me," he managed to say.

There wasn't anything we could do for him right now. I knelt beside him and asked urgently, "Where are the hostages?"

"Room," he muttered. He tried to say more, but his words burbled away into something indistinguishable.

I envisioned the base's schematics. *Cassandra will be in the control room. But the hostages? Where?*

Lien-hua grabbed the assault rifle.

"Go right," I directed her. "If you don't find the hostages, get to the control room and stop Cassandra!"

She darted right and I sprinted left toward the crew quarters.

90

8:57 p.m.
3 minutes until the transmission

"Amber!"

No answer.

The meds?

The sleeping pills?

No, no, no!

Tessa yanked out her phone, tried 911. The line was dead.

Pick the lock.

You have to get in that room!

The doorknob was like most bathroom locks—just a hole on the outside. Easy to get into if you have a barbeque skewer-thing or maybe a paperclip or bobby pin. Or a thick nail.

"I'm coming!" she yelled to Amber, though at this point she doubted her stepaunt could hear her. As fast as she could, Tessa rushed downstairs to Sean's workbench.

◼

The interrogators unfastened Terry's wrists.

While they were lifting him toward the bed, he went for Riley's gun, but as he snagged the weapon, it discharged, sending a round through Riley's pelvis. The guy shuddered to the ground, scream-ing. Terry dropped back into the wheelchair, and by the time he'd landed, he'd already swung the gun toward Riley's head. "Don't move!" he shouted to the other agents.

The two of them froze, tense, hands already on their weapons.

For a moment, Terry debated with himself about trying to kill them all but decided he probably wouldn't be able to do it without getting himself shot.

"Place your guns on the bed," Terry commanded. "If you try anything, Riley dies."

They didn't move.

"Don't test me. Guns on the bed. Do it now."

At last, unwillingly, they obeyed.

"Get out. If anyone comes through that door in the next twelve minutes I'll kill Riley."

"No, we take him—"

"Go."

The two men hesitated at first, then finally backed out the door. When they were gone and the door was closed, Terry repositioned himself to better cover it.

"Hang in there, Riley," Terry told him, then, thinking of the militants who would be showing up any minute, he added honestly, "I'm not going to kill you."

■

I flared around the corner, saw a woman in military fatigues straddling the rec room entrance, AR-15 aimed inside.

"Put down the—" I yelled, but she spun, faced me, laser sight on my chest. I fired. Three shots. Quick. Center mass.

She went down.

I rushed forward and found her alive, stunned, wearing body armor. I cuffed her, then scanned the room.

Three men in Master-at-Arms uniforms lay inside, as well as five other naval personnel all gagged and restrained with plastic handcuffs. Sometimes terrorists will tie up some of their own people along with their captives so if you free the hostages you'll inadvertently also free some of their men. There was no time to sort all this out now. I turned to leave.

No, Pat! There are ten or more Eco-Tech members. Cassandra ordered these people eliminated. Someone else will come by to kill them.

I found the ranking MA, a man whose name tag read T. Daniels, ungagged him.

Donnie loves his family. He would talk about them.

He would—

"How long have you known Commander Pickron?" I asked.

"What?"

"How long!"

"Six years."

"When did Ardis have Lizzie?"

He looked at me oddly. "She was adopted."

That was enough for me.

I flicked out my knife to cut him loose.

Tessa found a plastic container with an assortment of nails. Grabbed it.

Sprinted back upstairs to the bathroom.

I handed Daniels my knife. "Free everyone from your team. Secure this level."

Then I rushed toward the stairwell that would take me down to the control room.

Tessa slid the nail in, jiggled it, and within seconds the lock clicked. She threw open the door.

And saw Amber lying unconscious on the floor, an empty bottle beside her left hand.

No, God, please, please, please!

Tessa ran to her, called her name, but Amber didn't move. Tessa shook her, and Amber's head lolled listlessly to the side.

This isn't happening. This can't be happening!

Tessa felt for a pulse. It was there, thready, but present, and Amber was breathing, but Tessa didn't know how long she'd survive, how serious an overdose it was.

Obviously it's serious! The pills are all gone!

She snapped out her cell, found the number for the hospital in Woodborough, and when a woman finally answered, Tessa blurted, "Get me a doctor, now!"

"What's the emergency, ma'am?"

"An overdose! I need to wake someone from an overdose!"

She expected the woman at the hospital to ask her what kind of pills had been ingested, or how many had been taken, or the victim's sex or build, but instead she said, "Just a moment," and put Tessa on hold.

On hold!

Tessa set down the phone, turned on the speaker, said to Amber, "You're gonna be okay." After a quick search, she assured herself there were no more empty bottles around. The bottles of depression meds were still nearly full.

You need to get her to the hospital.

Amber's car was in the driveway. She could—

No, Amber might stop breathing on the way. You have to wake her up before you do anything!

Tessa had a friend who'd overdosed last year. She'd survived only because they got her stomach pumped in time.

Still no doctor.

Still on hold!

Tessa couldn't make Amber regurgitate while she was still unconscious—she'd aspirate on her own vomit.

Wake her up, you have to wake her up!

Tessa's eyes fell on the shower stall.

She grabbed Amber's armpits and dragged her across the floor.

Alexei reached the command level, found a militant waiting for him at the bottom of the stairs.

Using the eight-inch blade Ka-Bar Tanto he'd acquired from the man he'd disabled a few moments ago, he put the militant down—in less than a second, the blade was red, his adversary's neck was open, and with a soft and susurrus gurgle, he was fading to the ground.

Alexei allowed himself no time for regret but started through the electromagnetic production room toward the hallway to the control center—then heard footsteps on his left, readied the knife, and slipped behind a generator.

The female FBI agent he'd met a few minutes ago appeared at the doorway carrying an assault rifle, but an Eco-Tech militant burst from the side of the room, delivering a fierce punch that sent the rifle spinning to the ground. She went at the man with a powerful inner edge crescent kick, then a butterfly kick to the jaw, driving him backward.

So, it looked like she could handle things from here.

Alexei charged down the hallway to the command center.

91

Someone at the top of the stairwell shot at me, and I ducked low, spun around the corner. "Drop your weapon!" I yelled.

In reply he fired again.

I didn't have time for this. I did not have time!

A quick breath and I rounded the corner again, but another burst of gunfire sent me pivoting behind the wall.

My watch's alarm went off.

One minute left.

$$\blacksquare$$

Solstice stared at the screen. "What did you do?" she yelled at Donnie.

"I set it up for a retinal scan. And I won't initiate it unless I know Lizzie is okay. Unless I talk to her."

Without hesitation, Solstice whipped out her FN 5.7 and fired a round through Donnie's left knee. He screamed in pain.

"Lizzie is already dead. I killed her on Wednesday. Killed your wife too."

A dark cloud of confusion, of desperation. "What?"

She drew out her knife. "Send the signal now or I'll cut out your eyeball and send it myself."

$$\blacksquare$$

No more time.

I raced toward the stairwell. When the shooter flashed out with his gun raised, I fired at him until he was no longer a threat, then bolted past his body and down the stairs, reloading my weapon as I did.

———————————■———————————

Tessa sat in the shower, her stepaunt's head on her lap, cool water spraying down on them both.

But Amber did not wake up.

Oh, God, please. Don't let Amber die. Please don't—

A sweep of headlights washed across the bathroom window.

Someone was coming up the driveway to the house.

Patrick?

Sean?

Yes, good.

One of them had returned.

———————————■———————————

At the bottom of the steps I found a man's body, a pool of blood spilling from his slashed neck.

Hearing a harsh grunt in the machinery room to my left, I immediately peered inside and saw that on the other side of a wire mesh partition Lien-hua was fighting one of the terrorists. "Lien-hua!"

Too much machinery. Too much movement. I had no shot at her assailant.

Blade hidden behind his wrist, he feinted toward her, then whipped it out and went for her abdomen, slashing in a figure eight. "Get back!" I yelled.

She leaned to the right, away from the blade, then blocked his arm, backed into position for a kick. "Go!" she hollered to me. "I'm fine!"

I wanted to help her, wanted to—

She can take care of herself.

"I'll come back for you!" I shouted.

The control room lay at the end of the hall.

I dashed toward it.

The door was closed. I heard shouting inside, then a sharp crash.

A strangled scream.

And a dead stretch of dull, eerie silence.

92

I kicked open the door. "Do not move!"

Gun steady in both hands, I took in the room.

Workstations, control panels, computer displays, wall monitors. In the far corner, Cassandra Lillo was crouched behind a rolling chair on which Donnie Pickron sat clutching his knee, a fierce bruise on the side of his head, a look of horror on his face.

She held an FN 5.7 to his chin.

Alexei stood close to them, poised, bone gun in one hand, a bloody combat knife in the other. Just past him, an obese man lay unconscious atop a collapsed table.

Two other men stood near Cassandra. I recognized them from the photos Alexei had sent me: the Eco-Tech members Becker Hahn and Ted Rusk. They appeared to be armed only with Tasers.

"Put down the gun, Cassandra," I called.

"You first, Agent Bowers."

Donnie was in the way and I had no shot.

She held up her left hand to show me the remote control detonator for the TATP ordnance. "Put down the gun or I'll do it. If I press this button, the whole base comes down."

I didn't move.

A cursor was flashing on an expansive high-def screen mounted on the wall to her left, and a message: *Ready to transmit. Awaiting signal verification.*

Beside a keyboard on the desk in front of Donnie, a retinal scanner was futilely surveying empty air.

The signal hasn't been sent. The missile hasn't been fired.

"She killed my wife," Donnie screamed. "She killed my daughter!"

"Why Jerusalem?" I asked Cassandra.

"I said set down your gun!"

"You killed Tatiana as well." Alexei's voice was cool. Unflinching.

"I've killed lots of people." Cassandra's eyes flicked toward the screen. "Set down your gun, Bowers, or Donnie dies. And I'll blow the whole base if I need to."

I didn't have many cards. I threw one on the table. "We know about Terry. He wants to talk to you, to call it off."

"I don't believe you."

"Who's Terry?" Becker Hahn muttered. "What's going on? Who's Cassandra?"

"The CIA is willing to negotiate," I told her, making this up as I went, trying to buy time. "You don't want to kill those people in Israel. It's never been about that for you, for either of you. It's the challenge. I know that. The money."

Alexei edged forward. Honestly, he might have a better chance of taking out Cassandra than I did, and for a fraction of a second I was tempted to let him loose on her.

"Terry's in Egypt." I gestured toward one of the computers. "His interrogators have him online right now. They're—"

"Quiet! Put the gun down or we all die. You have five seconds."

I hated the thought that came next—

"Four . . ." she said.

—but it did come, and I had to balance it with the severity of the situation. *If this is really about a missile launch, you need to stop—*

"Three . . ."

—*her even if she detonates those explosives, even if the base goes down, you can save hundreds of thousands of lives if you—*

"Two—"

—*shoot through Donnie. You have to shoot through the hostage; you have to end this!* Hating what I was doing, but with no alternative, I took aim.

But apparently I wasn't the only one balancing those fatal thoughts, because before I could fire, Donnie spun to the side and went for the remote control detonator. Without hesitating, Cassandra sent a round through his jaw, and the lower half of his face exploded in a red, grisly spray.

I fired at her, but Alexei had leapt forward, and I pegged him in the left shoulder. "Get down!" He stood his ground. I leaned farther, heard another shot from Cassandra's gun, and saw a look of shock cross her face.

She brushed a hand against a wound in her abdomen, then quickly grabbed Donnie's head in both hands. He might've still been alive; I couldn't tell. I aimed at her neck just above her body armor, then squeezed the trigger and hit my mark. Her body lurched backward and buckled to the ground.

"No one move!" I hollered to Alexei, Becker, and Ted. They all remained where they were. Alexei finally looked at his shoulder, at the blood spreading across his shirt.

"Put the Tasers down," I ordered Becker and Ted.

They dropped them, kicked them across the floor.

Secure the TATP detonator.

Confirm that Cassandra is dead.

It seemed impossible that she'd survived, but I wasn't ready to take any chances.

Donnie's body was slumped forward, his head on the desk, his eyes wide open, staring into eternity. From his nose down, his face was gone. Blood spewed from the cavity that used to be his mouth, covered the keyboard, drenched his shirt.

Sickened, I moved toward Cassandra.

It was hard to decipher exactly what had happened, but it appeared that in his last few seconds of life he'd wrested the detonator from her, then twisted the gun, angling it up beneath her body armor before it went off. Whatever the exact chain of events, in his dying moments he'd saved us from the explosion and managed to take revenge on Cassandra for what she'd done to his wife and daughter.

On the wall monitor, the cursor was still blinking; still waiting.

It looked like we'd stopped it. The signal hadn't been sent.

As I crossed the room I could see Cassandra's legs, but her face and torso were still hidden by Donnie's body, which was slouched on the chair. I passed Alexei and he said softly, "I wanted to do that." His eyes were on Cassandra.

"Step back, Alexei, and drop the bone gun."

The door to the house banged open. "Patrick!" Tessa yelled. "Is that you? We're in here!"

"It's me," Sean shouted.

"Amber overdosed!"

"What?" He was pounding up the stairs. "No!"

"Hurry!"

"Valkyrie's dead," Alexei muttered. His bone gun was now on the floor two meters away from him.

Keeping an eye on him, I knelt beside Cassandra.

"She wasn't Valkyrie," Ted Rusk mumbled.

"What?"

"Quiet," I said. It didn't take long at all to determine that Cassandra was not going to be causing us any more trouble.

"What do you mean she's not Valkyrie?"

"Everyone quiet." I didn't need to check Donnie's pulse. He was gone. I pushed myself to my feet.

Rusk pointed at Becker Hahn. "He made me tell 'em she was Valkyrie. He told me that—"

Becker whispered something under his breath.

Is he Valkyrie?

"What did you say?" I demanded.

"I said, 'Dialogue when possible, action when necessary.'" He lowered his hands toward the table.

"Hands up!" I yelled.

But as he raised his hands, he grabbed a computer monitor and heaved it toward me. I fired, missed him, but sent a spray of electronics exploding from the screen. I had to turn my shoulder to take the blow from the monitor, and it hit my arm hard, throwing me off balance, knocking the gun from my hand. The Glock spun toward Cassandra's body, landed just beside her leg.

Alexei went for his bone gun.

Then.

Becker was vaulting over the desk toward Donnie. I rushed toward him, but he managed to grab Donnie's head and direct his eyes at the retinal scanner. *No! It hasn't been long enough! The eye is still perfused! It'll still—* I was almost to Becker, but Alexei beat me to him, planted the tip of the bone gun against the base of his skull.

"No!" I shouted.

Alexei engaged the device.

The sound of Becker's skull cracking was sickening, horrifying. His arms went limp and he dropped Donnie's head, which thumped off the desk, sending his body sagging to the floor. Alexei was lowering Becker beside him: "Easy, now. I don't want you to die yet."

I needed to stop Alexei, but my eyes jumped to the wall monitor.

Two words flashed: *Transmission complete.*

The ELF signal had been sent.

93

The USS *Louisiana* received the extremely low frequency signal, the algorithm Terry Manoji had designed synapsed through the system, the sub's third aft missile hatch opened, and a Trident strategic ballistic missile shot into the water on its way toward the city of Jerusalem.

■

I grabbed my gun, pushed Alexei out of the way, and bent beside Becker. He lay helpless on the floor, his hands twitching faintly by his sides. I wondered how long he'd survive with his skull shattered.

"How do we stop it?"

"What?" The word was strangled with pain. "Stop what?"

"The missile!"

"No, we disarmed—"

"You just sent a message to fire a nuclear missile!"

"It wasn't supposed to . . ." His lips trembled, his eyes went large. "We were disarming . . ."

He didn't know?

He's anti-nuke. Of course—

Movement at the doorway. Lien-hua.

She rushed in carrying the AR-15, flanked by Daniels, the Master-at-Arms I'd freed earlier.

Thank God she's okay!

"Cover Alexei," I told her. I pointed to the screen where a CGI missile was moving through a simulated sky, and asked Daniels, "How do we stop that missile?" From the graphics display I could tell the missile had been fired from a sub somewhere in the Gulf of Oman.

His face was ghost-white. "You can't."

"Can't it be disarmed in flight?"

"No."

"Intercepted? Could we fire another missile at it, shoot it out of the sky?"

He shook his head gravely. "Fallout."

"Redirected?" I pressed him. "New coordinates?"

"Not a Cold War nuke."

I smacked the desk.

Earlier, I'd had Margaret put the planes into play as a last resort, but now—

I slid into the empty chair next to Donnie's body, typed at the keyboard to put an online call through to her. As I did, I asked Chekov, who was standing stationary near the end of Lien-hua's assault rifle, "The Beriev A-60. Range, you told me five hundred kilometers. And it can shoot down a submarine-launched ballistic missile?"

"Yes, but with an SLBM it would only work in the boost stage." He spoke quickly, aware of the seriousness of the situation. "If you fracture the missile's outer casing after it begins final descent, the nuclear device contained in the missile will detonate."

A second-by-second countdown on the screen told me the missile's ETA was in ten minutes twenty-nine seconds.

Come on, Margaret, where are you!

I indicated to the screen and asked Daniels, "How long until final descent?"

"Six minutes. Maybe less."

It won't take Israel long to identify the speed and trajectory of the missile. They'll assume Iran fired it. They'll respond—

Margaret answered, but I cut her off, "You have to get Israel to hold off a kinetic response. It's the only way to save Jerusalem. They cannot fire, Margaret, you have to—"

"Patrick—"

"The missile was launched! Are the Beriev A-60s in the air?"

"Yes—"

"No retaliatory response. None! And get Nielson on the line. He has to tell Iran's Supreme Leader, not the presid—"

The signal went dead. All the computers went offline.

"What?" I shouted. "What happened?"

"The comm link on the first level." Rusk's words were flushed with shock. "Someone must have gotten up there, disabled it. You said a missile was *fired*? We were supposed to take 'em offline!"

We have until the final descent. You need to move.

You can still stop this!

I leapt to my feet, said to Daniels, "Is the elevator on the top level working?"

"I don't—"

"No!" Rusk interrupted, desperate now. "I disabled it!"

I started for the door. "Rusk, Lien-hua, you're with me." Lien-hua passed the rifle to Daniels, and I pointed to Alexei. "Shoot him if he tries to get away. Shoot him if he tries to approach either of the men on the floor. Shoot anyone who goes near that detonator switch."

As I left the room I heard Alexei accuse Becker, "You killed Tatiana."

Becker responded, just loud enough for me to hear, "I'm not Valkyrie."

"Then who—"

But by then I was out of earshot, hurrying with Lien-hua and Rusk toward the stairs.

94

Amber opened her eyes, sputtered, shivered, gasped for breath.

Thank God! Tessa nearly said the words aloud.

Sean lifted Amber, hurried to the bedroom. "Grab some towels," he called to Tessa, "and we need to find some dry clothes so we can get her to the hospital."

Tessa gathered the towels, but she didn't know how long Amber would remain conscious, not after that serious an overdose.

She had her phone with her, but no doctor had come on the line yet. After helping dry Amber and pulling on some dry clothes herself, Tessa went online and typed in the name of the drug, then searched for treatment strategies, and saw that the drive to the hospital would be cutting it dangerously close.

"Sean, we need to empty her stomach!"

Bypassing the clothes, Sean had decided to wrap Amber in thick, warm blankets for the drive. He was yanking them from the closet shelf. "What do you suggest?"

A finger down her throat? That doesn't always work; it's hard to do on someone else. Amber's a pharmacist. Surely she'll have some—

Tessa said to Amber, "Do you have any syrup of ipecac?"

"No." Her voice was weak.

"Hydrogen peroxide?"

A nod. "Medicine cabinet."

But when Tessa checked, she found the bottle nearly empty.

No!

All right, one last option.

Maybe, maybe, it's worth a try—

Tessa left for the kitchen.

"Where are you going?" Sean called.

"My friend Anisette had bulimia. She used dish soap."

■

Second level.

I was pushing forward as fast as I could on my injured ankle.

The entry bay stairwell wasn't far.

Toting sidearms, the ELF crew had secured this floor. However, *someone* had managed to disrupt that comm line, so it looked like at least one Eco-Tech member was still loose on the level above us.

As we rushed past the rec room, I told Lien-hua, "It's good to see you, by the way. What about that guy you were fighting down there?"

"He won't be bothering us."

I corralled two of the warfare information officers to join us.

"What are we doing, Pat?" Lien-hua asked.

"I need to talk to Margaret. The Iranians have planes, Russian-made Beriev A-60s. They're in the air and they can shoot down that missile if only we can convince them to do it."

"But it's heading for Jerusalem," she said. "Why would Iran stop a nuclear missile that's on its way to Israel?"

"I'm working on that." Then I asked the officers with us, "Is there any other means of communicating with someone outside of this base?"

"No," one of the men answered. "Both the sat comm and land-lines are down. RF has been jammed all night."

"You'd need to get to the surface," Rusk stammered, "but I told you, the elevator's been disabled!"

"I'm not going to use the elevator."

95

We emerged from the stairwell.

Stepped into the base's entry bay.

Even from here I could see that the comm line had indeed been yanked down, snapping somewhere in the middle. I hurried to the shaft, flicked out my Maglite, shone it up toward the maintenance building.

The light didn't reach the top.

No handholds.

No footholds.

I'd have to stem the whole way up, climb it like I would a crack or a chimney. I tossed off my jacket, asked the naval officers, "Is this shaft open on top?"

Lien-hua and the crewmen had their sidearms out and were scanning the area. "No," one of them said. "There's a cement cover that slides over the hole."

Great.

The schematics had said this shaft was twenty-seven meters long.

Just less than ninety feet.

Lien-hua guessed my plan. "Pat, no."

"It's all right. I'll be all right." She and the others were still watching for Eco-Tech members. I cranked my boot laces as tight as they'd go and told the officer, "You need to get that cover moved by the time I get up there."

"I'm not sure we can get—"

"Find a way." I pointed to Rusk. "This guy disabled the elevator, maybe he can help."

"Pat, if you slip—" Lien-hua began.

"I won't slip."

Speed climb this. Don't think. Just climb. You need to get up there and call Margaret.

470

I could do this: one foot and one hand on opposite walls, pressing out, using oppositional force, then working my way up one move at a time. I told Lien-hua, "I've done this in Yosemite."

"With climbing shoes. With ropes. With anchors!"

The track on which the concrete platform had ridden down was on one side of the shaft, but because of the shaft's width I wouldn't be able to use that wall to climb. However, I could use it to get off the ground. Grabbing one of the bars, I hoisted myself up and scissored out my legs and arms to span the width of the shaft.

If you slip, if you run out of strength, if they don't get the cover off the top, you'll fall, and if you fall—

I pushed those thoughts aside. "There's someone here, in one of these tunnels, Lien-hua. Cover these guys so they can get the hydraulics working again."

"Pat, swear to me you won't fall."

You can do this. Don't stand up too much. Outward pressure. Get solid, then move.

I locked my feet in place, rested my weight for a moment. "I'm gonna marry you someday, Lien-hua. There's no way I'm going to fall and miss out on that."

It wasn't exactly a proposal. I could clear that up later.

All right. Go.

Holding the Maglite in my mouth to keep my hands free, I began to ascend the shaft.

The dish soap had worked.

Sean was carrying Amber down the stairs so they could drive her to the hospital.

To help the doctors know what else was in Amber's system, Tessa grabbed the empty pill bottle as well as the depression meds, then hit the stairs.

"Get the door," Sean called.

She flung it open and they stepped into the whipping fury of the storm.

96

I wasn't even halfway up the shaft yet and my arms were already spent.

The width wasn't right for my arm span, and each time I positioned my hands, it took tremendous energy to hold myself in place while I made another move.

Focus.

Hand, foot. Hand, foot. Stem your way.

Go!

A wire of pain stretched from my ankle up through my leg whenever I put pressure on it, but I did my best to ignore it. I had to.

Hands out. Move. Smear your feet.

There was no turning back, no down-climbing.

I scrambled upward.

What are you going to tell Margaret?

I didn't have an answer. I climbed.

Without breaking my rhythm, I tilted my head back and aimed the flashlight's beam upward.

Still nine or ten meters to go.

A third of the shaft.

The planes are in the air, but the missile will—

But why would the Iranians shoot down the missile?

Think, Pat. Think!

Bribes? Lifting sanctions? A few billion dollars in aid? Allowing them to develop their own nukes? None of that seemed like enough to convince Iran's president to rescue a country he'd said was a fake regime that must be wiped off the map.

No, not the president . . .

My calves were burning, and I noticed my left leg twitching.

Hurry!

If not bribes, then what?

Five meters to the top, but I could see that the cement slab they'd told me about still rested on its stout metal arms, still covered the top of the shaft.

Come on, get that thing out of the way.

I climbed, thought of Iran, of politics, of weapons, of reasons . . .

The Supreme Leader of Iran. He has more pull than the president; he's the one who appoints the highest ranking members of the armed forces—anything like this would go through him, not the president.

Three meters to the top—

Breathe, just breathe.

But rescue Jews? Why? How would they save face in the Muslim world if—

I heard the rough movement of machinery, and, tipping my flashlight up, I saw the great arms moving, lowering the concrete platform, tilting it toward the side of the shaft.

Yes!

But then, too late, I realized I'd miscalculated.

I was too close. The slab was going to hit me as it swung down.

One choice.

One chance.

Gritting my teeth, I eased up on the pressure from my legs and hands, letting myself slide down, my palms scraping along the rough concrete, leaving a trail of blood behind.

Two meters.

Three.

I jammed my feet out and levered out my hands to arrest my descent. The platform crossed where my head had been only a moment earlier, and I waited, legs shaking, barely able to hold my weight, until it was out of the way.

The top of the shaft was clear.

Fighting the pain in my shredded palms and struggling against my fatigued muscles, I stemmed up the rest of the way and grabbed the lip of the building's floor, the blood on my hands making it slippery, hard to hold on—

For a moment that seemed to last forever I hung over the emptiness, trying to firm up my grip, to gather my strength, and while I did, I heard the roar of snowmobiles approaching the building.

Crying out from the effort, I heaved myself up, mantled out of the shaft, and collapsed onto the floor of the maintenance building.

Arms shaking from exhaustion and adrenaline, palms bloodied from the climb, I was barely able to speed-dial Margaret's number.

"They won't do it!" she exclaimed. "They—"

"Here's what Nielson needs to do. Now!" I gave her my instructions.

Man, I hoped this worked.

Prayed it would.

It'll work. It has to—

The snowmobiles stopped just outside the door.

Margaret ended the call so she could speak with Secretary of State Nielson, and I looked at my watch. We had only two, maybe three minutes before final descent.

Someone was turning the door handle.

Still lying on the freezing cement, I took aim with my Glock, tried to hold it steady in my torn, trembling hands as the door burst open and a cluster of flashlight beams blinded me.

"Stand down," I yelled. "I'm an FBI—"

"Pat, it's me!" Antón Torres shouted.

"Antón." *Yes, good!* I lowered my gun. "You're just in time."

"For what?"

"There are people down there who might try to blow up the base."

I wiped the blood from my hands and surfed to the DoD's Routine Orbital Satellite Database, punched in my federal ID number, and searched for the live satellite feed of the SLBM's contrail. "And we need to see if this missile can be stopped."

While Sean barreled his pickup through the drifts forming on the road, Tessa sat with Amber in the backseat, trying to keep her awake.

"We'll be there soon," Sean told them. "Hang in there."

Tessa closed her eyes and asked for divine intervention.

Even if God was angry at her for what she'd done, even if he couldn't forgive her for the thrill she'd felt when she took that man's life last year, maybe he could find enough mercy on this hellish night to give Amber a second chance.

97

I found the satellite image.

One of the SWAT guys handed me his jacket and I slipped it on, sat up. Stared at the screen.

With the satellite's magnification, the missile's contrail was clearly visible streaking over the Persian Gulf, and I waited for the SLBM to break apart, crack, fail, fall, die, but it did not.

No, it did not.

Over the next minute or so Torres's men quickly and expertly set up their anchors and lowered the ropes they'd brought with them to rappel into the base, and while they did, I gave them the rundown on the base schematics, the number of terrorists, the status of casualties and known injuries, the location of the TATP detonator in the control room, but most of my attention was on the phone's screen, on the contrail, on the missile that was not being blown out of the sky.

Come on.

Time ticked by. The missile streaked toward Jerusalem. I prayed for the bride, for the queen, for the people of God in that holy city. But the missile did not stop its fatal trajectory.

One by one the SWAT guys rappelled into the shaft while Torres and I silently watched the images on the phone.

"Come on," I whispered. "Come—"

And then, all at once it appeared: a thin red streak, faint and barely visible, cutting across the corner of the screen. It contacted the missile for two seconds, three—maybe four—then veered away again and was gone.

Just that. Nothing more.

No. That's not enough time!

But yet it was.

Without any dramatic explosion or pyrotechnic display, the SLBM ruptured, its fractured pieces fell toward Earth, and the contrail misted to a vaporous end.

And it was over. It'd worked. Iran had done it, but—

Hopefully, Israel hasn't already responded.

Hopefully—

I felt Torres's hand on my shoulder. "You did good, bro. I'm gonna go get those people out of there."

"Chekov is in the control room." I thought I might have already told him this a minute ago, but everything was sort of a blur. "Be careful with him, Antón. He won't think twice about killing your whole team or blowing the base if he needs to in order to get away."

"Right." He handed me his gloves and wool hat. "Stay warm. I'll see you in a bit."

Then Torres lowered himself into the shaft and I was alone in the chilled, empty maintenance building, catching my breath, decompressing, trying to keep from shivering from the rush of adrenaline, the frigid air, my wasted, quivering muscles.

Figuring that cable news would be as up-to-the-minute as the government, I surfed to CNN's website. Then I pulled on Torres's hat, wriggled my hands painfully into his gloves.

On my cell's screen, a reporter announced that, "According to our sources the missile is no longer in flight. We are waiting to confirm that—yes . . ." He spoke for a few moments about the SLBM's destruction, then finally mentioned that Israel had not fired retaliatory missiles, that "at this time it appears a cataclysmic crisis in the Middle East has been narrowly averted by the strident efforts of Secretary of State Nielson and an unlikely ally in the Supreme Leader of Iran . . ."

I was breathing out a deep sigh of relief when I noticed that I had a voicemail from Tessa. The icon flashed *highest priority.*

A tap at the screen, then I heard her words, frantic, desperate: "Patrick! It's Amber. She overdosed. She's unconscious. I need you! We're going to the hospital!"

What? Overdosed!

The message was from eight minutes ago.

I tried Tessa's number. No reply.

I dialed Amber's cell, their landline, Sean's bait shop—nothing.

Pushing myself to my feet, I hollered down the shaft to Torres, "Tell Lien-hua I'll be at the hospital. Amber's in trouble!"

He acknowledged that he'd heard me.

Legs still uncertain from the climb, I clambered out the door toward the snowmobiles that Torres and his team had left outside the building.

Terry heard two explosions, felt the building rumble.

It must have worked. The missile must have hit Jerusalem and now Abdul's men were here!

He waited, but no Al Qaeda militants came in to save him.

Instead, without warning, his door flew open and two CIA agents charged into the room, one shooting Terry's gun from his hand, the other kicking him in the face, dazing him.

Then they were both on him, pinning him down.

Riley, who was pale and breathless on the floor nearby, gasped that he needed help. "In a minute, buddy," one of the agents said. Then he leaned close to Terry, his breath stale and sausagey, his tone smug. "Your two buddies blew 'emselves into paradise right outside the door." He pressed his knee against the GSW tunneling through Terry's hand. White light blistered apart inside his head and he clenched his teeth, but he couldn't keep from crying out in pain. "Didn't account for American engineering, though. This place is built to withstand a lot more 'an that."

Trying to fight off the pain, Terry rolled his head to the side and saw a woman whom he didn't recognize enter the room. She wore a white coat and carried a medical kit and a large syringe.

Terry tried to wrestle free, but his legs were useless and he could barely move his arms or torso beneath the merciless grip of the two agents holding him down.

The woman knelt beside him. "Looks like you've been given a transfer order, Mr. Manoji."

Then, the man who'd ground his knee against Terry's wounded hand grabbed his head and forced the left side of Terry's face to the floor. Out of the corner of his eye Terry could see the woman positioning the needle against his neck.

"This comes to you compliments of FBI Director Wellington and CIA Director O'Dell," she said. "Don't worry. It's a transfer to a much better place."

And as Terry Manoji screamed, the woman in the white coat depressed the plunger of the syringe.

98

Tessa sat beside Amber's bed.

Her stepaunt was unconscious, on oxygen, a nasogastric tube inserted through her nose. The doctors had worked hard at empty-ing the drugs from her system, but she hadn't responded well.

Sean pulled the other chair to the bedside, took Amber's hand in one of his and with the other brushed a strand of hair from her eyes.

For the moment it was just the three of them in the room.

Tessa put out of her mind the unthinkable possibility that Amber wasn't going to make it. Her stepaunt was going to be okay. She was definitely going to be okay.

Yes, yes she was.

Having forgotten her phone at Amber's house, Tessa tried call-ing Patrick from the room phone, but he didn't answer. Neither did Lien-hua.

Scrolling through her mental database of names, of numbers, she tried Agent Jake Vanderveld's cell number and managed to reach him at the Schoenberg Inn, where he was searching for a snowmobile to get to someplace in the national forest. Tessa tried to tell him about Amber, but he cut her off and proudly announced that Patrick had just helped save the lives of a million people.

What is he talking about? Is he even being serious?

"Um . . ." What do you say to that? "Awesome." Yes, she was curious about what he'd said, but for the moment she stuck with the news of Amber's overdose, got through the summary.

"If Pat's in the base," Agent Vanderveld said, "he's out of cell contact. I'm not sure I can get him the message until I get there. Do you need me to come to the hospital?"

"I'm sure he'll fill you in later. Just, when you find him, tell him to get here as soon as he can, okay? How did he save a million people?"

"We'll explain it all later. I'll get him the message. I hope Amber is going to be all right."

"Yeah, me too."

Don't worry, she will.

As Tessa was hanging up, a nurse soundlessly came into the room to check on Amber, but evidently there'd been no change. A few moments later, she left after encouraging Sean and Tessa to hang in there: "Don't worry. Everything's going to be fine." But she didn't make eye contact with either of them, and the half smile she offered wasn't very convincing.

After they were alone with Amber again, Tessa and Sean sat quietly in the throbbing, ticking silence of the room. Between them, Amber breathed in the machine-fed oxygen.

And did not wake up.

She'll be okay, Tessa told herself. *She really will.*

Tessa hadn't been paying much attention to Sean, but now realized his eyes were moist. She figured that if there were times when it was okay for a grown man to cry, this was one of them. *But he probably doesn't want a teenage girl watching him—*

"I'm so sorry," he whispered to Amber. "I let you down."

After a short silence, Tessa said, "She loves you. She does. She felt really bad about everything."

He lowered his head into his hands, and ever so slightly his broad shoulders began to shake.

Leave him with her. He needs to be alone.

"Um, I'm gonna go grab us some Cokes." It was pathetic, but it was all she could think of to say. "Or something. I'll be back in a bit."

He nodded a quiet reply, and she eased out of the room.

When they'd entered the hospital, Tessa had noticed some vending machines in the lobby. So now, she took the elevator down one level to the ground floor.

It struck her that even though she'd helped Amber tonight, tried to do all she could, Amber still might not make it.

A good deed doesn't balance out a bad one. A kind act doesn't make scars disappear. Everyone dies eventually. You can't stop it, just forestall it.

Not the right thoughts to be having.

She left the elevator and was halfway to the lobby when she saw a sign to the hospital's chapel. A narrow window on the door revealed that the chapel was really just a sliver of a room with subdued lighting, six folding chairs, some kneeling cushions, and a small, unvarnished wooden cross hanging up front.

After a moment's deliberation, Tessa slipped inside and, figuring it would be a little too weird kneeling on a cushion, took a seat on the closest chair.

No one else was there, and the air was filled with a sterile hospitally smell but also something else, something fainter, some kind of gentle perfume, soft and floral and lingering from someone who must've only recently left the room.

Words from Tessa's mother came to her: "You need to learn to believe in grace as much as you do in pain, in forgiveness as much as you do in shame."

In other words, find a place where hope is real again!

Hope. Real hope.

"Please let Amber live." Tessa said the words audibly to give them more weight, to help convince herself that they were going to come true. "Give her another chance."

The cross at the front of the room was simple, wooden, and rough, and it made her think of the story she'd read, about the woman weeping at Jesus's feet, the woman who knew she was a great sinner, who knew she had a ton of stuff she needed to be forgiven for.

I want to believe, I do. Like that woman.

Like Amber.

Like Mom.

Tessa's conversations with her psychiatrist, with Patrick, with her stepaunt, about God and love and forgiveness all seemed to whirl around her: "I'm sinking into a place I can't climb out of on my own," she'd told her shrink . . . "When you ask someone to forgive you, you're really asking the other person to sacrifice for the benefit of the relationship," Amber had explained . . . "Denial isn't the answer. Somehow forgiveness, or making amends, or some sort of penance, has to be," Patrick had said.

And Jesus had reassured that weeping, broken woman, "Your faith has saved you, go in peace."

Someone needs to sacrifice for someone else to be forgiven.

At the house, Tessa had asked Amber which came first, love or forgiveness, but now it struck her that neither one does, that both love and forgiveness follow something else—

"Your faith has saved you, go in peace."

Tessa felt a tear easing down her cheek.

Denial is too cheap a cure.

And so, she did not deny it. She did not deny anything. *I'm sorry for the kind of person I can be, for the evil I'm capable of.*

And in the soft silence of the chapel, she heard a soul-whispered voice that seemed to somehow come from both inside her heart and also from someplace far beyond herself: *"I know."*

Will you forgive me? Please, I—

"I already have."

The sailboat painting came to mind, the one that'd seemed so real to her, that had invited her to step from one eternity to another, to arrive at the other side of the canvas.

And in that moment Tessa felt something pure wash over the part of her soul that had been dark and ruined for so long. Words came to her, just like they might've if she had her notebook in front of her, and the words were both a confession of her sins and an acceptance of blood-bought grace. Four simple lines:

i am the clever
architect of oblivion;
you are the wondrous
carpenter of hearts.

She waited for more poetry, more reassurance, but no more words came. The poem was over.

And please save Amber.

But the voice did not speak to her again.

She wiped away the tear that had escaped her eye.

"Please."

The perfume in the air dissipated, and only the pale sanitized smell of the hospital remained.

Tessa repeated her prayer for Amber, but no matter how earnestly she pleaded out this intercession for her stepaunt, she heard nothing but silence.

Unsettled by the sudden whiplash of emotions—from the bright glimmer of peace to a tightening knot of fear, Tessa stood and backed out of the room.

Maybe you were just imagining things. Wishful thinking, making up a divine response in order to cover your shame. To find a way to deal with your past.

Disheartened, confused, she reached the vending machines. And then, not far from her, on the other side of the lobby, the front doors of the hospital whisked open, and she saw Patrick, her father, emerge from the storm.

99

I heard Tessa call my name, and it took only a moment to find her near the soda machines. "Hey"—I hurried toward her—"how's Amber?"

"I don't think she's doing so well."

I felt my heart squirm. "Which room?"

"220. It seemed like Sean needed a little time alone with her. I came out here." She paused. "To get some Cokes."

Though anxious to get to the room, if Sean needed to be alone with Amber right now, it gave me a chance to catch up with Tessa on what'd happened. "Tessa, tell me what—"

"The kidnapped lady, did you find her?"

"Yes. She's fine. Listen—"

"How did you save a million people tonight?"

"No. I didn't. Iran did."

She looked at me questioningly. "A million people?"

"It's a long story. I'll explain later. Tell me what happened with Amber."

Finally, Tessa switched gears and, while I hurriedly purchased the cans of soda, she filled me in about the power outage, the overdose, her efforts to awaken Amber, Sean's arrival, their harried flight to the hospital.

The final Coke tumbled through the machine, I retrieved it, and we walked to the elevator.

I was struck by how, at every step of the way—from picking the lock, to waking Amber in the shower, to thinking of the dish soap and remembering to bring the pill bottles to the hospital, Tessa had exhibited clear, quick thinking under incredible pressure.

Then the elevator doors closed and we were on our way to the second floor. "So how are you doing through all this?" I asked.

She was slow in responding. "I went to the chapel. Something happened." She hesitated. "Earlier tonight you told me that somehow forgiveness, or making amends, or some sort of penance, has to be the answer."

"Yes."

"But if you have to do penance or make amends, then it means the forgiveness wasn't complete, right? I mean, if it was, there'd be no need for them. If you can make up for the past, why would you need to be forgiven for it?"

"I'm not sure I know what you're saying here."

She looked heavyhearted, distressed. "Apart from forgiveness, can you think of any way of dealing with your past that doesn't involve some form of denial or negotiation?"

I didn't know how to respond.

Mental compartmentalization, rationalization, justification, repression . . . all forms of denial or just different genres of excuses.

"No," I said frankly, "I can't."

The doors dinged open.

She took a heavy breath. "Anyway, the nurse keeps telling us Amber's going to be okay. So that's good."

"Yes." And, as abruptly as it had begun, our forgiveness conversation was over.

We exited the elevator. Passed room 210 . . . 212 . . .

Despite myself, I thought of the conversation I'd had with Lienhua about twists at the end of stories, how the people who deserve to live don't always make it. I refused to let myself consider such things.

216 . . . 218 . . .

We arrived at the room and I knocked softly. Sean called for us to come in, and when we entered, to my great relief, I saw that Amber was sitting up in bed. Conscious. A nurse was removing her NG tube.

"Amber?" Tessa stared at her dumbfounded. "How are . . . how do you feel?"

If Tessa had been right that Amber was unconscious just minutes ago, the turnaround was nothing short of extraordinary.

"I'm okay." Amber's voice was faint and scratchy. The nurse stepped aside. "Thanks to you and Sean."

As we gathered at her bedside, Amber tried to apologize for all the trouble she'd caused, for "how stupid she'd been," for making everyone so upset and scared, but none of us were accusing her of anything, no one was angry, we were just thankful she was still here with us. She shared her tearful, profound gratitude to Tessa and Sean for helping her, but they downplayed their role as "what anyone would've done."

Then, for what seemed like a long time but might've only been a minute or two, no one said anything. Finally, Sean was the one to break the silence, telling Amber plainly that he would change: that he'd give up drinking once and for all, if that's what she wanted, if that's what it took—anything—if she'd just give him, give their marriage, one more shot.

Amber looked past him toward the window, and when she didn't reply, I was afraid it might be too late for them, that whatever they'd had was over, but then she rested her hand gently on his arm, and the small gesture said as much, if not more, than any words would have.

"We can do this," he vowed.

"Yes," she replied softly. "Okay."

The moment was heartfelt and moving but short-lived because then Sean looked my way. "How's your jaw?"

"It'll be fine. But you throw one mean punch."

"You deserved that, you know."

"Yeah." I searched clumsily for the right thing to say. "I'm glad everything's out in the open."

Sean took Amber's hand in his own. "The past is past, all right?"

"I hope things can be—"

"We move on, okay?"

I gladly accepted the offer. "Yes. Thank you. We move on."

Amber nodded as well, then asked if she could have a few minutes alone with Sean, so Tessa and I slipped into the hallway, and, almost immediately when we were alone, Tessa said, "I need to tell you something, but I don't want you to make fun of me or anything."

"Of course not."

"You know how Mom used to say that I needed to learn to believe in grace, in forgiveness, stuff like that?"

"Yes."

"I think maybe I'm starting to."

"Tessa, that's fantastic. Why would you think I'd make fun of you for that?"

She was quiet. Then, rather than answer my question, she said, "You remember how you told me I was good at beating myself up?"

"I was only trying to—"

"No. It's okay." A nurse passed us, carrying a food tray toward a room farther down the hall. "But here's the thing: I'm not the only one. You're a world-class self-beater-upper. You never slept with Amber, right? And Sean's not gonna hold your little emotional fling against you, so you need to accept that. Like he said, move on."

I was quiet.

"All right?" she pressed.

"Okay."

"And this whole deal with believing or not believing him about the accident. Under the bridge."

"Gotcha."

"There's a chapel down on the first floor if you need to use it. Take care of business."

"Um. Thanks." I wasn't sure if she was being serious or not.

She looked as if she were going to respond, but held back. "You told me Iran saved a million people."

"They shot down a ballistic missile that was heading for Jerusalem."

"But Jake told me you saved them?"

"He was exaggerating. I just shared some thoughts on why it would be a good idea for them to stop the missile."

She looked at me dubiously. "What are you talking about? Iran hates Israel."

"Well, think about it like this: if you were Israel's president and a nuclear missile was coming at you from the general vicinity of Iran—"

"You'd assume they fired it."

"Sure, and you'd respond immediately, send missiles, bombers, whatever you had, against the country whose president had, for years, threatened you with annihilation."

"So you told Iran—"

"Well, the Secretary of State did, actually, it might've even been the president. I don't know who exactly—"

She rolled her eyes at me. "Whatever, you know what I mean—told them that the only way to save themselves—"

"Was to save their worst enemy."

She let that sink in, then shook her head. "No. That doesn't seem like enough."

I couldn't help but smile. "I wasn't sure it would be either, so I sent word for the Secretary of State to contact the Supreme Leader of Iran."

"The religious leader."

"Yes. As a matter of fact, in many ways, he has more influence than the president."

"I know that," she said impatiently. "I'm not completely in the dark about the geopolitical landscape of the Middle East."

"Oh. Right." *Yeah, this is Tessa, remember?* "Anyway, I suggested Nielson remind him that doing this would give Iran credibility on the world stage, a seat at the table, so to speak. And they could save face in the Muslim world by portraying the US as a rogue nation with nuclear weapons that it couldn't control—"

"But that they could," Tessa said, completing my thought.

"Precisely."

"And they come out looking more powerful than America." She nodded. "Nice, so you appealed to Iran's self-interest and pride."

"In a sense, I suppose."

"So, motives."

"Motives?"

"Right. You had to accurately assess their motives, then—"

"No, it was just logic."

She put both of her hands on my shoulders, looked me squarely in the eye. "Patrick, you helped stave off war in the Middle East only because you thought like a profiler. Lien-hua is gonna be so proud of you when I tell—wait." Tessa dropped her hands. "Is she okay? Where is she?"

"She's fine. She's still at the top secret underground military base helping round up the eco-terrorists."

Tessa blinked. "Oh."

I thought again of Valkyrie, who it might be—Cassandra? Becker? Manoji? Rusk? We could sort that through soon enough.

In the hallway beyond Tessa, I noticed the elevator doors glide open. "You should know that I told Lien-hua tonight I was going to marry her."

"You what?"

"I told her I was going to marry her."

"No, I mean you didn't *ask her* if she'd marry you?" Tessa said incredulously. "You *told her* you were gonna marry her?"

"Um . . ."

Jake Vanderveld left the elevator and came striding toward us.

"Oh." Tessa shook her head. "You screwed that one up big time."

"How's Amber?" Jake asked, eyeing the door behind us.

"Recovering." I was surprised to see him here. "Did you go to the base?"

"Without a snowmobile there wasn't any good way to get out there; I couldn't reach you by phone, and when I spoke with Lien-hua, she said I'd find you here. I decided to come and check on everyone."

His marked concern surprised me and made me wonder if maybe I'd misjudged him all these years.

"Tessa," I said, "can you give us a couple seconds?"

"Sure."

She knocked on the door to Amber's room, and Sean invited her in. As soon as she was gone I asked Jake, "What do we know about the base?"

"Torres and his men disarmed the explosives, and it looks like they caught all the Eco-Tech militants, but Chekov is missing."

"What!"

"Somehow he overpowered the MA who was guarding him. The guy'll survive, but by the time SWAT got to the control room, Chekov was already gone. Listen, we'll get him, though, right? Lien-hua told me you put a GPS ankle bracelet on him, so as soon as he surfaces we should be able to nail him."

Don't bet on it.

He saw the skepticism in my eyes. "Those things are a bear to get off, Pat."

"Yes, they are."

"You think he's still in the base?"

I shook my head. "He has a gunshot wound in his shoulder that needs to be treated. Also, he'd anticipate that the longer he waited, the more backup would arrive."

I doubted Chekov would use the Schoenberg tunnel to escape, since, after leaving a kidnapped victim at the Inn, he would know there'd be a heightened law enforcement presence there.

He could possibly be hiding in one of the other tunnels, but since they lacked rail tracks, there was no indication that they surfaced anywhere. Also, after his disappearance he would know law enforcement would search them eventually and he'd be trapped.

That left the tunnel to the sawmill, and what better place to cut off a tamper-proof, steel mesh GPS ankle bracelet than a sawmill?

"Jake, are you up for a drive?"

"To where?"

"Let's go catch us an assassin."

100

I drove.

Jake sat beside me, his iPad 2 on his lap, a tracking application for the GPS ankle bracelet open on the screen.

Before we left the hospital, Amber had assured me that she was fine, that I didn't need to worry about her; and Sean had been glad to let me borrow the pickup: "As long as it doesn't end up like my sled."

"Gotcha."

Now, Jake and I were about ten minutes from the sawmill, but so far, nothing had come up on the iPad's tracking program. Nothing at all.

So maybe this was a fool's errand. Another dead end.

Maybe.

Maybe not.

I'd spent the first part of the drive giving Jake my account of what happened at the base. In the end, he suggested that Rusk was probably Valkyrie. "He's a hacker," Jake said. "He's got a Carnegie Mellon computer science degree."

"But it doesn't fit. He's a hacktivist, that's all. There's nothing else in his background that matches Lien-hua's preliminary profile for Valkyrie."

"And what profile is that?"

"She believed Valkyrie would have law enforcement or covert operative training, be highly intelligent, well-traveled, midforties, linguistically skilled. Male."

"That's not much, Pat, hardly anything. Maybe Valkyrie is just a code name Manoji was using, or it could've been Cassandra after all."

"That doesn't explain how Valkyrie showed up in Russia last May. Terry was in a coma and Cassandra was in prison at the time."

Jake quietly monitored the iPad, and I had the sense he didn't want to discuss Valkyrie's identity anymore just then.

Wait.

The mind has to deal with guilt somehow. When it's overwhelming, escaping reality is sometimes the only choice.

Alexei might still be in the tunnel and offline. Or, he might not be.

Yes. Bait.

"Send me an email," I said, "asking me to confirm that I know Valkyrie's identity. Make it seem like I'm about to reveal to the Bureau who Valkyrie is."

"Send you an email?"

"To my Bureau account. Go ahead. Let's see how often Alexei checks my messages."

I found my thoughts flitting through the events of the night, and I remembered that earlier I'd made a mental note to follow up on any videos that might've been found of people in the Midwest being killed while Basque was in prison.

"When you're done with the email, pull up the Federal Digital Database. There are a few things I'd like you to check."

A couple moments later he finger-scrolled to a browser. "What do you need?"

I gave him the search terms I had in mind—the dates, the locations, the types of weapons, the victimology.

"What are we looking for, exactly?"

"Reiser's killer."

We tried a variety of searches but in the end didn't find anything helpful. If there were more victims, more videos, they hadn't been found.

Dead end.

"Think this through with me, Jake. Fourteen years ago we discover two sets of DNA at the scene of Basque's murders but aren't able to identify the second set until the homicide last June when you matched it to Reiser. Lien-hua and I were wondering if the records could have been falsified."

"But how?"

"Once Basque got out of prison, if he reconnected with his old partner and that person had access to the records, they could've set up Reiser by faking or switching the DNA analysis."

Jake considered that. "We could pull up a list of people who've accessed the case files or DNA records. See if there are any red flags."

With all of the lawyers, officers, and agents involved, I knew the list would be extensive, but it was worth a look. "Do it."

We could cross-reference the names against work schedules, the timing of the crimes, their locations, travel times from the crime scenes to people's residences . . .

Jake finished typing but said nothing. There was a stalled moment of silence.

"What is it?" I asked.

"One person's name keeps coming up."

"Who?"

"Torres."

"What? Antón?"

"Yeah. He's been in there half a dozen times. Including earlier this week. On Tuesday."

"That makes sense," I said, defending Torres. "He was doing prelim work for the mission on the trailer park."

"And it looks like he accessed the files two days before I identified the DNA sample last summer."

Torres was left alone in the kitchen when you and he entered the trailer. He could've planted—

No, it couldn't be Torres.

Three miles to go. Six, maybe seven minutes.

Torres is the one who told you there was DNA on one of the knives from a murder in DC, he sent you the videos, he lives in DC—

"Wait a minute," I said. "The clippings. The news footage. Yesterday you said Reiser was a scrapbooker."

"Yeah, and the ERT found—"

"Yes, yes, but which news shows? Which papers? It wasn't just cable news. It was local."

"Sure, WKOW in Madison, WTMJ in Milwaukee. We went through all this already today, Pat."

I remembered Lien-hua's words about someone who seems innocent for the whole story but then turns out to be the killer.

"But if they were local papers, the killer would've most likely chosen ones that were delivered to the places he lived . . ." I was thinking aloud. "Recorded news shows he could watch from home."

"Okay . . . ?" Jake said expectantly. "And?"

"Torres never lived in Wisconsin or Illinois." Caught by my thoughts I said, "Oh. Yes. Basque's partner left his footprints."

"Where?"

"Here." I tapped the map on the screen of his iPad. "Everywhere."

"What are you talking about?"

"He's been leaving them all over the place—Wisconsin, Illinois, Ohio, DC—I just haven't been studying them carefully enough."

"You're not making any sense, Pat."

"Okay, overlay the people on that list with the locations of—"

The GPS program sounded its alert.

The ankle bracelet was above the surface.

Jake swept his finger across the iPad screen. "Chekov's at the sawmill," he announced. "And he's on the move."

101

I brought the pickup sliding to a stop on the edge of the lumberyard, and Jake and I leapt out.

"Which way?" I said.

A few utility lights pinioned high on telephone poles tried to illuminate different sections of the lumberyard, but through the wild, blowing snow, everything looked wispy and half real, more like a painting than reality.

Pyramids of logs. Lonely buildings. Shadows lurking everywhere.

Jake glanced at his iPad, then pointed toward the sawmill building, the one with the conveyor belts, sorting stations, high-powered blades, and mammoth grinder that chewed logs into pulp.

I took the lead, and we crossed the yard quickly but cautiously, weapons out. We'd called Tait on the way to get backup over here, but now Jake phoned him again to confirm they were on the way.

The lumberyard was vacant. No movement in the night.

Though I tried to direct all of my thoughts here, now, on finding Alexei, I couldn't help but think about the Reiser case.

Torres accessed the files?

Torres—

No. That was too obvious. Someone skilled enough to be able to overlay digitized DNA records would be careful enough to use someone else's ID number. *So, a hacker? An FBI agent? Someone who could—*

We reached the sawmill.

Jake confirmed that the ankle bracelet was inside the building, then slipped his iPad under his jacket. Leaning against the door with my shoulder, I pressed it open and was once again overwhelmed by the smell of sweet pine and sawdust, just like I'd been when I first visited the mill. All the lights were off.

"Alexei?" I called.

Silence. No sound except the wind repositioning itself outside, whistling through cracks in the ceiling.

The killer taped local news shows.

Clipped local papers.

Local.

Reiser lived in La Crosse, Oshkosh, Superior, but the papers and news programs were from Rockford, Milwaukee, Madison—

Jake found a light switch, and the sawmill flicked into view, illuminated by a series of yellowish bulbs high overhead.

The ankle bracelet lay less than three meters away on the ground. A handsaw had been discarded nearby.

"He's close," I whispered to Jake, then I called into the cold air of the sawmill, "Alexei!" I scrutinized the area. "Come on out. Don't make me shoot you."

Jake edged left toward one of the workstations.

Lien-hua noted that the killer would be less dominant, more easily manipulated than Basque . . . He accessed the digitized files, early last summer, right after Dr. Renée Lebreau's murder, lived in—

Oh.

Fire coursed through my thoughts, bringing everything—the facts, the hypotheses, the duty to the truth, bringing it all into focus.

Sex and violence. The killer's psychological history will include a close association between sex and violence.

Be always open to the unlikely.

I wished I was wrong, hoped I was.

But—

Who asked to work the Reiser case? Who first reviewed the digitized case files, matched Reiser's DNA? Who lived in Rockford and Madison before moving to DC? And in Cincinnati fourteen years ago—

"Jake," I said softly. "Where is the *Business Courier* from? It's from Cincinnati, isn't it?" I looked behind me, but he wasn't there.

"Jake?" I heard shuffled movement to my right and turned.

Just in time to see Jake Vanderveld, Basque's accomplice, bring the shovel down toward my head.

102

I woke up on the conveyor belt to the wood grinder. My head was pounding and it took me a moment to regain my senses. When I tried to move, I realized my injured ankle was restrained, plastic-cuffed to the reticulated chain running along the side of the belt.

Awkwardly, I managed to roll onto my stomach.

Jake stood beside the control panel ten meters away adjusting the instruments. I felt my pockets; he'd taken my phone, keys, gun. All I had left was my flashlight.

"Where's Alexei, Jake?" I touched my head where the shovel had hit me. Couldn't help but wince.

Jake looked my way. "Oh, Pat. Welcome back. Haven't seen Chekov. I'm sure he's long gone by now." Both of our guns sat on the workbench in front of Jake. "So, the *Business Courier*? From when I lived in Cincinnati? That's what did it, huh?"

"You should have been more careful with your scrapbooking. You saved the newspaper clippings and recorded local news coverage from the places you lived, not the ones where Reiser did. That's not a very good way to set someone up."

"You couldn't just leave well enough alone, could you, Pat? The DNA should have been enough. It would have been for most people, but not for you—"

"Or Lien-hua. She knows too, or she will. She noticed it first."

"Lien-hua," he said slowly. "I see."

I suddenly regretted mentioning her name.

I tugged at my leg. I wasn't going anywhere. "Counseling rape victims? You got a thrill out of that, didn't you? Sex and violence. You just like watching women suffer. That's why you taped Basque killing them. How many other women died while Basque was in prison?"

"A few." Then he corrected himself. "More than a few."

I felt my anger rising. "Other partners? Accomplices?"

"None that are still alive."

How did he pull this off for so long!

I remembered my conversation with my brother at lunch yesterday, when I'd considered the fact that every killer, every rapist is friends with someone, is trusted by someone, loved by someone.

And my conclusion: *You can never really know someone, not really; at times every one of us acts in ways that are inconceivable to others, that are unthinkable even to ourselves.*

How true—

Jake was watching me curiously.

"So what's the story you're going to use?" I didn't have enough play with my ankle to stand, but I was able to push myself to my knees. "Alexei killed me? You chased him, but he got away? Is that it?"

"Something along those lines. Maybe that I was searching the sawmill office when Chekov attacked you down here. By the time I heard the motor running and managed to arrive, it was too late to stop your tragic, and rather grisly, death." He contemplated that for a moment. "I should be able to make that fly. I'm pretty good with this sort of thing."

"Why not just shoot me?"

"Come on, Pat, that really *would* be hard to explain, besides, by now you should know I like a little spectacle."

I thought of the videos, the soft chuckles of the person filming them. "Sooner or later," I said, "you knew we would've caught on that Reiser wasn't Richard's partner. That's why you killed him, so we'd stop looking, right? By killing him, you—"

"Yes, yes. Case closed. But it didn't quite work out like that, did it?" Sirens in the distance, still a few minutes out. "Okay, let's get things rolling."

"And Albuquerque and St. Louis—you know which cases I'm talking about—you stalled out those investigations, didn't you? To give the killers more time."

"Really, Pat. You should have been a profiler." He took a long look at me. "And so, first, though, the matter of Lien-hua. If, as you said, she knows, I'll have to hand her over to Basque, let him do what he does best. It should make for some really good footage. I always like those Asian girls. The way they writhe."

Anger.

Cutting loose inside me.

"Mmm. And what about Tessa? What shall we do with her? Oh, she'll be devastated by the death of her stepfather and his girlfriend. Maybe I could send her the video of Lien-hua's last few hours?" He paused, seemed to savor the thought. "No, as tantalizing as that is, I think watching that sweet little stepdaughter of yours squirm under Richard's blade is just too enticing. I think we'll do her too."

Easy, Pat, don't lose it!

I saw movement near the doorway, a dark blue parka, and I had an idea. "So you're saying you're going to kill a woman, kill a girl, just to watch them suffer? To watch them die?"

"I can't think of a better reason."

"Killing men isn't enough for you? You turn to women and children?"

"Patrick, trust me, the more helpless they are, the more satisfying it is."

"That was the wrong thing to say, Jake."

"Really?"

"You're going to regret threatening Lien-hua and Tessa."

He grinned. "Am I?"

"Yes," came a voice from the doorway. "Now, step away from the control board." I heard the sound of a shell being slammed into the chamber of a shotgun.

Alexei Chekov edged through the doorway, aiming the Remington 870 12-gauge from the gun rack in Sean's pickup at Jake's chest.

He must've read my email.

He'd come back.

And Alexei Chekov does not take it lightly when people threaten women or children.

103

"Step back," Alexei repeated to Jake. "I mean it." Maybe Alexei didn't typically use guns, but I was glad to see him holding one right now.

Obviously surprised but not appearing intimidated, Jake held up his hands, backed away from the panel.

"So, you enjoy killing women?" Alexei said. "Watching children suffer and squirm?"

The smugness on Jake's face evaporated. He said nothing.

Keeping the gun on Jake, Alexei called to me, "Who is Valkyrie, Agent Bowers?"

Oh no.

Not good.

Now Jake grinned. "Go on, Pat, tell him the truth. You don't have any idea who Valkyrie is."

Alexei eyed me. "Is that true?"

Not Terry. Not Cassandra.

Would Becker have lied while he was dying, his skull crushed? No. I doubted that.

So, not Becker.

Rusk?

"Well?"

My thoughts tumbled over each other, roaming, curling, turning in quick cycles, flipping through the facts. I could feel it. Everything coming together. The clues, the case, like an intricate puzzle, all clicking into place.

Whoever Valkyrie was he, or she, knew details of this mission, communicated with the Eco-Tech team.

Code names by high-level operatives are rarely chosen

indiscriminately. Valkyrie draws from images of death, eternity, beauty, marriage.

Fluent in different languages. Male. He has a specialty in communication technology and hacking.

Yes.

"Agent Bowers?"

To find out what lies at the core of someone's personality, you need to know more than what he wants . . . Only when you know what someone most deeply regrets will you know what matters to him most.

What he most deeply regrets . . .

"Tell him, Pat," Jake called. I said nothing and Jake went on, "In the car, Patrick had me send that email to his account noting that he knew who Valkyrie was—"

The mind has to deal with guilt somehow. When it's overwhelming, escaping reality is sometimes the only choice.

"But he made that up. Just to lure you—"

"I was speaking with Agent Bowers," Alexei said coolly. "I'd like you to be quiet now. Quiet alive or quiet dead. You choose."

Jake said nothing.

"Agent Bowers, tell—"

But before Alexei could finish his sentence, Jake went for his gun, and then I was yelling for Alexei to *Get down!* but Jake snatched up his Glock, aimed, Alexei fired the shotgun, the slug hit Jake in the torso, and he jerked to the side, crumpling to the ground.

Even if the magazine of the Remington 870 had a plug, Alexei had at least one shot left before he would need to reload. He turned the barrel toward me. "Who is Valkyrie?"

Careful, Pat. His GRU psych profile noted his "volatile and irregular temperament."

"Alexei," I ordered, "put down the shotgun and—"

On the other side of the room I saw Jake rise to his feet and reach for the switch to the pulp grinder.

"Behind you!" I yelled to Alexei.

But it was too late. Jake flipped the switch, the engine sprang to life, the blades of the log grinder began to churn, and the conveyor belt I was cuffed to lurched forward, carrying me toward the spinning blades.

Alexei trained the shotgun on Jake, but Jake fired again, sending him ducking for cover behind a workbench about three meters from the grinder. I could barely hear the shots over the roar of the motor.

All Jake needed to do was hold Alexei off for a couple minutes. Then I would be dead, backup would be here, and Jake would be the hero—wounded in the line of duty while apprehending an internationally wanted assassin.

As far as I knew, the only way to turn this wood grinder off was the switch beside Jake.

It's like a giant paper shredder.

And shredders can be jammed.

Hoping to stop the blade, I aimed my Maglite into the spinning blades, threw it in.

For a fraction of a second, the machine stalled, but then, with a sheer, screeching noise, the blades chewed through the flashlight's aluminum casing and batteries, sending shards of metal flying in every direction. Even four meters away I felt some of them blister across my face.

But it'd worked for a moment—

I just need something bigger. Something metal.

I scanned the area for something big enough to stop the blade.

The conveyor belt took me closer.

Nothing. Nothing within reach.

Hurry!

Closer now. Every second closer.

Yes!

I pointed to the shotgun that Alexei held and shouted as loudly as I could for him to throw it to me. I doubted he heard the words, but he must've understood my gestures because he heaved the shotgun up to me across the aisle that stretched between us.

Time seemed to slow as I rode the conveyor belt toward the blades and watched the shotgun rise through the air, parallel to the ground. I gauged my timing, reached for it, snagged the gun from its flight, swung the stock to my shoulder, and pivoted on my knee toward Jake.

He was eyeing me down the barrel of his Glock—

I aimed at his face.

Squeezed the trigger.

Dropped him.

Then I spun and faced the shredder again. I raised the shotgun high, targeted the spinning blades, and thrust the barrel into the wood pulp grinder as hard as I could so it wouldn't get kicked back out.

With a high-pitched cry, the blades fought to power through the metal, but the barrel was too thick. Still, somehow, the machine managed to draw the gun in nearly two feet before jamming completely. The conveyor belt lurched to a stop, a wisp of sour smoke coughed from the grinder's engine, and though they strained violently to devour the gun barrel, the blades no longer moved.

When I looked toward the control panel, I saw that Alexei was already there. He punched the kill switch, and the engine powered down.

"Nice shot, Agent Bowers."

"Nice throw."

He bent over Jake's body. "I really thought that I . . . Aha."

He held up the shattered iPad that Jake had stuffed into his jacket when we were just outside the door. The slug had gone through it, but the iPad must have deflected it enough to strike Jake in a place that allowed him to live long enough to try to kill again.

Sirens. Close. Maybe a mile out, maybe less.

Alexei approached me. "Do you know who Valkyrie is?"

I felt my heart hammering.

He flicked out the bone gun and placed the device's tip against the bone on the outside of my plastic-cuffed ankle.

"Alexei, think about this—"

"I'll start with the calcaneus and work my way up. Do you know who Valkyrie is or don't you?"

"I do."

He tightened his grip on the bone gun, positioned it carefully against my heel. "Who is Valkyrie?"

"You are."

Alexei stared at the agent. "What?"

"You're Valkyrie. You're the one who killed Tatiana, and when you did, something happened inside of—"

"No."

"You loved her and when you—"

"No!"

But even as he denied it, images were sliding across Alexei's mind, images of things he should not have been able to remember, not if he were innocent. The pictures came to him as if they were filtered through a screen, as if he were recalling someone else's life . . . attacking Erin Collet on Wednesday night . . . pressing the remote control detonator and blowing off Kirk Tyler's head . . . then leaving to read *The Brothers Karamazov* . . . having a conversation with . . .

Himself.

No!

Yes.

Valkyrie.

The sirens drew closer.

Valkyrie knew about the Tanfoglio in Italy. About Tatiana! He had contacts in Pakistan, first appeared in May, left the money at the dead drop. All of this, Alexei, all of this, because you were—

Images. Memories. Pain.

Seeing Tatiana, the look on her face when he raised the pistol, the terror in her eyes, the sound of the shot—

No!

Yes.

The day Valkyrie was born. The day Tatiana died.

Alexei removed the bone gun from Special Agent Bowers's calcaneus bone.

"If you leave here"—Bowers's words were steely and unflinch-ing—"I *will* find you. I'm going to bring you in."

"I have no doubt," Alexei heard himself say softly.

Blue and red lights were flashing, curling, through the blowing snow, flashing through the windows and the still-open door.

He backed away from the conveyor belt, and, as the patrol cars arrived on the property, Alexei pocketed his bone gun and disap-peared into the night.

104

Four days later

We did not find Alexei Chekov.

I expected him to use Sean's truck for his getaway from the sawmill, but he did not.

In the hours, and now days, following his escape, state patrol scoured the lumberyard, the roads surrounding the area, even the ELF tunnels and base.

Nothing.

That night, thinking that Alexei might try to catch a ride in one of the cruisers, I'd had the officers check their trunks before leaving the property. No sign of the assassin.

It was as if he really was a ghost and had stepped out of that sawmill door and slipped right into the invisible fabric of the air.

■

Alexei Chekov, shirt off, back to the mirror, stared over his wounded left shoulder at his reflection, studying the infected bullet wound beside his scapula.

He had managed to hide in the forest until the officers left the lumberyard, and then made his way down here to South Chicago one borrowed car at a time, and now he was in a motel that charged by the hour. He'd paid for four.

Alexei had purposely left the bullet in his shoulder, purposely left it untreated in order to make his wife's killer suffer. The day she died he had vowed to do so, and he was a man of his word.

Angry, red, infected lines fingered out from the bullet wound and snaked across his shoulder, down his arm, up onto his neck. Bearing this wound without complaint had also been his own private penance, a self-imposed sentence for slaughtering his beautiful bride.

But it had not been enough.

The memory flashes hadn't stopped, but each day became more and more frequent: conversations he didn't know he'd had, travels he'd been unaware of until now, crimes Valkyrie had committed against those whom Alexei never would have harmed.

There were two people inside of him. One who killed because it was his profession, the other who killed because it was his passion.

But this battle was going to end tonight.

Last week when he was in that jail cell in Wisconsin, Alexei had told Agent Bowers, "I have someone to take out my vengeance on; you have only God to blame."

Tonight he would avenge Tatiana's murder by putting a bullet in the brain of her killer.

Alexei put on his shirt, dressed for the cold, and then left the motel to find a pawn shop where he could purchase a handgun.

───────────◼───────────

Lien-hua and I arrived at Sean's house late for supper.

This afternoon's debriefing with Tait, Torres, Natasha, and Linnaman, the coroner, had gone longer than I'd thought, and when we arrived at the house, Tessa, Sean, and Amber were already seated at the table for the meal.

As Lien-hua hung up her coat, I noticed a small package addressed to me sitting on the table near the front door. The package had a Denver postmark, and I knew immediately what it was—the item I'd had my friend John-Paul send me.

The item I needed for tonight.

Surreptitiously, I slid it into my pocket so Lien-hua wouldn't see. "I'll meet you in the kitchen," I told her. "I need to run to my room for a sec."

"See you there."

───────────◼───────────

Alexei arrived at the pawn shop.

"Can I help you?" asked the greasy-haired man behind the counter.

"I believe you can." Alexei indicated toward the guns propped up in a large glass case on the wall.

"You got a Firearm Owner's ID card?"

"No. And I'm looking for something you have cartridges for, here in the store." Alexei pulled out a thick wad of hundreds. "This will be a cash transaction."

Sean stared into the wok. "It's called what, again?"

"Tofu," Tessa said.

"Tofu," he mumbled.

"Yes."

Amber slid some of the firm white squares onto his plate.

Sean tentatively prodded at them with his fork. "And it's . . . you said it's curd?"

"Soybean curd," Tessa answered. "You'll like it. Trust me."

"Soybean curd."

"It's really not that bad," I assured him. From across the table Lien-hua gave me a wry smile.

Margaret had wanted me to rest for a few days, Tessa didn't mind missing a little school, and Amber needed family around, so it'd been an easy decision to stay at Sean and Amber's place for the week. Additionally, with all of the follow-up on the cases, it hadn't been hard to get Margaret to sign off on letting Lien-hua stay in the area for a few extra days as well.

Obviously, Sean and Amber had a rocky road in front of them, but I figured if their marriage could survive everything that had happened last week, they might just be able to make things work after all.

"Mmm, not bad," Sean said, referring to the tofu. "It's kind of tasteless, but that's better than I expected." He offered Tessa a friendly wink.

"Hey," he said to me, "I've got something for you." He reached under the table. "The description you gave me of the tree wasn't perfect, but . . ." He produced my .357 SIG P229, retrieved from the snowbank near the Chippewa River, cleaned, just like new.

"Oh yes." This morning when he'd offered to go look for it, I hadn't thought he was serious, and when I realized he was, I hadn't thought there was any chance he'd find it.

"You're amazing." I took the gun from him.

And it was happy to be home in my hands.

Alexei made his decision.

A Rossi 351 .38 special. "Good choice." The clerk unlocked the cabinet to get the gun. "Simple. Small. Perfect for concealed carry. Reliable."

Reliable wasn't really the issue since Alexei was only going to use it to fire one bullet, but he decided he didn't need to mention that.

While the clerk pocketed his money, Alexei left for the motel, carrying the gun, the holster that came with it, and the cartridges, which only came by the box.

We'd put a moratorium on watching the news.

Listening to the ways that America and Iran were spinning the incidents of last week, watching the atmospheric rises and falls of the volatile stock market, hearing the political analysts drone on, was just too much.

Honestly, being here, isolated in the winter wonderland of northern Wisconsin, it felt like we were in another world.

And I wasn't sure I really wanted to go back to the old one.

After supper, when I was on my way to talk to Tessa to show her what was in the package from Denver, Sean called me aside.

"Listen," he said, "I'm driving over to Green Bay tomorrow—Tessa said she'd be glad to stay with Amber." They'd been taking turns making sure Amber wasn't left alone. It was part of the deal for us bringing her home from the hospital.

"Green Bay?"

"I've decided to tell him—to tell her son—the truth."

I still wasn't following. "Her son?"

"Nancy Everson. She had a twenty-two-year-old son when she died. I'm gonna tell him the truth about that night—that I'd been drinking, that I lost control of the car, and that's the reason his mother is dead."

"Sean, I'm really not sure you need to do that. There are statutes that—"

"Yeah, he could press charges. I know. I've thought about that. But he deserves to know the truth. It matters. I need to do it. Resolve this thing. It's as simple as that."

I realized that whatever the outcome of my brother's meeting with the man in Green Bay tomorrow, I was proud of him right now for choosing to entrust his future to the truth.

Yes, I was proud of my brother.

And for the first time I could ever remember, I told him so.

Right after my brief conversation with Sean, I headed down the hall and knocked on Tessa's door.

"Yeah, come on in."

I went in, closed the door behind me. Tessa was lying on the bed, writing in her journal, her teddy bear, Francesca, nestled up beside her.

"I have something to show you, Raven," I said.

Curious, she scooted forward, sat on the edge of the bed, and I held up the box containing the ring.

"What!" Her eyes were wide. "Can I see it?"

I gave her the box.

"It finally arrived this morning. I'm about to go ask her right now."

Tessa opened the ring box and let out a long, slow breath. "You did good." She admired it longer than I thought she would. "You did real good."

At last she handed me the box, and I slid it into my pocket. "Anyway," I said, "that's why I stopped by. I just wanted, one more time, to make sure that you're cool with—"

"Patrick." Tessa had chosen a parental tone. "It's been almost two years since Mom died. You have a life to live. Lien-hua is great. I couldn't ask for a cooler stepmom."

"Thanks." I gave her a light kiss on the forehead.

"You gonna tell her about DC?"

"Yes."

"A new adventure."

"That's right."

A small silence. I saw her tapping her leg. "Hey," she said, "did Amber ever teach you that game of hers, Guess the Plot?"

"Uh-uh."

"Well, you watch, like, a little snippet of a movie and then you try to guess the rest of the story. I was just thinking . . . you, Lien-hua, me—if this were a movie, how it would end."

"And?" I said, somewhat apprehensively.

"It looks like the guy finally gets the girl."

"That's my kind of story. What about the precocious teenager? Does she live happily ever after with the dashing and brave geo-spatial investigator and his exotically beautiful kickboxing bride?"

Tessa looked at me with mock incredulity. "You're dashing and brave, she's exotically beautiful, and I'm *precocious*?"

"In an endearing, fetching sort of way."

"Humph." She folded her arms but wasn't really angry. "Well, I think maybe she stops having trouble falling asleep."

"Really?"

"I think so. Yes."

"This is turning out to be the kind of ending I like."

"But as far as living 'happily ever after,' let's hope that doesn't happen."

"Let's hope it *doesn't* happen?"

"Yeah, I mean, just sitting around being happy all the time? Boring. I'm more into an ongoing adventure kind of thing."

I patted her arm. "Don't worry. I'm sure something bad will happen soon enough to keep things interesting."

Then I left to go ask Special Agent Lien-hua Jiang for her hand in marriage.

———————————◼———————————

In his motel room, Alexei Chekov addressed the six envelopes.

Each contained over $150,000, all of the money he had left from his trip to Wisconsin.

As a small way of showing recompense for the death of their husbands, he left one envelope to Mia Ellory, the deputy's wife, another to Annette Clarke, the wife of the truck driver he had killed. The third envelope he addressed to Erin Collet, because he had attacked her and allowed her father to die; the fourth was for Kayla Tatum, for mental duress suffered during her abduction and captivity; the fifth, for the maid who would find his body tomorrow. The final envelope contained enough money to pay for cleaning up the motel room.

Then, Alexei sat at the desk and carefully wrote a note to each of the women expressing his deep regret for the pain and grief he'd brought into their lives.

———————————◼———————————

Lien-hua was already waiting for me outside the front door in the lightly falling snow. Quietly, I took her mittened hand and we left the house, choosing the trail that led past the woodshed and toward the forest. Faint light from the patio glowed around us, gently illuminating the peaceful winter landscape.

After a few moments of silence she said, "I spoke with Director Wellington today. Asked her whatever happened to Terry Manoji."

Margaret was not the most forthcoming person I knew. "And how did that go?"

"She said, and I quote, 'My counterpart at the CIA has assured me that Terry Manoji will no longer be a threat of any kind to the United States of America.'"

"No longer a threat of any kind, huh? And what does that mean, exactly?"

"Well, I asked her that too, and she just said that in the scope of her conversation with CIA Director O'Dell, some things were left unsaid and some things were left unasked."

"Aha." I still wasn't completely clear on why Margaret hadn't been more available the night everything went down last week. Two days ago she'd curtly told me that the missile crisis was not the only disaster she was trying to avert at the time. It was hard for me to believe that there could've been anything as pressing as what we were dealing with, but she let it go at that.

Lien-hua and I took a few steps. I watched the snow swirl around us, thought of how I was going to do this. She said, "What do you think ever happened with Chekov?"

"Well, he was going to kill his wife's murderer. I can't help but wonder if he might've just gone ahead and kept his word."

I thought of Tessa's probing question at the hospital last week: *"Apart from forgiveness, can you think of any way of dealing with your wrongs that doesn't involve some form of denial or negotiation?"*

The question had been on my mind a lot over the last few days as we wrapped up these cases, as I considered all the crimes that Terry, Cassandra, Jake, and Alexei had committed. And in the background, always in the background, casting a long, thin shadow across the last fourteen years of my life, Richard Devin Basque and the women he'd killed.

Can you think of a way . . . ?

And I still had to answer Tessa's question "no."

If you don't find forgiveness, you'll never end up with peace, just get lost in a maze of comforting excuses.

A maze I decided I was not going to enter.

I felt Lien-hua reposition her hand in mine, grasp my fingers more tightly. "So have you decided?" she asked. "About teaching at the Academy again?"

"I'm going to take the job."

"So you'll be moving to DC?"

"Yup."

"Well, then, we'll be neighbors."

"I hope not."

"What?"

We stopped walking and stood on the edge of the night, snow falling lightly around us. "Lien-hua, do you remember how, in that ELF tunnel, I told you there was something I wanted to ask you?"

"Yes."

"And you made me wait until all that was over?"

"Yes."

"And then, when I was about to climb up that shaft, I sort of said I was going to marry you, and that's why I wasn't about to fall—because I'd miss out on that?"

"I think I recall something along those lines."

I took out the ring box.

Her eyes widened. "Oh, Pat," she said, drawing a mitten-covered hand to her mouth.

"Lien-hua . . ." I brushed a snow-dabbed strand of hair from the side of her face. "Since the first time I met you I've been under your spell. You're beautiful in all the ways that matter most, and the more I get to know you the deeper I fall in love with you. I'd do anything for you and I want to spend the rest of my life by your side. Lien-hua, would you marry me? Would you be my bride? My queen?"

She said nothing at first but then threw her arms around me, leaned up on her toes, drew herself close, pressed her lips against mine.

And said yes.

There is a fate worse than death.

The discovery that you're the one who killed the person you love the most. How do you deal with that kind of knowledge? That deep a sin?

Alexei raised the Rossi, placed the end of the barrel against his temple, and, in his mother tongue, Russian, counted down the last five seconds of his life.

Pyat' . . .

He would finally be reunited with Tatiana again.

Chetyre . . .

Justice meted out against her murderer.

Tri . . .

The pain of loss fading into night.

Dva . . .

Alexei closed his eyes.

Odin—

Valkyrie opened his eyes.

Lowered the gun.

Then breathed in deeply, savoring the moment, the feeling of air filling his lungs, the thumping beat of his heart in his chest, proving, proving, proving that he was alive. Yes, alive.

And finally, alone.

There was only one mind, one psyche, now.

Only one.

Valkyrie—the dark angel who decides who will live and who will die on the battlefield of life.

He went to the dresser, ripped open the envelopes, slid out the money, and destroyed the handwritten notes to the women.

Then Valkyrie began to pack his things.

After finding a doctor to treat his shoulder, he had some unfinished business to attend to in Pakistan concerning a certain Abdul Razzaq Muhammad, a man who had failed to transfer $100,000,000 to the offshore account Terry Manoji had opened, the one Valkyrie had obtained the password to and had planned all along to siphon the funds from.

Yes, a trip to Pakistan, and then . . .

Who knows?

The future would be wide open and bold with possibilities.

ACKNOWLEDGMENTS

A book like this could not be written without extensive research. I would love to publicly thank all of the people with whom I consulted, but some of them are in sensitive positions in our government. In order to protect the identities of my sources I'll just note your first names. You know who you are, and I couldn't have written this without you. Thanks to Harry, Jim, Jerry, Carole, Scott, Pat, Larry, Todd, Wayne K., Craig, Anita, Adam, Chris, Kristin, Wayne S., David, Pam, Trinity, Liesl, Jen, and Shawn.

Steven James is the author of many books, including four other bestselling Patrick Bowers thrillers. He has a Master's Degree in Storytelling and has taught writing and creative communication on three continents. Currently he lives, writes, drinks coffee, and plays disc golf near the Blue Ridge Mountains of Tennessee.

**Look for
Steven James's
next thriller
in fall 2012**

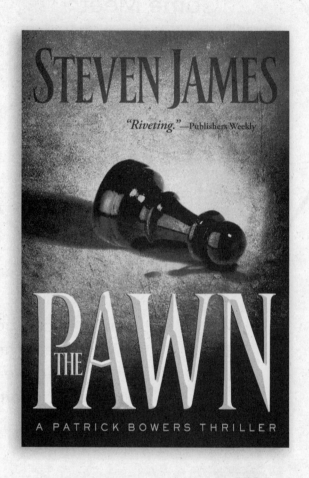

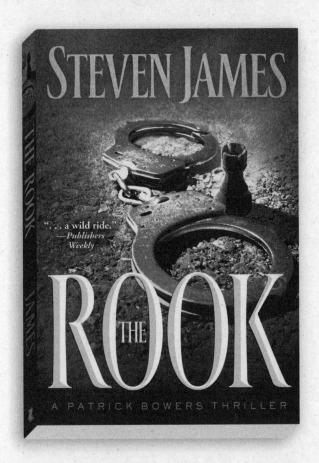

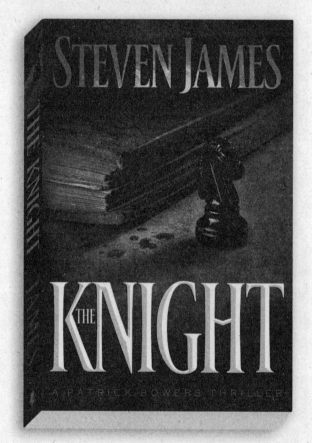

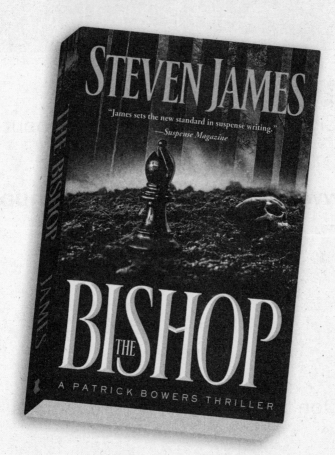